In Case You Missed It

Lindsey Kelk is a *Sunday Times* bestselling author, podcaster and prolific tweeter. Born and brought up in Doncaster, South Yorkshire, she worked as a sales assistant, a publicist, a silver service waitress and a children's editor before moving to New York and becoming a full-time writer.

Lindsey has written sixteen novels for adults, including the *I Heart* series, *The Single Girl's To-Do List* and *One in a Million*, as well as the children's book series, *Cinders and Sparks*. A fan of lipstick, pro-wrestling and cats (although not all at the same time), she now lives in Los Angeles with her husband, Jeff, and their two cats, BelleBelle and Anderson Cooper.

You can find out more about Lindsey on Facebook, Twitter or Instagram @LindseyKelk, and at http://lindseykelk.com.

In Case You Missed It

Lindsey Kelk

HarperCollins*Publishers*

This novel is entirely a work of fiction.
The names, characters and incidents portrayed in it are
the work of the author's imagination. Any resemblance to
actual persons, living or dead, events or localities is
entirely coincidental.

HarperCollins*Publishers*
1 London Bridge Street
London
SE1 9GF

www.harpercollins.co.uk

A Paperback Original 2020
2

Copyright © Lindsey Kelk 2020

Lindsey Kelk asserts the moral right to
be identified as the author of this work

Excerpt from 'The Love Song of J. Alfred Prufrock' from COLLECTED POEMS 1909-1962
by T.S. Eliot. Copyright © 1952 by Houghton Mifflin Harcourt Publishing Company,
renewed 1980 by Esme Valerie Eliot. Reprinted by permission of Houghton Mifflin
Harcourt Publishing Company. All rights reserved.

Excerpt from 'The Love Song of J Alfred Prufrock' by T.S. Eliot taken from *The Complete
Poems and Plays* by T.S. Eliot © 1952
Reprinted by permission of Faber and Faber Limited

A catalogue record for this book
is available from the British Library

ISBN:
978-0-00-838465-4

Set in Melior by Palimpsest Book Production Limited,
Falkirk, Stirlingshire

Printed and bound by CPI Group (UK) Ltd, Croydon CR0 4YY

For Jeff.
Thanks for making sure I didn't miss you.

CHAPTER ONE

The only difference between a fresh start and 'oh my god, my life is a complete failure' is a good attitude and the right Instagram caption.

Which was why I had my 'so happy to be moving home' social media declaration drafted and ready to post, even before the wheels of the plane had touched British soil. It wasn't a lie but it wasn't exactly the truth either, which I figured was OK, since that described roughly ninety-seven percent of the internet anyway.

Taking a deep breath, I pushed my wayward curls into some sort of recognizable shape, rapped three times on my parents' back door and let myself into the house.

'Knock, knock,' I called, heaving my bags inside. 'It's only me.'

'Look lively, Gwen, sounds like burglars.' I could hear my dad slapping his thighs all the way from the other side of the house.

'Yes, put your hands in the air and step away from

the baked goods,' I ordered as I bounced into the living room all jazz hands and forced smiles. I dropped my backpack on the floor and searched the room for snacks. 'Seriously, I'm not joking, where are the Fondant Fancies? I'm so hungry I could eat a horse.'

'Plenty of cultures eat horses,' Mum said, gathering me up in a trademark Gwen-Reynolds-hug, swinging me from side to side and making sweet, unintelligible noises. 'Probably better for you than a Fondant Fancy.'

Dad, the more stoic of my parents, opted for a pat on the shoulder and a curt nod before he disappeared into the kitchen to emote. He wasn't the touchy-feely type. At my graduation, while everyone else was sobbing and crying, my dad shook my hand and slapped me on the back so hard, my mortar-board went flying.

'How was the flight? Did you have any trouble at the airport? Did you get all your bags?' Mum asked as she settled on the settee and I took up residence in my favourite armchair. It was as though I'd never been away.

'Hers and half the plane's by the looks of things,' Dad called from the other room. 'Have you brought all of Washington back with you, Rosalind?'

'Not all of them,' I shouted back. 'Only the good ones.'

'Not many then,' he replied, muttering something about 'the bloody state of politics' to himself as I heard him turn on the tap.

I smiled and let myself relax for the first time in I couldn't quite remember how long. The living room looked almost exactly the same as it had when I left, same magnolia walls, same bookcase groaning with books, same painting of a peacock my parents bought on their honeymoon and refused to admit was hideous. It was all so reassuring, however questionable the aesthetic. I hadn't been back for a visit in more than eighteen months and it was a little over three years since I'd left London for my fabulous new job, producer at a radio station in Washington, DC. Somehow it felt like I'd been away much, much longer than that, and like I'd never been away at all, both at the same time. I wondered if everyone's family living room had the same time-warp effect on them.

'So,' Mum said quietly, tucking her smooth, straight hair behind her ears. I got my hair and my height from my dad but the rest of me, the freckles, the brown eyes, strong nose, wide mouth, were pure Gwen Reynolds. 'You're home. Is everything all right?'

I pressed my lips into a thin, straight line. So much for relaxing.

'Everything is fine,' I replied as confidently as I could. 'I told you on the phone.'

'You did and I'm not going to go on about it,' she said with an agreeable smile. 'But if there's anything you want to talk about, you know I'm here . . .'

'Here we are, here we are,' Dad walked back in with a heavily laden tray, matching china teacups for them, the novelty Care Bear mug I'd been drinking from since I was six for me. 'I got one of those fast-boil kettles, worth its weight in gold. Less than a minute, even if you get the water out the fridge.'

Mum reached across the tray for her cup and gave me a knowing look. She wouldn't say anything else in front of Dad, deep and meaningfuls weren't his cup of tea.

They both looked a little bit older, I realized, noticing a few more lines around Mum's eyes, a bit more grey in Dad's close-cut curls. It was the kind of thing you didn't notice when you saw someone every day but when it had been a while, you couldn't help but see it.

'Present time!' I said, setting down my mug and clapping my hands. I wrestled a very full duty-free bag out of my backpack. 'Perfume for Mum, bottle of whisky for Dad . . .'

I handed out the tax-free bounty and beamed. 'The man said that was his favourite whisky, I hope you like it.'

'And who are all those Toblerones for?' Dad asked, eyes on my backpack. I quietly pushed it around the side of my chair before he realized the Toblerones had already been eaten. It had been a long flight.

'Can't believe Jo's left home,' I said, changing the subject as I took in all the other details that spelled out home: the velvet drapes, the net curtains, Mum's late-nineties collection of Swarovski crystal bears. 'She says she's enjoying it?'

'Having the time of her life.' Dad lifted his eyebrows over the rim of his teacup as Mum spritzed herself with her new perfume and immediately sneezed. 'According to the one text message she has deigned to send me.'

No one would ever actually call my sister an accident (except me) but even if she wasn't planned, my parents couldn't have cooked up a better child if they'd tried. And they had tried (again, me). Jo was beautiful.

A perfect baby with silky, straight hair, a button nose and the biggest blue eyes you'd ever seen, which was why, when I passed all my exams at sixteen and jokingly told everyone I was the brains of the family and baby Jo was the beauty, I didn't mind so much that they agreed with me. It stung a bit more when she grew up and turned out to be an actual genius as well as shockingly beautiful. Where was the fairness in that?

'One in, one out,' Dad said as he passed me the biscuit tin. 'Just when I thought we'd finally got the house to ourselves.'

'Obviously, we discussed the timing,' I joked. 'Didn't want to leave the two of you here on your own to go mental.'

He fixed me with a look that suggested he got the joke, he just didn't think it was funny.

'I didn't think we'd see you back so soon, everything seemed to be going so well. Thought you'd stay over there a bit longer,' he added, his voice lilting up and down as he avoided asking his real question.

Why had I come home?

'It was the right time to leave,' I said airily, breaking a ginger nut in half and dipping it in my tea.

Dad passed me a napkin. 'And move back in with us?'

I chewed my biscuit thoughtfully. Anyone would think he didn't want his unemployed thirty-two-year-old daughter moving back in unexpectedly, fourteen years after she'd left home.

'I won't be here long,' I told them, wiggling my left big toe into the cuff of my right sock and prising it off. Ahh, sweet relief. 'As soon as I get a job, I'll be out of the way.'

'Any bites on the work front?' Dad asked.

'Lots of possibilities.' I busied myself by balling up my socks so he wouldn't see my face. My dad could always tell when I was lying. 'I'll be out of your way in a couple of weeks.'

'There's absolutely no rush,' Mum insisted before sliding her hand around the back of Dad's neck and giving it a rub. 'We're just happy you're home, aren't we, Alan? I never liked you being that far away anyway.'

I silently registered their PDA. This was new.

'You know, I might go and put my head down for an hour,' I said, stifling a fake yawn. Perhaps I was hallucinating from exhaustion. 'Before it gets too late for a nap. Got to beat the jetlag, you know?'

Mum and Dad caught each other's eye, furtive glance meeting furtive glance. I put down my mug and straightened in my seat. Something was up.

'Is everything all right?' I asked.

'It's more than all right,' Dad said. A big, bright smile spread across his face and I watched in horror as he placed his hand on my mother's thigh. Her actual, upper thigh. And then he *squeezed*.

'I could definitely use some shut-eye.' I stood swiftly, scooping up my socks and getting an unfortunate whiff of myself as I stood. Some shut-eye *and* a shower. 'Didn't really get a lot of sleep on the plane.'

And if my dad's hand didn't stop creeping up my mum's leg, I might never sleep again.

'Before you go anywhere,' Dad took Mum's teacup

and placed it back on the tray. 'We've got a surprise for you.'

'I think you're going to like it,' she added, a happy pink flush in her cheeks.

It was exactly what they'd said when they told me Mum was pregnant with Jo. If she hadn't been very vocal about going through the menopause several years ago, I would have been quite concerned.

'Come on, this way.' Dad stood up and beckoned me through to the conservatory. I followed as he opened the French doors and made his way down to the bottom of the garden.

'Shoes on,' Mum ordered as I made to follow in my bare feet. 'It rained earlier and the grass is wet. I don't want you catching your death on your first day home.'

'It's a thousand degrees out there now,' I muttered but I did as I was told, going back to the kitchen for my trainers before following them outside. Ducking low under the washing line, I met them both at the bottom of the garden.

'What do you think?' Dad asked, gesturing to a new shed with an out-of-character flourish.

I looked at the shed. Mum looked at the shed. Dad looked at the shed.

'It's a shed,' I stated.

'It's not a shed,' Dad said with a stern look. He produced a shiny silver key from his pocket and waved it in front of my face. 'Go on, open her up.'

Tired as I was, I took the key and offered them a wan smile in an attempt to show willing before I blocked up their Jacuzzi jets with half a bottle of Mum's Badedas. There was an upside to your dad running a company that installs bathrooms and that upside was the massive soaking tub in their en suite that I'd been dreaming about for the duration of my overbooked, overnight flight, stuck in the middle seat of the middle row for eight very long hours.

I pushed open the flimsy door.

It was not a shed.

It was every item from my childhood bedroom, taken out of the house and painstakingly reconstructed in a damp, prefabricated structure at the bottom of my parents' garden. Double bed, wardrobe, chest of drawers, Postman Pat beanbag and all.

'I – I don't get it,' I stammered, looking back into the garden where my parents beamed back at me. How had they got my enormous knotted pine bedframe into this tiny space? 'Why is all my stuff in here?'

'You know your dad loves a project,' Mum said, gazing up at my father with an expression I'd only ever seen in our house that time we all watched *Memoirs of a Geisha*. It was an uncomfortable evening and I didn't care to be reminded of it. 'He built this all by himself!'

'Peter Mapplethorpe helped a bit,' Dad corrected reluctantly.

'Are they repeating *Grand Designs* again or something?' I asked. I lingered in the doorway, key still in hand, so confused.

'Yes but that's not the point,' Dad replied, gently but decisively shoving me inside. 'What do you think?'

What *did* I think?

All my books were there on my bookcase, from Enid Blytons to my Sweet Valley Highs, via a few well-worn Virginia Andrews and a copy of Judy Blume's *Forever* that had a spine so cracked only I could tell which book it was without looking at the cover. All my CDs were stacked up next to my boombox and a legion of cuddly toys stared at me from the top of the wardrobe. Even my beloved terracotta oil diffuser from the Body Shop was in there. I wrinkled my nose at the tiny bottle of Fuzzy Peach oil that stood sentry beside it. It was practically rancid at the time, God only knew what it would smell like now.

The whole thing was altogether too much for my jetlagged brain to handle, like I'd walked out of the garden and into 1997. Wait, was that what had happened? I wondered. What if this wasn't some sort of bizarre art installation, 'Child's Bedroom in a Shed', but actually a time machine Dad had built at the bottom of the garden? He did spend an awful lot of time by himself and he was very handy.

'If you go through that door, there's a bathroom,' he explained, sliding past me and the pine wardrobe that matched my bed in both design and gargantuan proportions. 'It's small but perfectly formed, just like your mother.'

My mother tittered appreciatively. I did not.

'It's a compostable toilet,' he went on from behind the concertina door. 'Good for the environment. And the water from the shower goes into the garden! Waters the tomatoes. It's genius. Come and have a look.'

'It's really impressive, Dad,' I said, fighting back a yawn as I clambered over my bed to peer into the bathroom out of politeness, immediately finding myself wedged in between the bed and the chest of drawers. Shuffling free, I whacked my hip on the oversized round knobs I'd fought for in the middle of DFS so many moons ago. 'So, what's the plan, you're renting it out? Doing Airbnb?'

'Oh.' Dad emerged from the bathroom with a slightly crestfallen look on his face. 'No.'

'You know we're very excited to have you home,' Mum said as Dad and I shuffled awkwardly back and forth until he clambered on my bed and shuffled over on his hands and knees. 'And we know it might take a little while for you to get back up on your feet—'

'I'm not *off* my feet,' I replied quickly. 'This is just a fork in my road that will lead me on an unforeseen pathway to fulfilment.'

My flight had been delayed for so long, I'd caved and bought one of those inspirational books everyone raves about on Instagram from the airport bookshop. *Starting Over: A Woman's Guide to Getting It Right the Second Time Around.* It turned out to have more to do with getting over a divorce than anything else but, still, there were some very catchy sound bites in there. It really was dangerous to leave unattended humans in an airport for more than five hours at a time – another half an hour and I'd have been chatting with the nice-looking lady giving away biscuits and trying to talk to people about Scientology.

'I know my coming home was a bit of a surprise and I know not having another job waiting for me isn't exactly ideal but I'm so absolutely, one hundred percent fine.'

'Well, that sounds very nice but, regardless, we thought while you were here, it would be nice for you to have your privacy.' Dad coughed to clear his throat before looking to my mother for help. Mum looked at

Dad and Dad looked at me and I looked back at both of them.

'If all my furniture is in here, then what's in my room?' I wondered out loud, too tired to get it.

'The thing is, Rosalind, you're not a child any more,' Dad said firmly as the pieces of a puzzle I hadn't been prepared for began to fall into place. 'And while we're happy to have you home for as long as you need to be here, I think we would all appreciate a bit more space and a bit more distance and, well . . .'

Oh.

Oh no.

They hadn't put my bedroom in a shed.

The shed *was* my bedroom.

'You want *me* to live in *here*?' I asked, hoping they would laugh and bring me back inside with a clap on the back. Good joke, everybody laughs.

But no.

Dad slapped his hands together, breaking the tension with a thunderclap.

'I'll get your bags, will I?' he said brightly. 'I think they'll fit under the bed, otherwise you'll have to bring them in once you've emptied them and I'll put in the loft until you leave. Not that there's a rush for you to leave.'

'Everything works except the WiFi,' Mum said proudly as I adjusted to the reality of my situation. The reality of living in a shed. 'And the reception on the telly comes in and out but that'll all be fine once we've worked out the WiFi. There's a man coming next week.'

'Great,' I replied, steadying myself on my bedframe. 'No rush.'

After all, who needed television or the internet, especially when they were unemployed and looking for a new job?

'Thing is, we turned your room into an office so your dad can work from home a couple of days a week,' Mum said, fussing with the curtains, straightening the nets. She might have her daughter living in a shed but she was not a savage. 'And you said you wouldn't be back for long and it's so nice having him around more.'

'And Jo's room?'

'Jo only left a month ago!' She turned to stare at me, positively aghast. 'We couldn't very well upend her room when her bed was still warm, could we?'

'I suppose not,' I replied, definitely not thinking about how they moved Jo into my room the same day I left for uni because she needed a bigger room. When she was four.

'Exactly.' Mum cleared her throat. 'But I have put all her furniture in one corner and I'm using it as a yoga studio. I'm really getting there with my downward dog.'

What I wouldn't have given to see my sister's face at that moment.

'If you cook anything, be careful,' she went on, picking things up then putting them down. My Pikachu piggy bank, an unopened bottle of bath pearls from Christmas 2004, a framed photo of Justin Timberlake that Sumi had given me for my birthday in the first year of uni that Mum had given pride of place, clearly mistaking JT for an actual friend. 'We took the batteries out of the smoke alarm because it kept going off every ten minutes and we could hear it up in the house. Very distracting.'

No WiFi, no TV and no smoke alarm. I could see it now: exhausted from being forced to read an actual book, I would fall asleep with a Pop-Tart in the toaster, the toaster would set on fire, I'd die of smoke inhalation and no one on Instagram would ever even know.

'Right, I need to get back into the kitchen and put the chicken in the oven for dinner. Unless you'd like to have us over to your place?' Mum asked with a theatrical wink.

'Perhaps I should try not to set it on fire the first night,' I joked weakly as Dad returned with my bags.

Or maybe I should, I thought, eyeing the toaster across the room.

Closing the door behind the horny pod people who had replaced my parents, I cast an eye over my domain – all three hundred square feet of it – before dropping down on my bed. The uncertain, ancient frame complained at my weight but the protest wasn't loud enough to get me back up on my feet.

'You have so much to be grateful for,' I told myself, staring up at the ceiling. 'You have your health, your parents, your friends *and* a highly flammable roof over your head. It's more than a lot of people have. It's not as nice as what you had before but it'll be OK. You'll get a job, you'll get a flat, you'll burn that poster of Tom Cruise and you'll be fine. Everything will be fine.'

The more times I said it, the closer it felt to being true.

A smile found its way onto my face. I'd have loved this place when I was a teenager, I thought. A bolthole at the bottom of the garden, all to myself? Maybe it was actually amazing and I was just too tired to realize. The smile disappeared as a single drop of water fell from the roof and landed right in the middle of my forehead. I rolled over onto my side and watched as it began to rain, a summer storm tap, tap, tapping on the corrugated roof of my new home.

'It's all going to be fine,' I said again, more determined this time.

I only hoped I was right. I hadn't always been that reliable in the past.

CHAPTER TWO

One of the most wonderful things about London was, no matter how much it changed, at its heart, it always stayed the same. They could open as many coffee shops and co-working spaces and Brewdog after Brewdog after Brewdog but the bones of the city stood strong, happy to slip on a new skin from time to time but always knowing its true self, underneath it all. As I emerged from the tube station at London Bridge, I took a deep, familiar breath of murky city air and smiled. I'd missed home so much.

After university, I'd lived nearby with my best friend, Sumi, and our friend, Lucy, the three of us crammed into a tiny two-bedroomed terraced affair with no functioning kitchen to speak of, a living room that doubled as Sumi's bedroom and a bathroom that didn't have a bath. Since we only had a fridge-freezer in the hallway and nowhere to sit that wasn't some-one's bed, we met at The Lexington Arms almost every evening after work to eat and drink and catch each other up on every last little thing that had happened during our day. It was a wonderful, crappy old pub round the corner, beloved by us for its fish finger sandwiches, cheap white wine and the landlord's willingness to let us upstairs when he had a band on without paying for a ticket. Sumi was in law school, Lucy was training at beauty college and I was making tea for whichever local radio station or desperate DJ would have me. It sounded hideous but they were happy times, really, they were the happiest.

As I waited for the green man, I gazed across the cobbled street at Borough Market. It was all together too cool for us back then but Sumi insisted I meet her here tonight. It was closer to her office, she said. This new bar she'd started going to was far nicer than The Lex, she said. A complete and utter betrayal, I said. And there had been no word on whether or not they served fish finger sandwiches.

Dodging the tourists with their giant backpacks and the locals with their bulging shopping bags, I walked around in circles, searching for the bar but only succeeding in getting lost in a sea of artisan food stalls.

'You can't afford fancy cheese,' I reminded myself as I stared longingly at a wheel of brie in the window of the cheesemonger's. Besides, who needed a baked camembert and a fresh-from-the-oven baguette when they could buy a Dairylea Dunker from Tesco Metro on the way home? Christ, I groaned inwardly, it had been a long time since I'd had been this broke. I had to find a job sooner rather than later.

Eventually, I spotted it, nestled between a boulangerie and a cheese shop, a tiny sign stencilled on a huge plate-glass window in antique gold lettering. Good Luck Bar was about as far away from The Lex as it was possible to be, figuratively speaking. Instead of a dark, dank, old man's boozer, this place was one of those café-pub hybrids with too many mirrors and not enough dry-roast peanuts. One side of the room was taken up by oversized sofas in the perfect shade of pink for faux lounging while you took a thousand Instagram photos. The other side was filled with communal tables and a dulled metal bar that ran halfway down the room, lined with tall barstools and Edison lights hanging down overhead. It looked like a steampunk hairdressers, if a giant strawberry yoghurt had exploded inside. Not that it mattered what I thought, the place was absolutely packed, the sofas were swarmed and the communal tables full of people nursing an almost empty coffee cup while they abused the free WiFi.

With no other options, I hopped up onto an empty stool, resting my bag on the bar. A woman appeared on the other side and gave me a big smile. Her hair was woven into a long, elaborate braid you couldn't help but respect and a heavy leather work apron covered her white shirt and blue jeans.

'What can I get you?' she asked.

'A white wine please?' I replied with a quick glance at the happy hour menu. 'A large white wine?'

I might not be able to afford expensive cheese but there was always room on my credit card for a drink.

'One of those days?' The bartender pushed an enormous glass of Sauvignon Blanc towards me.

'Something like that,' I agreed, tucking my own long hair behind my ears and taking a grateful sip. I liked her already.

The day had been a challenge. Between my jetlag and a pair of randy rutting foxes that had seemingly chosen the back of my shed as their love nest I'd barely slept a wink. Which meant I didn't cope very well when my dad apologetically explained he'd moved all my clothes from the washer to the dryer without asking me and accidentally shrunk more than half of them. And that was before I'd got to the freezing-cold water in the shed shower or the utter horror of the compostable toilet. My parents might be happy to have me home but home did not seem happy to have me.

'Oh my god, it's you, it's you, you're really back!'

Without warning, a black leather tote bag, filled to overflowing, thumped down beside me at the bar with a short South Asian woman attached.

'I am so happy to see you,' I told her, squeezing my friend so tightly she squealed in protest.

'I'm happy to see you too,' Sumi replied, delight all over her face. She'd always hated being short and lived in four-inch heels but she loved that she was, in her own words, 'a thicc bitch', all confident curves and zero-fucks attitude. Her hair was long and dark and her face was a masterpiece, glowing skin, huge eyes and a mouth that always seemed to be smiling.

'I'm gagging for a drink,' she said, waving to the bartender and pointing at my glass before giving her a thumbs up. The woman threw her a wink and went to work. 'So, tell me everything. How does it feel to be back?'

'Weird,' I admitted as we fell right back into our rhythm. I hadn't physically laid eyes on Sumi since she came out to visit a year ago but one way or another, we'd spoken every single day without fail. We didn't miss a beat. 'I'm happy though, I've missed everything about home so much.'

18

'You picked the right three years to be gone,' she replied. 'I'd have gone with you if I could have. How's the flat-hunt going?'

'Can't get a flat without a job,' I pointed out. 'I'm totally broke. If I'd known I'd be leaving so suddenly, I'd have tried to save more.'

I shuddered at the thought of winter in the shed.

Sumi took in the news with her trademark sympathy. 'You'll work it out,' she said, patting me aggressively on the back. Sumi was a corporate lawyer who would never be out of work as long as companies continued to do dastardly things to each other – which basically meant she'd be loaded forever. 'Everyone will be champing at the bit to give you a job. Your CV must look amazing, who else in London has three years' experience at American Public Radio? You're a rockstar, babe.'

'Yeah,' I agreed weakly. 'That's me.'

She lifted her head slightly to examine me, an expression I knew only too well.

'You still haven't really explained what happened. Did you quit? Was it layoffs?'

'I was ready to come home,' I said, also ready to draw a line under the conversation. 'It's a long, boring story, not worth the waste of breath.'

She gave me a sideways glance as her wine arrived. Sumi, ever the lawyer, knew when a case was closed.

'Your mum and dad must be thrilled to have you home?'

'They're making me live in a shed.'

Sumi's eyes lit up. 'I have many follow-up questions.'

'You may not ask them,' I replied. 'But you can help me set up my new phone if you like.'

I pulled a sexy black slab out of my bag and modelled it with my best game show hostess hand movements while my friend contributed the appropriate 'oohs' and 'ahhs'. Even though I couldn't really afford it, I had to have a phone. I'd had a work one in DC and the moment I'd handed it back in, it was like having my arm cut off. The ancient handset I'd been using in the interim was so slow, it would have been easier to send my friends telegrams than it was to text.

'My phone is so old you practically have to put twenty pence in the back to make a call,' Sumi muttered, admiring my new technology. 'But I can't face learning how to use a new one. I've gone full Luddite.'

'Oh, I've got no idea how to use it but look how pretty it is.' I gazed lovingly into the glossy screen and blinked with delight as it unlocked itself, opening up the home screen. 'Look at that! I didn't even have to press anything.'

'Facial recognition,' she said darkly. 'Another reason not to upgrade, I don't need the Russians saving my face to some mad database.'

'Why the Russians?' I asked, peering at the virgin, unscratched screen. So beautiful.

'It's always the Russians,' Sumi said, a knowing look on her face. 'The Russians or Mark Zuckerberg. Or both. In fact, do we even know he's not Russian?'

'Yes, Sumi,' I replied, holding my phone at a safe distance and studying it carefully. 'We do.'

My sister, Jo, could pick up any item of technology and, within three seconds, she'd have a gluten-free, vegan pizza on its way, her favourite music playing through an unseen speaker and five potential dates lined up for the weekend, all while checking her blood pressure and livestreaming footage from the Mars Rover. I had to work a little bit harder. The woman in the shop had set up the basics but I was going to have to figure out the rest for myself. For the last three years, I'd had to listen to all my albums on shuffle because I was too embarrassed to ask anyone how to turn it off.

Sumi took a deep swig of her wine and sighed with pleasure. 'Have you downloaded the apps yet?'

'Give me a break. I've had the phone for half an hour, this is the first time I've looked at it since I left the shop,' I replied, sighing at her impatience before casting my eyes towards the floor in shame. 'I downloaded Tinder.'

She pulled a bowl of snack mix down the bar and began popping peanuts into her mouth as her eyebrows wiggled up and down suggestively. Free snacks on the bar were definitely a plus point for this place.

'Don't get excited,' I warned. 'I downloaded it, that's all, I didn't activate my profile. I think I should probably find a job before I start looking for a shag.'

'Absolutely, one hundred percent agreed, you'll hear no arguments from me,' Sumi said right before she grabbed my phone, held it up in front of my surprised face, swiped, tapped and, five seconds later, my Tinder profile was reactivated.

'You're a monster,' I told her as she sat beside me, swiping through my options. Dozens of different faces gazed up at us, a smorgasbord of available men just waiting to be tapped. 'You know I've never had any luck on the apps, no one does, it's totally pointless. Besides, I'm not ready.'

21

'I met Jemima on an app, Lucy met Creepy Dave on an app,' Sumi reminded me, as though invoking Creepy Dave might help her argument. 'Look at your pictures, they're amazing! You look fit and nice and not like a complete arsehole. That's Tinder gold.'

'Thanks.' I cringed at a clearly staged photo of me with my mouth open laughing at absolutely nothing. 'Fat lot of good they've done me so far.'

'No bites?'

'The last date I went on arrived thirty minutes late, dripping in sweat, wearing his running gear and, because that wasn't bad enough, his knob kept falling out of his shorts.'

'If his knob was big enough to fall out of his shorts, you might have been a bit more understanding,' Sumi, a lesbian who had literally never even touched a penis, suggested.

I reached across her to nix a photo of a white man proudly displaying his dreadlocks. Immediate red flag.

'And if his mum hadn't been waiting for him outside the bar, I might have been.'

'Maybe his mum was an Uber driver who needed some practice?'

'Maybe he was the next Norman Bates?'

Sumi frowned at London's love offerings. Man with a baby tiger, man skydiving, man on top of a mountain. Man on top of a mountain holding a baby tiger immediately after skydiving.

'I know you're going to tell me you're too busy to be in a relationship right now but I do think a good shag would sort you right out,' she said, causing the man sitting to my right to choke on his gin and tonic. 'It's good to clear out the cobwebs, you know?'

'I'm not against the *idea* of being a relationship,' I told her, politely pretending not to notice as my seat neighbour sopped up his drink with several napkins. 'I'm against the idea of *dating*. I don't have the time or energy to waste drinking overpriced cocktails with people I never want to see again.'

'Oh, of course,' Sumi agreed innocently. 'Because you're so busy living in your parents' shed not working?'

'Put that down as my headline,' I told her, catching my own eye in the mirror behind the bar. I looked tired. 'I do want to find someone, eventually. No one wants to be the weird single friend that shows up to family parties in last night's eyeliner and scares the children, but it's too much right now.'

'But a good first date is the best.' Her eyes sparkled as she gazed into a memory. 'All the laughing and talking and finding reasons to touch each other, wondering who's going to make the first move, wondering if they'll ask you out again, wondering when they're going to text . . .'

Sumi's first dates sounded as though they'd been a lot more fun than any of mine. 'That sounds great,' I said, giving her a look. 'But *Frasier* isn't going to rewatch itself, is it?'

Her smile softened into something more understanding. 'I think you need to get back on the horse. I think you might have forgotten how much fun horses can be, if you give them a chance.'

'All the horses I ever rode were destined for the glue factory,' I reminded her.

'To new horses,' she said, tapping her glass against mine. 'Sexy, clever horses with their own teeth, financial stability and a home that isn't a shed.'

'What about a stable?' I suggested.

'Only if it's Jesus,' she replied.

Laughing, I tucked my hair behind my ears and shook my head. I had missed her *so much*.

'Before I forget,' Sumi said, tapping a long, black acrylic fingernail on the screen of my phone. 'You need to send me your new number before I accidentally call some random American in the middle of the night.'

'I need to send everyone my number,' I told her, rubbing peanut dust on the leg of my only pair of jeans. 'They updated my contacts from the cloud so I've got everyone's details but no one has mine. Is there an app for that or have I got to text everyone I ever met?'

'You sweet precious baby,' Sumi said with a fake swoon. 'There's an app for everything, even I know that.' Her nail rattled across my screen and, in just a few taps, a little green icon appeared on my phone. 'This is what we use for group texts at work. End-to-end encryption, no one can hack it.'

It was fair to say Sumi was more than averagely engaged with conspiracy theories.

'Hit that, connect it to your contacts and open up a group message. Then you can text your number to whomever your heart desires.'

'How did I manage three whole years without you?' I asked, marvelling at the wonders of modern technology.

'It is a question I ask myself every day.'

Editing radio shows was easy, iPhones were a whole different story. This was why I didn't dare download TikTok. Fear of the unknown.

I stared at the screen, trying to come up with just

the right message. How was I supposed to say 'Hi, I'm back in London, please don't ask me any questions about my surprise return that was one hundred percent my choice and also I live in a shed now' without sounding completely pathetic?

'You're sending people your new number, you don't have to write an essay,' Sumi climbed down from her stool, peering over my shoulder to see my fingertip poised over a blank screen. 'I'm going for a wee, see if you can finish it before I get back.'

'Good to know, enjoy it,' I told her as she click-clacked off through the bar in her stilettos.

Hi, it's Ros Reynolds, I typed out before I could overthink it. Overthinking was one of my greatest talents. Given the chance, I could talk myself out of literally anything in under five minutes. Instead, I took another glug of the wine while I tried to imagine what I would say if I were writing it for someone else.

Hi, it's Ros Reynolds. This is my new number, I just moved back to London! Let's catch up soon.

One exclamation mark, no emojis. Short, sweet, to the point and, most importantly, not pathetic. It was a winner. I tapped the little arrow in the corner and saw a small white box pop up.

Group Text wants to access contacts? I hit 'Allow'.
Choose recipients or select all?

'Can I get you another drink?'

I looked up to see the woman behind the bar smiling at my empty glass.

'Could I get a water?' I asked, my head suddenly swimming with the realization that I'd absolutely chugged an entire glass of wine on an empty stomach. Not the perfect start to a Monday night. Or was it?

25

Rubbing my tired eyes, I looked back at the screen. *Choose recipients?* I started scrolling and clicking, scrolling and clicking, scrolling and clicking. It got very boring, very fast.

Yawning, I flicked my thumb upwards, sending the screen whirring all the way back to the top of the page. I clicked on *Select All*.

And then I pressed send.

CHAPTER THREE

'Someone's popular,' Sumi said on the return from her mission to the loo. On the bar, my phone flashed with unread message after unread message.

'Turns out a lot of people are bored and on their phones on a Monday night,' I replied as the 'welcome home', 'let's get a drink' and 'who is this?' texts flooded in. 'I don't even know why I have half these people in my contacts, I never text anyone apart from you, Adrian, Lucy and my sister.'

'I am honoured,' she drained her wine glass. 'Shall we have another drink?'

'Oh, go on,' I said, pushing my water away. 'Which way are the loos?'

'Downstairs, all the way to the end,' Sumi replied, already lost in her own phone. 'Ladies on the left.'

I set off on my mission, checking my latest text as I went. Domino's Pizza. At last, someone who was truly excited to have me back in the country.

*

The ladies' loos were massive, all rose gold fixtures and well-lit mirrors, perfect if your primary reason for being there was taking excellent selfies but if you needed a wee you were bang out of luck. The room was huge but some genius had only installed two toilets, both of which were occupied as I waddled up and down in front of the sinks.

'Two bloody toilets, what is the bloody point?' I muttered under my breath, sounding more like my dad by the second.

There was only one thing for it and I was far too close to having an accident to be picky. Besides, we were living in a post-gender world and I was a dying-for-a-wee girl. I scooted out of the women's toilets with my knees clamped together and cautiously opened the neighbouring door.

'Is anyone in here?' I called, poking my head into the gents.

No one was.

Ecstatic, I flung myself into one of the stalls, relieved to see it was spotless. Not as nice as the ladies but at least they had individual toilets with floor-to-ceiling wooden doors and each stall piped in both air freshener and music – both of which, I assumed, would be a bonus in the men's toilets.

The idea of drinking a glass of water with every alcoholic drink was all well and good but unless you happened to be wearing an adult nappy, it really was a supreme test of bladder control. I pulled my phone out of my pocket to see the screen light up with yet more returned messages. Robot numbers, failed connections and the odd and deeply unflattering, 'new phone, who dis?' Nestled in the middle of the mess was one text that screamed with capital letters.

Hi Ros!!! Long time no see but perfect timing??? CALL ME! ASAP!!!!

According to my contacts list, it was from Dan. But who was Dan? And why were they so intent on using every punctuation mark in their phone? Then it dawned on me. Could it be? I leaned back against the white porcelain tank, pressed call and waited for my phone to connect.

'Ros bloody Reynolds, is it really you?'

'It is,' I replied happily. 'Hello, Danielle.'

'I can't believe you're back,' she shrieked. 'This is amazing. Perfect timing, meant to be.'

Danielle and I started out as interns at the same radio station on the same day. We were first-day-of-school friends, joined at the hip and so excited. We took our tea breaks together, went for lunch at the same time, inhaled two-for-a-fiver cocktails at the Wetherspoons across the road, starry-eyed and rosy-cheeked and still so optimistic about our first forays into the job market. At least, we were for the first three months, then we realized we really didn't have anything in common other than the place we went to work every day. Slowly, we stopped hanging out so much – fewer lunches, far less tea and eventually, zero cocktails – until Danielle left for another job and that was that. She faded into a shadowy existence as nothing more than a Facebook friend and a number in my phone I'd forgotten I even had.

'I would love to have a proper chat but I'm on a plane and we're about to take off,' Danielle interrupted without pausing for breath. 'We should have a real

29

catch-up when I'm back *but* I have the most incredible opportunity of all time, I'd be doing it myself but I'm out of town for the next few weeks. PodPad needs a producer basically yesterday and I know you'd be insane at it. Is there any chance, the slightest possible hint of a chance, I might be able to tempt you to come and work for me?'

'PodPad?' I repeated. 'You're at PodPad?'

'Babes, I'm running PodPad,' she laughed. 'The programming at least.'

I knew PodPad. I turned down a job at PodPad to take the job in DC.

'That's amazing,' I told her, the sound of a politely irritated flight attendant asking her to end her call crackling through my phone's speaker. 'I'm so pleased for you.'

'It's pretty wonderful,' she agreed. 'So, producer job. Are you interested?'

'Um, I'd love to hear more about it,' I replied, trying very hard not to sound as desperate as I felt. What if she wanted to know why I'd left? What if she wanted a reference?

'You're incredible, this is the most incredible thing that has ever happened,' she cheered down the phone. Danielle, I remembered, was prone to hyperbole. 'Can you come in tomorrow?'

'Yes, absolutely,' I confirmed, pushing negative thoughts away. 'Let me know when and where and I'm there.'

I thought back to a chapter of *Starting Over* I'd read at three a.m. while the foxes behind my shed rogered each other senseless. This is what happened when you stayed positive. *Take your time, stop running.*

Stand still and the clouds will clear, allow life to show you the way.

'I'm texting you the address, be there at ten tomorrow morning and I'll love you forever,' Danielle threatened. 'I'm so pleased you texted me, Ros. I was just about to offer the job to a complete wanker and you've saved my life. Meant to be or what?'

'Miss, please put away your phone or—'

Three short sharp beeps in my ear declared the call over.

I was officially the first person on the face of the earth who had accidentally sent someone a text message and it had gone right. I made a mental note to buy a lottery ticket on the way home. It had to be my lucky day.

Flushing the loo, I slipped my phone into my back pocket so I could look myself in the eye and pretend I wasn't the kind of person who reads their phone on the toilet (even though everyone did it, there were many reports on the matter). Pushing against the heavy toilet door with all my weight, I groaned, hoping the added vocalization might somehow make me stronger but it didn't budge.

'What do they do in here that they need hermetically sealed cubicles?' I asked, not really wanting an answer to the question, before hurling myself at the door one more time. It stuck for a second then creaked open, sending me stumbling out into the toilets and—

'*JESUS FUCKING CHRIST.*'

I immediately locked eyes with a man using a urinal.

'*OH MY GOD,*' I screamed, covering my face with my hands before remembering I still needed to wash them. Thrusting my arms out in front of me, I closed my eyes instead, stumbling around the gents like a blind zombie.

'What are you doing?' the man shouted. 'Get out!'

'I'm going, I'm going,' I promised, still holding out my arms and fumbling my way forward. It seemed foolish to keep my eyes closed now, especially since I'd seen *everything*, but I had been raised to be polite. And not to use the men's toilets, but still.

'Shit,' he grunted as he zipped up his fly. 'You made me piss on my shoes.'

I winced, opening my eyes just a crack to find the sink. Sure, I might read my phone on the toilet but I always, *always* washed my hands.

'No, really, take your time,' I heard the man say over the sound of many, many paper towels being dispensed. I purposefully pumped the soap dispenser.

I opened my eyes a crack and saw him rubbing at a dark stain.

'I'm going to wash my hands,' I said primly, rinsing my hands. 'I'm not a monster.'

He looked up but his dark hair was covering most of his face. 'Says the woman using the men's toilets.'

'How dare you assume to know my gender identity,' I mumbled as I grabbed my own paper towels.

'I'm so sorry,' he said, even if he didn't sound as though he was. 'What *are* your preferred pronouns?'

'Prefer not to say.' I clocked the furious set of his jaw before I made a beeline for the door. Dark hair, dark eyes, murderous expression. Got it. 'Sorry about your shoes.'

Running back up the stairs, I grabbed the fresh glass of wine that was waiting for me and downed half of it in one gulp. Sumi's eyes opened wide.

32

'What happened to you?' she asked. 'Did a rat climb out the toilet or something?'

'Let's say yes,' I replied, taking a breath and then going back for the rest of the glass. 'I'm starving. Why don't we go and get some food? Or go to The Lex?'

'Ros, I told you, no one goes there any more. They got a new landlord and it's basically a crack den,' Sumi pulled a face. 'It was always basically a crack den, we were just too poor to care before. If you're hungry, they've got really good food here. Adrian loves the burger, have that.'

'I really want to go somewhere else,' I said, looking over my shoulder. 'I know you like it here but this place is so pretentious and totally overpriced. Let's go and get a pizza or something.'

Sumi set down her glass with concern. 'What on earth's wrong? Did something happen to you downstairs?'

'Nothing happened to *her*,' a voice answered from behind the bar. 'And we've got pizza. But it might be too overpriced and pretentious for you.'

And there he was. The man from the gents, strapping a leather work apron over his white shirt and his damp blue jeans.

'John!' Sumi leaned over the bar to press kisses on either side of his annoyed face. 'What are you doing here on a Monday?'

Of course, they were friends. Of course they were.

'Mostly being attacked in the men's toilets,' he replied, never once taking his dark eyes off me.

'I didn't attack you, it was an accident,' I muttered. I attempted to hide my face behind my masses of hair, utterly mortified. 'It's not my fault you pissed on your shoes.'

'Is that what I can smell?' Sumi sniffed the air and made a face.

'Could be the pizza,' I suggested.

Sumi looked from me to John and back to me, a confused smile on her face. As much as I loved my friend, she did like to stir up shit and there was clearly shit here to stir.

'So, it seems like you've already met but we'll do introductions anyway. John, this is my best friend, Ros, the one who was in America. Ros, this is John McMahon, the greatest bartender in all of London.'

'Nice to meet you,' I mumbled, holding out my hand. He stared at it but did not move. 'What? You know it's clean.'

'Nice to see you, Sumi,' John said with a nod. 'If you'll excuse me, I'm needed in the kitchen.'

Leaving my hand hanging over the bar, he turned and disappeared down a staircase I hadn't noticed before, hidden behind an enormous wine rack.

'Well,' Sumi turned back to me and took a long sip of wine. 'Someone made an impression.'

'Not the one I would have chosen,' I replied curtly. 'So, you were saying something about a burger?'

'Drink your drink,' she ordered. 'I'm buying and you're not working, let's get pissed.'

'Actually, I might have a job after all.' I gave her a happy grin, accompanied by my best jazz hands. 'Do you remember Danielle who I used to work with?'

Sumi frowned. 'Was she the very, very keen one?'

'Was and still is,' I nodded. 'She got my new number text and she reckons she might have a job for me. How mad is that?'

Sumi's face began to scrunch in on itself until her

nose was the only discernible feature left. 'Were you weeing or were you down there texting everyone you've ever worked with? On a public toilet? In *London*?'

'No,' I said quickly. 'I was *reading* texts on the toilet and making one very quick phone call. Perfectly acceptable according to millennial social etiquette. I only sent that one text.'

She suddenly stared at me with very wide eyes.

'Ros, did you send that text to every number in your contacts?'

I nodded.

'And you thought that was a good idea?'

I nodded.

'Have you got any idea of the number of dick pics you're going to get in the next twenty-four hours?'

I considered it for a moment then decided I definitely did not want dick pics. Yes, I was going through a dry spell but still. Unbidden dicks were not nice to look at. Even bidden dicks failed to make the prettiest of pictures. There was a reason there was no 'hall of knobs' at the Louvre.

'No one in my contacts would send a woman dick pics,' I stated. 'I'm sure of it.'

I was not sure of it.

'So it is written, so shall it be,' Sumi declared. 'Thou sendeth a group text to unknownst numbers and ye shall receiveth pics of dicks. Even I get dick pics and talk about a waste of time.'

I grabbed my glass of wine and took a deep sip. 'You're so lucky to be a lesbian.'

'And don't I know it,' she agreed.

*

By ten o'clock, I was safely tucked up in bed with *Starting Over*, slightly buzzed, learning how to tap into my limitless ass-kicking optimism and waiting for my phone to stop vibrating. The shed was feeling more and more like a Twilight Zone version of home – from the Forever Friends jewellery box to the Groovy Chick pillowcase – but it was all just a little bit off. To make matters even more confusing, just as I got into bed, Mum popped in to put all my dryer-shrunk clothes away in my drawers and, at some point in the day, Dad had been by to hook up an ancient VHS to the useless television. I now had the thrilling choice of watching any number of mid-nineties Disney films, six episodes from season two of *Sex in the City*, or a live rendition of *Les Misérables* Mum had taped off BBC about twenty years ago and, for some reason, protected with her life. I'd never had it so good.

As the words in my book began to blur together, I gave up on reading, sliding the book down the slender gap between the bed and the wall and checking my morning alarm for at least the fifteenth time.

'See?' I told the ceiling of the shed as I wedged my phone underneath my pillow. 'I am not a failed loser who is going to die alone, I am loved by my friends and family and an in-demand professional who is open to love and new experiences and also drinking wine on Mondays.'

I hiccupped and smiled happily, hugging my pillow tightly as I closed my eyes and went straight to sleep.

CHAPTER FOUR

Ten o'clock the following morning, I sat, patiently waiting in the waiting room, wearing a pair of trousers left over from the turn of the millennium that the internet assured me were due to come back into fashion any second now and my mother's second-best shirt. There had been no time to shop for a better interview outfit and since Dad had destroyed all my nicest things, I was forced to be a trendsetter.

PodPad, according to the research I'd done on my way into town, was no longer the tiny startup I'd rejected three years ago but a terribly cool company that made terribly cool podcasts about terribly cool things, like paleo diets and radical politics and serial killers. People loved podcasts about serial killers. Probably a societal red flag, I thought, reading through the list on their website: Murderville, The Killer Nextdoor. Murdered to Death. Probably something we ought to be more worried about, as if we didn't have enough to be worried about already.

A tall, gangly, red-haired man, who looked like he'd

shaved for the very first time that morning, stuck his head out the door. He glanced at me once, frowned and desperately searched the otherwise empty room for someone who was not me.

'Ros?' he asked, eventually giving up his pointless quest.

'Hi.' I stood and held out my hand. He took in my trousers, shiny shoes and freshly ironed shirt before taking my hand, shaking it and turning away with an audible sigh.

Off to a brilliant start.

'This way,' he said, leading me out of the waiting room and into a very different environment. I looked back through the door and blinked; it was like walking into hipster Narnia. Gone were the bare walls and hard plastic chairs, and in their place was a farm full of happy-looking people clicking away at computers, sitting on bold, colourful sofas, lounging next to gorgeous floor-to-ceiling windows that let in all the light. They even had the requisite ping pong table that seemed to be a contractual obligation in modern media offices. It meant this was a Cool Company and I had always wanted to work for a Cool Company. They probably had a fridge full of beers that you could have whenever you fancied and someone who came in on Tuesdays to make tacos.

'Danielle says hi,' the man said, his hands gripping his upper arms, squeezing an assortment of colourful but seemingly unconnected tattoos. I saw Mickey Mouse in his *Sorcerer's Apprentice* outfit; a Pepsi logo; an Indian-looking symbol I was sure I recognized from a yoga class; and a face that was perhaps supposed to be Kurt Cobain's but, under the tension of the man's

38

grip, looked more like Postman Pat's. 'She's in the New York office for the next couple of months so I'm looking after content while she's away. She said you've just come back from the States, yeah?'

'Yes,' I confirmed, desperate not to sound as nervous as I felt. 'Just got ba—'

'And you were working for APR, yeah?' he interrupted. 'Cool, cool. My favourite radio station. Not that I really listen to radio.'

'Thanks, it was a really good pla—'

'You were a producer? That's choice.'

Apparently he was going to interview himself on my behalf.

'Dream job, right there,' he said, stopping suddenly and perching his very tiny arse on the edge of a desk. 'Why did you leave?'

I looked around the office, with its bright colours and happy, busy people, and I wanted to be part of it so badly.

'It was time for a change,' I said. No need to go into specifics unless specifics were asked for. 'I learned a lot there but I'm ready for the next challenge.'

He considered my answer as I squeezed the strap of my handbag tighter and tighter and tighter. Was he really going to interview me in the middle of the office, in front of everyone? I cast my eyes around the room and saw everyone pretending they weren't watching.

'I'll cut to the chase,' the man said, staring hard into my eyes. My hand rose to swipe at any stray mascara that might have migrated where it was not wanted. 'We need a producer ASAP. Someone who can think fast and work hard. Danielle says that's you. Is that you, Ros?'

'I think so?' I said hesitantly, taken aback by his sudden intensity.

'We don't do "I think so" here,' he said, eyes burning directly into mine. 'We do passion.'

'I'm so sorry,' I said, coughing to cover an awkward attack of the lols that threatened to burble up and out of my mouth. 'I just realized I didn't catch your name.'

'That's because I didn't tell you my name,' he replied, re-crossing his arms over his T-shirt and covering up a slogan that was either very funny or very rude, depending on how you felt about vegans. 'What's your deal? Who is Ros? What does she want?'

I'd been working in radio for ten years and no one had ever asked me what my deal was. They'd asked me about my experience, they'd discussed my qualifications and, once, a breakfast presenter had asked for my bra size but you really couldn't get away with things like that any more, thank god.

'You want to know about my deal?' I repeated, hoping I hadn't heard him properly.

'What's your deal?' he said again, karate-chopping his own hand to emphasize each word. 'Why do you want to work at PodPad?'

'Because I'm truly passionate about sharing the truth with people and I believe radi— I mean, podcasting, is the greatest medium we have to communicate the stories that matter to the people who need to hear them,' I said carefully. It was a never-fail interview line but he just carried on staring at me, not speaking or moving.

'Why do *you* want to work at PodPad?' I asked,

starting to get annoyed. 'And seriously, what is your name?'

'We'll get to names if I decide to offer you a position,' he said, completely ignoring my first question with the hint of a smirk on his face.

For the first time in my life, I longed for an awkward, stilted interview across an MDF desk conducted in an HR dungeon by someone called Brenda. I had taken my Brendas for granted and I was regretting it. You always knew where you were with a Brenda. Was I wasting my time? Why would a company like PodPad want to hire me anyway?

'I'm here because I need a job,' I said plainly. It was cards on the table time. 'I'm thirty-two, I'm living in a shed in my parents' back garden, no one is hiring in radio between here and the Outer Hebrides and, if I don't get a job soon, I'm going to have to retrain as either an optician or an international assassin.'

The redhead's smirk grew into a fully fledged grin.

'Why an optician?'

'Seems like a good job,' I said with a shrug. 'Decent hours, good money. I've spent a lot of time sitting in little dark rooms so that seems like transferrable skill. Oh, and some opticians work in Boots and I love Boots.'

'And international assassin?'

I chewed on the inside of my cheek.

'I like to travel?'

'But you'd have to kill people.'

'Every job's got its downside,' I reasoned.

We stood face to face in the bright, busy office for slightly too long a moment and stared at each other in silence until the redhead stuck out his fist. For a split second, I thought it was going to punch me and instinctively shirked away. And then I realized he wanted me to fist-bump him and I died inside.

'I'm Ted,' he said as I reluctantly tapped my knuckles against his. 'Welcome to the team.'

CHAPTER FIVE

'To our working girl! Wait, no, that sounds terrible.'

Adrian raised a glass of sparkling wine while Lucy and Sumi cheered loudly enough to attract the attention of everyone in the bar who wasn't wearing AirPods. Which, to be fair, wasn't that many people.

'If I hadn't got this job, it would have been a very real possibility,' I replied as we clinked our glasses together. 'Not sure I'd have made a lot of money though.'

As soon as I'd messaged my friends to let them know the PodPad interview was a success, they insisted we all get together for a celebratory dinner that evening, just like old times. The only downside was, they also insisted we meet at Good Luck Bar, despite my protestations. The food was amazing, Lucy said. It was the most convenient place for everyone, Sumi insisted. And John always took a chunk off the bill, Adrian added. And so, there we were, installed in a baby-pink velvet booth that made me feel as though we were sitting on a particularly comfortable blancmange, but it was worth it to have the three of them together at such short notice. I hadn't seen them all together in one place since the last time I'd been back for Christmas, almost two years ago and that was far too long to go without your best friends.

'Tell us about the show you're producing,' Lucy said, full of encouragement as usual as she topped up my water.

'I don't actually know much about it,' I admitted. 'They were all so busy today they didn't really tell me anything. I've got my induction tomorrow. When you work for a network like that, you could be doing a million different things, it's so exciting.'

'I can't believe you found such an amazing job so quickly,' Adrian said with a congratulatory punch in the arm. Adrian and I had known each other since we were babies. His parents had lived next door to mine until his granddad died when we were fifteen and they moved into his fancy pile of bricks twenty minutes down the road. 'What happened with the old one, anyway?'

'Oh, it's just . . .' I opened my mouth, looking for the words. They were my best friends, I could tell them, surely?

'She missed us so much she had to come home,' Sumi interjected loudly. 'And now she's on to bigger and better things.'

I threw her a grateful look and agreed with a nod.

'I'm very happy for you, although I was hoping you'd slack off for a while and hang out with me,' Adrian said, throwing his arm around my shoulders. 'I hardly ever see these two, always too busy for me.'

'Some of us have to work for a living,' I replied,

needling him gently. 'Some of us don't have houses bought for us by our parents.'

'You *kind of* do,' Sumi reasoned with a grin.

'Show me the photos again,' insisted Lucy, her lovely face shining. 'I can't believe your dad built it for you, it's so sweet. Like a grown-up Wendy house.'

'Do you think the Lost Boys made her a compostable toilet?' Sumi asked sweetly.

'Where's the waitress?' I asked, keen to change the subject even as Sumi rustled around in my handbag, searching for my phone. 'I'm starving to death over here. A working woman has to eat.'

'Got to order at the bar,' Adrian replied as Sumi and Lucy pored over pictures of my shed. 'Is that a framed photo of Justin Timberlake?'

'Is that a Groovy Chick duvet cover?' Lucy asked. 'Oh my god, what a flashback.'

'I'll go,' I offered, shuffling out of the booth, taking a menu with me. 'Be right back.'

Pitching up at the bar, I earned a welcoming smile from the same waitress I'd met the night before.

'You're Sumi's friend,' she stated, reaching an amiable hand across the bar. 'I'm Camille.'

'Ros.' I navigated my arm through the taps to return her firm handshake. 'Hello again.'

'I'll let John know you're here before you order,' she asked, pointing at the menu in my hand. 'Chef's trying out some specials I know he'll want you all to try. You lot are our official guinea pigs.'

I glanced behind her into the kitchens and saw tall, dark and angry from the night before, deep in conversation with an equally tall, very pretty blonde. 'Don't worry,' I insisted, politely trying to avoid another confrontation. 'Looks like he's busy.'

'With her?' Camille turned up her tiny nose with ready indiscretion. 'She won't be staying long. Fingers crossed.'

'Girlfriend?' I asked. They were talking intently but they definitely didn't give off a colleague vibe.

'The wife.' She made little air quotes with her fingers and, from the look on her face, it seemed as though there wasn't much love lost between them. I couldn't help but be curious.

'Does she work here?'

'Hmm,' she confirmed, looking over at the two of them as the blonde laughed at something we couldn't hear. I inched my bag up my shoulder and watched as she picked a fleck of dust from his shoulder. 'When she feels like it.'

I kept one eye on John and his wife from a safe distance. What if he'd told her how I walked in on him in the bathroom? I was too British to live with that shame. And how was it that they were both so tall? Did they meet on a dating app for giants? Shouldn't they both be with shorter people to try and share those genes around? Their kitchen had to be amazing, they could both reach all the cupboards. What a gift. Before I realized I was staring, John looked up and caught my eye. I switched my gaze to the menu, boring holes into the heavy paper and reading our selections out to Camille.

'I'll have it all out as soon as,' she said as she tapped it all into the iPad in front of her. 'Nice to meet you properly, Ros.'

'Nice to meet you too,' I said, catching her boss's eye again and wishing I could say the same for him.

*

'Remember when our idea of a dream meal was a fish finger sandwich and an entire box of potato waffles?' I said loudly, once I was safely back at the table. 'Oh, to be twenty-two again.'

'You couldn't pay me to go back to my twenties,' Adrian declared. 'Not for every fish finger on the face of the earth. Too many fuck-ups, too many lessons learned the hard way.'

'Nor me, I'm so glad life is easier now,' Sumi agreed, even though she'd taken four Nurofen Plus since she'd arrived and had dark circles under her eyes that would have had Nosferatu asking if she was feeling OK. 'I couldn't go through it again. All those hours studying? No one taking you seriously? The five years it took to convince my grandmother I was gay? No thank you.'

'You work every hour god sends, you constantly complain about the other partners taking the piss out of you and your gran still thinks you're just waiting for the right man,' I reminded her. 'Lucy? Back me up.'

'I did love my twenties,' she agreed, running her palm over her belly in soothing circles. 'But, you know.'

I did know. We all knew. Lucy was the most pregnant pregnant woman that had ever existed.

'If you had to relive one year over again, which one would you choose?' I asked. They all muttered and shrugged. 'I would be twenty-eight in a heartbeat,' I said, answering my own question. 'All of us living together, loving my job, not having to worry whether or not *Friends* is problematic . . .'

'Cough, straight white privilege, cough,' Sumi spluttered. Lucy immediately reached out to rub her back as though she really had a cough and I smothered a smile with my hand.

'Not to mention that's when you met Pa—' Adrian began before he squealed and grabbed himself under the table. Someone had clearly given him a swift kick. 'Ow, what was that for?'

'We don't. Mention. Him,' said Sumi, shooting a warning look in Adrian's direction.

'Oh, come on,' I said with a light laugh even as I felt myself flush. 'It's fine. It's the past. I'm not going to start sobbing if someone says his name.'

'Really?' Lucy asked, one eye on me and my steak knife.

'It's been years,' I laid it on as thick as I could. 'Do I wonder what might have happened if I hadn't taken the job in America? Yes. Was he the love of my life? Probably. Is this a conversation I want to have right now or ever? No.'

They all gazed back at me, the same doubtful expression on three different faces.

'I am completely and utterly over Patrick Parker,' I declared. 'I am fine.'

'Good, I'm glad to hear it,' Sumi replied. 'He led you up and down the garden path so many times it was ready for repaving.'

'He was always all right with me,' Adrian said. 'I liked him.'

'You mean you were totally in love with him because he got you tickets to the FA Cup Final,' I corrected. Adrian didn't argue.

'I remember the first time we met him,' Lucy said, pressing her hand on top of mine. 'You brought him to that Christmas party and I thought, oh gosh, what a stone-cold fox. But I still think you did the right thing by leaving. You'd have regretted it if you hadn't.'

'You definitely did the right thing,' Sumi agreed. 'Imagine if you'd turned down an amazing job in America for a man.'

'Imagine,' I agreed, as if I didn't imagine it all the time.

'Everyone has a Patrick,' Adrian reasoned. 'Someone you'll always wonder about, imagine what might have been. You're contractually obliged as a human. He's the one that got away.'

'More like a bullet dodged,' Sumi muttered into her drink. 'I never saw the appeal myself.'

'He was very clever,' Lucy answered on my behalf. 'And he was a writer, that's very alluring.'

'And he was incredibly sexy,' Adrian added as we all gave him a look. 'What? A straight man can't say when another straight man is fit as? I'm secure in my masculinity, Patrick was a sexy man.'

'It wasn't just a physical thing,' I said, twisting a strand of hair between my fingers. 'His writing was beautiful and he was passionate and confident and—'

'He was horny and arrogant and up his own arse,' Sumi corrected. 'But then that's always been your type.'

'Patrick isn't why I'd go back to being twenty-eight, anyway,' I said, not wanting to argue about it. She wasn't necessarily wrong, I did have a type and that type was terrible. 'Twenty-eight is the perfect age. People stop treating you like you're too young to be taken seriously but you're not too old either, there's still so much potential to do things. Or undo things.'

'Like terrible romantic decisions,' Adrian suggested brightly. 'And liver damage.'

'It wasn't terrible with Patrick,' I said, my voice cracking just a little. 'Until the end.'

'Doesn't matter, does it? It's the past,' Sumi held up her hands to wrap up that conversation. 'You can't go back, even if you wanted to.'

'Who would want to? We're all killing it,' Adrian replied. Me and the girls exchanged a look. All of us? 'Well bloody done on getting a new job so soon.'

'I knew she'd find something right away, she's brilliant,' Sumi said proudly before she leaned across the table to smile at my oldest friend. 'But what about you, Adrian, had any more thoughts about getting one of those job-type jobs like the rest of us?'

'Lucy hasn't got a job!' he protested.

'I'm on maternity leave,' she exclaimed, clutching her belly to protect it from his accusations. 'You try giving people a facial when you've got a belly bigger than Santa's and you have to go for a wee every fifteen minutes.'

'Good try, Adrian,' I said with a smile. 'When *was* the last time you had a job?'

'I work!' he insisted. 'I drove for Uber last year, remember?'

A shiver ran down my spine as I imagined Adrian pulling up as my Uber driver. He was the worst driver on the face of the Earth. It would be like getting into a taxi driven by Mr Bean after he'd taken a Glastonbury's worth of Molly.

'And I'm working on my screenplay again.'

We all groaned as one.

'My baby is going to be doing its GCSEs before you get that thing finished,' Lucy predicted. 'If not its degree.'

'As if your kid is getting into university,' he replied with a snippy grin.

Lucy shrugged and carried on stroking her stomach. Lucy never rose to anything. Lucy was an actual saint.

I listened as they bickered back and forth, laughing and poking and prodding at each other, just like they always did. Lucy beamed as she cradled her belly and, for a moment, I felt a glow of familiar, old happiness. A tug back to a time I thought had gone by. *Starting Over*, much like Sumi, said you should never go back, that your old life was the past and the past was over, but I wasn't so sure. My old life was sitting right around this table and it looked pretty good to me.

'Before I forget, Mum and Dad are having a wedding anniversary thing on Saturday night,' Adrian said, inhaling deeply on a Marlboro Gold outside the bar as soon as Lucy and Sumi were out of sight. There was every chance he was the last person I knew who still smoked actual cigarettes. 'Will you come? They've been asking after you.'

'Are Lucy and Sumi coming?' I asked.

He shook his head. 'Lucy has a Creepy Dave thing and Sumi has a Jemima thing. She's off to Madrid to build a cathedral or something so they're going to visit for the weekend.'

Sumi's girlfriend was an architect, which meant she was very clever, very rich and an endless source of exciting minibreaks. I was sure there were many wonderful things about being in a relationship but having a lifetime-long reason to get out of doing things

51

you really didn't want to do had to be right up there with the best of them.

'Come on, Ros, it'll be a laugh,' Adrian said with a wheedling whine.

'No offence to your parents but it absolutely will not,' I said, rummaging around in my bag for chewing gum. The hake crepe that Lucy had demanded had left a very unpleasant aftertaste in my mouth, which wasn't too surprising since it had tasted very unpleasant. Fish finger sandwiches were definitely better. 'Surely you'd rather take someone who might actually have sex with you afterwards?'

'Yes, of course I would,' he replied without so much as blinking. 'But I've turned over a new leaf. I'm the new Adrian, I don't do that any more.'

'Why?' I asked, suspicious.

'Because I'm only interested in forming a deep and meaningful relationship with someone I care about,' he said, pouting. 'I'm a reformed character, Ros, I haven't had a shag in ages.'

I gave him a questioning look.

'Fine, it's been a slow summer and I haven't had any offers,' he admitted. 'But please come, it's their ruby wedding anniversary, it's a big deal. There's going to be an ungodly amount of food and drink and you know you want to.'

I really *didn't* want to but I couldn't say no. It wasn't as if I had anything else to do and Adrian would cross hot coals for me if I asked.

'Ros?' he wheedled. He took one last draw on his cigarette, stamping it out as a black Prius with a glowing Uber badge pulled up beside us. I let out a very heavy sigh and nodded. 'Fantastic,' he said as he opened the car door and hopped inside. 'Come any time after seven, can't wait. See you Saturday.'

Without the money for a taxi, I wandered back down the street towards the tube station. It had been so good to see my friends but I couldn't help but feel a little empty as I took myself off home instead of linking arms with the others and laughing all the way back to our shared house. The late-night milk runs, doing our makeup in each other's rooms, snuggling up together on the sofa to watch a film. I couldn't think of a time that I'd been happier. Now they had new homes to go to, new partners to snuggle up with. But not me.

Just like everyone else who happened to be walking alone down a busy city street at ten o'clock on a Tuesday night, I automatically slid my hand into my pocket and pulled out my phone. I was still getting replies to my texts: my great-aunt who hadn't realized I'd been away, my university friend Alison who wanted to know if I'd accepted Jesus as my Lord and Saviour since the last time she'd seen me (at our ten-year reunion with me hugging one of the student union toilets after a regrettable pint of snakebite and black). I wondered what new messages might have arrived since I'd last checked.

And then I saw it.

My heart pounded, my stomach lurched and I started to sweat, a horrible conviction that I was about to see the hake pancake again washing over me. I stuttered out of the flow of people on the street and leaned against a cold stone wall, staring at my phone, quite sure I was seeing things, quite sure it would disappear.

But it didn't. It stayed right where it was, shining up at me and willing me to open it.

I held my breath.

I opened the message.

Two words.

Hello, stranger

The text was from Patrick.

CHAPTER SIX

Everyone has a Patrick.

Adrian's words echoed in my ears all the way home to my shed. Was it true? Did everyone have someone who made them feel this way? Light-headed and loose-limbed and like they might have forgotten their own name? Because if they did, someone should have warned me before things got as bad as they did. No matter how many songs I heard or books I read or films I watched, no one had ever quite managed to put into words how I'd felt about Patrick Parker. The whole time we were together, I melted at the thought of him even as I seized up with fear that I would somehow breathe the wrong way and ruin it all. He made the sun shine, the moon glow, I had a secret smile that was just for him and there was nothing I wouldn't have done if he'd asked. He took my breath from the moment we met and I didn't get it back for nine whole months.

And then it was over.

I turned the music up in my earphones as I rounded

the corner of my parents' road, trying to drown out the memories.

Sumi once told me everything in life was an equation, that everything had a value and could all be worked out with maths. With relationships, you took the length of time you were together, added how desperately in love you were, then multiplied it by the degree of pain of the ending to find out how badly it would affect you. There were other variables: the amount of time you'd been crushing on someone before you got together (add ten), how good the sex had been (multiply by a hundred), unforgiving habits or unappealing fetishes (subtract accordingly) and, eventually, divide by the amount of time since the end of the relationship. That was how long it would take you to get over someone.

It was a straightforward solution for Sumi; her friend was the happiest she'd ever been and then, in a matter of moments, became the most heartbroken human alive, meaning there was only one conclusion: my ex was evil. But for me, it was more complicated. I needed more than just maths to figure out Patrick and me. Maybe one of those fancy calculators they'd made us buy in Year Eight but literally never showed us how to use. Was this what the 'sine' button was for?

All that was left now was a bittersweet aching, tender at the heart but warm around the edges. It was the kind of pain that felt good to press on from time to time. When I looked at my phone I was anxious and excited and sad and scared but also, there was no point lying to myself, incredibly turned on.

Instead of walking down the driveway directly to my shed, I pulled out the key to my parents' front door and skipped up the steps. There were no lights on inside, my parents were probably asleep already, but I'd left all my old diaries in the loft when I went away and I needed them. The written word was more reliable than memories.

The house was quiet, except for the ticking of the hallway clock and the occasional clack of the boiler in the understairs cupboard. It didn't matter that it was July, a day did not go by when my mother did not have the heating on. What if the queen was driving past, her car broke down and she wanted a bath and we didn't have any hot water? It just wouldn't do. What would the neighbours think?

I was rifling through the post in the hall when I heard a sound coming from the living room.

'Bugger me, that's cold.'

Clearly my dad, clearly complaining. Even though all I wanted to do was get my diaries and retreat to my shed with my memories and the enormous bar of chocolate I'd bought at the train station, I couldn't imagine a version of events where I didn't get an almighty bollocking for not coming in to say hello before I started creeping around in the loft.

'Only me,' I called, as breezy as I could manage, pushing open the living room door. 'I'm going to pop into the loft and – *oh my God.*'

My parents were sitting at the dinner table, or, to be more specific, my mum was sitting at the dinner table, a pair of chopsticks in her hand, and my dad was on top of it, his eyes wide open, mouth clamped shut and his naked body covered in sushi.

'Hello, love,' Mum said calmly, standing to reveal she was wearing nothing other than a full-length apron featuring a blacksmith's body on the front, which I remembered Jo bringing back from a school trip to Ironbridge. She leaned across the table and puffed out a candle burning awfully close to a sensitive part of my father's anatomy, which thankfully had been covered with a napkin.

'We thought you'd already gone to bed,' she said, her face fixed in a tense smile.

'And I thought *you'd* put the chain on the door,' Dad muttered through a clenched jaw, not moving so much as a muscle.

Horrified, I was stuck to the spot. Why did this keep happening to me? Why couldn't I have walked in on something civil, like some nice armed robbers, instead?

'Are you hungry?' Mum asked, smiling at me with manic eyes.

'I don't think I'll ever be hungry again,' I replied. 'I mean, no. I'm fine, thank you. This is all fine.'

'You said you're going into the loft?'

I nodded, holding onto the door handle as though it were the only thing keeping me upright.

'Be careful with the ladder,' Mum cautioned lightly as a salmon roll slid slowly off Dad's chest and fell onto the carpet. 'Your dad oiled it when we put Jo's stuff up there and it sometimes comes down a bit fast.'

'OK, thanks, good to know,' I said, walking backwards out of the living room and closing the door firmly behind me. 'Perhaps it'll hit me in the head and I'll get amnesia and forget everything I just saw.'

When I got upstairs, I looked at my hand and saw I was still shaking. Did I need to start wearing a bell around my neck? What was wrong with people? I took a deep breath and tried to concentrate on the task at hand rather than the tuna rolls that had been covering my dad's nipples.

'Get the diaries,' I mumbled to myself, using the torch on my phone to light up at least four lifetimes' worth of cardboard boxes. 'Get the diaries, go back to the shed, bleach your eyes and go to sleep.'

Ignoring the boxes marked 'Books', 'Ornaments' and 'Kitchen stuff' in my block lettering, I reached for a smaller box labelled 'Ros's Shit'. It was nice of my sister to help me pack up, I thought, frowning at her looping handwriting. Holding it tightly under one arm, I made my way carefully back down the ladder.

'Night Mum, night Dad,' I shouted as I dashed past the living room and into the kitchen, making a beeline for the back door.

'Christ almighty, Gwen,' I heard my dad screech. 'Careful with the bloody wasabi.'

Once I was showered, scoured and tucked up in bed, I opened up the box. It wasn't just my diaries I'd kept, there were all manner of mementos, including one special shoebox dedicated to all things Ros and Patrick. A beer mat from the bar we went to on our first date, an Indian takeaway menu he'd scrawled his number on, the 'Do Not Disturb' sign I'd nicked from the hotel when we'd gone on a minibreak to Dublin.

Dublin . . .

I turned the flimsy cardboard sign over in my fingers, remembering the thrill of first-time hotel sex, tearing each other's clothes off as soon as we walked in the room, not even making it to the bed. But there was also the terrible afternoon we'd spent traipsing around

59

the city in the rain, looking for the house from *Dubliners*, only to discover it had been knocked down years before. He'd been so annoyed, I'd tried to assuage him with a trip to a whisky distillery and given myself my worst hangover of the decade, which only annoyed him further. It was impossible to vomit subtly in a hotel bathroom. But those parts were easy to forget when I remembered the first day, spinning through the streets hand in hand, eyes only for each other, laughing and breathing and feeling so free. And did I mention the hotel sex? I would never be the same woman again.

This diary still felt new compared to some of the others in the box, the ones covered in stickers and scribbles, postcards of bands stuck to the front, whose songs I could barely remember now, but had meant everything to me once upon a time. The creamy pages were thick and lush between my fingers – total stationery porn – and my illegible handwriting looped and sloped all over the place, ballooning off the lines on some pages, slanted with the speed of my script on others. The first few entries were full to bursting, words running into each other as I documented my every thought and feeling, from meeting Patrick at some ridiculous party I'd been dragged to by my parents, to the first date, the first touch, the first kiss, the first everything else. It was all written down, the things I couldn't say out loud, not even to Sumi or Lucy. It felt alien to me now: had I ever felt this strongly about anything? I certainly hadn't felt even a fraction of this since we broke up. My love bled through the page with blistering vulnerability and it was almost too painful to read. Cool, composed, sophisticated, intellectual, passionate, gorgeous, bold, brave, adventurous Patrick was mine and I was ecstatic.

And then the anxiety crept in. The concerns, the worrying, the second-guessing. He cancelled a date, was he over me? He forgot we made plans, did he not care? Was I ever even good enough for him? It was a side of myself I didn't care to be reminded of.

By the time we got to the end of the nine months, twenty-two days and fourteen hours, my writing didn't flow quite so freely and I'd eased up considerably on the adjectives. Just the facts, ma'am. I told him about the job offer in DC, he said I should take it, he wanted to go travelling anyway. A clean break is always for the best. No hard feelings, let's stay in touch, yeah? And then nothing. I'd left this diary behind and given up keeping one altogether. The only record of my time in America was in photo form, tiny digital squares of memories saved on my laptop and not nearly as affecting.

A handful of photographs fell into my lap, blurry, overexposed candids, a million miles away from the pictures we took on our phones. Every photograph I took now was ruthlessly cropped, filtered and edited, and anything less than deeply flattering was immediately discarded into the digital wasteland. These were different. I leafed through them, smiling. It wasn't that long ago but we all looked so much younger, sharper angles but softer edges. We took disposable cameras everywhere that summer, me, Sumi and Lucy, determined to break free of our phones, an ahead-of-the-curve digital detox. It lasted exactly one month until Sumi balked at the price of film development and I ran the camera we'd taken to Lucy's hen do through the wash.

There was a rush in these photos you couldn't get in phone pics, I realized, tracing the curve of my arm in another photo: it was slung carelessly around Patrick's neck, my head thrown back, him holding a hand out towards the camera to wave the photographer away but still laughing. So much genuine emotion packed into one frame that I suddenly had to wonder if our ancestors had been right all along. Did the flash steal your soul? Did we give a piece of ourselves away with every selfie?

There was one photo in particular, curled at the edges and sticky on the back from a time it had taken pride of place on my wall, one photo that hit me right in the heart. It was me and Patrick at Lucy's wedding. Lucy had given it to me, rather than keeping it for the album, it felt too personal, too intimate, to share with strangers. The sun was behind us, a bright white light sharply lining our features, and we were holding hands, eyes on each other, as though we were the only two people on earth. Our faces were inches apart, either pre- or post-kiss, I couldn't recall, but we looked so happy. So, so happy. And three weeks after it was taken, we broke up.

Slipping the photos back in the diary, I threw it as far as I could. About four feet. The shed really wasn't very big. I pulled the sheets up to my chin and let out a loud huff. Probably not the best idea right before bed, I thought as I threw my hot and bothered body around, my legs tangling themselves up in the bed clothes as I went.

Grunting, I reached for my phone and opened my messages.

There it was, bold as brass, clear as day.

Hello stranger.

I placed the phone back on the nightstand and draped one arm over my face, covering my eyes. Maybe if I lay there long enough, stayed still enough, I would forget about the text and fall asleep.

I lasted ten seconds.

With a loud sigh, I reached for my phone again.

Hello stranger.

It was going to be a long night.

CHAPTER SEVEN

'Tell me you didn't text him back.'

'I did not text him back.'

It was the truth. I had not replied to Patrick's text. I'd slept for what felt like fifteen minutes, taken two cold showers, listened to the foxes living and loving in my parents' back garden, eaten half a tub of Nutella straight out the jar, read several chapters of *Starting Over*, chosen my least-worst New Job outfit from my limited wardrobe and hunted for my ex up and down the internet to no avail but I had not replied to Patrick's text.

Striding down the street, on my way to my first morning at work, I lifted my chin to feel the sun on my face.

'I didn't text him,' I said. 'But I really want to.'

A short, exasperated sigh whistled down the line.

'I know you do,' Sumi said kindly after collecting herself. 'But you can't, Ros. Honestly, I don't know why you even still have his number in your phone.'

'I didn't have his number in my phone, it was in

the cloud!' I protested. 'When the girl in the shop downloaded all my information to the new one, she used a back-up from the cloud. She said it would be quicker than doing a phone-to-phone transfer.'

'You never save anything to the cloud!' Sumi admonished me. 'You don't really want all your personal information flying around out there in cyberspace, do you?'

I shrugged. If it meant I didn't have to remember my passwords or credit card numbers when I wanted to order a pizza, I was happy to be part of the problem.

'Please don't text him, Ros,' she pleaded. 'It's such a bad idea.'

'Is it?' I wondered out loud. 'Because I was thinking about it last night and I think closure might be a good idea.'

'I'll give you closure, we'll role-play.' She cleared her throat and deepened her voice. 'Hello, Ros, I'm Patrick. I think I'm really clever because I've read a lot of books and written one or two but I've actually got the emotional maturity of a shoe and not a very nice one.'

I shook my head and smiled as I walked past a coffee shop, remembering the coffees and pastries he'd brought back to his flat the first morning after the first night before.

'Do you think he misses me?' I asked. 'Do you think that's why he sent the text?'

'I don't know what he's thinking,' Sumi admitted. 'But I do know he broke your heart and I'm not down for you to give him a chance to do it again.'

'Probably just being nice,' I reasoned. 'Replying out of politeness. I did send him the first text, after all.'

Sumi burst out laughing. 'Ros. When was Patrick ever nice? Or polite?'

It was a fair point. He was a lot of things but nice wasn't one of them. But who wanted nice? Nice was just a polite word for boring. Patrick was adventurous and passionate and bold and even though I tried so hard not to, now he was back in my head, I missed him so much I could taste it.

'It has been a while, what if he's changed?'

'He could have been turned into a unicorn that's been tasked with protecting the Holy Grail and I still wouldn't think it was a good idea to text him,' she replied, blunt as ever. 'You were together six months and it's taken you three years to get over him. Don't do this to yourself.'

'It was nine months,' I corrected. 'Almost ten.'

Nine months, twenty-two days and twenty-three hours if we were being precise. Accuracy was important to me.

'You were together nine months, almost ten,' Sumi repeated. 'Then you were offered an amazing job opportunity that didn't mean you had to break up but he knocked the whole thing on the head without giving it a second thought.'

'I know,' I said softly. 'I was there, I remember.'

'I just don't want you to get hurt again,' Sumi groaned. 'This is *so* like him, so casual, so vague. What if you reply, get your hopes up, and then he tells you he's married with kids?'

The thought of Patrick being legally tied to someone else hit me like a wet haddock. I slowed down in the street, suddenly sick to my stomach.

'And you already know it's a bad idea,' she added,

her voice softening slightly. 'If you'd wanted someone to tell you to text him, you'd have called the soft-touch, not me.'

She meant Lucy. Lucy was, in fairness, very persuadable.

'Enough about that Twat-Faced Wank Chops,' Sumi said, invoking her favourite nickname for him, before I could add fuel to the Patrick Parker conversation fire. 'Are you excited for your first day at work?'

'Nervously optimistic?' I replied. Patrick's message had worn the edges off my giddiness but I was still a bundle of happy nerves when I thought about it. 'I've got loads of ideas, I think it's going to be good.'

'It's going to be brilliant,' she corrected. 'Have fun, be amazing and do not spend the entire day thinking about Patrick "I've got a PhD and not in the dirty way" Parker.'

'But also in the dirty way,' I reminded her.

'Thinking about his knob is not going to improve matters, so stop it,' Sumi warned. 'No thinking about him, no looking at photos of him and definitely no texting him. These are my commandments, Ros, I command thee. Thou hast been commanded.'

'I'm sure I'll be far too busy for him to even cross my mind,' I assured her even though we both knew I could be put in charge of air traffic control at Heathrow and I'd still manage somehow. 'I'll talk to you later. Love you.'

'Love you,' Sumi replied. 'Don't text him!'

'Sorry for all the smoke and mirrors yesterday,' Ted said, leading me out of the bright and colourful PodPad HR office and down a markedly less bright and colourful staircase I hadn't seen the day before. 'But we've signed a million NDAs for this show and I couldn't tell you anything until you'd signed a contract.'

'No problem,' I answered without hesitation, jogging closely behind him. Why were we leaving the Cool Office? Why was he leading me into the basement? 'My curiosity is officially piqued. What's the show about?'

Ted stopped at the bottom of the stairs and gave me a grin. 'What was your last show about?' he asked.

Someone enjoyed exercising power wherever he could find it.

'The Book Report?' I replied. 'It was a culture show, book-based, obviously, clue's in the name. The host interviewed a different author every week, asked them about their favourite books, you know, from different stages of their life. I developed it from scratch, got to work with the authors, the publishers, everything.'

He fumbled with an enormous ring full of keys and opened a heavy security door. 'You like books?'

'Yes,' I nodded. 'A lot. You?'

'Eh,' he grimaced as he pulled open the door in a pantomime of chivalry. 'Not really a book man.'

Not really a book man.

'Is the new show book-related?' I asked as we walked down a dimly lit corridor, a prickle of excitement running up my spine as fluorescent lights clicked into life one by one above us. 'Because it's a great format, super easy to put together. If we find the right host, it could be up and running in a few weeks.'

'Here's the thing,' Ted stopped short in front of one of six identical plywood doors. 'We've already got a show for you. PodPad signed an incredibly talented person and they have the potential to be massive but they need the right producer to help them. Someone creative, someone who isn't afraid to take risks, someone who can get a brilliant show out of a brilliant mind.'

'And I'm that producer?' I asked, a little surprised but pleasantly flattered.

He clicked his tongue and shot at me with double-finger guns.

'So,' I said, bracing myself against the sudden drop in temperature. Downstairs was much colder than upstairs. 'Who is the incredibly talented person and why are we in the basement?'

'This is where the studios are, soundproofing, yeah?' He opened the door to a tiny, dark, dingy room and suddenly I was very nostalgic for the home comforts of my shed. 'And you're not going to believe it when I tell you. It's insane that we've been able to get him, totally mad. Even I can't believe we got him and I'm the one who signed the massive cheque for the bastard. He's a genius. And not a book genius, like, a proper genius normal people have heard of.'

My heart began to pound and not just because I was incredibly claustrophobic. Here it was at last, my opportunity to put myself on the map, show everyone what I could do, working with a non-book genius. Who could it be? Lin-Manuel Miranda? The Rock? Anyone but Kanye.

'OK, the anticipation is killing me,' I said, watching Ted flick six switches on at the wall only to see half as many bulbs light up. 'Who is it?'

He sat down in a beaten-up leather office chair that

had been patched up with duct tape one too many times and grinned. 'He's an athlete.'

'David Beckham?' I guessed, heart pounding. I couldn't do it to Posh and the kids obviously but a feverish flirtation would probably be morally acceptable.

'Bigger,' Ted grinned.

'Roger Federer?'

'Even bigger,' he replied, eyes closed and hands up in the air, ready to conduct an invisible orchestra. 'It's Snazzlechuff.'

It was at that precise moment I realized I had followed a man I did not know into a soundproofed basement with no idea about his mental state and, to make matters worse, I was wearing shitty kitten heels that would never in a million years be able to penetrate his skull if I needed to use them as a weapon.

'Excuse me?' I said, very politely.

'It's Snazzlechuff,' Ted repeated. 'Snazzle. Chuff.'

'Are you having a seizure? Should I get help?' I asked, looking around for signs of human life besides the two of us. I knew I shouldn't have listened to *Murdered to Death* on the train to work.

'You've never heard of Snazzlechuff?'

I shook my head as I calculated my best possible route of escape. Probably bash him in the head with my backpack, bolt back upstairs, grab one of the free beers and launch myself through the plate-glass window.

'He's literally the most famous person in the entire world,' Ted said, not even trying to hide the disdain on his face. 'He's got the most successful gaming channel in history, more than 15 million followers across all platforms and you've never even *heard* of him?'

He shoved his phone in my face, waving it around until I grabbed it out of his hands.

'This is him?'

Ted nodded.

'Why's he got a dog's head?'

The picture in front of me showed a skinny body, clothed head to toe in a bright red tracksuit, with an enormous Wes-Anderson-looking Dalmatian's head on its shoulders.

'He always wears a mask,' Ted explained. 'It's part of his mystique.'

'What's his real name?'

'No one knows,' he replied, waving his fingers around and making spooky noises. 'He's an enigma.'

'You said you signed his cheque?' I said as I swiped through the photos. 'Surely that had his name on it?'

'Cheque went to his agent.'

'I thought you said he was an athlete?' I said, deflating by the second. Bye-bye David Beckham, farewell Roger Federer, see you in my dreams. Both at the same time, hopefully.

'He's an *e-sports* athlete,' he explained. 'He's a god on YouTube.'

'Then that explains it,' I replied, folding up my dreams of a workplace romance and storing them neatly next to my Ted-might-be-a-serial-killer anxieties. 'I'm not really a YouTube woman.'

He sat forward and peered at my forehead.

'How old are you?'

'Thirty-two but very dehydrated,' I said, tossing my hair to cover as much of my face as possible. 'So, when am I meeting this superstar? Is he here?'

'Course not,' he answered. 'It's Wednesday, he's at school.'

It just got better and better.

'How old is he, Ted?' I asked.

My new boss scratched his stubble thoughtfully. 'I want to say fifteen but he could be a tall twelve. It's very hard to tell with kids these days, isn't it?'

'It is,' I agreed readily, wondering whether or not I could drive the heel of my shoe through my own temple if I was truly dedicated to the act.

'He's not like a normal kid though,' Ted assured me. 'He's clever. And funny! So it doesn't matter that you're not.'

I looked around the studio, such as it was. Cheaply painted dark grey walls covered in black sound-proofing, like foam egg boxes that had been dipped in tar, flickering fluorescent overhead lights and a filthy sheet of glass that separated the producer's bay from the recording booth. It was covered with so many handprints it looked as though it had recently been used to reenact that scene in the back of the car in *Titanic*. God forbid I ever turn a black light on the room, I thought to myself. The whole place was crying out for an anti-bac wipe. Or a nuclear blast. One or the other.

'If I'm being totally honest with you, I haven't really done anything like this before,' I said, tugging at the sleeve of my smart white shirt. 'Not that I'm not up for the challenge but it isn't something I have a lot of experience in. You're all right with me learning on the job?'

Ted waved away my concerns with an unmoved 'pfft'.

'Mate,' he replied, even though we were not mates.

'If you can make books sound interesting enough for people to tune into your show, think what you'll be able to do with a genuinely fascinating subject like e-sports!'

'You really mean that, don't you?' I asked, glancing around the studio-slash-dungeon one more time.

'I most certainly do,' he said with a grave nod. 'You're welcome.'

'And this is only the studio? I don't have to stay down here all the time?' I asked, afraid I already knew the answer. 'My desk's upstairs, right?'

'Thing is,' Ted sucked the air in through his teeth like he was about to tell me my carburettor needed replacing. 'We're short on desks at the moment. But you can do a bit of decorating if you like? With your own money.'

He rapped his knuckles on the desk and its loosely attached drawer crashed to the floor.

'We can probably get you a new one of those,' he muttered, kicking it away as I held my breath.

Run, commanded the voice in my head. Run far and run fast. But I refused to listen, that was just fear talking, according to *Starting Over*. The fear of failure and the even more powerful fear of success. I would not stand in my own way, I would embrace this opportunity and succeed. I would also bring in my own cleaning products from home.

'Just so I'm absolutely, one hundred percent clear about everything,' I said, running a finger along the mixing desk and balking at the filth. 'The job I just signed a contract for is to produce a podcast about e-sports with a YouTube child star?'

Ted gave a single, eyes-askance nod.

'Didn't you say you lived in a shed?' he asked.

'So,' I said, taking a deep breath in and giving my new boss a bright and glittering smile. 'When do I meet Mr Snazzlechuff?'

After Ted left me alone to wallow in my pit, I sat at the desk and stared at my reflection in the glass partition between the studio and the mixing desk. The look of despair on my face was altogether too clear since I'd gone at the bloody thing with a full bottle of Windolene I'd found in a cupboard, oddly enough unopened.

Ten years of working every hour god sent and suddenly my career depended on a teenage gaming addict who liked to cosplay as a mid-2000s Jay-Z from the neck down and the saddest Good Boy from the neck up. Where had it all gone wrong?

'It's going to be fine,' I told my own face, even though I didn't look as though I believed me. 'You're lucky to have this job. It's different and new, that's all. Everything was different and new once, you'll be fine.'

But a very large part of me was completely over different and new.

Three years ago, I'd jumped at different and new, lost Patrick, left my friends and whole life behind and for what? To end up right back where I'd left off, only now I was alone and I lived in a shed. Everything was confusing and exhausting, I couldn't get to grips with any of it: how to decide what to watch in the evening, which politicians were the most evil, who had been cancelled and why. What was I allowed to like, what was I allowed to dislike and where was indifference permitted? No, different and new were on my shitlist.

I wanted old and familiar. I wanted easy and under-standable. I wanted tried and tested, simple and straightforward, comfortable and known and, without thinking, I picked up my phone, opened Patrick's text and tapped out a reply, hitting send before I could stop myself.

Hello, stranger, his text said.

Hello yourself, I replied.

'Well, that's that,' I whispered, taking a deep breath and watching a single grey tick appear next to the message, followed by a double grey tick. Message delivered.

Three years of stopping myself from contacting him, three years of having to sleep with my phone in the other room every time I came home drunk or went on a rubbish date or experienced even a flicker of yearning. All of it over in an instant. I looked up, expecting to see some flags fly out, a winged pig zooming past overhead, or to at least hear a distant fanfare, but there was nothing. Life-changing moments were supposed to come with a soul-stirring soundtrack, something to acknowledge their gravitas and importance, but all I had was a soundproofed studio-slash-cell, a half-eaten apple and a bag of Mini Cheddars.

'The stuff dreams are made of,' I muttered, yawning before I bit down on the apple. 'Now let's see if he bothers to reply.'

The clock on my wall announced the time as ten a.m.

A long night, followed by an even longer day.

CHAPTER EIGHT

'Having fun?'

'Never had so much fun in my life.'

I clinked my glass of Pimm's against the one in Adrian's hand and nodded across his parents' vast lawn.

'Mr Carven told Dr Khan he didn't want one of your dad's sausages because they weren't cooked all the way through,' I said, discreetly pointing at the middle-aged gents, bickering around the barbecue like a bunch of schoolgirls.

'And my dad heard him?' Adrian asked, sipping his drink like so much tea. 'He'll have his guts for garters.'

'They're currently trying to decide which sausage to cut open to end the debate,' I confirmed with a nod. 'Mr Carven wants one from the outside of the grill but your dad wants one from the middle of the grill and Mr Khan is very concerned that if they wait much longer, all the sausages will be burnt and the experiment will be compromised.'

'Aren't you glad this is how you're spending your

first Saturday back?' he said, resting his arm on my shoulders. 'Is there anything more British than watching a load of old men fight over barbecued sausages?'

'It is strangely compelling,' I agreed as the men settled on a sausage and sliced it open. Adrian's dad hooted with joyous conviction, brandishing the perfectly cooked sausage in his supposed friend's face. I hadn't seen anything quite like a British barbecue in a long time. I smiled, my stomach rumbling. Mostly I was just glad to be outside and able to see the sky. I'd stayed late at work all week and not only because my friends were all too busy to see me. I really, really wanted to do a good job and, since I knew absolutely nothing about gaming, it had been a steep learning curve.

'Mum's so happy you're here,' Adrian said, nodding over at his mother resplendent in her garden party florals. 'But be warned, she's definitely going to ask you if you've come back to make an honest man of me.'

'How much to tell her I'm pregnant and it's yours?'

He threw his head back and barked out my favourite laugh. 'She'd have you up the registry office wearing her wedding dress before you'd even finished your sentence.'

At least once a year, one of Adrian's parents would ask me, in person or – my favourite – by commenting on an unrelated post on my Facebook wall, why it was he and I had never got together. The truth of it was, we had kissed once. Both very drunk on alcopops, faces smushed together on the dance floor of the only local nightclub that didn't check IDs closely enough to see that neither of us was eighteen. It was such a rousing success that I burst out laughing, Adrian's penis disappeared back up inside him and neither of us had ever mentioned it again. I'd always assumed we must be related in some weird, 23andMe kind of a way, because, love him though I did, it really wouldn't have mattered if he was the last man left on the face of the earth, I would rather have had sex with my own foot than make a go of it with Adrian Anderson.

'Christ almighty, is that your mum?' he gave me a nudge as my parents approached. 'She looks well fit.'

'Shut up before I remove your testicles with my house keys,' I replied, my cheeks flushing the exact same shade as my mum's strappy sundress. Everyone else at the Andersons' party was wearing exactly what you'd expect: a bit of Jasper Conran here, a touch of M&S there, plenty of floaty and floral. But not my mother. The hem of her dress barely flirted with her knees, clung to her tiny waist and strained over her absolutely massive chest. I looked down at the round-neck, loose-fit watercolour-print Zara midi dress I'd bought on the way home from work the night before, feeling like a complete frump.

'She looks fantastic,' he said, waving them over. 'I don't think I've ever seen her out of jeans before. What has she been doing?'

'More like who she's been doing,' I grumbled. 'Her and my dad are "getting to know each other" again, if you know what I mean.'

'I don't but I'm dead serious, your mum could get it,' he whispered before throwing his arms open for a hug. 'Mr Reynolds, Mrs Reynolds, so nice to see you. It's been a dog's age.'

'Adrian, how many times do I have to tell you? It's Gwen to you,' Mum said, tittering as my friend kissed her hand and spun her around, making the handkerchief hem of her dress flare outwards.

Dad wasn't nearly as impressed. Ever since we were little kids, he'd never been especially keen on Adrian and Adrian hadn't really done anything to change his mind, whether he was kicking a football through his greenhouse or suggesting that the very expensive and beautiful steam shower Dad had designed for Adrian's parents' new bathroom was 'cool in a sexy gas chamber kind of way'.

It was fair to say he didn't help himself.

'We must go and say hello to Simon and Sheila,' Dad said, unwinding my mother from Adrian's arms and casting a cool look in his direction. Adrian fended it off with a wink I was sure I'd be hearing about later. 'Will you be wanting a lift later, Rosalind?'

'Don't worry, Mr Reynolds,' Adrian answered before I could. 'I'll get her home safe and sound.'

Dad gave him another thunderous look and marched on, barbeque-bound, with my mother leading the way.

'You make it worse every time,' I said, suppressing a smile. 'Although, maybe if we told my dad you'd got me pregnant, he'd let me move back into the house.'

'If we told your dad I'd got you pregnant, we'd be moving him to the heart ward at the Royal Brompton and me to the cemetery,' Adrian replied. 'But whatever it is your mum's doing, you should consider doing the same.'

'I don't think I'll be doing what my mum's doing any time soon, thank you,' I muttered into my glass. The cursed image of sushi night flashed in front of me.

'How's the job going?' Ade asked as I watched all the attending dads eye up my mother and all the attending wives glare at the dads. 'What's the latest?'

I pulled at the high collar of my dress, as my mum, surrounded by middle-aged men offering her sausages, hooted with laughter.

'It's interesting,' I said diplomatically. I'd spent all week immersing myself in all things Snazzlechuff and I still had no idea what I was going to do. 'As soon as I work out how to best display the talents of a near-mute fourteen-year-old, I'll be killing it.'

'Snazzlechuff,' Adrian whispered, holding one hand aloft and squinting his eyes as though he were delivering a Shakespearean soliloquy. 'It's this generation's "Rosebud". I want it to be my dying word.'

'You're going the right way about it,' I assured him. 'Hey, isn't that the bartender from Good Luck Bar?' I pointed over to a tall man with black hair who was busy behind the bar. 'What's he doing here?'

'That's John,' he confirmed. 'He's my anniversary present to Mum and Dad. Custom cocktails to get everyone so slaughtered, they don't blame Dad's barbecue skills when they're throwing up tomorrow.'

'You're such a good son,' I replied, wrinkling my nose at the platter of chicken legs that was currently marinating nicely in sunshine and salmonella. 'And you're buying me a pizza later.'

'Agreed,' he said, sinking his Pimm's. 'Shall we test-drive the cocktails?'

'Let's,' I agreed, my desire to avoid John from Good Luck outweighed by my desire to get tipsy enough not to worry about my mum having a wardrobe malfunction. The delicate straps of her dress were doing work they were not built for.

Adrian leaned against the bar with a knowing smile on his face while we waited for John to finish rummaging with bottles at the back of the bar.

'OK, I've waited long enough, out with it.' Adrian reached across the bar and plucked a maraschino cherry from a little black pot while John's back was turned. 'What did you text back to Patrick?'

He popped the cherry in his mouth in one, gurning like a madman while he attempted to knot the stalk with his tongue.

'There's literally nothing sexy about that, you know,' I told him. 'You look like you're having a seizure.'

'You'd be amazed at how many times this has worked,' he replied right as his eyes bugged out of his head and he coughed up the stalk, spitting it elegantly onto the lawn. 'Answer the question. What's going on?'

'Sumi told you?'

'Sumi told me,' he confirmed. 'No judgement.'

A likely story.

'Maybe I didn't text him,' I said with an unconvincing shrug.

Adrian brayed with laughter.

'Fine, yes, I messaged him back,' I said, coiling my hair into a high ponytail to get it off my sticky neck. 'But don't look at me like that, it's not that weird. Lots of people are friends with their exes.'

'Oh, I see,' Ade replied, nodding. 'You want to be

81

friends with Twat-Faced Wank Chops. OK, sure, definitely, that's your plan, is it?'

'Maybe,' I shrugged. 'Maybe not. It actually makes sense to me. Why waste my time, my incredibly valuable time, on dates with complete strangers who are most likely going to turn out to be utterly shit, when I could dig into my contacts and see if there's anyone worth a second chance?'

Adrian shook his head, refusing to play along. 'Ros, your contacts are where dates go to die. You only keep your exes' numbers so you know not to answer when they call.'

'Speak for yourself. I can think of a couple of people I went out with once or twice but the timing wasn't right. *Including* Twat-fac— including Patrick,' I said, beginning to feel flustered. 'What if I messed up something good with him when I left? And why not skip all that awful getting-to-know-you stuff and pick up where I left off with someone who's already seen me naked?'

I gave my head an aggressive toss to make my point and caught a passing pensioner in the eye with my ponytail. 'Oh, Christ, I'm sorry. Are you OK?'

'I just had my cataracts done!' he wailed as I grabbed a handful of napkins off the bar. Behind me, I heard a muted chuckle.

'Have you thought about wrapping her in bubble wrap before you let her out the house?'

John the bartender leaned against the opposite side of the bar, he and Adrian both wearing the sort of bemused smile that made me feel extra punchy. I pressed my stack of napkins into the older man's hand, apologizing profusely, as he swiped at his watering eye before a woman in a dusky-blue two-piece rushed up and whisked him away, giving me a filthy look as they went.

'You look like you could use a proper drink,' John said, eyeing our empty glasses. 'Two anniversary specials?'

'Two anniversary specials,' Adrian confirmed. 'And make them strong enough to loosen her tongue. I promised Sumi I'd get it out of you before they cut the cake.'

Ooh. Cake.

'Fine, yes, I replied to his text *to be polite*.' I kept my eyes on John as he mixed our drinks. There wasn't nearly enough bottle-twirling for my liking, I'd seen *Cocktail*, I knew how this was supposed to be done. 'I wasn't brought up to be rude, Adrian.'

'Is that right?' John muttered under his breath.

Adrian grinned as I gave the bartender a double-take.

'Here you go,' he said loudly, sticking a steel straw into one of the drinks in front of him to taste his concoction. 'Two Ruby Wedding Fizzes.'

'It's perfection,' Adrian said, closing his eyes in rapture as he took a sip. 'John, have I ever told you that I love you?'

'Son?'

I turned to see Adrian's less-than-woke dad staring at his only child with a look of intense concern on his face.

'Not like that, Dad,' he said, clapping the older man on the back. 'Please don't have a stroke during your own party.'

'Although he could do a lot worse,' John muttered not-quite-under his breath.

Mr Anderson blustered as I politely looked away, biting my lip to stop myself from laughing. 'It wouldn't matter to us, you know that,' he waffled. 'Your mother and I just want to see you settled and happy and—'

'What's up, Dad?' Adrian asked, mercifully cutting him off mid-stream.

'Your mother needs a hand getting the cake out the kitchen,' he said, lowering his voice to explain further. 'It's, uh, quite heavy.'

'It's a triple-tier fruitcake,' Adrian explained for our benefit. 'She made it herself.'

I nodded, understanding all. Mrs Anderson's fruitcakes were things of legend. I could have hollowed one out and lived in it and it definitely would have been more of a solid structure than my shed. 'Do you need me to help as well?' I offered.

'I think two of us should be able to manage it,' Mr Anderson said with an appreciative smile. 'Lovely to see you back, Rosalind. We must have you over for dinner, I'd love to hear about America. Perhaps you could bring your boyfriend with you? If you're seeing someone?'

'Let's go and get the cake,' Adrian said with an exasperated sigh. 'Come on.'

The two of them traipsed off into the house, Adrian slightly taller, his father slightly broader, but both of them cut from exactly the same cloth.

'I know he won't thank me for saying it but he's so like his dad,' John said as they disappeared into the house.

'He won't but he is,' I agreed. 'I was thinking the same thing.'

He leaned over the bar, arms resting in between a bevy of bottles. 'And you won't thank me for asking this but who did you text when you weren't supposed to?'

I cast a glance over my shoulder, one eyebrow raised.

'Bartender's privilege,' he said with a lopsided grin. 'I'm entitled to ask about any and all gossip I hear during a shift and duty-bound never to repeat a word.'

It was a new one on me.

'There's an oath, is there?' I asked, smiling.

'I'm practically a doctor,' he confirmed.

'Or a lawyer,' I suggested. 'Or a priest.'

He paused and looked up at me, meeting my eyes just for a moment.

'Maybe not a priest.'

I sipped my cocktail and tried not to think about what I'd seen in the gents toilets.

'All right, let me guess, I'm good at this,' John said as he pulled out a small knife to peel back the foil on another bottle of prosecco. 'It's an ex, clearly.'

'What makes you say that?'

'I didn't hear all of it but I heard enough.' John began mixing more drinks while he talked. 'What's interesting to me is that your friends clearly don't think you should text him. Also, you told Sumi but not Adrian and you know those three, they tell each other *everything*.'

I fought off an indignant flush of outrage. They weren't 'those three', we were 'us four'. How dare this random bar boy group my friends into a trio when we were definitely, absolutely, always-had-been-always-would-be, a quartet?

'Fine, it's an ex,' I admitted, tightening my ponytail. 'But that was obvious, you're not exactly psychic, are you?'

He smiled mildly as he poured what looked like a never-ending stream of gin into a cocktail shaker.

'What's the deal?' John asked. 'How come they don't want you talking to him?'

'We broke up when I moved to America for work,' I told him, reluctant to go over the details of one of the worst times of my life with a man I knew nothing about other than that he worked in a bar, mixed a mean cocktail and was circumcised.

'Bad break-up?'

'Complicated break-up.'

'He didn't want you to go?'

I chewed on my bottom lip, unbidden tears burning the back of my eyes. Damn that Pimm's on an empty stomach. 'It wasn't that. We'd only been together for a while but I suppose I thought it was more serious than it was.'

'Oh,' John said, rounding out the word and stretching it into oblivion. 'I see.'

'But who knows what would have happened if I'd stayed?' I added. 'He didn't want to do long distance and I took it fairly badly, so my friends don't like him. Standard ex stuff. That's all there is to it.'

'That's the reason they don't like him?' John asked. 'Because *you* left for a job in another country?'

I paused and took a drink.

'It's possible they didn't all get on terribly well before that,' I replied. 'But, you know, your friends don't always get on with your boyfriend. None of us are exactly in love with Creepy Dave.'

'No, but I've never heard Adrian call him "Twat-Faced Wank Chops" either,' he said. 'Seems to me they don't think he's good enough for you.'

Oh good, I groaned inwardly. He was going to mansplain my own friends and their opinions on my break-up to me. His poor, beautiful, giant of a wife. Imagine having to put up with this all the time.

'How long has it been since you texted him?' John asked, fitting a pint glass into the top of his cocktail shaker. 'One day, two days?'

'He texted me on Tuesday, I texted him on Wednesday,' I replied, watching as he shook his drink into next week. Now, there was some proper Tom-Cruise-level cocktail crafting, I was almost impressed. His biceps bulged against the stiff cotton of his shirt with the strain of his effort but his face was completely impassive. Maybe I could start an exercise class using cocktail shakers as weights. Get a workout and a drink at the same time, what could go wrong?

'Three days,' he said, squinting at the maths. He knocked the cocktail shaker against the bar to loosen the pint glass he had wedged in the top and poured the frothy pink liquid into four waiting glasses.

'It's fine, it's whatever,' I said hurriedly. 'He's probably not going to reply.'

'Oh, he is,' John replied. 'He'll text you tonight, ask what you're doing later.'

'And how do you know that?' I asked, suddenly panicking that he was about to pull off some incredible mask and reveal that ah-ha, he, John the mild-mannered bartender, had been Patrick all along.

'If he messaged you in the week, he would have

had to make real plans with you.' He topped off the cocktails with prosecco and added them to a silver tray already laden with drinks. 'This way, it's a far more casual, no-obligations situation. A no-pressure hang-out. Classic arsehole behaviour.'

'Is that right?'

His absolute certainty, the complete and utter self-assuredness of his answer, rubbed me up entirely the wrong way. I did not like John the bartender.

He nodded. 'In the words of a certain singing teapot beloved by young and old, it's a tale as old as time.' He wiped his hands on the white bar towel that hung over his shoulder. 'I've seen it a thousand times, Rose.'

'It's Ros,' I corrected.

He tossed the towel down on the bar as a passing waiter scooped up the tray of drinks and melted away into the crowd. He pushed his wavy, black hair away from his face and I strongly considered suggesting to Adrian's mum that he really ought to be wearing a hairnet.

'He'll text and you'll reply and we'll be having this conversation all over again next week. Unfortunately it's very predictable, *Ros*.'

'I'm predictable, am I?' I asked, the fingers of my left hand curling into my palm, fingernails stabbing at my flesh. What a cock.

'The *situation* is predictable,' he corrected. 'When you work in a bar, you get used to hearing these stories. No need to take it so personally.'

'Well, you're wrong about one thing,' I informed him as I placed my unfinished drink back on the bar.

'Yeah? What's that?'

'We won't be having this conversation again,' I declared. 'Or any conversation if I can help it.'

I turned and walked away before he could reply, marching across the garden. Who did he think he was? And what on Earth did Sumi and the others see in him? I searched for a friendly face that might bring down my blood pressure.

'Rosalind, there you are.'

Instead, I found my parents.

'I'm so glad we found you,' Mum said, her cheeks pink and eyes bright. 'We've something to tell you. Do you want to do it, Alan, or shall I?'

'You tell her,' Dad replied, kissing the back of her hand all the way up her arm like an about-to-be-fired 1980s waiter.

'No, you do it,' she insisted, all giddy. 'It was your idea.'

It was still so strange to see my parents engaged in any kind of physical display of affection. I knew other people's parents got touchy-feely on occasion but mine just didn't, especially not my dad and especially not in public. But here he was, M&S sweater draped over his shoulders, socks pulled halfway up his calves and a spring in his step I'd never seen before. And, if I was being brutally honest, My Horny Dad didn't feel like something that had been missing from my life.

'Well, one of you needs to tell me,' I cut in, fighting back the hordes of theories popping up in my mind. They'd started a swingers' club. They were taking up naked tennis. They were starting a naked tennis swingers' club. 'Out with it?'

'It was all this romance,' Dad said, gazing around

the Andersons' back garden, seemingly seeing a very different party to the one I was attending. 'It got me thinking. We've got our ruby wedding anniversary coming up in a few weeks and I thought, rather than celebrate the past, why not celebrate today? Why not do it again?'

'Do what again?' I asked, eyeing John over Dad's shoulder. He was happily chatting to Mrs Danvers from down the street, my epic putdown clearly not weighing on him in the slightest.

'Your dad asked me to marry him!' Mum said, clinging to her husband like a loved-up limpet.

'But you're already married.' I blinked at them, confused. 'Wait, you *are*, aren't you? You didn't get secretly divorced or anything?'

'It'll be a second wedding, a vow renewal,' Dad clarified. 'Our first one was so long ago, this time we want to celebrate with everyone who makes our lives so special.'

'And the first one wasn't necessarily everything it could have been,' Mum added, Dad nodding along in solemn agreement. 'I want this time to be perfect.'

It had never really occurred to me before but I didn't know much about my parents' wedding. They didn't have a single photo up anywhere and they never talked about it the way my married friends did.

'And I know you're going to say no but I would very much like you and your sister to be my bridesmaids. It would mean a lot to me if you would at least consider it.'

'While you're living with us, rent free,' Dad added, clearing his throat with a subtle cough.

I smiled and wrapped them both up in a giant

Reynolds sandwich, throwing as much enthusiasm as I could muster into the mix.

'This all sounds lovely,' I told them, a giant smile pasted on my face. Who wouldn't want to be a single thirty-two-year-old bridesmaid for her own parents? What a dream come true. 'Anything I can do to help, just say the word. While I'm living with you, rent free.'

'There is quite a lot to plan,' Mum agreed, her fingers woven tightly through my dad's. 'But I think we'll make short work of it all together.'

'Anything you plan will be perfect, Gwen,' Dad replied, shoulders straight, tall and proud. If they hadn't been my parents, it would have been adorable to see the two of them nuzzling, so very much in love.

But they were, so it wasn't.

I turned away, pretending to be checking something in my handbag as they snuggled into each other, mutterings of love turning into noisy public kisses.

There it was. My phone lit up, quietly announcing one new text message from Patrick Parker.

I stopped for a moment, paralysed.

Until I opened the message, it could say anything. It could be an apology or a declaration of love. It could say 'I'm good thanks' and nothing else ever again. It could be a wedding photo, a christening announcement, that GIF of the husky that looked like it was telling you a terrible joke. I could delete it now and never know. Or I could open it and live with the consequences.

Shuffling away from my parents, I opened the message.

Doing anything tonight?

I looked back the bar where John was happily chatting away with Adrian's mum and silently cursed him and his precognitive powers.

Not really, I replied quickly. Fancy a drink?

CHAPTER NINE

It took me exactly four minutes to make my excuses, get out of the party and into an Uber.

For three years, I had dreamed of what would happen if I ever saw Patrick again and there were a thousand variations on the theme. I imagined walking past him on some romantic street, usually Paris (because it was my fantasy and why the hell not?) and I would always be bundled up in a fabulous coat, walking by the river at night, trees filled with twinkling fairy lights. We would spot each other at the exact same moment, stunned that fate had delivered us back into each other's lives, and time would stand still, right up until we fell on each other, lips on lips, body to body, heart to heart.

On other occasions, I imagined myself opening the post, only to find a long handwritten letter from him, an epic essay in his beautiful handwriting, telling me how much he missed me, how he still loved me, how he couldn't go on another day without me, and then, as a perfect single tear fell down my face and dropped onto the letter, there would be a knock at the front door and Patrick would be waiting, with red-rimmed, pleading eyes. 'Did you get my note?' he'd ask and then we'd collapse into each other's arms, never to be parted again.

And then there were the nights I lay awake, staring at my ceiling and dreaming of tearing his testicles from his body and gouging his eyes out with a rusty spoon.

My feelings were complex.

Memories, possibilities and worst-case scenarios all raced around in my head as the Uber I'd splurged on rolled to a stop. It was like Christmas morning, my birthday and the first day of the school holidays all mixed together with exam results day and that one horrifying time I had to take a pregnancy test after sleeping with someone I met on holiday in Ayia Napa. The best of times and the very, very worst of times. I wondered if Charles Dickens had ever been on an 18-30s holiday of his own. If he hadn't, he ought to be made to revisit that statement.

'Lucy, I'm about to do something really stupid,' I said into my phone as I climbed out of the car and paced a hole in the pavement, two doors down from the pub.

'Then don't do it,' she said through a yawn.

'I'm on my way to meet Patrick.'

'OK.'

I stood back to let a group of friends armed with bags of chips and unrestrained laughter jostle past. Mmm, chips.

'You're not going to tell me not to go?' I asked.

I heard her take a deep breath in as she considered her response.

'Ros, we all knew you were going to see him as

soon as he messaged you,' she said as kindly as she could. 'And we both know you would have called Sumi if you wanted someone to tell you not to go.'

These were both excellent points.

'Now tell me, do you look fabulous?'

I fanned myself with the skirt of my dress and checked myself out in the car window. 'I look fine.'

'Which is Ros for "I look drop-dead gorgeous",' Lucy replied. 'So, get in there, show him what he missed out on then leave with your knickers on and your dignity intact. I'm deadly serious, go and meet him but if you even think about dropping trou, I will feel ripples in the force and send Sumi out after you. If he's even considering trying to win you back, he has to earn you.'

'It's just a friendly drink,' I said, wondering whether or not that was true. 'I swear that by the time I go to sleep, it will be in my own bed and these knickers will not have left my person.'

She made a doubtful sound down the line.

'Are they nice knickers?'

'Yes,' I admitted. 'You go out, you put on a nice dress, you wear nice knickers. It's just what you do. I wasn't planning on anyone seeing them.'

Although it never hurt to be prepared, hadn't they taught us that in Brownies? I wasn't sure this was the situation Brown Owl had in mind when she told us that but, we were where we were.

'Fine, fine, fine,' she said with another yawn. 'I'm going in for a scan first thing Monday morning, shall we get dinner Monday night? You can tell me all about Patrick and I'll bore you with all the hideous baby details. Dave's away all next week and I wouldn't mind the company.'

95

'I could come to the scan with you if you like,' I offered, starting down the street towards the pub. I could do this. I was doing this. 'I don't have to be in the office until ten.'

'Ooh, if you don't mind?' Lucy brightened quickly. 'Sumi came to the first one but she's so busy I hate to ask. Adrian came last time but they asked me not to bring him again, he was dicking around with a speculum and broke it.'

'Dave didn't go with you?' I asked, although I wasn't nearly as surprised as I should have been. That man did not deserve her.

'He was ill when I had the first one and away working for the second one,' she explained. 'And you know how much he hates hospitals. It's honestly easier to do it without him.'

Because scheduling work trips around your wife's hospital appointments for your first child was entirely unreasonable. I deeply disliked Creepy Dave.

'I'd love to be there, text me the details,' I told her, standing outside the pub and peering through the dirty windows. 'Right, I'm going in.'

'Call me if you need me, I mean it,' she said, blowing kisses down the line. 'I'll be asleep in half an hour but I have to get up for a wee seven times in the night so I'll probably be able to reply before you do anything stupid.'

'Thanks, Luce, love you,' I said as I ended the call and checked Patrick's last message one more time.

The Fox and Crown, seven thirty, can't wait

I was outside the Fox and Crown, it was seven thirty-four and I didn't have to wait another second.

*

The day had been hot and humid and Patrick's pub of choice was all the more disgusting for it. Close and dark was the best description, but at least it was a proper pub, unlike Good Luck Bar. This was the kind of pub where we'd made all our mistakes growing up: dark wood, red velvet and a squishy carpet underfoot, perpetually sodden with a century of spilled pints and not-so-empty threats. Classic London boozer.

I couldn't see him when I walked in but my heart stuttered with every step, knowing any second now, he'd be there in the flesh. Suddenly my hair felt wrong, why had I taken it down when it was so sticky out? I pulled it up into a ponytail and then immediately let it back down again. Patrick loved my hair up. I was trying too hard. My midi dress was another mistake, the synthetic fabric was soaked through at my lower back. What was sexier than an incredibly sweaty woman with too much hair on the verge of an anxiety attack? I fished around in my bag for a Polo to give my brain and my body something to do. You could always rely on a Polo.

A man stepped onto a small stage at the back of the room and tapped a microphone, causing a squeal of feedback that made everyone jump.

'Right you are, we've got a turn on tonight,' he muttered, beckoning a slight woman holding a guitar onto the stage. 'This is our Karen, she's going to sing us some songs. Keep quiet for fifteen minutes and don't be arseholes about it, clap will you?'

Scattered applause danced around the room as the girl positioned herself on a high stool and turned her brilliant smile on the room.

She could be in an advert for toothpaste, I thought,

running my tongue over my own teeth. And conditioner. And makeup. And oh, shit, is she wearing my dress? I looked down at my floral frock and grimaced. Fucking Zara.

It was a sign and I knew it. Patrick was late, there was a musically blessed supermodel in the same room wearing the same dress as me and it didn't matter what I did with my hair, it would never be right. The universe did not want me to meet Patrick, the universe wanted me to throw my phone under a bus, go home and leave this sweaty rag of a dress out for the foxes.

Mind made up and heart in tatters, I turned on my heel to march out the door and back into my senses.

And there he was.

Our eyes met and the light of recognition brightened his face. In the dim gloominess of the pub, he was all I could see. Blond hair, blue eyes, easy smile, exactly how I remembered.

'Hi,' he said as Karen strummed her first chord.

I opened my mouth to reply but nothing came out. I smiled and tried again, managing a strangled squeak.

'Ros?' Patrick asked, placing a warm hand on my shoulder. 'Are you OK?'

I gave him a thumbs up as I doubled over, spluttering, the ground rushing up towards me altogether too fast. My eyes were watering, my face was burning, I couldn't breathe. Oh my god, I was choking on a Polo. This was perfect, I thought as I dropped to my knees and people around us began to mutter. I'd waited three years for this moment and I was going to choke to death on a Polo. At least I was wearing nice underwear.

'Ros? Ros!'

As the room began to close in on me, I felt two hard thumps in the middle of my back, a shard of white flew out of my mouth and I drew in a long, loud, sharp breath.

Combing my hair out of my face, I looked up to see Patrick, just inches away from me, holding me in his arms.

'Saved your life,' he said softly.

'Thank you,' I replied, my voice barely above a whisper.

A squeal of feedback reeled out from the stage.

'Is she OK?' asked Karen with the guitar.

'She's OK,' I confirmed, still doubled over, staring at the remains of the Polo and wondering if perhaps death by mint wasn't the worst way to go.

Slowly, I stood up, tossed my hair over my shoulder and wiped at my wet eyes, two smudges of mascara on my fingers. Patrick looked like Patrick, calm, confident and slightly bemused, still holding me up, one hand on my arm, one on my waist. I looked like a pound-shop Kardashian.

'It's good to see you, Reynolds.'

'It's good to see you, Parker.'

And just like that, three long years melted into nothing.

It was still light outside, still not even nearly dark, but the edge had been smoothed off the sun, leaving the streets sticky in the almost-dusk. Patrick leaned against the wall of the pub while I stood, uncomfortably straight, half hiding underneath a tree heavy with tiny pink flowers.

'So,' I started, swirling the glass of wine he'd bought me. 'Long time no see.'

Patrick smiled but said nothing.

'How've you been keeping? Been anywhere nice over the summer?' I asked, filling the silence with a steady stream of hot bullshit. 'Warm, isn't it? Can't believe the weather, it's so close, that's the problem, so humid. I've barely slept a whole night since I've been back and—'

'I love your hair that length,' he said, interrupting my ramble with exactly what I wanted to hear. 'It suits you long.'

Was it longer than the last time I'd seen him? I didn't think so. Bigger, almost definitely. The humidity was real. I looked at the people around us, either busy with their own conversations, staring at their phones as they smoked or sat or sipped their drinks. I wanted to shake them, explain what a momentous occasion this was and have them acknowledge it. Just an average Saturday night to them, a second chance with my soulmate for me.

'It really is good to see you,' Patrick said, finally filling the gaps as my words failed me. 'I'm surprised you were free, I was sure you'd be too busy to fit me in.'

He rolled his glass against his lips before finishing his whisky. Had they always been that full? I wondered. God, I hoped our children had his lips. No, bad Ros! You are not having children with this man, you're not having sex with this man and you're certainly not having a destination wedding in Hawaii, just the two of you, on the beach at sunset with dolphins leaping out of the waves to anoint your blessing.

'Not too busy,' I squeaked, racing with myself to find the right words. I knew so many of them, I used them all the time, literally every day. Why did they have to fail me when it mattered the most?

'I'm glad you could squeeze me in for a drink,' he replied, completely in command of his extensive vocabulary. The words I wanted hovered on the edges of my mind but every time I reached for them, they were replaced by a clown intermittently blowing a trombone and shouting 'YOU LOVE HIM' at the top of its voice.

'Yes,' I said, making myself say something, anything, before I gave up and mounted him in the middle of the street. 'I squeezed you in.'

Practically poetry.

Now we were outside in the warm evening light, I could see him a little bit better. There was a scattering of salt and pepper in his hair, just around the temple and lines running down his cheeks, brackets for his smile, but they only added to the appeal. I waged war on my own burgeoning laughter lines, drowning them in the most expensive lotion or potion I could afford at any given time, but on him, they looked good. I studied them carefully, wondering who had made him smile, who had made him laugh, what moment was responsible for each and every new mark on his face. Physical manifestations of the three extra years of Patrick the rest of the world had enjoyed while I had missed out.

'So, how have you been?' he asked, his voice already husky and whisky-tinged.

'OK, no, I can't, I'm sorry, I thought I could but I can't,' I blustered, spinning around to rest my wine glass on the closest window ledge and only just managing to catch it when it immediately fell off. I spun back to face him. 'What's going on? What is this? What are we doing?'

Patrick knitted his eyebrows together and gave me a pleasant, questioning look.

'What do you mean?'

'What's going on here?' I asked, waving at the space between us. 'With us?'

'Oh.' He leaned past me to put down his glass, placing it next to mine on the ledge. His glass did not fall.

'I mean, I'm very happy to see you,' I said, all the words that had been MIA now pouring out of me like they might never stop. 'And I was so pleased when you messaged me but I'm a bit confused because it's been forever and we haven't been in touch and I just need to know what this is, because you said you didn't want to see me again but here we are.'

I took a sharp breath in as though I might add to my speech but instead my mouth snapped shut and I waited for him to speak.

'Ros,' he started slowly. 'You messaged me, I messaged you and now we're here. I hadn't really thought past wanting to see you.'

'I sent a group text, you know,' I replied. 'To everyone.'

'Sure,' he replied with a shrug. 'OK.'

'And you wanted to see me as friends,' I added. 'Right? You wanted to see me as a friend? This is a friendly drink?'

'We're drinking, we're friends,' he stepped closer and picked a stray petal from my shoulder. 'I suppose that makes it a friendly drink.'

'Good, that sounds good,' I said, more to myself

than to him. 'Because it really has been a long time and I don't know what's been going on with you, what you've been up to or where you've been or . . .'

Patrick came closer until we were face to face. He raised his hand, thumb tracing the line of my jaw as he curled his hand around the back of my neck, his fingers weaving their way into my damp hair.

'I really have missed you,' he said, his voice a low rumble. 'Have I said that already?'

My bottom lip trembled as I opened my mouth to respond.

'I think you have, yes.'

'And do you think you might have missed me?'

I answered with a nod, not quite able to raise my eyes to meet his.

'Ros,' he whispered.

'Yep?'

'Can I kiss you?'

He moved closer until we were millimetres apart, his breath prickling my lips, his features fuzzy against the burning orange sunset. My heart pounded, my legs felt deeply unreliable and there was nothing to hold onto but Patrick himself.

'I would like to go on record as saying this probably isn't a very good idea,' I murmured before leaning in, unable to wait a single second longer. 'But yes, go on then.'

I touched my lips to his, melting as he tightened his grip on the back of my neck. My mouth opened to him and the rest of my body was dying to follow suit. It was overpowering, new desire mixed with old memories, knowing how incredible it would be rushing at me, layered with the heady excitement of anticipation.

My first time with Patrick, all over again. People had killed for less.

'This is a bad idea,' I said, already completely out of breath as I tore myself away.

'Terrible idea.' His voice was equally as ragged, his fingers firmly circled around my wrist tethering me to him. 'But . . .' he paused and swallowed hard. 'I want you.'

A familiar warmth pooled in my stomach and I knew it was too late to turn back. Any remaining traces of self-preservation or commonsense was utterly consumed by just how much I wanted him too.

I took a deep breath and held out my hand.

'Then what are we waiting for?' I asked.

CHAPTER TEN

Exactly thirty-eight minutes later, I collapsed on Patrick's floor in a tangle of arms and legs, discarded clothes and condom wrappers.

'I have to admit,' I panted, staring up at the ceiling and searching for patterns in the plaster swirls. 'This is not how I'd expected today to end.'

'There are worse things you could be doing with a Saturday evening,' Patrick pulled me in towards him as I repositioned myself to rest my head on his chest. We were only a few feet from the bed we hadn't made it to but the floor seemed like the safest place to be right now. I didn't trust my legs to carry me.

'Like arguing about sausage cooking times with my friend's dad?' I yawned, slinging one leg over his legs, stretching my arm over his chest, taking as much territory as I dared. He looked at me, confused. 'Long story,' I said. 'Don't worry about it. I'm very happy with where my Saturday evening ended up.'

He kissed the top of my head and laughed.

'You knew this was on the cards as soon as you

sent me that text,' he accused. 'Don't pretend this wasn't your evil plan along.'

I lazily traced my fingertips down his collarbone. He had the best collarbone. 'Evil plan?'

'Hi everyone, I'm back, I have a new number? Let's hang out? You know, you could have just called me.'

'That wasn't an evil plan, it was a stupid group text,' I said, rolling onto my stomach and discreetly tucking my left breast back into my bra. 'I sent it to everyone in my phone.'

'OK, Ros,' he closed his eyes and smiled. 'I believe you even if thousands wouldn't.'

'You can believe what you want,' I replied primly, slightly annoyed to have my postcoital glow tainted. 'It was a mistake, I deleted you from my phone years ago but it must have been saved in the cloud. I never would have messaged you otherwise.'

'And why not?'

Resting my head back in his nook, I looked around his flat. His bed was in his living room, in the place of a settee, and what would have been the bedroom was set up as an office, his huge, cluttered desk taking pride of place next to the dormer window that looked out onto the street below. It was a new place but he had filled it with all the same stuff. Worn leather armchair he'd got from his dad, framed maps all over the walls and bookcase upon bookcase upon bookcase. I'd have guessed it in a heartbeat had we been playing Through the Keyhole. Who would live in a house like this? Absurdly expensive custom-made shoes? Eight different vintage editions of *Jane Eyre*? Enough single malt whisky to get an elephant bladdered? It's got to be Patrick Parker.

'Because we haven't spoken in more than three years and, the last time we saw each other, it didn't go that well?' I reminded him. Now that the sex seal had been broken, my words were coming thick and fast. 'Or have you forgotten?'

Patrick gently shifted my head and sat upright.

'Do you have any idea how hard it was on *me* when you ended things?' he asked, standing up and walking over to the front door to retrieve his pants. I was both proud and uncomfortable in equal measures. 'I never got in touch with you because I didn't want to hear all about your new life and your new friends and – at the risk of sounding pathetic – new men, while you left me behind.'

I opened my mouth to speak but had no idea what to say. *When I ended things?*

He slipped into the bathroom, ran the tap for a moment then returned in his boxer shorts. 'I've been wondering ever since if I'd hear from you.'

'I didn't end things with you,' I said slowly. 'I told you I had been offered the job in DC, then you said I should take it and it would be better for us to have a clean break.'

'Yeah, because I'm a shit man with a massive ego and I couldn't stand the rejection,' he said, looking at me as though I was the one who was being obtuse. 'Christ, Ros, I thought you might suggest we try long distance or something but no, you agreed with me straight away. You wanted to leave without the baggage. I get it, that's fine, but don't make me out to be the villain when you're the one who left.'

I felt as though I'd been punched. Had I agreed with him? I didn't remember it that way. I certainly had not said I wanted to leave without baggage. I very much wanted baggage, I wanted Patrick-shaped baggage more than an Away suitcase and I wanted an Away suitcase so badly. Bloody Facebook advertising. What I remembered, was the feeling that the world was ending and, as I recalled, I didn't *say* much of anything. I told him about the job, he told me I should go and I ran out the door, only stopping to cry in the street before I flagged down a cab.

'You could have told me you didn't want me to go,' I said. I reached for my dress and draped it over my body, too vulnerable to be so naked.

Patrick sat down on the edge of his bed and sighed. 'And tell you not to take the job? What kind of a shit would that make me?'

'You said it was good timing because you were going travelling,' I reminded him. 'You said it was for the best.'

'I did go travelling,' he confirmed. 'And then I came back. Alone.'

I folded myself up like a deckchair, arms wrapped around my legs, hands knotted together around my shins. Even though it was still hot and sticky in his flat, I suddenly felt a chill.

'I don't know what to say,' I admitted.

With a deep breath in and a heavy breath out, Patrick joined me back on the floor.

'Then don't say anything,' he said, kneeling in front of me. 'I missed you, Ros, and now you're here again, I think that's enough. Can we agree that the past is the past and take it from here?'

Something lifted inside of me, a weight I'd been carrying around for so long, I'd almost forgotten how heavy it was. I felt so light, I could have leapt up and touched the ceiling.

'I feel like such a dickhead,' I said, pushing all my hair back out of my face. 'What would have happened if you hadn't got that stupid text?'

Patrick took my face in his hands and kissed me softly. 'But I did.'

'OK,' I breathed, wrapping my hands around his wrists to lock him into place. Patrick missed me. Patrick wanted to try again. Before I could stop it, a tiny laugh escaped from my mouth.

'What's so funny?' he asked with a curious grin.

'Nothing? Everything?' I replied. 'This, us. I feel like I need to know everything that's happened since I last saw you. I've got about a million questions.'

He kissed my forehead then broke my grip on his wrists before standing up to stretch.

'Like what?'

'I don't know.' I scrambled semi-upright and placed myself on the bed, hugging one of his pillows as he wandered off into his study. Everything felt bright and electric and like it wasn't quite real. 'What were you doing two years ago today?'

'Two years ago today?' he called back from the next room. 'I believe I was in Bhutan.'

'Bhutan?'

'Yes.' Patrick reappeared with a bottle of whisky in his hand. 'It's in South Asia, near Tibet.'

'I know where it is,' I replied. I didn't, but I could have.

He climbed onto the bed and stretched out. His body looked more muscular than I remembered, not that I was complaining. I pulled the covers over my body, wondering what comparisons he was drawing about me.

'Of course you know,' he said as he opened the bottle. 'I was just answering your question. Your turn. Where were you two years ago today?'

Thanks to Facebook memories, I knew exactly where I had been. Two years ago to the day, I was beside myself with joy because I was on my way to Ikea to buy my very own Klippan sofa.

'Um, I think I was at a lecture,' I lied, nodding to myself. 'Salman Rushdie in conversation with Malcolm Gladwell.'

'Wow,' Patrick replied with raised eyebrows. 'Really?'

'Two very interesting men,' I confirmed, hoping he had absolutely no follow-up questions. 'What were you doing in Bhutan?'

'Living? Existing?' He breathed in deeply. 'Whatever it was, it was better than this.'

I sucked the air in through my teeth. 'Could you at least wait until I have my knickers back on before you start insulting me?'

Actually that was a good point, I thought, peering around the room. Where were my knickers? I had a horrible feeling they might be on the wrong side of the front door . . .

'I didn't mean literally this, I meant living in London,' he rapped my arm with a tap just the wrong side of playful. 'I miss travelling.'

I considered this news with a quiet nod. Patrick could absolutely go travelling. We would FaceTime every day, he could get an Instagram account so I could follow the stories. Maybe I'd even be able to meet up

110

with him for a couple of weeks. Or maybe I'd take a sabbatical and go for a couple of months. Not that I was rushing anything, of course.

'I've always wanted to go to Thailand,' I said as I rolled onto my stomach, pulling a sheet with me as I went. 'Have you been?'

'I've been to Thailand so many times,' he said, taking a swig of whisky straight from the bottle before handing it to me. 'But you should go, you'd like it. It's a good starter trip. They've got some nice hotels for people who don't want to rough it.'

'And I do not,' I confirmed before I took the tiniest sip. I couldn't stand the taste of whisky but I knew he wouldn't have anything else in the house. Patrick was exclusively a whisky drinker. 'Out of everywhere you've been, where is your favourite place in the entire world?'

Patrick sat up and looked at me with an odd look on his face.

'What?' I asked as he bounced off the bed and into the kitchen. 'Where are you going?'

'Stay there,' he commanded.

What was he doing? Why had he left the room? I turned over and cursed myself for asking so many questions. It was late, he was tired, I was totally pushing my luck. He'd probably gone to retrieve my pants and call a taxi, not necessarily in that order. From the bed, I could hear cupboards opening and closing, cans clicking and fizzing and the occasional muttering from Patrick.

'I think this is the quickest way to deal with this,' he said as he strode back into the bedroom, laptop under his arm and a tray full of food in his hands.

111

Ooh, food. Snacks were my love language and he knew it. He pulled a map down from the wall and laid it on the bed in front of me, placing the tray in my lap and opening up the computer.

'What's all this?' I asked, poking in what looked like a bowl of brightly wrapped sweets. He slapped my fingers away and smiled.

'This is the last three years of my life.' The laptop sparked into life with a familiar chime and Patrick pointed over at the map. 'All the countries in purple are the places I visited while I was researching my book.'

I glanced down and saw a lot of purple. In the last two years, I had been to exactly two countries, the one I was born in and the one I ran away to. Patrick had been to places I couldn't even pronounce.

'And on the tray, you have some of my favourite foods from said countries,' he said, handing me a cold red can of fizzy pop. 'That is Future Cola from China.'

'Future Cola is good,' I confirmed after taking a sip. 'What's this?'

'*Awadama*, from Japan,' Patrick replied, unwrapping one of the sweets and holding it out for me. 'It translates to "foamy balls". Very popular.'

'Thank you,' I muttered as it fizzed up in my mouth. 'Very foamy.'

'Probably shouldn't have given it to you at the same time as the Future Cola,' he replied with a grimace. 'We've also got Vietnamese sesame rice balls, Tapita from Costa Rica, Doña Pepa from Peru and Chinese Ore No Milk Candy.'

'Ore No?' I replied, opening one of the little white

packages to find a hard, white ball that looked like any other boiled sweet. 'What does that translate as?'

'It's milk-flavoured,' Patrick said as I put it in my mouth and almost immediately spat it back out. 'It roughly translates as milk candy for tough guys. Or tough guy's milk.'

'I really didn't want that in my mouth,' I said, taking another swig of Future Cola to wash away the taste. 'And don't you dare say that's what she said.'

He held his hands up to protest his innocence but with a huge smile on his face.

'And what's on the laptop?' I asked.

'Photos,' he replied, climbing back onto the bed and pressing his body against mine. 'Lots and lots and lots of photos.'

'You're going to show me your holiday photos?' I asked, utterly delighted.

'I'm going to show you my holiday photos,' he confirmed as he rested his chin on my shoulder. 'Shall we start with China?'

I nodded, far too excited for someone about to endure someone else's travel pics. But this felt very different to Lucy and Dave's three-hour-long honeymoon video from their trip to Sandals St Lucia. This felt like discovering they'd made three new seasons of your favourite TV show and bingeing on them all at once.

'Who's that?' I asked, as Patrick began flicking through the photos.

He skipped back to a shot of himself, posing with his arm slung casually around the shoulders of a beautiful blonde woman. He was smiling into the camera but she was gazing at him with an expression I knew all too well.

'That's Judith,' he replied.

'She looks nice,' I said in a bright, tight voice.

'She is nice,' Patrick said, matter-of-factly. 'We met in Beijing. She teaches English out there.'

I took a sip of my Future Cola. It was already flat.

'She still in Beijing, is she?'

'She is,' he confirmed, amused with my response. 'And yes, we were seeing each other for a while but no, we're not seeing each other now. I'm sure you haven't been living like a nun for the last three years, have you?'

'Nun-like,' I replied. 'Nun-adjacent.'

'Nun-adjacent, I like that,' he laughed lightly, sliding his legs underneath the covers. 'When you get to the photos of the pretty brunette in Mongolia, her name is Shana and we went on three dates before she binned me off for an American footballer called Brad.'

'You're making that up,' I muttered, clicking through the photos faster and faster. He stroked my hair, nuzzling into the back of my neck.

'Does it matter?' he asked as he slid his hand down my back until he reached the hooks of my bra. 'She's not here, eating my tough man milk sweets, is she?'

Quietly, I closed the laptop and placed the tray and the map down on the floor beside the bed before turning to face him.

'I really did miss you,' Patrick whispered when we were nose to nose, the oxygen burning out of the air in between us.

'I really did miss you too,' I whispered back, closing my eyes as I lay back against the bed.

One minute we were just talking, the next, we were together. There was no precise moment or second on the clock you could point to, we weren't and then we were. His hands were hot on my skin as they followed familiar paths around my body, touching me in ways I'd only dreamed about for so long. The light seemed to fade, the bed got bigger and the room got smaller and everything became hazy at the edges as my body took over and my mind let go.

CHAPTER ELEVEN

'You're in a lot of trouble, young lady,' Lucy said, grinning at me over her massively pregnant belly.

'You're the one with your legs in stirrups,' I pointed out, shovelling a packet of salt and vinegar Discos into my mouth in between yawns. They tasted like heaven. The sky was bluer, the birds sang more clearly, my morning cup of tea was like the nectar of the gods. I was even having a good hair day. At long, long, long, long, long, long last, all was right with the world.

Lucy pulled at the hem of her gown, attempting to cover things it was far too late to attempt to cover. 'It's back on, is it?' she asked. 'You're a smitten kitten, all over again?'

'I don't think I've ever been this happy,' I replied, too full of joy to come up with anything clever or funny. 'I know none of you are going to be ecstatic about it but truly, Luce, it just feels blissful. All the time I was missing him, he was missing me and now we get another chance.'

'What did Sumi say when you told her?' she asked.

'It wasn't so much what she said as how she said it,' I answered thoughtfully as I recalled our phone conversation from the night before. 'Or rather screamed it.'

'She'll come round eventually. Remember how you all hated Dave when I first met him? And now you're practically best mates.'

I stuffed my mouth full of crisps and looked out the window.

'Anyway, I'm very pleased for you and insanely jealous.' She held her hand out for a crisp and I dutifully handed over the entire bag. Her need was greater and I no longer needed the sustenance of food. I had achieved the impossible: I had reconnected with the one that got away and reeled him right back in. 'I've had the raging horn for the last month and Dave won't come anywhere near me.'

Classic Creepy Dave. Actually, was that less creepy or more creepy? I would have to check with the panel.

'There are a lot of things I would do for you but that is not one of them,' I told her, wiping my hands on the legs of my jeans and then wiping the crisp crumbs off my jeans and onto the floor. 'And I don't care how long it's been for you, I know it's been much longer for me because the evidence is about ten centimetres from staring me right in the face.'

She rested the crisps on the top of her belly and turned her head to look at me. 'Go on then, tell me all the disgusting details, I know you're dying to.'

'Do you *really* want them all or do you want me to blush and say something like, there's not that much to tell?' I asked, already regretting handing over the crisps. Her needs were not greater, I needed to replace all the calories I'd burned over the weekend.

'Give me everything,' she nodded, taking a deep breath. 'I can take it.'

'Fine but remember you asked for it.' I closed my eyes, my shoulders pinching together with the memories. I'd only left his flat a few hours ago and I was still tender if I pushed in the right places. 'So, we met at the pub but there was a singer on and she was rubbish but then I choked on a mint.'

'Ooh, it's practically *The Notebook*,' Lucy cooed, delicately placing a crisp in her mouth.

'Shut up. So we left the pub and we were standing outside, sort of looking at each other in the sunset, and it was all intense and so I said, what's going on and he said, I'm going to kiss you and—'

'Ros,' Lucy interrupted, looking down at my feet. 'You do know your sandals don't match?'

I looked down at my feet. One brown leather sandal, one leopard print.

Shit.

'Do you want the story or not?' I asked.

'Not really,' she admitted. 'It's giving me heartburn.'

'Too much salt is bad for you,' I said, seizing the opportunity to reach across her and nab the Discos back.

'This is the most wonderful part,' she sighed, a dreamy smile on her face and her legs up in the air. 'When it's all shagging and talking and more shagging and breaking for snacks and then more shagging. Have you even slept? Are you utterly delirious?'

'I no longer need sleep,' I replied. 'I am as a god.'

Lucy smiled.

'And when are you seeing Mr God again?'

'Don't know,' I said as I chomped. 'We just spent

two days shagging and he did not appear to be utterly repulsed, that's good enough for me. I'm not expecting a proposal until at least next week.'

Although that didn't mean I hadn't spent every second since I left his flat staring at my phone and willing him to text me. But that wasn't Patrick's style. He'd once told me he considered his phone an 'interloper on his sanity' and I'd automatically covered mine with my hands so Siri wouldn't be offended.

'Then it all sounds wonderful, very romantic,' she said, folding her hands together on top of her belly. 'I just want to make sure you're going in with your eyes open.'

'They're wide open,' I insisted. 'They're *Clockwork-Orange*-open. I know you're worried about me but you don't have to be, I promise you, I'm fine. We had this incredibly beautiful, honest conversation about what happened last time and then he went down on me until I thought I'd gone blind so I really think it's going to work out this time.'

'All right, that's enough, that's enough,' she replied, slapping her hands over her ears. 'I can't take any more.'

'The stars aligned,' I declared, holding a completely round Disco up to the window in awe. 'And so did our genitals.'

'Hello, hello, how are we getting along in here?'

The door to the office opened and a rather large man in a rather brown suit let himself into the room. 'Mrs Warren, is it? I'm Mr Appleton.'

Lucy raised a hand and gave a meek smile. 'Is Dr Abara not here today?'

'Off sick,' the man replied with a frown as he

snapped on a pair of medical gloves. 'Right, what are we doing today? Thirty-five weeks and you wanted to do an extra scan, I see? Baby's almost fully cooked, why are we doing the scan today?'

Even though Lucy was the world's sweetest human, her parents were among the most anxious living beings I'd ever met and some of that had filtered into their only child. The downside of this meant Lucy couldn't even climb a ladder at home alone without calling one of them before and after, but the upside was they'd offered to pay for her to go private with her pregnancy. They were not prepared to take any chances with their first grandchild, even though it was entirely unnecessary, according to Lucy. I'd scoffed at it when she first told me but now I was here, I couldn't help but notice this place was more like a fancy hotel than a normal hospital. Much as I loved the NHS, I didn't think I'd be able to turn something like this down either.

'The nurse didn't say Dr Abara wasn't here,' Lucy said in a slightly strangled voice. 'Will she be back tomorrow? I could reschedule?'

'No need,' the doctor replied, leafing through some papers on the desk. 'I'm here.'

It should have sounded reassuring but it really didn't.

'But I could come back tomorrow?' Lucy said again, looking over at me. I slyly wiped my hands on my jeans and tucked the rest of my crisps into the tote bag resting by my feet. 'I don't want to be difficult, it's just that we've seen Dr Abara at all the other appointments and her team is going to be delivering the baby so, um, I would quite like to stick with her. Last time I came in the baby was breech and she said

I could come in again this week for another scan if I felt like nothing had changed.'

'They usually move on their own, you mightn't be able to tell if anything has changed,' he said, completely ignoring her as he reached for an extraordinarily large bottle of lube, the likes of which you really didn't expect to see outside of certain shops on Old Compton Street. 'I can always turn you if need be.'

'Oh no,' Lucy gasped. 'You don't need to do that.'

I'd heard and seen enough.

'I think we'd really prefer to come back tomorrow and see the other doctor,' I said politely as he loomed over my cowering friend. 'If that's possible?'

The doctor stopped what he was doing and stared at me.

'You're the "other mother"?' he asked, definitely thinking air quotes, even if he didn't use them. It was hard to do bunny ears when you were manhandling an epic bottle of lube. 'Didn't see that in the notes.'

'I'm sorry, I don't think I caught your name,' I said, smiling sweetly and not bothering to correct him. 'Are you the nurse?'

Over in her stirrups, Lucy's eyes widened.

'I'm the senior obstetrician at this hospital and I can assure you I am more than qualified to perform *a scan*.' He enunciated the word to make sure we were entirely clear that this appointment was beneath him. 'I understand this is your first pregnancy and you're probably confused as to what's going on, but I have a full schedule today thanks to the absent Dr Abara and really don't have time for this debate. Can we please get on with this, *ladies*?'

The first time I met Lucy was on the second day of

university when she staggered into me and my three Smirnoff Ices after literally headbutting a disgusting boy called Vernon who was trying to take a photo up her skirt in the student union. Lucy was an iron fist in a velvet glove, wasted in peace time really, she would have absolutely shone during the war. And yet, here she was with one single, perfect tear trickling down her beautiful rosy, red cheek all because of this absolute twat in his dogshit-brown suit.

I wasn't having it.

'I'm sure you're very qualified, but we'd be much more comfortable seeing our usual doctor,' I replied. 'Wouldn't we, Luce?'

She nodded fiercely. 'Yes,' she said. 'I think so.'

Mr Appleton put down the lube with a look I imagined had passed over the faces of many men who had been made to put down lube when they really wanted to use it. He inhaled sharply through his nose, a sour look on his face.

'I would be more comfortable seeing my doctor,' Lucy reiterated, as I helped her out of the stirrups. Being really pregnant looked properly shit at times like this. Just when you wanted to make a speedy and dignified exit, you were forced to roll around on an elevated bed like an oversized Weeble.

'Also, you're very rude,' I added. 'Just so you know.'

Without another word, he snapped off the surgical gloves and tossed them in the bin, marching straight out the door and leaving it swinging behind him.

'That was great but what if they don't let me come back again?' Lucy asked as she struggled back into her pants. 'This little bugger could make an appearance any day, I don't want to get blacklisted. This is the best maternity hospital in London, you know.'

'So help me god, don't you dare mention Meghan Markle,' I warned.

She pouted. No one loved Meghan Markle as much as Lucy loved Meghan Markle.

'There's nothing to worry about,' I assured her. 'If they kick up a fuss, we tell Sumi about the condescending doctor and have her write a threatening letter. Honestly, it's like you forget you've got a lawyer for a best friend on purpose.'

'You should get shagged more often, you know,' she said as she forced her swollen feet back into her flip-flops. 'I like this Ros.'

I smiled and held my arm out to my friend.

'Thanks,' I said, escorting her out the room. 'I like her too.'

CHAPTER TWELVE

Three sharp knocks on my shed door woke me up at seven a.m. on Tuesday morning. I blinked at my Bart Simpson alarm clock, quite prepared to have a cow. Between reliving every moment of my weekend and stressing about work, I had barely slept a wink.

'Morning, Sleeping Beauty,' my mother opened the door and poked her head inside. 'Are you still in bed?'

'Yes,' I replied, pulling a pillow over my face. 'Because it is the crack of dawn. Please go away now.'

What was the point in being banished to the bottom of the garden like a common Womble if my parents could still let themselves in my room whenever they wanted? Surely that kind of intrusion warranted full-time washing machine rights?

'I thought you'd want these,' she said, throwing the door open wide and carrying in the most enormous bouquet of flowers in sunset colours. 'They came yesterday but you got home so late and the lights were out by the time I looked in on you.'

'They're for me?' I asked, bouncing out of bed.

Flowers! I had flowers! But that didn't mean the flowers were from Patrick, they could be from Lucy for kicking that awful doctor's metaphorical backside or from that man on the 521 bus who put his hand a little bit too deep into his trouser pocket every morning when I got on. Not even a very meaningful glance at my #TimesUp badge had put him off.

'They're for you,' Mum confirmed, setting them on the collapsible dining table and handing me the little white envelope that only ever came with flowers.

There was no name on the card, just a quote.

Oh, do not ask, 'What is it?' Let us go and make our visit.

A line from his favourite T.S. Eliot poem. No doubt about it, they were from Patrick.

'All right then, what does it say?' Mum asked, the same smile on my face spreading across hers.

'It's just a bit from a book,' I replied, keeping the card safely in my hand. 'They're beautiful, aren't they?'

'Gorgeous,' she affirmed. 'Whoever he is, I already like him better than the last one.'

I fluffed out one of the sunburnt orange blooms and said nothing.

'I love dahlias. Grace, honesty, kindness, commitment and positive change,' Mum said, pulling the language of flowers from some corner of her brain that hadn't been corrupted with the names of all the different Instagram filters. 'Your dad used to send me dahlias when we were first courting.'

'And what do foxgloves mean?' I asked, combing through the other flowers in the arrangement and wondering how much research Patrick had done when he was choosing the bouquet. Had he known all that

125

or were these just the nicest bunch? Maybe they'd been on offer. Maybe it was the first bouquet he saw. Or maybe I could stop trying to ruin this for myself and just revel in the fact that Patrick had sent me flowers.

'Mostly that foxes are snazzy dressers.' She settled down on the arm of my tiny sofa and cast an eye across the room, taking in the pile of shoes, the dirty clothes next to the wash bin and the dishes in the sink. In my defence, I'd been very busy shagging all weekend and domestic tasks hadn't been my top priority. Or any sort of priority. But I would have to tackle the washing soon or I'd be out of knickers and forced into a lunchtime trip to Primark. The worst of fates.

'Foxgloves are complicated. Some people think they're good luck, some people think they're bad but they're often associated with honesty and magic.'

'Miracles, more like,' I mumbled as I tore into the pack of flower food and sprinkled it into the bottom of the vase.

'Perhaps we should have dahlias at the renewal ceremony,' Mum said. 'If they're in season now, I'm sure they'll still be available in a couple of weeks.'

'A couple of weeks?'

Mum and Dad's wedding anniversary was on the ninth of August, which was . . . in a couple of weeks. Well, bugger me. Time flies when you're living in a shed.

'It's on a Saturday so your father and I thought it rather makes sense to have it on the day than wait any longer. I was hoping you might pop to the shops with me over the weekend. We're both going to need new frocks, don't you think?'

I hadn't been clothes shopping with my mum since I was fifteen and she made me try on bras over my clothes in M&S and Caroline Beaumont, Shari Singh and Thomas McCall from the lower sixth all saw me and took photos and stuck them up all over the sixth-form common room. There was a reason I hadn't lost my virginity until university.

'I don't need anything,' I said automatically even though I very much did. 'But I'll come and help you find an outfit.'

'Don't laugh but I thought it would be nice if you and Jo wore the same thing,' Mum said, busily rearranging my flowers. 'Since you're going to be my bridesmaids.'

Oh god, I'd forgotten. An adult bridesmaid wearing the same dress as my gorgeous younger sister, for my mid-sexual-renaissance, sixty-year-old mother. Maybe Patrick *hadn't* sent the flowers, maybe the universe sent them as a preemptive apology. Jo was not going to like this at all.

'Does Saturday work?' I asked, staring at my dahlias and channelling their grace.

'Saturday is wonderful,' she hopped up to her feet. 'I'll see if I can book us a table somewhere nice for lunch, we can make a day of it.'

'Perfect,' I said, pulling the covers back up over my face. 'Is Jo coming?'

'I think Jo might be too busy to come back from Cambridge for the day,' Mum said, not-so-discreetly running a fingertip along the windowsill. 'So you get the deciding vote on your dresses. And I did think it might be nice if you wanted to help us plan the actual shindig, I haven't organized a party since you were nine.'

A sudden flashback to my dad accidentally water-boarding Adrian when we were supposed to be bobbing for apples.

'I'd love to, Mum,' I told her. 'It'll be perfect, I promise.'

'And you never know,' she gave my flowers a knowing look. 'Could be good practice for your own wedding.'

'All right, enough's enough,' I said, waving her out the door. Not that I hadn't already worked this very bouquet into my wedding speech already but still. 'Please lock it on your way out.'

'I'm going, I'm going,' Mum laughed as she let herself out. 'Oh, and Rosalind, please tidy up in here before you leave for work, it's a disgrace.'

I knew she wouldn't be able to help herself.

It took me all the way to work, two very large coffees and a forty-five-minute deliberation in the group text before I decided how to reply to Patrick's flowers. Eventually I got two-thirds approval to say 'Thank you for the flowers, they're beautiful.' Simple, honest and safe. Sumi was the holdout and lobbied hard for 'Stick them up your arse' but our official friend group rules said you only needed a two-thirds majority approval to send a text. Had it been a photo, things might have been different but it wasn't so she was outvoted.

'I just don't trust him,' she yelled down the phone after the text had been sent. 'One bunch of flowers does not a decent human make. It's every arsehole's go-to move.'

'So sending flowers is worse than not sending flowers?'

I was never going to win. Patrick could reveal he

was the second coming of Christ and Sumi would still say he was trying too hard.

'In his case, yes,' she replied with trademark bluntness. 'Next you'll be wanting to bring him to my birthday dinner.'

I saw my horrified face reflected back in the glass of the recording booth. Sumi's birthday. She hated parties, detested surprises and was universally accepted as the most difficult person to buy for on the face of the earth and yet, every year, she insisted we 'do' something, even though she refused to give any sort of direction as to what the something should be, where it might take place, at what time or for how long.

But I was up to the challenge. In fact, I was going to ace it.

'Sumi.'

'Ros.'

'Did Jemima book anywhere yet?'

'No,' she replied, already distracted. 'She's been away, she's not back until Friday.'

'Let me plan your birthday,' I said, suddenly feverish with excitement.

Sumi paused before she replied as I pressed my hand against my forehead to check I wasn't actually feverish. What was I thinking?

'You know I don't want a fuss,' she replied.

This was a lie.

'Something quiet, just us.'

Another lie. A previously prepared guest list would be forwarded at some point in the next hour and it would include at least seventeen people. It always did.

'It'll be perfect,' I promised, already scribbling down

ideas on my notepad. 'Just keep Saturday night free and await further instructions.'

I heard her breathe in, second-guessing herself before she spoke, and I knew exactly what she was going to say.

'You're not going to bring him, are you?' Sumi asked.

'Not to be an arsehole but yes,' I said, kind but firm. 'I would really love it if you could give him one tiny chance to prove he's not actually Satan himself.'

She huffed down the line. 'And I would really love it if Kristen Stewart showed up on my doorstep with two cats and a minivan but that doesn't seem very likely either.'

'Don't give up on that dream just yet,' I said, scribbling down notes. 'I've got four days to make magic happen.'

'Ros Reynolds, if you throw me a *Twilight*-themed birthday party, so help me god, I'll murder you.'

I crossed out my first idea.

'I promise he'll be on his best behaviour and, if he isn't, you can be incredibly horrible to him and hunt him for sport. Please can I invite Patrick?'

Sumi considered the request.

'I can hunt him for sport?'

'Yes.'

'Like in *Hunger Games*?'

'You can go full District 12, with my permission.'

'Then he may attend.'

'You won't regret it,' I promised.

'I almost certainly will,' she replied. 'But I want to be proven wrong. Right, I've got to go.'

'Important lawyering?' I asked, firing up my computer.

'I have an all-day arbitration session scheduled to

try to resolve a dispute between two hotel development groups and the Dominican Republic that could result in a two-billion-dollar lawsuit,' she replied.

'A hotel is suing a country? How does someone sue a country?' I asked. 'Did they fall down a pothole or something?'

'Yes, Ros, that's exactly what happened,' Sumi answered with a sigh. 'I've got to go. Love you.'

I ended the call determined to plan Sumi the greatest birthday party of all time. When we were younger, we'd gone on so many wild, spontaneous adventures but for anything other than an evening out, I'd have to get approval from Jemima and it couldn't be too energetic or Lucy wouldn't be able to participate. And while Adrian might be able to splash out on a ten-course tasting menu at some super fancy restaurant I had never even heard of, I was on a tight budget if I ever wanted to live somewhere that wasn't a shed. I needed something fun but not too physically demanding. Affordable but still exciting. Something that would make Sumi so happy, she'd forget to be shitty to Patrick and they would end the night as BFFs.

'Piece of piss,' I whispered to myself as I scrolled through my options. 'It's going to be the best birthday ever.'

CHAPTER THIRTEEN

Second Chances was full of inspirational advice on how to open yourself up to new opportunities and allow magic into your life. What it was not so good at was telling you how to do so when you were trapped in the bowels of your office with no natural light and a rancid stench that crept in through the walls and was in no way improved by the addition of half a can of air freshener.

'Ready for the big meeting?' Ted said, knocking on the studio door before letting himself in. 'Our boy'll be here in two minutes.'

'Ready as I'll ever be,' I agreed as I gathered my notes and knocked four empty cans of sugar-free Red Bull into the bin. I'd spent my first week deep in prep but today was the big day. I was finally meeting Snazzlechuff.

'Come on, we'd better be in the meeting room when they get here, his agent doesn't like to be kept waiting.' The corner of Ted's mouth flickered.

'What's the agent like?' I asked as we climbed the stairs.

'Impressive,' he replied.

'That's an interesting way to describe someone,' I said as we emerged back into daylight. I took a deep breath in, slightly relieved to discover the world was still there.

'Wait until you meet her,' Ted said, holding open the meeting room door and waving me inside. 'I think that's their car outside.'

I looked out the meeting room window to see a huge white Range Rover pulling into the alley down the side of the building.

Ted frisked his oversized hoodie for imaginary crumbs and took a deep breath in.

'I'll go and get them. Get ready, Ros, your life is about to change forever.'

I rolled my eyes as I helped myself to a Hobnob from the plate in the middle of the table. The meeting room was nice, big, airy. Just the sort of room in which you'd like to spend eight hours of your day, five days a week, rather than a mouldering pit. According to the pop art painting on the wall, this was the Alexander Graham Bell room. All the PodPad meeting rooms were named after icons of telecommunications: Bell, Samuel Morse, Guglielmo Marconi and, for reasons best known to someone who was not me, Keith Chegwin. Every time I walked past his meeting room, with its bright Cheggers mural on the wall, I couldn't help but shudder.

'Ros Reynolds, are you ready to meet a superstar?' Ted shouted from outside the door. I stood up then sat down then stood back up. What was the correct protocol for meeting internet-famous children? I felt like Mary Poppins without the magic bag. Or the chimney sweep. Or the songs. I didn't feel that much like Mary Poppins.

Ted flung the door wide, an enormous smile on his face as he ushered in a furious-looking woman with the biggest white leather handbag I had ever seen on her shoulder and a coffee the size of a fire extinguisher in her hand. She had to be the impressive agent. She was followed by a sad-faced man holding a set of car keys in one hand and a four-pack of full-sugar Red Bull in the other. Bringing up the rear of the strange party, was what I assumed to be a Snazzlechuff. He was a shortish human in blinding white jogging bottoms, matching oversized track jacket and enough gold chains to weigh him down to the bottom of the Thames tottered in behind the adults. The outfit alone would have been disturbing enough but, perched on his shoulders was a bizarrely lifelike, furry panda head.

'This, is Snazzlechuff,' Ted breathed, holding out his arm as though he were presenting the Christ child.

'Hey,' squeaked the panda.

'Hi,' I replied, not sure whether to shake his hand or call social services. 'I'm Ros.'

'Snazzlechuff,' he replied, as though he could be anyone else. 'You can call me Snazz if you want.'

'Snazz it is,' I said. I was trying so hard not to stare.

'We haven't got long. We need to be in Milton Keynes for the opening of a Tesco Metro by half eleven,' barked the woman with the handbag as everyone got themselves seated around the table. 'Let's hear the new girl's ideas.'

'So, I'm Ros,' I said brightly, holding out my hand. The agent stared at it as though I were offering her a shitty stick. The man didn't move. Slowly, I pulled my hand back in towards me and bit my lip.

134

'Veronica, Ros just joined us from America,' Ted offered. 'We've brought her in especially for the project, the result of a global search for the perfect producer.'

I looked over at my boss without saying a word. What *was* he talking about?

'Fan-fucking-tastic,' Veronica replied, rattling her fingers against the table before pulling a pen out of her bag and slipping it between her fingers as though it were a cigarette. 'Let's hear what she has to say then.'

'Obviously we know Snazz has a lot of fans,' I began, watching as the panda reached across the table for a Hobnob, broke it into four pieces and carefully fed it up underneath his mask. 'And we want to offer them something with the podcast they can't get anywhere else.'

Veronica nodded, winding her finger in the air, signalling for me to continue.

'Well, one idea would be . . .' I looked down the table to see the panda staring back at me blankly, not moving, not breathing, just a dead-eyed panda with black, blank pits boring into me. I stared into the abyss and the abyss was a YouTuber. 'One idea would be for Snazz to choose some vintage video games and tell the story of how the game was developed, any social significance, interesting founder stories, stuff like that?'

Veronica looked over at her young charge. He did not move.

'He hates it,' she declared. 'What else?'

I took a deep breath and opened my notebook, pretending to be pleasantly surprised by what I saw when in fact the page was filled with a shopping list of things I needed to pick up from Tesco on my way home from work.

'What if he interviewed other inspirational young people? I'm thinking Greta Thunberg, Millie Bobby Brown . . . Malala?'

Veronica quite rightly choked on her coffee.

'Next,' she barked.

'He's not very chatty, is he?' I said as Snazz pulled the zip on his jacket up and down and up and down in silence. 'All my ideas involve quite a lot of him talking.'

'He'll be fine,' Veronica replied. 'I'll give him some Red Bull and a Mars Bar.'

Snazz snapped another Hobnob in half and tittered under the mask.

'Red Bull and a . . . ?' I whispered, wondering if the number to Childline was still the same.

She fixed me with a cool, level glare. 'Do you have any more ideas? Because these are just as bad as the ones we heard before.'

Glancing down at my notebook, pages full of suggestions and a dozen or so failed attempts at drawing a house without taking the pen off the page, a cold sense of dread gripped me in my seat. I could not lose this job, I just could not.

'Ros?' Ted's voice cut through the tension like a rusty bread knife.

'What if he just sat around and talked to his mates while they play video games and we call it Snazzlechuff Says?' I blurted out.

Ted gasped with either joy or despair, it was far too difficult to tell.

'CHUFF,' Veronica barked.

The panda snapped to attention.

'Snazzlechuff Says,' she repeated. 'Yay or nay?'

His narrow shoulders pinched together in what seemed to be a shrug.

'He'll do it,' Veronica declared, snapping her fingers twice.

'We could record live at WESC,' Ted suggested, popping up and down inside his too-big hoodie like a designer meerkat. 'Make a big noise for the first episode.'

'Love it, two birds one cheque,' she replied, standing up and clapping in the sad man's face. 'Let's go.'

While Ted saw them all out, I loitered in the staff kitchen, admiring the big pink fridge and reading all the different kind of coffee pods. The longer I could stay upstairs, the better.

'Good work in there,' he said, striding back into the office, his chest puffed out like a peacock. 'Snazzlechuff Says, it's got a good ring to it.'

'Why did you tell them you'd brought me in from America to do this job?' I asked, pocketing a bag of Mini Cheddars to take back down to my lair.

'It's more or less true,' he muttered.

'No, it isn't,' I countered with a laugh. 'What's the matter, could you not get anyone else to do the show or something?'

Ted continued to show a very peculiar interest in his shoes and I realized I'd accidentally worked out the truth.

'I thought this was a dream job anyone would kill for?' I said, turning my accusatory glare on the rest of the producers in the open-plan office, all of who suddenly seemed very interested in their computer screens. 'Wait, what did Veronica mean when she said she'd heard ideas before?'

'Thing is,' Ted said before clearing his throat. 'Everyone else here and half a dozen freelancers have already had a crack at it. We were on our last chance with Veronica today.'

My eyes widened and I felt an ever so slightly smug smile growing on my face.

'Oh,' I said, possibly a little too pleased with myself. 'So what you're saying is, I sort of saved the day today.'

'You could say that,' Ted agreed. 'Sort of.'

'Well,' I sucked the air in through my grin and reached for a shiny green apple from the fruit bowl, tossing it up in the air and just about managing to catch it. 'Well, well, well.'

'But um, just so you know,' he said, picking up an apple of his own and shining it on his T-shirt. 'If this doesn't work out, we won't really have a reason to keep you on. So let's give it everything you've got, yeah?'

What are you doing tonight? I really want to see you. Southbank Centre at seven?

I fizzed as I reread the text from Patrick that had sent me sprinting across Waterloo Bridge on a Thursday lunchtime tour of London, readying myself to leave for our second first date. Superdrug for makeup essentials, Chanel for a spritz or seventeen of nice perfume, Topshop to replace my greying old granny pants with a more acceptable date-night thong. I had an entire debate with myself in the changing room. I knew a pair of knickers could not change the course of mine and Patrick's relationship but I bought the black lacy

138

thong anyway. It never hurt to have one in your arsenal even if, I realized only after I got back to the office, it did really rather hurt my actual arse.

After applying roughly eighteen coats of mascara, slathering my new lip gloss all over my lips and throwing an optimistic toothbrush into my handbag, I left work on time, waving to Ted through his big, beautiful window as I went, and set off to meet Patrick.

He was standing by the railings on Southbank, all of London laid out behind him, and my insides seized up as he turned around and smiled. He wasn't just there, he was there to meet me. On purpose. By choice. Ridiculous.

'Hey,' I leaned forward to meet him for a kiss.

'You made it.' Patrick's face shone with a smile of his own as he cocked his head towards the cinema behind me. 'Come on, I don't want to be late.'

'Late for what?' I asked, anxiety washing over me. Had I got the time wrong? Had he sent another message I'd missed? And then I saw the tickets in his hand. 'We're seeing a film?'

'Two films,' he corrected. 'It's a Fassbinder retrospective. I was supposed to come with Carlton but he cancelled and I knew you'd love it.'

'Really? A Fassbender retrospective?' I was somewhat stumped. Didn't seem like Patrick's kind of thing. 'As long as they're not showing *Shame* because I saw that when it came out and I don't think I could sit through it again, not for all the naked Fassy in the world.'

Patrick laughed and took my hand in his, pulling me through the throngs of people wandering more aimlessly up and down the South Bank. 'Not Michael

139

Fassbender, *Fassbinder*. Rainer Werner Fassbinder? The German filmmaker?'

'Oh,' I cleared my throat and nodded with great knowing. '*That* Fassbender.'

'Fass*binder*. Tonight they're showing *The Bitter Tears of Petra von Kant* and *The Marriage of Maria Braun*.'

'It'll be great to see him on the big screen,' I said, choosing my words very carefully. 'I've never seen his films in a cinema before.'

This was all true, although it would be more accurate to say I'd never seen any of his films anywhere before. But lies of omission were allowed in the early stages of a relationship. If everyone practised nothing but radical honesty from the off, we'd have never made it out the caves.

I looked longingly at the stalls of books which lined the embankment outside the lobby as Patrick squeezed my hand and hurried me inside the huge concrete building. All of mine were still in storage. No room for literature in the shed.

'What are you doing Saturday night?' I asked.

This was the best way to do it, ask him outright at the beginning of the night rather than spending the entire evening worrying about his response when you had no idea what he was going to say.

'Not sure, why?' Patrick replied, showing an usher our tickets and grunting quietly when she told us the cinema was still being cleaned and we would have to wait in the lobby for a couple of minutes.

'At least we weren't late,' I remarked, trying to sound as frustrated as he looked. 'Anyway, about Saturday night.'

'Do you want to do something?' He gave me a smile

that made me ache. I hoped *The Bitter Tears of Petra von Kant* wasn't a long movie. 'There's an exhibition of collages on at the ICA from this young American woman who was just sent down for murdering her best friend and I've been dying to see it. Apparently she used the same knife to kill her friend that she used make the collages. It's very intense. Let's do that then make dinner at my place. I'll show you how to make real pad Thai.'

'While that sounds *fascinating*,' I started, holding his hand tightly to stop myself from gipping, 'it's Sumi's birthday and I'm organizing her party. Will you come?'

He stared over my head, mouth open, response not fully developed.

'Patrick?'

'Eesh!'

He let go of my hand and clapped another man on the back in an official buddy hug.

'Here for Fassbinder?' the man asked, giving me a polite smile.

'We are, we are,' Patrick confirmed.

His friend's eyes skittered back and forth between the two of us.

'I'm Ros,' I said, sticking out my hand towards him.

'Ishai,' he replied as he gave it a good shake. 'Big Fassy fan?'

'Huge,' I confirmed. 'The hugest.'

He and Patrick both laughed and I smiled. It felt like passing a test.

'Right, well, I've got to get some supplies before they let us in. Can't make it through a Fassbinder marathon without snacks to offset the emotional trauma,' Ishai said. My heart sank: so this wasn't going to be a spiritual companion piece to *Jurassic Park*. 'Monica's running late but she'll be here in a minute. We should all get a drink after.'

'We should, definitely,' Patrick agreed, raising his hand to wave him off. 'Good to see you, mate.'

'Nice to meet you,' I called, wondering if we should also be stocking up on reinforcements. If I was going to be bored and/or offended, I should at least get a bag of Maltesers for my troubles. I glanced up at Patrick. 'Do you want to meet them for a drink after?'

'God, no,' Patrick scoffed as the usher opened up the door to our screen. He rested his hands on my shoulders, walking behind me, leaving me Malteser-less. 'Ishai's fine but Monica I can't deal with. She works in publishing which means she knows everything. She's always trying to give me advice and it's incredibly patronizing.'

'Maybe she's trying to be helpful?' I suggested.

'She's edits children's books,' he replied. 'She doesn't understand literary travel memoirs in the slightest.'

It did, in fairness, seem as though Patrick's chosen genre was somewhat niche.

My eyes adjusted to the darkness of the small screening room, following Patrick up to the second-from-back row, making our way to the two centre seats.

'How is the book going?' I asked as we sidled past the two men already situated on the end of the row. When someone approaches your row, you stand up, I fumed silently, you don't shuffle your legs to one side and force me to slide my arse over your knees. Down with the patriarchy.

'Ugh,' he rolled his eyes and gagged. 'Slowly. I really

shouldn't be out of the house. I should be chained to my computer until the end of time.'

'Right, sounds tough,' I agreed, wondering if he fancied being chained to me instead. 'I got a date to record my first podcast with Snazzlechuff today. We're recording it live at this thing called WESC in a couple of weeks.'

He took his seat and grinned as the screen glowed white in front of us. 'I only understood about a third of those words and I'm a writer. You'll have to explain it all to me on Saturday.'

'So you'll come?' I whispered, shifting my inside voice to my inside-the-cinema voice. 'To Sumi's birthday?'

He turned his light blue eyes onto me, lit up in the semi-darkness.

'I'm not saying no but Sumi doesn't really like me, does she?' he said. 'Are you sure she actually wants me there?'

'She's desperate for you to come, they all are,' I lied. 'What makes you think Sumi doesn't like you?'

'Besides the Facebook message she sent me telling me to fuck myself up my own arse with a cheese grater the last time we were dating?' he replied.

I pressed my lips together as I tried to come up with a positive way to frame that.

'Well, you don't have Facebook any more,' I reasoned. 'And she's a lot more friendly these days.'

'If it's important to you, I'll come.' He lifted the armrest between us and wound his arm around my shoulders, pulling me in towards him. 'As long as it's OK with the birthday girl.'

'It's more than OK,' I promised, sinking into my seat

and resting my head on his shoulder and smiling. Future plans. Future plans with friends. 'Thank you.'

He kissed the top of my head as the curtains parted, the movie began with everyone speaking in German and my heart flew so high, not even the prospect of four hours of subtitles could bring it down.

CHAPTER FOURTEEN

'What about this one?'

My mother stepped out of the John Lewis changing room, a big smile on her face and not a lot of dress on her body.

'I love it,' she said as she tugged the already plunging neckline so far south, I could almost see her caesarean scar. 'What do you think?'

'It's a beautiful colour,' I replied, casting my eyes to the heavens.

If I'd tried to leave the house wearing the same frock fifteen years earlier, my father would have sent me out with a bin bag duct-taped to my body. It was nearly neon pink with slinky spaghetti straps that ran from her shoulders, all the way down her back until the fabric decided to at least have a go at being a dress, coming together just in time to cover her arse. It was Smirnoff Ice turned into an outfit. A dress that said 'I give no fucks' while proving that some-times, just sometimes, it was necessary to give at least one or two.

'It's very slimming.' She turned to the side and ran her hand over her stomach. 'And your dad loves it when I wear pink. I've got this satin nightie teddy that's just this shade.'

I squeezed the sides of my second giant iced coffee so hard the lid popped off.

'Don't take this the wrong way,' I said as she tested the limitations of the dress with a quick burst of the pony. 'But do you really think it's appropriate for a second wedding? I know it's not a normal big-white-frock affair but it's still a relatively formal occasion, isn't it?'

Mum reached around to the back of the dress, scrabbling for the price tag and both her boobs fell out.

'One hundred and forty pounds,' she muttered. 'There can't be more than ten pounds' worth of fabric in it.'

'At most,' I replied. 'At the absolute most.'

'You never like anything I like,' Mum said as she hoiked herself back into the dress, jiggling her breasts back into place while I silently prayed to the goddess that my boobs would be as tenacious as my mother's. 'And it's my party, I want to wear something fun.'

'I know strippers are really having a moment right now but I don't think that's the look you should be going for at the vow renewal,' I said. 'Why don't you try on that nice lace one I pulled out?'

Mum turned and looked at the very respectable periwinkle blue lace sheath I'd selected.

'Don't take this the wrong way but it's hideous,' she declared, snatching back the curtain to her cubicle in disgust. 'The queen mother would think it was too frumpy.'

'The queen mother's been dead well over a decade.'

'And she still wouldn't wear it.'

The curtain flew open again, revealing a bright green mini-dress with balloon sleeves and a slit running all the way up to her left hip, rendering any and all underwear unwearable. Very early period J.Lo if early period J.Lo made her own clothes out of Muppet remnants.

'It's all right for you,' she said as she paraded out the cubicle and proceeded to strike an assortment of poses in front of the mirror. 'You've always been able to wear whatever you want and get away with it.' I looked down at my eighteen-year-old jeans and dodgy trainers and wondered where she was going with this. 'That's because my generation fought for you to have that freedom, freedom we didn't have!'

Narrowing my eyes, I finished my coffee. 'Mum, you were a teenager in the seventies, not during World War One.'

'Well, I wasn't allowed to wear whatever I wanted when I was a teenager,' she sniffed before lowering into a squat and attempting to twerk. 'And when I left home, I went straight into teaching, which meant I had to dress respectably in and out of school. There would have been hell to pay if the head had seen me dancing at Park Avenue on a Saturday night, dressed up like a dog's dinner. And as soon as I had you, I had to dress like a mum. What does that even mean, dressing like a mum? I'm sixty years old and I'm dressing for myself for the first time. And I like this dress.'

The fourth-wave feminist in me wanted to stand up and cheer but the eternal child just could not get over the fact that I could one hundred percent see my mother's vulva.

'Mum, I think you're amazing and we should definitely be celebrating that,' I said, trying very hard not to look at It. 'But that dress just isn't special enough. We need to find something that's worthy of you.'

She gazed at herself in the mirror before casting a disparaging look at my choice of dress. 'Your nana wouldn't wear that blue frock.'

'Is Nana coming to the ceremony?' I asked, clutching non-existent pearls at the thought.

'Christ, I suppose she'll have to,' Mum muttered. 'Perhaps it's not too late to call the whole thing off.'

'We'll get her drunk and make Adrian talk to her,' I said, shaking my head. 'She loves Adrian.'

My nana loved Adrian because my dad hated Adrian. It was simple family maths.

'Everyone says you'll feel terrible when your children leave home.' Mum trotted back into her stall and drew the curtain with considerably less vigour. 'Empty nest syndrome, they said. Thought your dad and I would be rattling around the empty house without a clue what to say to each other but to be entirely honest, Ros, we've never been happier.'

'Jo *was* a handful,' I nodded sympathetically.

'Not just Jo,' Mum replied with a pointed peek through the curtain. 'Do you remember Avaline who did the accounts for your dad?'

I nodded even though I didn't. No need to make the story a thousand times longer than necessary.

'She went totally loopy when her youngest went off

to uni. Left her husband, shacked up with a woman and started dressing head to toe in leather. Invited everyone at work to join her Facebook group for BSM, very awkward business.'

I sucked on my straw until my coffee was empty, frowning at myself in the mirror.

'She was moonlighting for the British School of Motoring?'

'No, not that BSM,' Mum stuck a disembodied head out of the curtains. 'Whips and chains and all that malarkey. There's a club down on Swinnow Street that has swingers' night on a Tuesday. You'd never know to look at it from the outside.'

My eyes grew so big, I thought they might fall out. If she'd just told me this story the moment I arrived home, I'd have *offered* to sleep at the bottom of the garden.

'I'm sure you don't want to hear it but staying married for forty years isn't exactly a walk in the park, especially when thirty-two of those years are mostly taken up by keeping two other human beings alive every day.'

'Also known as your children,' I added. 'Who you love very much.'

'Of course we love you both,' she replied from behind the curtain. 'But that doesn't make parenting any easier on a relationship. I gave up a lot for our family, Ros. I didn't tell you at the time but I was up for a spot at Oxford when Jo came along.'

I guessed that this was the wrong time to suggest she should have known what caused pregnancy by the time she was forty-two. There really was no excuse for it, we had five TV channels and a satellite dish by then.

'And what did your dad give up? Nothing. Most of my friends were celebrating their kids moving out and getting their lives back and there I was, being forced out of a job I loved to stay at home with a stroppy teenager and a gifted toddler, while your dad went mincing off around Europe on an awful lot of business trips.'

A horrible thought crossed my mind that I couldn't keep off my face.

'I do remember him going away a lot,' I said, putting two and two together and coming up with a number I didn't like the look of at all.

'Everything is fine between me and your dad now but it wasn't always. Back then everyone just assumed I'd give up my career to look after you girls while your dad kept doing whatever he wanted.'

'You're talking like it was a million years ago,' I mumbled. 'Jo's only eighteen.'

'Exactly,' she said, emerging in her usual Prince of Wales checked trousers and a black silk shirt I would never again take for granted as long as I lived. 'And don't you forget it. As soon as we make an inch of progress, we write off yesterday as though it were ancient history. We'd all do a good deal better to remember what happened yesterday. It was this millennium, not the dark ages, and I was passed over for a job I was more than qualified for and was as good as promised, all because I went in to interview with a room full of men when I was six months pregnant. We tend to assume we're entitled to the things we have, we rewrite history to make life easier for ourselves. It's not the case, Ros.'

'I know, Mum,' I said quietly.

'Your dad tried but he was never very good at the hands-on parenting,' she said, straightening her hair in the big mirror. 'And as much as he loves her, he never really knew what to do with your sister. She's always been a handful.'

'I knew it was Jo's fault,' I whispered into my coffee.

'Because you were such a great help with her,' she added with a lashing of unnecessary sarcasm. 'None of it matters. Your dad doesn't go on nearly as many business trips as he used to and we're back on the right track. I just want you to know it wasn't always easy.'

'What about your work?' I asked. 'Do you think you'll go back to it?'

She shrugged as she tucked herself in. 'We'll see.'

'I think you should,' I told her. 'I hate that you had to give up something so important for us.'

'And I'd do it again,' she said, clapping her hands together. 'Right, shall we attempt to find me a dress before it's dinner time? Since you hate everything I've chosen for myself?'

'You need a showstopper,' I declared, filled with love and pride for my mother. It was much easier now I couldn't see her areolas. 'Something extra special.'

She looked wistfully at the strips of sparkly satin, held together by diamanté straps and bad intentions hanging in her cubicle.

'Step away from the manmade fibres,' I ordered. 'I'm almost certain we can find a happy medium between Nana's Big Day Out and first evictee from *Love Island*.'

'Just can't get into that but your dad's obsessed,' she muttered, adjusting her collar. 'Right, what would you suggest?'

'Something radical,' I said as I tucked my empty Starbucks cup behind the leg of my chair. It wasn't littering if it was in a shop and you hid it. 'Let's try a different shop.'

Mum looked aghast. All special occasion Reynolds outfits had been purchased at John Lewis since time immemorial.

'Where else is there?'

'You're just going to have to trust me,' I said, standing up and giving her the look.

'Well, we can go somewhere else but I reserved a table on the terrace at twelve for lunch,' she replied, face flushed with fear. 'Will we be back in time?'

'If we're not, we can always eat somewhere else.'

It was as though I'd slapped her around the face with a trout.

'Now *that's* a dress.'

Shoulder to shoulder with an exquisitely turned-out bridal consultant, I applauded as Mum stepped onto the raised dais, glowing under the soft lighting, clad in a beautiful ivory satin wrap dress that skimmed her amazing figure and swept the floor as she moved. A quick Google and one pleading phone call had seen us abandon Oxford Street for a tiny bridal salon, tucked away behind the Big Shops, which had managed to squeeze us in between their other appointments.

'It is very nice,' Mum said, twisting and turning in the gown, admiring herself in every one of the million mirrors that covered the walls of the dressing area. 'But is it me?'

'It's a very elegant choice,' the consultant said. 'It looks as though it was made for you.'

'Yes, it does,' I said, encouragingly.

'Would you ladies like some champagne?' the consultant asked.

'Yes, we would,' I said, encouragingly.

'They say it's free but you know you end up paying for that,' Mum said, still making eyes at herself in the mirror as the consultant drifted away. 'I can't begin to imagine how much this dress costs.'

'It's four hundred quid and you're buying it,' I told her. 'You look amazing, Dad's going to die.'

'He does like a bit of cleavage,' she replied, juggling her boobs in the front of the frock. 'But I don't know.'

'Mum,' I said in my most serious voice. 'Does this dress make you feel like your most fabulous, wonderful, complete self?'

She pouted and tied her hair up into a loose topknot.

'It's four hundred pounds, daughter.'

'And aren't you worth four hundred pounds?'

A hint of a smile appeared at the edges of her mouth.

'You can always save some cash by not having bridesmaids,' I suggested. 'I for one am prepared to make that sacrifice.'

'So generous, Rosalind,' she said, looking back at me in the mirror. 'Fine. I'll get it.'

I dipped into a low bow, catching sight of my knackered trainers.

'You're going to need shoes,' I said as the consultant returned with our champagne. 'Do you have shoes?'

'Of course,' she replied smoothly. 'What size?'

'She's a four,' I said, taking a sip from my glass and kicking back in a particularly comfortable armchair while Mum continued to make love eyes at herself in the mini hall of mirrors.

My work was done.

CHAPTER FIFTEEN

Once I'd put Mum back on the train with her dress, a beautiful pair of not-stripper shoes and, god forbid, some tasteful lingerie, I moved on to the next task at hand, Sumi's birthday.

'This is going to be the best party she's ever had,' I told Adrian, marching purposefully down the street from the bus stop with a bouquet of birthday balloons in my hand. 'I'm deadly serious, she's going to enjoy herself if it kills her.'

'*Someone* spent an entire day with her mother,' he replied, skipping to keep up. 'Where's Patrick then?'

'Meeting us later,' I said, pushing down the excitement that bubbled up in my belly. 'He had to work today.'

'Work?'

'Write,' I clarified. 'He's on a deadline for a book he's writing. It's about his travels in South-East Asia, it's amazing.'

'Hmm.' Adrian jumped as a very big mouse or, more likely, a reasonable-sized rat scampered out in front of us. 'For Christ's sake, woman, where exactly are we going?'

'Somewhere brilliant,' I said as I took a sharp left off the main street and down a somewhat suspicious-looking alley that cried out for you to hold onto your handbag. Yes, this was exactly how I remembered it. Fantastic. 'Do you honestly not remember?'

'The only thing I know around here is a gay bath-house and please don't ask me how I know because I'm not at liberty to say,' Adrian said. 'I haven't been to Vauxhall for aeons. In fact the last time I was here, I think it was . . . Oh, Rosalind fucking Reynolds, you didn't?'

'I most certainly did,' I replied, throwing my arms out to present our destination. The Moonlight Roller Rink. 'How amazing is this?'

Adrian's face dropped.

'Do *you* honestly not remember?'

'I remember we used to come here all the time and we always loved it,' I said, hopping up and down as we reached the front door. 'Stop being an arse. Everyone's skating again, Adrian, it's what all the cool kids are doing, have you not seen *Euphoria*?'

'No?'

'Well, neither have I but I read a recap that said they all went roller skating,' I said as I handed him a neon-pink towelling headband. 'So please try to enjoy yourself. We'll skate, we'll drink and then we'll go dancing. Best. Birthday. Ever.'

'Oh, Ros,' Adrian said, slipping the sweatband over his head before reaching out to pat my shoulder. 'Dear, sweet, stupid Ros.'

'Stupid like a fox,' I argued. 'Sumi is going to—'

'Moonlight Roller Rink?' my friend's voice boomed over my shoulder. 'You're kidding me?'

'Sumi is going to remind you the last time we were here, that Samantha girl she was obsessed with broke up with her and she fell over and shattered her ankle,' Adrian whispered in my ear.

'Happy birthday,' I exclaimed weakly, handing over a huge helium balloon. Lucy and Jemima waved awkwardly and a gaggle of other women, referred to exclusively by Sumi as her Lesbian Lawyer Coven, loitered in the background. No one seemed quite sure of what to say, which was a big deal when you considered how many lawyers I was dealing with.

'Roller skating? Fuck yes.'

I peered past Sumi's giant balloon to see John the bartender striding down the alleyway, waving a hello. 'All right everybody? Happy birthday, Sumi.'

'You're up for this?' Sumi asked, looking more than a little bit surprised.

'It's been a while but it's got to be like riding a bike, hasn't it?' John replied as he made the rounds, hugs and cheek kisses for everyone, pausing when he got to me and making do with a bright smile and an arrogant wink.

'I don't know,' Sumi said. 'I do not have time for a broken ankle right now.'

'No one has time for a broken ankle,' Jemima said, hooping her arms over Sumi's head. 'Come on, it'll be fun. I haven't been roller skating since I was about twelve. I'm game for a laugh.'

'I would if I could,' Lucy added, pointing at her belly. 'But I'm very happy to sit and watch you all.'

'It'll be grand,' Adrian cheered, holding open the

157

door and ushering everyone inside. 'And if it's not, drinks are on Ros.' With an uneven mix of reluctant mutters and enthusiastic cheers, we poured into the skating rink and the blissful air conditioning.

'Drinks are on me as long as everyone's on the Panda Pops,' I muttered to Adrian as I handed out headbands and wristbands and birthday girl badges. 'I maxed this week's budget on the accessories.'

'How come you're so broke, anyway?' he asked, doubling up on neon sweatbands as the others ran off to get their skates. 'Were they not paying you in Washington?'

I shrugged; trying to work out where my money had gone was like trying to work out how certain people had been voted president. I understood it logically but it simply made no sense.

'It was expensive out there,' I reasoned. 'I was living on my own, which cost a fortune, ordering in food all the time because I never had time to cook. Money just goes, doesn't it?'

Adrian frowned. He was the wrong person to take part in this conversation.

'I wish I'd come out to visit more, I really wanted to do a proper American road trip,' he said. 'Figured you'd be there longer, you always seemed like you were having so much fun.'

'I was,' I replied stiffly. 'Go and get your skates, we've only got two hours here before dinner.'

With a swift salute, he headed off to the check-in desk, trotting along happily. One of the best things about having Adrian as a friend was that he didn't ask too many questions. I imagine it was easy to accept whatever people told you was true if you'd grown up wealthy; you never had to dig any deeper because nothing really mattered.

'I'm going to the bar, can I get you a drink?'

I turned to see John beside me, a neon-pink sweatband holding back his black hair. He looked ridiculous.

'I'm fine, thanks,' I told him, marching over to the check-in desk to pick up my own skates.

'This was such a fun idea,' Lucy said as she settled herself into a wildly uncomfortable-looking chair beside the roller rink as Sumi, Jemima and Adrian happily daubed themselves with the glitter gel I'd pulled out of my birthday bag of tricks. 'You're so clever to think of it.'

'I was just trying to think of the places we used to go,' I reasoned, pausing in lacing up my skates to watch Sumi dump half a tub of silver sparkles in Adrian's hair, howling with laughter as she wiped the remainder onto her leggings. 'We always had so much fun here. Well, apart from the last time.'

'I'd forgotten all about it,' Lucy admitted. 'Too much going on these days. I can hardly remember what happened last week, let alone ten years ago.'

I bent over to finish doing up my skates, wheeling my feet back and forth in my seat. Why did I feel so unsteady? I used to be a roller skating goddess. Skating forwards, backwards, spinning around with a drink in one hand, and, well, drink in the other most of the time.

'Who invited John?' I nodded at the bartender as he whizzed around the roller rink on unsteady legs. He was too tall, limbs too long, angles too sharp. It felt as though he was defying the laws of physics every moment he remained upright.

'Sumi asked me to text him,' Lucy replied. 'Why?'

'We never used to hang out with the bartender at The Lexington,' I pointed out as he took another wild turn, spinning around Jemima with windmills for arms. 'I don't get the appeal, if I'm honest. He's so pleased with himself all the time.'

'He's not just the bartender,' she said. 'He owns it.'

My head snapped up with surprise. 'He *owns* Good Luck?'

'Good Luck and another place in Shoreditch,' she confirmed. 'Buena Suerta, it's tapas, you'd love it, we should go.'

'Then why is he always behind the bar?' I asked, puzzled. 'And why was he mixing drinks at Adrian's parents' party?'

'Because he works hard and he's nice?' she suggested. She leaned back as far as she could in her hard plastic chair and shuffled until she looked as though she was somewhere near comfortable. 'I don't know, why don't you ask him?'

'Well, I still think he's a tit,' I muttered. 'He's arrogant.'

'Just your type then,' Lucy said with a small smile before tittering at my dark expression. 'What time *is* Patrick joining us?'

'He's meeting us for dinner,' I said as I attempted to stand. So far, so no-broken-bones. 'He had to write all day.'

'Didn't fancy the skating?'

'He didn't say that but . . .' I moved my stiff legs back and forth, clutching the back of Lucy's chair.

'Go on then,' she instructed as I grabbed the side of the rink and made my way to the gate. 'I want to see you bust some moves.'

'Bust my arse, more like,' I muttered as I wheeled slowly away.

The music in the roller rink was deafening, all the better to drown out the screaming, I thought to myself as I staggered over, half-walking, half-wheeling, all petrified. What was I thinking? Women over the age of thirty had no business on roller skates. What if I had early-onset osteoporosis and didn't know it? My nan had it and yes, she was in her late eighties, but still. As the bass thumped, the disco lights shimmered and shone, spinning even faster than the people already racing around the roller rink.

'Maybe it's actually easier when you're drunk,' I reasoned, rolling one foot out onto the rink. I had certainly never shown up sober before but that was what your twenties was for, wasn't it? Always drunk, never hungover. No wonder I missed them so much . . .

'Whooo! Go, Ros!' Lucy cheered and clapped from the sidelines as I propelled myself forward, keeping one hand within grabbing distance of the railing, my upper body a half-second behind my lower half.

OK, I thought, relaxing into myself and skating a little faster. It wasn't so bad, I could definitely do it. Enjoy it? Maybe not but do it, definitely.

'Ros, this is the best thing ever!' A dark-haired flash spun by me, sending me crashing back into the side of the rink. It was Sumi, whizzing by backwards before executing a perfect spin and stopping right in front of me. 'I can't believe we stopped coming here, you're a genius. Thank you so much!'

'How is she still so good?' I gasped as she roared away across the floor, only stopping to pirouette around Jemima and then race off to the bar.

Determined to find my roller-girl mojo, I pushed myself away from the side. My jeans felt too stiff, my sleeves too restrictive and my carefully blown-out hair was all in my face. Everything was wrong. Everything took so much more thought these days; back in our early twenties, we just did things. I didn't care what I was wearing or what the consequences might be but now, ten years on, I felt tight and awkward and couldn't bring my brain back to the present moment. It was far too comfortable working three steps ahead, in a reality where I'd already fallen, broken my neck and ended up in a home, right next to my nan while she sat and crowed, morning, noon and night, *all because she wanted to go roller skating*.

No, I told myself, sliding one foot in front of the other, the air rushing past my face as I slipped back into something like a familiar rhythm. You are a gazelle, a gazelle on wheels. You're Zendaya and Jessica Simpson and some other celebrities that roller-skate that I couldn't think of in the moment. You are graceful and capable and you're not thinking about all those celebrities who broke their legs on *Dancing on Ice*. It's all coming back, it's coming back to me now, you are Celine Dion and this is fantastic and—

'Oh, shit!'

My left foot crossed out in front of my right and, before I knew what was happening, my legs tangled around each other and I hit the floor hard on my backside, my left cheek taking the brunt of the fall.

'Ros! Don't move!'

I looked up from the floor to see John skating over, crashing to his knees beside me. I opened my mouth to reply but all the air, along with my pride, had been knocked right out of me and I absolutely, positively knew I was going to cry.

'Is anything broken?' he asked, frisking my legs with brisk authority. 'Does it hurt anywhere?'

'My arse,' I choked as I fought back tears. My face was bright red and, I was quite certain, I would have a backside to match by morning.

'Well, I don't think you've broken your arse, so come on.' He pulled me to my feet and dragged me over to the side. 'It was a good effort.'

'I haven't skated in ages,' I replied, my words coming out staccato, pinched by several sharp intakes of breath. My left bum cheek was killing me. 'I think I slipped on something.'

'Yeah, you did,' he agreed, unloading me into a seat next to Lucy who thrust herself upright to grab my hands, face awash with concern. 'Your own feet.'

My bottom lip trembled dangerously and even though I had a thousand snappy comebacks at the ready, I kept them to myself for fear of bursting into tears.

'Are you all right?' Lucy asked, handing me her carton of Ribena. 'You poor thing, that looked rough.'

I nodded, sucking through the tiny straw and wallowing in her pity. 'I'm OK,' I said bravely, adding a sorrowful sniff for good measure. 'Might sit it out for a bit though.'

'Still wish I could have at least one go around,' Lucy said, watching wistfully as our friends tore around the rink. 'Just for old times' sake.'

'We can come again,' I promised. 'Once you've had the baby.'

Lucy laughed. 'Yes,' she agreed. 'Let's put a date in the diary for a time when it no longer relies solely on me to exist.'

'There's always Dave,' I reminded her.

Lucy replied with a look.

'Fair enough,' I muttered. 'We'll come back as soon as it gets married and they've left for their honeymoon.'

John stood beside us, still in his skates. With the added inches, he looked as though he was about to climb down a beanstalk. There ought to be a height maximum for men in skates, I decided. Anything over five ten was ridiculous.

'I've got an idea,' he said, quirking his mouth into a smile. 'Stay right there.'

Carefully, he padded over to the check-in desk, pointing back at me and Lucy as he turned his sleepy smile on the girl behind the counter.

'What's he doing?' I wondered aloud as she nodded eagerly and disappeared into the little room where they kept all the skates.

'Maybe he's asking if they've got kneepads for you,' she replied. 'Or a nice helmet.'

I narrowed my eyes and slurped through the straw until her carton was empty.

'Here we are.' John returned to our spot with a proud look on his face and an ancient wheelchair in his hands. 'Let's go.'

'I fell on my bum,' I said, shifting in my seat to test said body part. Nope, too sore to sit on. 'I don't think I need a wheelchair.'

'It's not for you,' he replied pointedly before nodding at Lucy. 'It's for you. Hop in and I'll take you round.'

Lucy clapped gleefully, transferring herself into the other chair and cheering as John pushed her onto the rink. Propping my chin up in my hand, elbow on the table, I watched them circle the floor, Sumi, Jemima, Adrian and the rest hooking onto John's waist in a long conga line of skating-rink goodness.

'Ros!' Sumi wailed. 'Get your fucking arse back out here.'

'It's my fucking arse I'm worried about!' I shouted back, blanching as a woman and her young daughter walked by. The little girl's eyes bulged and she grinned. 'Sorry,' I said, apologizing profusely to the mother and forcing myself to my feet. 'Very sorry.'

With an awkward limp, I shuffled back onto the rink and waited for them to circle back around.

'Watch out!' yelled Adrian at the back of the train. 'Here we come!'

I reached out my arms and grabbed hold of him around the waist, squealing with laughter as I was pulled along by my friends.

'Feels like we were just here yesterday,' Adrian shouted over his shoulder.

'I know,' I replied, happily clutching his belt loops and ignoring the throbbing pain in my left hip as we whirled around, more and more people joining the back of the chain until everyone in the rink was part of it, all of us skating together. 'Isn't it brilliant?'

Sumi's birthday party was officially a success.

CHAPTER SIXTEEN

'Another round?'

John stood up, nodding at the assenting murmurs that passed around the table. Roller skating was thirsty work and, according to all the empty plates that covered our table, hungry work on top of that.

While my roller rink plan had turned out to be a resounding success, my plan to eat at the American diner next door was less of a winner. We had literally walked in, taken one look at the place and walked back out. It wasn't my fault, Sumi assured me as we jumped on the tube back to Good Luck Bar. How could I have known the supposed retro restaurant hadn't seen so much as a Dettol wipe since the turn of the century? It had a very fancy Instagram that didn't once mention the rats running around outside by the bins.

And so, we were tucked away in an upstairs room at Good Luck Bar I hadn't known existed until tonight and, credit where credit's due, it was utterly gorgeous. Exposed concrete walls, huge windows and soft pink velvet chairs to match the booths downstairs. Even with my broken bottom, they were so comfy, if I could have got one in my handbag, I would have. Hanging overhead at either end of the room were two beautiful chandeliers and, at the very, very back, I saw two huge double doors that led to a cluttered, closed-off roof terrace beyond.

'This is the best birthday ever,' Sumi cried, waving her still very full glass high above her head and splashing the contents in her hair. 'I love you, John.'

'Don't let your grandmother hear that,' Adrian accessorized his warning with a hiccup. 'It's not fair to get her hopes up at her age.'

'He's so good though,' she slurred as our host let himself behind the bar and began mixing drinks. 'I'm so grateful for you, John. It's so hard to make new friends when you get older. Ones that aren't shit, I mean. And you're not shit at all. We're all *so* grateful for you.'

He looked up from the bar, just long enough to show off an awkward, faux-embarrassed grin. I rolled my eyes and emptied my glass at the same time.

'Everyone go around the table and tell me what they're grateful for,' Sumi demanded, banging her hand on the table. 'Ade, you go first.'

'Remember that time we got so drunk on her birthday that we woke up in France?' I whispered to Lucy.

'Paris is beautiful this time of year,' she nodded with a nostalgic sigh.

'All right, what am I grateful for?' Adrian said, missing his glass when he reached out for it. 'I'm grateful for a roof over my head and food in my belly and my wonderful friends. Also tits.'

'Tits!' Sumi clapped her approval. 'I'm grateful for Adrian's beautiful honesty. Lucy, what about you?'

'I'm grateful for my new best friend,' she said, gazing down at her stomach. 'Whom I can't wait to meet.'

'What are you going to do if it turns out to be a serial killer?' Adrian asked while Sumi booed Lucy's answer. 'Or even worse, what if it's ugly?'

'How is ugly worse than a serial killer?' John asked. He returned to the table with a pitcher of fresh margaritas, holding it aloft to rapturous applause.

'Serial killers charismatic are at least.' Adrian held out his glass for a top-up. 'If the baby is ugly, there's nothing we can do. Until it's old enough for surgery.'

'He is joking, isn't he?' Jemima asked me.

'It's easier to assume he is,' I replied. 'I know he's not ideal but we just don't have the energy to interview for a replacement and you've got to have a boy in your group so someone can answer the sports questions at the pub quiz.'

'I will love my baby even if it's an ugly serial killer,' Lucy announced before knitting her eyebrows together. 'Which it *won't* be.'

'And what about you, Ros?' John reached his arm across my face to fill my glass. 'What are you grateful for?'

Sumi leaned forward to stare at me with unfocused eyes, her face and her hair falling into the remains of her Barnsley chop as she did so.

'I'm grateful for a lot of things,' I replied, pursing my lips as John took the empty seat to my left that I was still saving for Patrick. Two hours after he was supposed to meet us. 'Mostly, I'm grateful for old friends.'

'To old friends and new ones,' John said, raising his glass into the air.

'To friends!' Sumi repeated, throwing the contents of her glass up into the air so that it splashed down on her friends in a light, sugary margarita rain. 'Wait, didn't I already say friends? You can't say something I already said, go again.'

I thought hard for a moment, fully aware that Adrian was filming me on his phone. If he was posting this to Instagram, I would kill him.

'Then I'm grateful for second chances,' I said.

'Bleurgh,' Sumi stuck her fingers down her throat and I responded in kind with a finger of my own.

'Didn't I hear your boyfriend was coming tonight?' John asked, leaning his head over to one side while Jemima brushed Sumi's hair back from her face and dodged her sloppy, drunken kisses.

'Yes,' I replied without correcting his terminology. It was perfectly all right for other people to call Patrick my boyfriend, even if it was a bit early to be claiming it myself. 'He is. He will be here very soon.'

I glanced down at my phone. No reply to my last three messages, the one letting him know we were ordering dinner or the two I'd sent to make sure he was OK.

'Sweet Ros,' Sumi sighed, resting her head on a pile of jackets and jumpers she had pulled onto the table. 'Sweet, naïve Ros.'

'He's coming,' I insisted. He'd said he was coming, he had no reason to lie. 'He's just caught up with his writing.'

'Or he's been abducted by aliens,' Adrian suggested. 'Or he's run off to join the circus.'

'I do hope he's all right,' Lucy said, rubbing her stomach. 'The circus isn't as safe as people think.'

'He's not coming,' Sumi whispered to the coats, pressing a finger to her lips as she shushed them.

'He's fine and he *is* coming,' I repeated. 'I didn't know there was a time limit on when people could celebrate Sumi's birthday?'

'I'd say usually before midnight,' John suggested, taking a sip of his drink. 'But that's just me. I'm old-fashioned like that.'

'And preferably before the birthday girl passes out,' Adrian added, nodding down the table, where Sumi was resting her head on her hands, eyes closed, mouth open.

'I'm not passed out,' she replied without moving. 'I want to go dancing.'

'Yes, brilliant idea!' I exclaimed, jumping up too quickly and forgetting about my roller rink injury. It wasn't half going to hurt in the morning. 'Let's go dancing. Where's the best place to go around here?'

'Dancing, yeah,' Sumi cheered quietly, face planted on the table, waving her arms from side to side.

'We *could* go dancing,' Lucy suggested, pulling at her tights. 'Or I could go home to a nice elasticated waistband and my pregnancy pillow.'

'Pregnancy pillow, yeah,' Sumi cheered quietly, face planted on the table, waving her arms from side to side.

'We should get her home,' Adrian said. 'If she falls asleep, we'll have to carry her.'

'Again,' John added.

'But it's so early!' I protested, even though I already knew the party was as good as over. All around the table, people were folding up their napkins and ferreting around in handbags. 'And look, we've got a fresh round of drinks, we can't go yet. Adrian, it's Saturday night and it's only just eleven. There's no way you're going home.'

I grabbed the jug of margaritas and began pouring them into everyone's glasses, ignoring their protests.

'Sorry, chuck,' he said, ruffling a hand through his gingery blond hair. 'I'm afraid I'm tapping out. I've signed up for CrossFit in the morning so I need to be fresh-ish at the very least.'

'CrossFit?' I was dubious at best. 'But you hate exercise. And you're *always* the last one to call it a night. Don't let me down, Adrian.'

'What can I say?' he said with a shrug. 'I've turned over a new leaf.'

I glared at him with narrowed eyes.

'You're trying to crack on to a girl at CrossFit.'

He shook his head, no. 'I'm trying to crack on to the girl that *teaches* CrossFit.'

'It's Sumi's birthday,' I reminded everyone as I saw the Uber app open on one phone after another. 'This is supposed to be the wildest night of the year and you're all going home before midnight?'

'It's been a really long week,' one of Sumi's friends commented.

'It's been a long year,' added another.

'And roller skating really took it out of me,' Jemima added to a chorus of agreement. 'Sorry, Ros, but I'm really old.'

'You're thirty-four,' I wailed. 'You're a baby!'

'This was a really fun night,' Lucy declared,

officially calling an end to proceedings. 'Thank you so much for saving the day, John.'

'Ah, no worries,' he said, waving away her appreciation with a smile. 'We don't get to use this room often enough anyway and you know chef is always looking for guinea pigs to test new recipes on.'

'You must let us pay for drinks,' she said, fishing around in her handbag for her wallet. 'It's the least we can do.'

'Not at all,' John said. 'My treat. What's the point in running a bar if you can't get your friends pissed on their birthday?'

Slowly, Sumi was raised from the table, her arms draped around Jemima and Adrian's shoulders, and carefully led downstairs as everyone buzzed around one another with kisses on cheeks and vague promises of getting together 'sometime soon'. At the back of the pack, I waved them all off, making sure everyone was in their taxi, their Uber, setting off for the right bus stop, before I checked my phone one last time.

Still no word from Patrick.

'Not in a rush to get home then?' John asked as I lingered in the doorway.

'Not really,' I admitted, my stomach sinking further with every passing second. The thought of returning the shed and its dripping roof did absolutely nothing to soothe my mood.

'Want to finish off those margaritas?'

I crossed my arms over my chest and considered my options. Drink very strong cocktails with a man I was less than keen on or get back on the bus to my pimped-out shed and wonder endlessly why Patrick hadn't bothered to turn up?

'It would be terrible to let them go to waste,' I said, resignedly following him back upstairs.

John placed an exceptionally large margarita in front of me and took a seat on the opposite side of the table. Sitting face to face as he quietly savoured his drink, I couldn't help but be impressed by how shiny his longish black hair was, lit by the chandeliers overhead. There was no denying it was good hair, the way it curled against the nape of his neck and messily pushed back away from his face. I wondered what it would look like if he let it grow longer. Would it be as curly as mine? His eyes were deep brown and his complexion had a warm olive tone, although he looked as though he could stand to see the sun a little bit more often. Objectively a fox, I decided, kicking my shoes off underneath the table. I was out of practice in heels, definitely needed to build up my tolerance. Unlike my tolerance to tequila, which seemed to be doing just fine.

'So, you've been back how long now?' he asked, in between sips.

'Two weeks.'

'And how are you enjoying being home?'

'It's fine.'

'Work's going well?'

'Not really.'

He laughed unexpectedly as he licked the salt from the rim of his glass.

'I love how talkative you are,' he said. 'This really is a thrilling conversation.'

'I'm sorry,' I said with a big sigh. 'This time it's not actually you.'

'Didn't think it was.' John raised his glass across the table. 'Cheers.'

'I wanted tonight to be perfect,' I explained, lifting my glass in his direction. 'Sumi's birthday always used the biggest party of the year and I didn't want to let her down. Tonight was fine but it wasn't that extra, was it? No wacky adventures, no shenanigans to speak of. Just a perfectly ordinary Saturday night.'

'With roller skating,' John added.

'Once on Sumi's birthday, she ended up on stage during a touring production of *Cats* in Reading,' I replied.

He looked equally impressed and afraid. 'My worst nightmare. How did you organize that?'

'Oh, we didn't organize it,' I said. 'It's surprisingly easy to get backstage in a lot of regional theatres. And Sumi does a very good Rum Tum Tugger.'

'I bet she does,' he laughed. 'But you're worrying about nothing. She seemed pleased with the evening as far as I could tell, and now she's drunk, happy and home safe. As someone who has worked in bars for most of their life, trust me when I tell you, things could have gone a lot worse.'

'But it used to be different,' I said, staring out the window at the dusky sky. I had always loved a British summer and the late light nights. 'When we all lived together, we used to go out every weekend and we didn't come home until the sun was up, you know?'

'Things change,' John replied simply, wrapping long, strong fingers around his glass. 'Just be grateful you're not going to wake up on the night bus with someone drooling on your shoulder at three o'clock tomorrow morning.'

'But when did they change?' I wondered aloud. 'One minute, things were one way and now they're another. It feels as though it all happened at once. Lucy's pregnant, Sumi's asleep at the table and Adrian is going to CrossFit on a Sunday morning. Was there a meeting? Did I miss a memo?'

He grabbed a wedge of lime from a plate in the middle of the table and squeezed it into his drink, mixing it with a tiny metal straw. His hands were massive, I noticed. Long fingers, short nails, a strong forearm resting on the table and just a hint of an equally impressive bicep hidden by the sleeve of his grey T-shirt.

'I just wish everything was the same as it used to be,' I said, closing my eyes on it all.

'I've got to say,' John tapped the metal straw against the rim of his glass. 'You're not at all how I'd imagined you to be.'

I opened my eyes and looked at him across the table.

'When were you imagining me to be anything?'

As his face broke out into a smile that still turned down at the edges, I noticed a dimple in his left cheek that I hadn't seen before. Probably because I hadn't seen him smile all that much.

'I was curious,' he replied. 'They would talk about you all the time, Sumi and the others. It's only natural to wonder.'

Leaning my elbows on the long table, I considered him with more interest. It was a strange feeling, to find out there had been a complete stranger walking around, forming an opinion about you without your having any say in the matter.

'What is it about me that isn't what you expected?'

'I don't know,' John said slowly, his brown eyes lightly scanning my face. 'They all talked you up so much.'

'And the real-life me is nothing but a disappointment?' I asked with a deprecating laugh he didn't return. Instead he raised his glass to his lips and held it there for a moment before taking a sip.

'Not in the slightest.'

I felt a flush in my cheeks that had nothing to do with the amount of tequila in my drink. Well, maybe a little bit to do with the amount of tequila in my drink.

'I'm very good at reading people,' he said, holding my eyes with a steady gaze. 'But I can't read you at all. It's like trying to do a crossword puzzle, only the clues I've been given aren't quite right.'

I matched his gaze, searching his face for the answer to a question I wasn't sure I'd asked.

'This is what you call a birthday party?'

Almost three hours late and carrying a white cardboard box in his arms, Patrick appeared at the top of the stairs.

'You're here!' I cried, jumping to my feet. 'I thought you weren't coming.'

'I'm so sorry, I got caught up in work and lost track of the time,' he said as my heart thudded in my chest. The drink, the staring contest, the Patrick of it all. It was too much. 'Where is everyone? Did I miss dinner?'

'They've gone and you did,' I said, breathless. He pressed his lips to mine, catching the side of my mouth as he turned his head at the last moment to look at John.

'Oh, um, Patrick, this is Sumi's friend, John. John,

this is Patrick.' I touched the side of my lips with my fingers, covering up our almost kiss. It was always awkward to have an audience.

'You must be the boyfriend,' John said, holding out his hand without standing up.

'John runs the bar,' I added before Patrick could answer.

'Owns the bar,' he corrected from his seat.

'Nice place,' Patrick replied, ignoring John's hand and turning his attention back to me. 'I can't believe I missed the party, I brought cupcakes as well.'

He placed the big white pastry box on the table and opened it up to reveal a rainbow of sugary goodness.

'This is what happens when I try to make a good impression,' he said, showing off his easy smile. 'They really went home already? Even Sumi?'

'See?' I said, grinning at John. 'I told you! This is very out of character for her.'

He replied with a short, sharp shrug. 'I wouldn't say that. Yes, Sumi likes a drink but she also likes to be in bed before *Love Island*.'

'Sumi doesn't watch *Love Island*,' I scoffed before doubt softened my voice. 'Does she?'

'I can't believe I came all this way and they're not even here,' Patrick said with a groan, flipping the lid of the box up and down. 'What are we going to do with all these bloody cupcakes? Even you couldn't eat all of them.'

'That's what you think. I could take care of more of them than would make you comfortable,' I promised. 'Seriously, at first you'd be impressed, but by the end of it you'd just be worried about my blood sugar levels.'

'I don't want you to eat yourself into type two

diabetes, I can't stand needles. How about we leave them here?' he suggested, pushing the box towards John. 'You can give them out to the staff, if you'd like?'

'Very generous of you,' John replied. 'Why don't you take a photo of them to send to Sumi?'

'Good idea,' I agreed, plucking two cupcakes out the box and handing them to Patrick. 'Say happy birthday Sumi!'

Patrick held the cakes up to his face, mountains of frosting obscuring his features.

'You get in the picture as well,' John instructed. 'I'll take it.'

I handed over my phone with an appreciative smile before taking one of the cupcakes from Patrick. Before I could do anything, he swiped a dollop of frosting onto my nose right as I was blinded by my phone's flash.

'If the party's over, maybe we should just go back to mine,' Patrick said in a low, promising voice, licking the remaining frosting from his finger. I cleaned my nose off with a napkin as he slid his hand into mine. 'You look amazing by the way.'

'We should stay and help tidy up,' I offered, even though I really just wanted to get out of there. The atmosphere was thicker than the frosting on the cupcakes. 'John, what can we do to help?'

'Not at all, you go,' he said, staring at the screen of my phone before he handed it over, a too-big smile on his face that didn't quite make it all the way up to his eyes. 'I'll get this taken care of.'

'Only if you're sure,' I said, immediately edging towards the stairs. I couldn't quite say why but having him and Patrick in the same place without the buffer of other people just felt wrong, 'Thanks for hosting.'

He raised two fingers to his temple in a semi-salute, one side of his mouth turned upwards in a crooked smile.

'No worries,' he replied. 'Oh, and Ros?'

'Yes?' I called back from halfway down the stairs.

'Just so you know, I always figure out the puzzle eventually.'

CHAPTER SEVENTEEN

'I can't believe you brought cupcakes for everyone,' I said, clutching Patrick's hand tightly as we climbed the last few steps in the tube station nearest his house. My friends might have called it an early night but the rest of London seemed in agreement that it was a perfect evening for late-night adventures, the street was still so busy. 'That was so sweet of you.'

'Why do you sound so surprised?' He swung my hand back and forth, a wolfish smile on his absurdly beautiful face. 'I'm very sweet.'

'You are a lot of things,' I smiled at a group of girls, blatantly checking him out as they walked by. 'But I wouldn't call you sweet.'

'I can absolutely be sweet,' Patrick replied, stopping in the middle of the pavement and wrapping his hands around my face. He lowered his face to mine and placed the softest kiss on my lips. Down the street, I heard the group of girls sigh in chorus. 'See?'

'That was a good effort,' I murmured, pushing up onto my tiptoes to secure another kiss.

'I've always wondered what's in this garden,' he said, lifting his gaze over my head. I turned as far as I could without letting go of him to see a private park, the tall black railings lined with trees and bushes, obscuring whatever might be hiding inside. 'What do you reckon?'

'Portal to another reality, probably,' I replied as he disengaged his arms from around my neck and wandered off to peer into the bushes. 'That or it's a secret meeting place for the Resistance.'

He looked back at me with an affectionate smile. 'You're an odd girl,' he said. 'Do you know that?'

'Yes,' I answered before licking my lips thoughtfully. 'I don't suppose you've got any more of those cupcakes back at yours?'

'I bet,' Patrick said, his strong eyebrows set with determination. 'If I gave you a leg-up, we could get inside.'

My own eyebrows lifted in disbelief.

'But it's private,' I whispered. 'We're not allowed inside.'

He laughed, clearly delighted with my response. 'And that's why it's fun,' he said, squatting down and linking his hands together. 'Come on, up and over.'

'What if we get arrested?' My head swam with police sirens and flashing lights and disappointed parents and tequila even as I did as I was told. I was one hundred percent that girl who would jump off a cliff if all my friends were doing it.

'You know, you used to be a lot more spontaneous,' Patrick admonished. Before he could say another word, I had one foot in his palm, the other swinging over the fence. A sharp pain shot through my backside as

I hurled myself over the fence and my skating injury came back to haunt me. With a less than elegant tumble, I crumpled to the floor then sprang back up, determined not to let him down.

'Amazing,' he said, glancing over his shoulder. 'There should be a latch on the inside of the gate, there, to your left. Got it?'

I fumbled with it at first; the latch had been painted over with thick, black paint at least hundred times, and the warm summer weather had turned it into something like tar.

'Got it,' I gasped as I released the latch and pulled the gate in towards me. Patrick stepped into the garden easily, as though he took an evening constitutional every single night of his life, closing the gate behind him.

'Wow,' I breathed, weaving my fingers through his as we walked inside. 'It's beautiful.'

And it was. A crisp green lawn was set at the centre of the garden, bordered by tall trees and thick bushes, and pretty periwinkle blue plants, which I was fairly sure weren't periwinkles, wove themselves in and out of the branches. A bus whooshed by on the other side of the fence but safely behind the black bars of the garden, we were in another world.

'We shouldn't be in here,' I said, looking back at the gate as Patrick lay down in the grass, stretching his arms up behind his head. 'What if someone comes in?'

'It's eleven thirty on a Saturday night. No one is nipping into the park now.'

'We're here,' I reasoned. 'Anyone could come in.'

'Unless you're the terrible sort of person who would

break in, you have to have a key to get inside,' he replied. 'And only rich people have keys. Rich people don't like to cause a fuss. If someone comes in, we'll just quietly let ourselves out.'

I couldn't argue with his logic.

Carefully, I lowered myself down beside him, rolling onto my side to avoid my tender injury. Patrick shifted onto his side until we were nose to nose.

'I hope you didn't have too much fun without me tonight,' he said softly, running his finger along the line of my cheekbone, all the way down to my lips. 'I am sorry I was so late.'

'I understand,' I told him as I kissed his fingertips. 'And I would have had more fun if I hadn't completely decked it at the roller rink and fallen flat on my arse. It's going to be black and blue by morning.'

Patrick laughed and leaned in to replace his fingertips with his lips. The kiss was long and warm and lazy and, for several seconds, I couldn't feel anything else at all. 'Can't leave you alone for a minute, can I?'

'Do you remember that time we went ice skating at Somerset House and I went absolutely flying?' I asked as he pulled away, our eyes still locked on one another. 'It was even worse than that. How I haven't broken my neck before now, I'll never know.'

'Hmm,' Patrick replied, his eyes misting over for a moment. He rolled onto his back and I moved with him, resting my head on his chest. 'That guy back at the bar,' he said. 'What's his deal?'

'John?' I asked, practically purring as he combed his fingers through my hair. 'He's a friend of Sumi's.'

'Seems like a bit of a twat.'

'Definitely doesn't give a good first impression,'

I agreed, coming to as he pulled his hands away. 'I think he might be all right though.'

It was the nicest thing I'd ever said or thought about John McMahon.

'He's married,' I added quickly, not quite sure why. 'His wife is really tall.'

'Oh.' Patrick shifted suddenly and my head slipped off his chest and onto the hard ground. 'I didn't care for the "You must be the boyfriend" remark.'

'No?' I sat back up, rubbing the sore spot on my head. 'Why not? Do you not want people to think you're my boyfriend?'

'It's not what he said, it's the way he said it,' he replied, eyes up on the darkening sky. 'I am obviously flattered that anyone would think I am your boyfriend.'

I wove my fingers into the grass, wrapping my fingers around the long, green blades and smiled.

'But it was the implication that I'm *just* your boyfriend. It's reductive. You wouldn't like it if I went around introducing you to people as *just* my girlfriend, would you?' Patrick went on. I said absolutely nothing. Because I would love it. 'Besides, we just started seeing each other again and I know you don't want to go around slapping big labels on things.'

I yanked a handful of grass right out of the ground. Patrick had always had an ego but it didn't bother me, I considered it well earned. He very much wanted people to know how clever he was, what a brilliant writer he was. I'd always assumed that if I were as clever and as successful as him, perhaps I would feel the same way.

'I know it's early days and things are still delicate,' I said slowly, wiping off my hand and pressing the displaced clump of grass back into the earth. 'But I would be perfectly happy if you wanted to put a label on this. I mean, it's not as though we only just met, is it? And you did bring Sumi cupcakes, that's fairly boyfriend-y behaviour. Boyfriend-ish at the very least.'

'I can do lots of things that are boyfriend-ish,' he grinned, sliding his hands inside my shirt and glancing over at the gate to check for passersby. 'How quiet can you be?'

'Not that quiet,' I breathed, yielding to his wandering hands, my words catching in my throat. 'You're not really annoyed that he called you my boyfriend, are you?'

He pulled back so I could see his clear light eyes and his huge, dilated pupils.

'Do I look annoyed?'

He didn't. He looked handsome and horny and like someone who left his important work to come out on a Saturday night to meet me and my friends with a box full of freshly baked cupcakes.

'Let's go,' he said, removing his hands from inside my shirt and leaving a chill. 'I'll come up with a way to work off those cakes.'

'Sounds like a plan,' I agreed, clambering to my feet and chasing him back to the entrance, just as an elderly man walking a stately Dalmatian placed his key in the lock on the other side of the gate.

'Evening, sir,' Patrick said as I rubbed at the grass stains on my backside before we both burst out laughing and ran off down the street.

CHAPTER EIGHTEEN

'Now, do you think we need this many peanuts?'

I stared at my father from behind the enormous red trolley, already jam-packed with more food and drink than any assembly of humans would ever be able to consume.

'Yes,' I replied. 'People love peanuts.'

With an unintelligible grunt, he wedged a jar of peanuts as big as a carry-on suitcase into the trolley.

Nothing said love like a father–daughter excursion to the cash and carry on a Sunday afternoon.

'Your mum loves peanuts,' Dad reasoned as he dragged the trolley onwards. 'I want to make sure we have enough.'

My plan had been to stay in bed with Patrick until I lost the use of my legs and yet, here I was, traipsing around the Croydon Costco (not the closest Costco but Dad's *favourite* Costco), buying up the entire store in preparation for their vow renewal. I'd had a panicked call from my mother first thing this morning, asking me to accompany Dad on his shopping trip while she took one for the team and went to visit my nan who had apparently been 'causing trouble' at the nursing home and had her phone confiscated. Again.

'I don't think she's going to spend the entire day shovelling KP Dry Roasted down her throat,' I said while he considered a family-sized tub of wasabi peas. 'Aren't there other things to organize first?'

'Such as?'

'Venue, invitations, music, flowers, decorations, favours,' I replied, counting off on my fingers. 'And I'm assuming you've got something to wear.'

'I'm wearing my suit.' He swapped the wasabi peas for a giant box of Bombay Mix, then pointed at the label. 'Can you still call it that?'

'I think so,' I said, even though I wasn't actually sure. He shrugged and dumped it in the trolley. 'You don't mean your old grey suit?'

'It's a perfectly good suit.'

My dad was a man of few words and even fewer clothes. He wore his jeans until they fell apart and then he had Mum hem them into regrettable denim shorts which wore until the crotch split in two. And the less said about that particular family holiday to Lanzarote, the better.

'It's just, Mum's gone all out on the dress so you might want to think about getting a new one,' I suggested as I took in his stripy polo shirt and cargo trousers, each and every pocket filled to bursting with some sort of dad essential. 'And you've had that one for a while, could be time to invest in a new one.'

He considered this, stroking his unshaven chin as we walked. Sunday was the only day my dad did not shave. It was a treat he held sacrosanct, along with his Chelsea bun from the village bakery and forty-five unquestioned minutes, in the toilet, with the newspaper.

'It was good enough for your graduation,' he said, turning his blue eyes on me. I had Dad's hair but Mum's eyes. Alan Reynolds had been blessed with dark brown hair and blue eyes, a startling combo he'd passed on to his youngest daughter, leaving me with Mum's dark brown peepers. I knew they hadn't done it on purpose but still, it was very genetically selfish.

'And I graduated eleven years ago,' I reminded him, the strain of doing the maths showing on his face. 'Maybe it's time for a refresher.'

'Maybe I'll see what they've got in Debenhams,' he relented as he reached for a forty-eight pack of Mini Cheddars. 'How's work going?'

'Good,' I said, pushing the trolley on ahead. 'It's going well.'

'You think you'll stick this one out then, do you?'

My dad had worked the same job since the day he left school. Literally, he finished his last exam and went directly to my granddad's shop and started training as a plumber. From there, he started to specialize in fitting kitchens and bathrooms and eventually opened his own bathroom design company, Reynolds' Bathrooms. It wasn't the most creative name since the dawn of time but it did what it said on the tin. I knew he was still half heartbroken that I hadn't followed him into the family business but what could I say? Low flush toilets left me cold. And I couldn't really see Jo leaving Cambridge with a degree in physics to join him on a January jolly to the Kitchens, Bedrooms and Bathrooms Expo in Cologne.

'I think it's very romantic, you know,' I told him as we trundled around the corner and up the chocolate aisle. I lingered in front of a plastic pyramid of Ferrero Rocher.

'What is?' Dad asked, distracted by what claimed to be the world's largest tin of Quality Street.

'The second wedding.'

'Oh. Hmm.'

When we were growing up, Dad wasn't around very much. I'd never really thought about it until Mum's changing-room confessional because, at the time, it didn't seem that strange. I knew everything about my friends' mums but I knew next to nothing about anyone's dad. Some mums worked, some mums didn't, but all of them took the lead with their kids. Dads went to work, dads came home and dads were, for the most part, not to be disturbed. Mums were there to answer questions and help with projects while dads were tired and only available to drive you to the ice rink on Saturdays if they really had to. When my mum was told she'd have to have a caesarean with Jo, I vividly recalled a long and involved debate between my parents as to whether or not I'd have to go and live with my nan for a few weeks, since Mum would be unable to take care of me. I'd made a very vocal case at the time, about how I was fourteen and hardly needed a babysitter, but that was how hands-off my dad was. Sure, he was occasionally around to crack a joke, give a girl a piggyback or destroy my burgeoning sense of self with a casual comment about how my Doc Martens would make all the boys think I was a lesbian, but we really didn't know each other that well.

But I was tenacious and, apparently, a miracle worker.

If I could get Patrick Parker back in my life, I could get a two-way conversation out of a middle-aged man in Costco on a Sunday morning.

'Dad?'

'Rosalind?'

'How did you know Mum was the one?'

He stopped in the middle of the aisle and pulled his glasses up off his nose, resting them on the top of his head.

'Any reason in particular you're asking this right now?' he asked. 'Is there something we should know about the young man who sent you those flowers?'

'No,' I replied, respecting his attempt to deflect my question. 'I genuinely want to know.'

'You've heard the story of how we met a thousand times,' he said, dragging the trolley forwards, and me with it. 'Now, booze. Do you think just wine and beer or do we need spirits as well?'

'Spirits as well,' I replied without hesitation. 'And I'm not asking how you met, I know that.' At the chip shop where they argued over the last battered sausage. A love story for the ages. 'I'm asking how you knew she was the woman you wanted to marry.'

'Well, it's just what you did in those days,' Dad wandered on, plopping his glasses back down on his face to inspect the price of a jug of gin. 'As soon as your mum got pregnant, I had to propose.'

I looked down and saw my knuckles turning white against the bright red of the trolley's plastic-coated bar. I opened my mouth but the words got stuck on the first attempt.

'Can I interest either of you in a cheese puff?'

'No!' I yelped at a kindly-looking woman holding

190

out a plate full of sample snacks. She shrank back into her tabard, slowly lowering the puff. 'I mean, no thank you,' I corrected. Clearing my throat, I turned back to Dad and tried again. 'What do you mean, when Mum got pregnant?'

'You know your mum was pregnant when we got engaged,' Dad said, sliding the gin in next to the peanuts, the Bombay Mix and a giant box of Walkers crisps. 'I'm sure we've talked about this before.'

'We definitely haven't,' I croaked. But why hadn't we? Mum had never, ever, ever mentioned it. Was the baby planned? Was it a boy or a girl? If they'd had that baby, would they have still had me? These were not the kind of existential thoughts I wanted to entertain in a Costco.

'What happened?'

'She lost the baby, obviously, but by that time, the wedding was all arranged. Besides, I was fairly sure I was going to ask her anyway so we went ahead with it,' Dad said, clucking his tongue as he considered two different kinds of whisky. As though he hadn't just delivered the biggest family truth bomb I'd heard in, well, a week. I grabbed my phone and opened a message to my sister while Dad kept right on talking.

Did you know mum and dad only got engaged because she was pregnant and then she had a miscarriage?

'I got to thinking about it when we were at Simon and Sheila's party. It wasn't exactly the wedding of your mum's dreams and she deserves something special. That's why I wanted to do the whole renewal thing, not just some party. We both missed out on a lot when I was working every hour god sent and she was up to her eyeballs in you and your sister. I have to say, it's been a nice discovery, getting to spend so much time together since Jo left home. Like getting to know each other all over again.'

'That's nice.'

'Even with you back.'

'Right.' I was very ready to change the subject before he mentioned the sushi incident. 'So, what sort of wine were you thinking about?'

But it was too late. Dad had turned into one of the giant cans of Pringles in our trolley. He had been popped and he could not stop.

'People think having a gifted child is a blessing,' he went on, folding his arms and shaking his head at the ceiling. A man with a trolley chockfull of Blu-Ray players waited patiently for him to move before giving up and attempting to manoeuvre around. 'And of course we're proud of your sister, she really got a double dose of brains, that one, but it was a lot. All those extra classes, all those extra activities. You must remember how she was when she got kicked out of the Brownies, or had you left for university by then? That tantrum lasted a full week. Wouldn't eat, wouldn't sleep, screamed all day long, from sun-up to sun-down. According to your mother, that is, I was in Switzerland looking at a prototype for a tap that produced boiling hot, filtered water at the time. Ground-breaking, it was. Back then, anyway; every-one's got it now. You can make tea, right out the tap, you know?'

'I've seen them, yeah,' I replied, still somewhat struggling to get past the bombshell.

'It's a lot of maintenance,' he shook his head. 'You've got to get the filter changed every couple of months, take the whole thing to pieces if it breaks. No, it's not worth it. Not when you've got a fast-boil kettle. Anyway, back to your sister.'

'You know, this all looks lovely,' I interrupted him and nodded at everything in the trolley. 'But given how much you want to make the renewal extra special, maybe we should get a caterer to do all the food? And drink? Maybe we just get an event planner to do the entire thing?'

Dad considered this for a moment.

'You want me to get an event planner *and* a new suit?'

I nodded.

'No, I don't think so.'

Without a word, I grabbed a two-litre bottle of vodka from the shelf and placed it in the trolley.

'Come on, Rosalind,' he said, immediately putting it back. 'You know better than that. Vodka is for Russians, alcoholics and students.'

Three groups of people he held in equal contempt.

'Everything all right with the shed?' Dad asked, making a wide left into the baked goods aisle.

'I think there might be a leak in the roof,' I said, eyeing a twenty-four pack of chocolate chip muffins. 'Every time you hilariously hit it with the hosepipe at six a.m., I get dripped on.'

He chuckled softly to himself, missing my sarcasm completely. 'There's no leak,' he replied decidedly. 'Must be condensation. We'll get you a dehumidifier.'

My phone vibrated against my hip with a message from my sister.

So?

Oh to be eighteen and not give a fuck. A second message buzzed through before I could turn it off.

1 in 4 pregnancies result in miscarriage. It's more common than you think.

Jo hadn't even started her first semester and she was already well into the 'I know everything and you are deeply stupid' phase of studenthood. I remembered it fondly. The wonderful day I sat Mum and Dad down and explained the horrors of the dairy industry all while Dad enjoyed a Mini Milk.

btw can you ask m+d if I can bring my gf to the wedding? She wants to meet u all, idk y

Jo had a girlfriend and expected me to tell our parents.

So, that's how my day could get worse.

CHAPTER NINETEEN

I hadn't realized quite how far away Lucy had moved until it took me a bus, two trains, another bus and a fifteen-minute walk to get to her house on Sunday evening. Wandering down her road, following the little blue dot down a Google Map, I marvelled at all the restored Victorian houses. When I was younger, when we first all moved into the city together, I was obsessed with Georgian mews houses. I'd imagine what it would be like to live in a whole house, all by myself, with my husband and then maybe even our kids. There was usually a cat in the mix as well, sometimes a dog, depending on whoever filled out the man-shaped gap in my fantasy. Patrick was definitely a dog person but I already knew who would be taking it out for a walk in the rain when he was on a deadline.

Regardless of how far away it was, the house was a beauty, I thought as Lucy let me in, leading me down the narrow hallway, past the living room, through the kitchen and out into a carefully designed, dinky back garden. The lawn was perfectly mowed, the plants all pruned to perfection. Someone had spent a lot of time out there, making sure every blade of grass met its rigorously maintained size and colour, and I was almost certain that person was not Lucy.

'This is very impressive domesticity,' I told Lucy as she set a teapot down on the table between us.

'Dave is proud of his garden,' she confirmed, casting an approving glance over the flowerbeds. 'Ever since I got pregnant, I haven't been able to keep him in the house. I think he's afraid if he accidentally bumps into my belly, the baby will fall out.'

I looked up at the painfully blue sky, dotted with little white puffballs here and there. What we really needed was a storm – the humidity had been rising for days now – but according to the weatherman, the heat would hold out for at least another week. I poured the tea, to save Lucy the effort of having to pick up the teapot.

'It was planned, wasn't it? The baby, I mean?' I asked, trying not to think about Dad's casual Costco reveal. I had a feeling it wouldn't exactly be a dream topic for Lucy, the first-time mum-to-be.

'Totally planned, we talked about it for literally months before we started trying,' she confirmed. 'He did seem surprised I got pregnant so quickly though. He actually said he thought only virgins got pregnant on the first try.'

'I know we used to make fun of the kids that went to Catholic school when we were little but what a sweet, innocent way to live,' I said with a sigh. 'Does he think women are like milk? That we go off once we've been opened?'

Lucy snorted her tea through her nose. 'He doesn't

think anything about that kind of stuff. He does the garden. Look at my tomatoes, aren't they amazing? Don't let me forget to give you some before you leave, I'm up to my tits in them. I even started pickling. Pickling! What have I become?'

I wondered what university Lucy would make of pregnant and pickling Lucy and pressed my lips together to hide a little smile.

'Do you remember our old Sunday night ritual?' I asked, eyeing a bottle of Shiraz on the kitchen counter.

'Face mask, bottle of wine and two videos for a fiver from Blockbuster?' Lucy replied. 'How could I forget? That was the only time in my entire life I didn't have Sunday dread. Feels like forever ago now though, hard to believe it's not even been five years.'

I leaned forward, resting my arms on her wooden table, wedging the points of my elbows between the slats. 'For me it feels like yesterday. You probably don't miss it at all.'

'I do actually,' Lucy countered, brushing her long blonde hair out of her eyes. She had so much more hair than she had the last time I'd seen her. Pregnancy definitely suited our Lucy. 'But I miss it in the same way I miss getting an ice cream on the way home from school or not having to worry about which TV presenters might be secret kiddy fiddlers. That's the past, that time's over, we're all on to the next thing now. One day, we'll miss this.'

'Not all of us are on to the next thing,' I replied with a touch of regret. 'The only half-decent part of my present *is* my past. If my future is all sheds and Snazzlechuffs, I think I'll wallow in my nostalgia a bit longer, thank you.'

Lucy dropped a sugar lump in her tea and stirred slowly, a thoughtful look on her face. 'Come on, I can tell you're dying to talk about it. What happened to Mr Perfect last night?'

'He was working and turned off his phone and lost track of time,' I said, letting it all out in one big breath. 'But he showed up and he brought us cupcakes! Isn't that amazing? It's hardly his fault Sumi randomly decided to become a lightweight on her birthday. But he did show up, you can ask John, John saw him.'

'Oh, I know,' she said, eyebrows arching slightly as she drank her tea. 'I heard.'

'What's that supposed to mean?'

'Nothing,' she replied, a small smile on her face. 'Just that John texted us to say he'd met Patrick.'

'That's it?' I asked, very unhappy about this group text that I was clearly not a part of. 'That's all he said, that he'd met him?'

Lucy laughed and pushed the biscuit barrel towards me. 'I think John might be the only person on the planet who doesn't have your number,' she replied. 'Had any more weird texts lately?'

'Yes, several, all shit,' I replied bluntly. I snatched up a cookie but she had to be a fool if she thought she could placate me with anything less than a caramel chocolate digestive. 'What else did John say?'

'He said Patrick brought cupcakes,' she said, picking up her tea and taking a long sip.

'And?'

'He said Patrick brought cupcakes and that he was a bit rude,' she admitted. 'Maybe he misunderstood something, I'm sure Patrick wasn't openly rude.'

'No, he wasn't,' I corrected. 'He gave John the cupcakes, that's not very rude, is it?'

'No,' Lucy replied with a firm shake of the head. 'Very generous.'

It was fair to say, I thought, watching a tiny bird dart in and out of the hedge at the bottom of the garden, that Patrick wasn't always the sort to bend himself over backwards with new people, but he wasn't talking shit about people he'd just met in a group text either. Neither Patrick or John were about to win a Miss Congeniality award.

'It's a shame we didn't get to see him, I would have liked to have said hello,' Lucy said, ever the diplomat. 'Things are still going well though?'

Happiness blossomed in my belly, smothering any lingering annoyance. 'Luce, it's so good,' I confirmed, a blush rising in my cheeks. 'Like picking up exactly where we left off. Maybe a few days before we left off, the same but different.'

'Please don't start talking about all the amazing sex you're having or my baby will just fall out,' she said, holding up a hand to stop me. 'I can't bear it.'

'I wasn't going to talk about the sex,' I replied. I was absolutely going to talk about the sex. 'Everything's wonderful, not just the shagging. Last night, after we left Good Luck, we snuck into this little locked garden and just lay in the grass and talked and, well, did some other things you don't want to hear about, but trust me, it was very romantic.'

'Whatever you do,' Lucy said with pleading eyes. 'Do not tell Sumi that story. She will not care for it and you *will* get punched. I'm glad it's all going so well though.'

'There was one weird moment,' I said, keeping my voice light and my biscuit close. 'John called Patrick my boyfriend and he got a bit "ooh, let's not have labels when we're just starting over". Felt a bit random.'

'Hmm.' She made a noise into her teacup. 'Well, men can be funny about things like that.'

'I think he's trying to protect himself,' I rationalized on Patrick's behalf. 'You know, because of how I left last time.'

'Hmm.'

'Luce, men can be victims of the patriarchy too, it's harder for them to be vulnerable and admit things like that than it is for us,' I said. 'You can't hold every little thing I tell you about our relationship against him forever or I won't be able to talk to you about anything.'

'I'm not, I'm really not,' she replied, rummaging around in the bottom of the biscuit barrel to produce a chocolate Hobnob. 'But you know I'm contractually obliged to be Team Ros until the end of time. Until we see Patrick on his knees, proclaiming his love for you, preferably in song and with jewellery, we won't be entirely happy. You know no one will ever be good enough for you as far as we're concerned, let alone someone who's already had a really good go at breaking your heart.'

I rolled my eyes but smiled at the same time, reaching across the table to give her hand a squeeze. And nick the chocolate Hobnob.

'So, apparently Jo is gay now,' I said as I took a bite. 'Or bi. Or fluid. I'm not sure which one.'

'Oh, that's fun,' Lucy replied, hunting down another

chocolate biscuit. 'How did she break the news? Instagram announcement? TikTok? I hear the kids are all about TikTok nowadays.'

'She asked me to ask Mum and Dad if she could bring her girlfriend to their wedding,' I said as I pressed a finger into a sudden throbbing in my left temple. 'Which I'm absolutely not doing.'

'That'll be delightful,' Lucy rubbed her hand around and around on her belly. 'I very much look forward to going into fake labour that morning so I don't have to be there when your nan hears the happy news.'

'You're so lucky,' I grumbled, looking back up at the bright blue sky. 'I wish I were pregnant.'

'No, you don't,' she replied. 'Have you ever had haemorrhoids?'

I shifted uncomfortably in my seat. I was still suffering from my roller skating injuries and they were quite uncomfortable enough.

'Time for more tea,' I said, grabbing the teapot and ignoring her wicked laugh. 'You stay there.'

She waved me off into her kitchen, staring contentedly out at her patch of the world while I fished around in different jars and tins for teabags.

It really was a lovely house, I thought, admiring the neat paintwork, the carefully restored radiators, the stripped wooden flooring. Lucy had always been good at making things beautiful. Where were all her things? I wondered, hunting for invisible clutter. The contents of my handbag spilled out onto her butcher's block table, receipts and lip balms and pages from notebooks and random flyers I'd accepted out of politeness. Lucy projected nothing but serenity whereas I took my own personal brand of chaos with me everywhere I went.

What would mine and Patrick's home look like? His flat was so him, his personality indelibly stamped on every surface. I hadn't decorated my flat in DC, never quite sure how long I was staying, and the main style reference for my room in our shared house before that was 'I bought it at Ikea like everyone else'. Maybe we wouldn't stay in London. Maybe we'd travel before we settled down. Either way, I was happy for him to take the lead on the decorating. Or maybe I could ask John who had designed that upstairs room in the bar. As much as I hated the pretentious steampunk, Insta-friendly downstairs, upstairs was beautiful, a perfect balance of classic and contemporary, masculine and feminine. I wondered if his wife had done the decorating or if they'd used a professional. Or maybe he'd done it himself. I really had no way of knowing.

Running the teapot under the tap, I thought back to our conversation last night. A crossword puzzle with the wrong clues. What was that supposed to mean?

'Not that it matters,' I said out loud over the singing teapot.

'What did you say?' Lucy called back, twisting as far as she could in her seat. 'I zoned out for a minute. Baby brain.'

'It's nothing,' I replied, smiling back at her and wiping the thought of John from my mind. 'Absolutely nothing at all.'

CHAPTER TWENTY

Having spent what felt like hundreds of hours watching his livestreams and his YouTube videos, I had gleaned a few facts about my new co-worker before I set out in Mum's Mini Cooper on Monday morning for a meeting at Chateau Snazzlechuff. I knew he was fourteen, I knew he had more money than I would ever have in my entire life and I knew his followers worshipped the ground he mostly seemed to sit on. Every time I checked, he was online, playing some game live for all his followers to watch. They didn't even play along, they just watched him. It was bizarre. Mostly, I was amazed his legs hadn't wasted away altogether so his body could send more precious resources to his thumbs.

After what felt like an age of tootling along the motorway, Google Maps led me out of six lanes of traffic and into a small village. I kept watch, looking for the mega mansions that usually went with the kind of money Snazz was bringing in, but there was nothing. Just semi-detached new builds and a surprisingly large number of supermarkets. Just when I seemed to be running out of village, the map took me into a perfectly normal-looking cul-de-sac. At least, it looked perfectly normal until I pulled up to park in front of number 18. A sea of teenagers were milling around a tall metal gate, none of them actually talking to each other, all of them staring at their phones.

'At least I know I'm in the right place,' I muttered, climbing out of Mum's car and beeping the alarm.

'They won't let you in,' one boy said as I pressed the buzzer on the gate. He wiped his nose along the sleeve of his white training jacket, a knock-off version of the one Snazz had worn the first time I met him. 'They don't let no one in.'

'What are you all doing here?' I asked, ignoring the tallest of the group who was either winking at me or needed to see an optometrist. I very much hoped it was the latter. 'Shouldn't you be in school?'

They all began to snort and laugh, kicking stones with their very white trainers. No wonder Jo had started going out with girls.

'OK, OK, get out the way,' I told them, ignoring the muttered assessments of my tits, and pressing the buzzer again. A clicking noise, a sigh and then, very suddenly, the gate opened just a crack. I breathed in, squeezing myself through to a chorus of 'oohs' and 'ahhs' as each of the teens began snapping my picture.

'Get your arse inside,' Veronica barked from the front door, cigarette hanging out of her brightly lipsticked mouth as I bolted up the path. She stubbed it out on the side of the house and called out to the assembled teenagers at the gate. 'We've got a limited edition drop going livo on the shop in seven minutes,' she screeched. 'We aren't announcing it, you're the only ones that know!'

They silenced themselves with a collective gasp, lifting their phones to their faces as their attention turned from me to whatever delights awaited in the Snazzlechuff shop.

'What's the drop?' I asked, slipping inside, door slamming behind me.

'Nothing.' She tossed the half-smoked cigarette butt in a huge bin full of them. 'But they'll refresh the website all day before they risk missing out on something so you probably won't make an appearance on Reddit for at least another couple of hours.'

I frowned at the thought and wiped my shoes on the doormat before following her through the house. From the outside, it looked like a very normal semi-detached house and I assumed once upon a time, it had been. But at some point, it had become some sort of Premiership-footballer-meets-Justin-Bieber Frankenhouse. The normal-looking front was just the tip of the house iceberg. Gazing around at the bizarre architecture, it appeared number 18 and its semi-detached twin had been knocked into one giant house and extended out at the back, creating an absolutely humungous downstairs area, filled with oversized sofas, armchairs and beanbags bigger than a king-sized bed. And the televisions. So. Many. Televisions. The largest of them all hung on the wall, twice the size of a school blackboard.

Did schools still have blackboards? I wondered. Didn't seem as though Snazzlechuff was the right kid to ask.

All the soft furnishings were, against all kinds of

common sense, stark, bright white, and all the technology was black, giving the room the air of a very fancy chessboard-slash-asylum as designed by Kris Jenner, a feeling only enhanced by the fact that literally everything was either padded or had rounded edges. The effect was at once calming and unnerving. I couldn't hurt myself in here whether I wanted to or not, and the longer I was here, the more appealing the idea became.

'Coffee?' Veronica asked, pushing me through the millionaire's soft-play centre and into the next room. A considerably smaller but no less swish kitchen.

'Thanks,' I nodded, taking a seat at an island in the middle of the room. 'This is quite a house.'

She answered with a cackle. 'Isn't it though? They bought it when he first started making money and now they don't want to leave, so they just keep adding on and adding on. I've told them it's fucking ridiculous but they won't listen to me. When they want to sell, who's going to buy it? A million-quid mansion in the middle of a bloody cul-de-sac and only half a mile from the prison and the dog track. They'll be queuing up . . .'

'Maybe they could buy the neighbours out,' I joked. 'Take over the entire street.'

'They've offered but no one wants to sell,' she said plainly. 'All the neighbours are trying to cash in on him one way or another. Sad, really.'

I gave a low whistle, for the first time feeling oddly sorry for the junior millionaire.

The end of the room was made of glass and I looked out on the back garden. An assortment of dirt bikes, scooters, Segways, football nets and bouncy castles all stood sentry, patiently waiting to be played with. It had to be every boy's dream.

'Don't know why his mum keeps ordering all that shit,' Veronica commented, following my gaze. 'He never goes outside. I try to make him go out for his lunch but he won't have it.'

'Even prisoners get at least one hour a day,' I replied. 'What sort of state is his skin in under that helmet?'

'He makes Darth Vader look healthy,' she said with a shrug. 'It'd be easier to flay him alive than it would be to peel him out that gaming chair. I'm surprised his mother hasn't started giving him sponge baths.'

I pulled a very sour face that she caught before I could look away.

'This job is not without its challenges,' she added as she dropped a coffee pod into the Nespresso machine. 'Which leads me to wonder, how come you want to spend your life putting more of his nonsense out into the world?'

'His nonsense?' I repeated with a smile. 'That's a funny way to talk about your own client.'

Veronica opened the enormous American-style refrigerator and fished around for some milk, holding it up for my approval.

'I used to represent a different kind of talent,' she clarified as I nodded at the semi-skimmed option. 'Photographers, makeup artists, stylists, that kind of shit, but now there's no money in that. Someone needs a makeup artist, they don't call me, they go on Instagram and see who has the most likes. Same with a photographer. People think knowing how to use filters is the same as knowing how to take a great photo. Photography is an art. Don't come to me demanding ten grand a day until you've got a herniated disc in your neck from holding up a fucking reflector eighteen hours a day for five years. No one wants to learn the skills, no one wants to pay their dues. Drives me fucking insane.'

'So you decided to work with a grizzled old veteran like Snazzlechuff?'

She snorted out a laugh that turned into a prolonged smoker's cough.

'He might be a little twat but he is talented,' she replied, pressing a hand against her chest as she finished her hacking. 'Admittedly, that talent is not curing cancer or even being able to remember to shower twice a day, but at least it's honest. Someone was going to take him on, I figured it might as well be me. Every wanker with a pair of AirPods thinks he's an agent these days and they're all out to take advantage, lining their own pockets rather than looking after the client. I am actually attempting to look after the little bastard.'

Who would have believed it? Underneath it all, Agent Veronica had a heart.

'But you didn't answer my question,' she continued, pushing my coffee across the island. 'What's gone so wrong that working with my little shitstain is the best you can do with your life?'

Or maybe not.

'I think all kinds of stories have value,' I said, clinging to something I once thought was true. 'Snazz has a perspective to share that no one else does. There aren't many people in the world in his position.'

'Thank fuck,' she replied flatly.

'In all honesty, the job came to me but I'm really

glad it did,' I said, trying to sound convincing. I wrapped my hands around the mug, freezing cold in my jeans and T-shirt, even though it was still scorching outside. Snazz wanted you to know his house had air conditioning and he was not afraid to use it. 'I was in radio before this, producing news shows, culture shows. I worked on a show called The Book Report, you might have heard of that?'

Veronica locked her steely eyes on mine before bursting out into a throaty cackle that, against all the odds, I found endearing.

'You're funny,' she gasped. 'I like funny. No, Ros, I haven't got time to *read* a book, let alone listen to a podcast *about* reading books. Last novel I read was that one about that daft slag who had everyone thinking her thick husband killed her but then it turned out she staged it all because she was a mental.'

I digested her capsule review for just a moment.

'Do you mean *Gone Girl*?'

'That's the one,' she nodded. 'What a waste of fucking time. Went on a mad rampage just because she didn't like taking it up the arse. Just dump him, love, there was no need.'

'I don't remember that being her entire motivation but I hear what you're saying,' I replied weakly. We'd interviewed Gillian Flynn on The Book Report and I wished we'd had Veronica's capsule review back then. 'Maybe you ought to have your own podcast instead of Snazz.'

Veronica clacked her long, blood-red nails on the kitchen top.

'Sad truth is more people will take an hour out of their day to listen to Snazz and his mates chatting shit than they would to listen to a forty-eight-year-old woman with something useful to say,' she declared with a resigned shrug. 'The world's fucked.'

'You never know until you try,' I said, avoiding the sad fact that she was probably right by checking the time on my phone. 'Is the young master ready for me?'

'He is,' she said with a deep breath in. 'But I'm not sure what you're hoping to get out of him. PodPad came to us with the idea of doing a podcast, he said he was into it and so I did the deal, but I've got to tell you, you're fighting an uphill battle. Don't take this the wrong way but I think they'd have done better pairing him with someone who didn't mind doing all the work themselves.'

'I'll do the work,' I said quickly. 'I'm not afraid of hard graft.'

'That's not really what I meant,' she replied, leading me back through the designer asylum. One Flew Over the Kardashian's Nest. 'They should have given him a producer who wanted to lead the show and just have him there for colour. You don't seem like someone who's interested in the limelight.'

'Oh,' I nodded as we passed what looked suspiciously like a baby shark, darting around a fish tank bigger than my first car. 'Yeah, that's not really my thing. My job is to make everyone else look great, in an ideal world no one even knows I'm there.'

'You're a dying breed,' Veronica said, voice full of regret. We climbed the stairs rather than taking the glass-encased lift and took a sharp left at the top of the landing.

'Just out of interest,' I said, following her down a

hallway covered in photos of Snazz wearing assorted masks and posing with every celebrity you could think of, from A-list movie stars to at least four different heads of state. 'How did the two of you meet?'

'Me and Snazz?' She pulled a packet of cigarettes out of her pocket and knocked one loose into her hand. 'He's my godson. His mum's my best mate.'

I thought she couldn't shock me any more than she already had. I was wrong.

'I'm more or less his second mum. Sharon has her ups and downs, not for me to go into, but yeah, I've known him since he was born. The boy's a nightmare but he's my nightmare,' she said as we stopped in front of a black lacquered door. 'Anyway, enjoy your chat. Snazz, get your hand out your pants, Ros is here to see you.'

She threw the door open, a cloud of Lynx body spray, Wotsits and feet blasting onto the landing.

'I'll see you back downstairs in two minutes,' Veronica said. 'I'll have a bottle open.'

'Thanks but I drove,' I replied, steeling my senses.

'Didn't say it was for you,' she said, sparking up as she went. 'Oh, and don't touch anything that looks sticky.'

Words to live by.

'Knock knock,' I said as I entered the room. People always say women turn into their mothers but my default setting was definitely more embarrassing dad.

I was expecting some sort of Las Vegas hotel suite crossed with the Playboy Mansion, meets the NASA Jet Propulsion Laboratory, but Snazz's bedroom was just that. A bedroom. Slightly larger than the usual

211

teenage boy's den but, compared to the rest of the house, peculiar only in how average it was. The curtains were almost entirely closed, parted just enough for a slender crack of sunshine to slice the room in two with a full company of dust particles dancing in the shaft of light. I stepped carefully, trying to avoid treading on abandoned Funko Pop boxes, takeaway containers and carton after carton after carton of Ribena. The boy had a problem and it was blackcurrant flavoured.

'Hi Snazz, it's Ros from PodPad. I'm here to talk about the podcast.'

He had his back to me as he sat in the far corner of the room in an enormous black chair. An oversized head, complete with pair of pointed ears, was silhouetted against three different active screens. Was I meeting a teenager or a cat-human hybrid Bond villain? It was impossible to say. Over his bed was a built-in cabinet that stretched all the way to the ceiling, full of different animal heads. Not disconcerting at all.

'Not interrupting, am I?' I asked, looking around for somewhere to sit. Unmade bed? Nope. Beanbag covered in clothes so dirty they were stiff? Definitely not. The floor? I tried to find a square foot of carpet that looked like it wouldn't give me a rash. Well, they did say sitting was the new cancer.

'No, I'm not streaming,' he squawked as the three screens froze all at once. I nodded as though I had any idea what he was talking about. 'Veronica said you wanted to talk about the pod stuff.'

'Yep,' I replied, slowly edging my way towards the window and reaching out for the curtain. This might have been enough daylight for him but, as someone

212

who prized their eyesight and didn't want to drive home with a migraine, I needed at least a little more. 'Is it OK if I open the curtains a bit?'

With a trademark teenage sigh, he slumped down in his chair before spinning it around to face me.

'Whatever,' he groaned. 'But, like, stay out the window or they'll get a photo of you.'

I peeked around the curtain, expecting an army of paparazzi, but there was nothing out of the ordinary.

'How will anyone get a photo from inside your bedroom?'

'Telephoto lenses,' he replied as though it was perfectly ordinary. 'The neighbours let them hang out in their bedrooms and take pictures.'

'That is extremely disturbing,' I replied as I snatched the curtains closed as fast as I could. 'Is that why you wear your mask in your room?'

He scratched at his neck, right beneath the opening of his furry guinea pig head.

'Yeah,' he squeaked, tossing a complicated-looking controller onto his bed, accidentally choreographing another dust ballet. 'And, you know, means I haven't got to shave.'

Hmmm. I wasn't so sure he needed to worry too much about that.

'So, about the podcast,' I said. 'What I'm thinking is, we pair you with a couple of co-hosts, people you're comfortable with, and we pick a different game each week to play and discuss. Could be an old game, could be a new one, maybe a game that's famously considered to be bad?'

The guinea pig clasped his hands together in his lap.

'Like what game though?'

'I don't know.' I desperately tried to remember the names of any of the games I'd literally heard of for the first time over the last seven days. 'Grand Theft Auto? Halo?'

He giggled, the mask bobbing back and forth on his narrow shoulders. 'They aren't bad, they're iconic.'

'I'm going to level with you,' I said, inching my bag a little higher up on my shoulder. I really didn't want it to touch anything in the room. 'The last game I played was Snake and it was on a Nokia phone that belonged to my dad.'

The guinea pig looked entirely unmoved.

'But it doesn't matter, a lot of our listeners won't know that much about the games either. So we'll know that if I get it, they'll get it too.'

'But why would someone listen to a podcast if they don't know anything about the thing they're talking about?' Snazz asked.

'I really don't know but they do,' I replied. 'Why did I spend two hours watching nineteen-year-old makeup artists bitch each other out on YouTube last night? I barely know how to put on mascara. People are weird these days.'

Said the woman to the guinea pig.

'Can I have my mates on the show?'

'Why don't you send me a list of people you think would be good co-hosts and I'll get in touch with them,' I replied. 'But we do need to do it fairly quickly if we're going to record the first episode at WESC.'

I heard what I took to be an agreeable sniff from underneath the mask before Snazz turned his chair around, picked up another controller identical to the one on the bed and fired all three screens back into life.

214

''K,' he said, his back to me once again. 'I'll ask 'Ronica.'

A clammy sense of dread washed over me as I watched him barrel headfirst into battle, eviscerating an alien horde with nauseating realism. My career, my livelihood, depended on this rodent-headed child. He didn't need the money, he could drop out at any time. If he quit tomorrow, he'd still have enough cash to keep himself in guinea pig heads until the day he died. Maybe I should start a gaming channel. Computer games for the woman that knew nothing. I was clever, I'd taught myself how to program Mum's Sky+, how hard could it be? And then I felt myself throw up in my mouth as Snazz sliced open a screaming lizard man, green guts spraying onto the screen.

Maybe not.

CHAPTER TWENTY-ONE

'Anyway, it was completely insane,' I told Patrick as I tore back up the motorway. 'Wait until I tell you about the fish tank—'

'I can't talk right now but I can't wait to hear about it,' he replied, his voice crackling over the Bluetooth speaker in the car. 'When am I seeing you?'

My eyebrows knitted together as I mentally checked the date. 'Aren't we having dinner tonight?'

'Oh shit, we are,' Patrick groaned. 'I'm so sorry, I just this second said I'd meet my publisher. He wants to go over the chapters I was working on last week. Can I meet you after?'

'After's OK,' I said, annoyed at myself for feeling so disappointed. The man had to work, didn't he?

'Could be quite late,' he said, his warning softened with regret. 'But you could stay at mine? Late supper with an early breakfast on the side? I am sorry, I clean forgot. This book is taking up so much brain space.'

'It's fine,' I assured him, all the air going out of my

day. 'Don't worry. And honestly, I don't mind late. Maybe I can meet Sumi after work.'

'Yes, why don't you do that.' He sounded relieved. 'Just don't tell her I fucked up again or she'll be round to mine with the cheese grater.'

I laughed as we said goodbye and I put my foot down, undertaking an elderly lady in a Ford Fusion with a bumper sticker that read 'Hot Rod Granny'. He was busy, it was all reasonable. So why was I so annoyed?

'How did it go?' Ted asked, jumping on me the moment I got back to the office. 'Is everything OK? Did he agree on guests? Have you got anything I can give to the marketing team?'

'It was good,' I started. 'I think—'

'Great, choice, you write up the notes and send round a memo. We need to get things moving, Ros, moving and shaking and rocking and rolling.'

I was not the sort of person who would assume a co-worker was taking cocaine at work but if I were . . . Ted walked away, snapping his fingers and repeating the words 'Snazzlechuff Says' to himself over and over and over.

Grabbing a Diet Coke from the fridge, I looked back at the sunny, potentially class-A-riddled office and opened the door to the staircase. Time to return to where I belonged.

It was only Wednesday but I'd already spent every night since Sunday in my shed, all on my own. By the time I got home from work, I didn't have the energy to talk to my parents and there was always the threat of a repeated sushi incident. Lucy wasn't feeling up to coming into town and I wasn't feeling up to crossing the length and breadth of London when I knew Creepy Dave would be there as well. Sumi kept cancelling on me and Patrick had his meeting. Which left my oldest, greatest, would-never-let-me-down, best-in-the-world friend, Adrian.

'Can't,' he said from the screen of my phone. 'Sorry.'

'You're sure?' I pleaded, batting my eyelashes and puckering up my lips as Adrian reared away in mock disgust.

'If I wasn't sure already, that mug has made my mind up for me,' he replied, pretending to yak over his shoulder. 'I've told you, I can't. I've got a big date.'

'You've always got a big date,' I said, deep in the bowels of PodPad. 'Cancel it and come to dinner with me.'

'Afraid I really can't.'

I stared at his face in the giant screen, his big green eyes staring right back at me.

'What's going on?' I asked, crushing a stack of Pringles that would have to pass for lunch into my mouth. 'Since when are you such a smitten kitten?'

'Since I met Eva,' he replied.

'And who's Eva?'

'The CrossFit instructor,' he answered, proud as Punch. 'You'll meet her at *la bebe* fiesta on Saturday, she's amazing.'

It was almost enough to make me fall off my chair.

'You're bringing a girl to a friend thing? A girl you actually like?'

'A girl I really like,' he confirmed, eyes as big as saucers. He kicked his legs up behind him, swinging them back and forth like a teenage girl in the movies.

'I asked her for coffee after class on Sunday morning, we went out for dinner on Monday, we were texting all last night and tonight we're going for dinner. If things carry on this way, we'll be engaged by the weekend.'

'Adrian, this is amazing and terrifying and I can't see out a window down here so could you be a doll and look outside and check for flying pigs?' I asked, still in a state of shock.

'Ros, she's so beautiful,' he sighed, eyes skyward. 'But it's not just that. She's so funny. She's the funniest woman I've ever met. And she's got amazing stories about everything, I could listen to her talk about anything for hours.'

'Wow.'

I didn't know what else to say. I'd known Adrian for my entire life and I'd never, ever known him talk this way about a woman. Or a man. Or any living thing. 'So, what I'm hearing is, the sex is amazing?'

'Maybe tonight.' I watched him pick at a loose thread on what looked like a fresh-out-the-packet duvet cover. 'Or do you think I should wait longer? It's too soon, isn't it? I don't want to rush things.'

'Adrian Anderson,' I said with a gasp. 'You are blushing. If I didn't know better, I'd think you were in love.'

'Whatever, who cares, so what?' he mumbled, his face beetroot red. 'What's going on with you? How come you want to hang out with me when you could be balls deep in Patrick Parker?'

'Wouldn't he be balls deep in . . . never mind,' I replied, frowning at the sex maths. 'He's got a meeting with his publisher. I'm seeing him later.'

'What about Lucy?' Ade suggested.

'She said something about dinner with the antenatal girls tonight,' I replied, screwing up my face.

'Sumi?'

'She said she'd try but she'd probably be working late.'

'She's cancelled on me loads lately, work must be chaos,' he acknowledged with a nod. 'Question. Do you think roller skating would be a good date? Show Eva I'm fun?'

'Oh my god, you really are in love,' I laughed happily. 'Yes to skating. It'll be lovely, you'll hold hands, very romantic.'

'What if she falls over and breaks her leg?' he asked, face crumpling with concern.

'You'll take her to the hospital and have a great story to tell the grandkids.'

'Christ,' he sighed. 'Is this how it is? All the time?'

I smiled at my friend through the screen. 'Is what how it is?'

'This,' he rolled onto his back and held the phone over his face. 'I'm desperate to see her, can't stop thinking about her, can't stop talking about her. And so far I've gone through my entire wardrobe five times and can't find a single thing to wear tonight.'

'And the worst part is that feeling that it could all go to shit any second,' I agreed. 'Like, oh my god, don't let me say the wrong thing and fuck this up. One minute you're high as a kite and the next you're ready to chuck yourself under a bus.'

'Thanks for the heads up,' Adrian replied, his voice weighted with sarcasm. 'I haven't got to that part yet.'

I cleared my throat and put on a strangled smile.

'Maybe you'll be lucky and that's just a girl thing,' I suggested. 'You don't run through conversations after you hang out and worry about what you said?'

'Can confirm, I do not,' he said. 'Perhaps that's just a *Ros* thing.'

'I'd better go,' I said, suddenly desperate to get off the phone. 'I've got to call a load of children and ask their mums if they can come and play on my podcast.'

'Sweet,' Adrian said as I heard a keyboard clacking in the background. 'Is it too much if I send her flowers at work today? It's too much, isn't it?'

'Send them tomorrow,' I instructed gently. 'You're already seeing her tonight. Flowers in the morning will be a nice surprise.'

'See her tonight, send flowers tomorrow,' he repeated, closing his laptop. 'Thanks, mate. I'm so glad you're back. Sumi would have laughed in my face.'

'And I didn't?' I replied, waving goodbye.

CHAPTER TWENTY-TWO

At seven o'clock on the dot, I walked into Good Luck Bar to meet Sumi for dinner, only there was no Sumi waiting for me. Instead, I found a smiling John waving from the bar and beckoning me over to an empty high stool right in front of him.

Shrugging my arms out of my backpack straps, I trotted over to the only space left, straightening the sleeves of my T-shirt and giving myself a surreptitious sniff as I went.

'Evening,' John said, placing a large wine glass in front of me and filling it with Sauvignon Blanc.

'Evening,' I replied, gratefully lifting the glass in his direction and taking a sip. I had made a deal with myself to stop drinking in the week but it wouldn't do to be rude.

'Good news,' he said as he put the bottle back in the fridge. 'That's on the house. Bad news, Sumi isn't coming.'

'What do you mean she isn't coming?' I asked, immediately checking my phone.

'She's caught up but she didn't want to tell you because she didn't want you to spend the evening sat on your own in that shed,' he recited from his own phone before slinging it back by the till. The cracked screen made my heart hurt. So little regard for the precious. 'I thought it was a bit rude to refer to your place as a shed but you know her better than I do.'

Yes, I do, I thought to myself. I picked up the wine.

'No, she's being literal. I'm living in a converted shed at the bottom of my parents' garden.'

He crossed his arms and leaned against the back of the bar.

'Is it a nice shed?'

'It is not.'

'Then why are you living there?'

I looked at him over the rim of the wine glass. This drink was not free. This drink had a very high price tag indeed.

'Haven't got anywhere else to go,' I said. 'In case you haven't noticed, London is really expensive. It's going to take a while to find somewhere I can afford.'

'There'll be an article about you in the *Daily Mail* next week,' he said with a disbelieving chuckle. '*London Rents So High, This Professional Has to Live in a Shed.*'

He pushed his black hair back from his eyes, revealing a strong, straight hairline. His forehead was paler than the rest of him, he must have been out in the sun since Saturday. The first time I'd seen him, I thought his nose was too big for his face but as soon as he started talking, it made perfect sense. Slightly larger than average, a little bit crooked, but perfectly at home with the rest of his generous features.

Gazing down at the glass of wine on the counter, I sighed. I was exhausted. If Sumi wasn't coming, could I really stick it out all evening on my own until Patrick showed up?

'I'm getting the feeling you've had a not-brilliant day,' John said. 'Trouble at the mill?'

I breathed in through my nose and pulled a hair elastic off my wrist, twisting my hair up into a topknot.

'You could say that,' I confirmed as a large man placed himself on the newly vacant stool at the side of me. My eyes widened in momentary panic as I realized he was a white man with dreadlocks. My forever nemeses. 'How much do you know about e-sports?'

'I've dabbled in Twitch from time to time,' John replied with a shaky hand gesture. 'But my knowledge is limited to Halo, StarCraft, a little bit of Fortnite. But I'm far from an expert.'

'You know more than I do, I might have to hire you as a consultant,' I admitted, more than a little bit surprised. I inched my stool to the right away from my neighbour who was fumbling around under the bar near my knees.

'S'there a plug socket?' he grunted at John.

'Sorry, no,' he replied. 'All the plugs are over by the sofas. If it's your phone you need, I can plug it in behind the bar?'

The man huffed in response before heaving a huge beige plastic case onto the bar top. My tiny bowl of snack mix jumped an inch off the counter in surprise. I glanced over at John and raised my glass to my lips, quietly watching. What on earth was inside?

'Can I get some tap water?' he asked.

224

'Sure,' John replied, reaching for a glass. 'You want a menu?'

'No.'

Aware that I was staring, I shifted my attention to our reflections in the mirrored wall behind John. It was a weird shape for a laptop bag and altogether too beige to be from this decade. Unless it was something from the last Yeezy collection and I was just terribly out of it. I knew Kanye loved his neutrals.

'How come you're worrying yourself about gaming?'

Somehow, John managed to tear his eyes away from the man and turn his attention back to me.

'Um, I'm producing a podcast for a gamer,' I said, too distracted to get into it. *What was in the case?* 'Not that exciting.'

'Have to admit, it took me a while to get into them but now I'm obsessed with podcasts,' John said, resting his elbow on the bar and cupping his chin in his hand. 'I can't run without one now.'

I quirked an eyebrow.

'You run?'

'I run,' he confirmed with a grin. 'But yeah, love podcasts. I started with that one about that man who got done for killing his girlfriend, even though he said he didn't? God, that was fascinating.'

I forced a smile and nodded. A hundred years from now, historians were going to look at all these murder podcasts and wonder what the hell were they thinking? Nothing like dumping a metric ton of hints on how to get away with murder into the public domain. You know who found that kind of stuff useful? Murderers.

'But I can't listen to all that gory stuff now, the world's too depressing as it is.'

'I'm sorry but can you please keep it down?' said Mr White Man with Dreadlocks. 'Some of us are trying to work.'

And then he unclipped the sides of his big beige case to reveal a giant, electric typewriter. With lips pursed tightly together, I looked back at John, wide-eyed. His hand was clamped firmly over his mouth as he tried to look apologetic.

'Very sorry, sir,' he said before taking the wine he had poured me out of the fridge, grabbing a second glass and nodding over to a small table with two chairs in the corner of the bar. A closer inspection showed a small triangular sign that declared it reserved.

'You're sitting at a reserved table?' I gasped, following him, wine in hand.

'It was reserved for seven o'clock,' he replied as he topped off my glass before filling his own. 'Either it's a no-show or they sat somewhere else.'

'And you're sure you're not too busy?' I asked. I really didn't want to be on my own.

John nodded. 'It's fine. Camille is technically in charge tonight anyway and we're not that busy.'

I looked over my shoulder at the crowded room. Seemed pretty busy to me.

'Do you get that in here a lot?' I asked, eyes lingering on my former neighbour. He had spread out happily, the lid of his typewriter case shoving my bar mix out of his way. Gah, the bar mix. Gone but not forgotten.

'Rude people?' John replied, folding himself into the velvet-upholstered chair. 'Morning, noon and night.'

'Electric typewriters straight out of the eighties,' I

clarified. 'And rude people. I can't believe he's going to sit there and not order something.'

'Give him three minutes and he'll start eating your leftover nuts as well.'

He smiled, a quick, fleeting smile that still had turned-down edges, even when it lit up his light brown eyes. Where everything about Patrick was easy, John seemed at odds with himself. He was too tall, too angular, afraid to smile, sharp and spiky. Patrick was smooth and languid and sure of himself, so much more relaxed. Both of them put me on edge in different ways.

'*You* should have a podcast,' I said, exhaling into my chair and flipping one foot in and out of my shoe. 'You must have a million brilliant stories.'

'Bartender Confessions?' he replied with what was supposed to pass for a mysterious look.

'This week we explore the curious tale of the man with the electric typewriter,' I picked up the theme and ran with it. 'Is he a famous author? A man who has shunned modern technology and social media and writes steamy thrillers under a sexy pseudonym?'

'Wait, look, he's going for the nuts!' John whispered, excited.

The man reached out a furtive right hand and slowly dragged my abandoned bowl towards him before snaffling a palmful directly into his mouth.

'It must be weird,' I said, watching as he began to attack the keyboard of his typewriter with great ferocity. 'You have to deal with so many different people every day. I can literally go an entire day at work talking to two people but you have to talk to everyone.'

'It's a lot of people,' he agreed with a genial shrug. 'But in a place like this, they're much of a muchness. That's the thing I figured out pretty early on into working behind a bar. People are pretty much all exactly the same. At the end of the day, most of us want one thing.'

I wondered if we were officially friendly enough for me to unfasten the top button of my jeans. I'd worn corsets that were less constrictive. Not for a while, my raving days were one thing I was happy to leave in the past, but a girl never forgot these things.

'And what do people want?' I asked, ignoring my rumbling stomach.

'It's not hard to work out,' he replied. 'Safe place to sleep, warm food in their belly, someone to laugh at their jokes at the end of the day.'

Entirely unable to stop myself, I laughed awkwardly under my breath.

'Is that what everyone wants?'

He looked me in the eye, holding my gaze while he sipped his wine.

'Isn't it?'

'I just want to not live in a shed,' I said, reaching under my T-shirt and unfastening the top button. It was time.

'You want more than that,' John pushed. 'You want to feel appreciated, you want to be doing something you feel is worthwhile, or at least not beneath you.'

'I don't think what I'm doing is beneath me,' I argued, a little stung. There was his know-it-all arrogance again. 'I just think there are a million other stories out there that are more important than this one. I mean, this one isn't even a story, he doesn't even want to do the podcast, it's a cash grab by his very clever agent. If they had any sense, they'd be doing a series about his real life, the behind-the-scenes stuff. This kid hasn't even finished puberty and he's an entire industry. Wouldn't you rather listen to that while you're running than the ramblings of Snazzlechuff and his amazing friends?'

'You're working with Snazzlechuff?' John gasped, sitting bolt upright. 'That kid's a legend! His Fortnite streams are masterpieces.'

'You're a monster,' I informed him with a straight face. 'There is no hope for humanity.'

John relaxed into his chair, shaking his head in wonder.

'What mask did have on when you met him?'

'Today it was a guinea pig, the first time it was a panda.'

He touched his fingertips to his lips and blew them away with a chef's kiss.

'Literally everyone on earth should have a podcast before that child,' I insisted. 'He should be riding his bike around the park and drinking Kiwi 20/20 under the slide.'

'That's an alarming glimpse into your childhood that I can never unsee,' John replied. 'Also, he's far more likely to be off his tits on Adderall and watching hardcore porn on his phone than he is to be riding a bike. Sorry to break your heart.'

'What do you think *he* wants?' I asked, settling back in my chair and taking down my topknot. I pressed my fingers into my temples, trying to squeeze out a headache before it could begin. 'Snazz, I mean?'

'Probably a time machine for ten years from now

when he realizes what a ridiculous name he's saddled himself with,' John suggested. 'I honestly don't know. When I was his age, I wanted a PlayStation, some Air Jordans and a naked photo of Jenny McCarthy. I'm fairly certain he's got a PlayStation, all the Air Jordans on earth and couldn't give a flying fuck about Jenny McCarthy so I'm not really sure. He's got everything, hasn't he? What else could he want?'

'Not to have to sit in his bedroom with the curtains drawn and a giant guinea pig mask on his head?' I suggested.

John considered my response and I considered him. He wasn't that bad, I admitted grudgingly, at least not when you got him on his own and he was plying you with free wine. He was funny and quick, probably had to be, working behind a bar all the time. And he definitely wasn't bad to look at. If you liked tall, dark interesting-looking types.

He leaned across the table towards me, a lock of dark hair falling in front of his face. 'Why do it if you hate it?'

'I don't hate it,' I replied, surprised.

He half-nodded as though he was only reluctantly accepting my response.

'I don't,' I repeated. 'I love what I do. Admittedly, if I could do it somewhere else for someone else, that might be nice.'

'Then why don't you?' he asked. 'Why stay where you are?'

I lifted my shoulders and looked around the room. 'I'm lucky to have a job at all,' I replied, still making sure to focus on anything other than John. 'If I can make a success of this, it'll be easier to move on to something else. Then maybe, in a few years, I'll be able to do something I really want to do.'

He pulled a face that said fair enough before leaning across the table. Instinctively, I copied, edging forward in my seat. 'I know what you really want,' he said in a whisper.

A warmth crept up my neck as I shifted in my chair. 'You do?'

'I do,' he replied. 'You want to eat. Your stomach's screaming as though it thinks your throat's been cut. What'll it be?'

'Oh, God, food,' I pressed my hand against my white T-shirt and blew out a heavy breath. 'Yes, please. What do you recommend?'

'Well, nothing too pretentious, of course,' John said. He stood up and tossed his apron over his arm. 'And we'll give the overpriced pizzas a miss. Burger?'

'Burger sounds amazing,' I agreed, the flush spreading up to my cheeks as I recalled our second conversation. It burned even harder when I remembered our first.

'OK if I eat with you?' he suggested, looking around the bustling bar.

'They won't miss you?' I asked, surprised at how much I hoped his answer would be no.

Happily, he shook his head. 'They're more annoyed when I'm lurking. No one wants the boss watching your every move.'

'Why *do* you work behind the bar?' I asked. 'If you own the place, isn't that a bit weird?'

'Because I love it,' he said simply and I could tell that he meant it. John pointed at my half-empty glass of white. 'I'm going to put our order in. You up for more wine?'

There was still at least one full glass left in the bottle on the table but I was his guest and I didn't want to be rude. Sending him off with a thumbs up, I picked up what was left in my glass and got to work.

One burger, two hours, and an untold number of chips later, the bar was emptying out but John was only just getting going.

'No, I'm serious,' he said, almost knocking over the table between us as he gesticulated wildly, arms and legs flying everywhere. 'He comes in with a ten-foot Christmas tree on his back, needles going all over the place – in people's food, in their drinks – and I can tell he's wasted—'

'And he's dressed like Father Christmas?' I spluttered, splashing wine into his empty glass.

'Oh yeah, red suit, white beard, full gear, and he comes in and shouts "Merry Christmas, you bastards!" before collapsing in front of the bar, flat on his back and singing the dirty version of "Good King Wenceslas". Me and Cammy had to pick him up and carry him out, kicking and screaming like a toddler.'

'What did you do with the tree?'

John took a hasty sip of his drink.

'What were we supposed to do?' he replied, arms thrown out wide. 'I went down to Superdrug, bought some lights, job lot of tinsel and decorated it. Only problem is now I'm going to have to buy a tree this year and do it all over again.'

'Well, you can't rely on a pissed-up Santa delivering one to you every Christmas,' I said as I massaged my cheeks. My face actually hurt from laughing so hard.

'Does that mean you were on the nice list or the naughty list? I can't decide.'

'Oh, the nice list, definitely,' he nodded confidently. 'Never been on the naughty list in my life.'

'Never?'

'Not in a long time, anyway,' he replied with a guilty grin.

'See, you really would make a brilliant podcast,' I said with a sigh.

'So would you,' John countered, waving at someone as they called out their goodbye. According to the massive clock on the wall, it was almost eleven. We'd been talking for three hours. Talking and drinking. 'You could do an entire series on moving to another country.'

I swallowed hard, coughing as my wine went down the wrong way.

'You don't talk about it much,' he said, narrowing his eyes so slightly. 'Your time in America, I mean.'

'Not much to tell,' I said, switching my wine for water and taking a cautious sip. 'I was there and now I'm back.'

'My mum always used to say you have to take a step back to make a running jump. Which I am certain is very wise or something.'

'Your mum should start a hashtag inspo Instagram account,' I agreed. 'She's clearly a very clever woman.'

'Was,' John corrected lightly. 'She died last year.'

'Oh, I'm so sorry, I didn't know, I'm so sorry,' I babbled, thrown off course. I never knew what to say in moments like this. My mum's parents and Dad's dad had all died when I was a baby and, monster that she was, Nan was going to outlive all of us. Other people's grief always scared me a little.

'It's OK,' he said with a softer smile. 'You didn't know. Now you do, no big deal.'

We sat for a moment, John sipping his wine, me picking at chips, neither of us breaking the semi-companionable silence. Until he did.

'What happened in Washington?' he asked bluntly.

'What happened?' I repeated. 'What do you mean, what happened?'

'You never bring it up, you change the subject when anyone else does, and right now you look like you'd rather throw yourself out a window than carry on with this conversation,' John said. 'You can talk to me, you know.'

Picking up my wine, I tilted the glass back and forth, watching the liquid coat the inside and then run back down into the bowl.

'Bartender's privilege?' I replied. 'You know, you really are like a priest.'

'My cross to bear,' he said with another fleeting, downturned smile. 'But I really would like to hear about it if you want someone to talk to.'

I looked up at him from under my hair. 'It's not an exciting story,' I said, the words itching to come out. 'It's nothing dramatic. Which almost makes it worse.'

John shrugged and swept his arm across the table, giving me the floor.

'I got sacked,' I said quietly but clearly. The first time I'd said it out loud since I got back. 'Clever little Ros went off to America, gave up my job, gave up my friends, gave up my boyfriend and, when I got there, I couldn't hack it and I got sacked.'

He poured another trickle of wine into my glass. 'These things happen, why so secretive?'

'Because I'm embarrassed!' I exclaimed, almost ready to laugh. I couldn't believe he was just brushing it off like that. 'Who gets sacked these days? I was mortified.'

'How come?' he asked. 'How come they sacked you?'

'Because I wasn't good enough,' I replied, picking up my glass and then putting it down. A hangover tomorrow morning wouldn't help. 'They were making cutbacks and they brought me in and explained how they were promoting my assistant and letting me go. They felt as though there had been a "marked decline" in my work. Apparently.'

'Was there?' he asked.

'Probably,' I admitted. 'I hated it.'

It felt good to say it out loud.

'You hated the job?'

I watched as the man who had sat beside me at the bar packed away his typewriter, drained his third glass of tap water, emptied his second bowl of free nuts and got up to leave.

'Living in a different country was fun at first, everyone came to visit, everything was a novelty,' I explained. 'But I never really made friends there, not like the friends I've got here. And the job was a lot, I was working all the time, every evening, every weekend. By the end it was literally work, home, sleep, work, home, sleep. And the whole time, I could see everyone else's lives going on back here without me. I missed it so much.'

'You could have moved back, no one would have thought any less of you,' he said kindly.

'I thought if I stuck it out, it would get better,' I said. 'I thought I would get used to it and stop feeling so down all the time but I didn't.'

He offered a warm half smile but didn't respond, just waited for me to get the rest of it out.

'But everyone kept acting like it was the most amazing thing in the world, I didn't know how to tell them I was miserable. It didn't seem right to complain about my life when the entire world was going through so much shit, you know? And everyone was so impressed when I was offered the job. They head-hunted me, I didn't apply, they found me and offered me this amazing deal to go over there.' I groaned, pressing my fingers into my throbbing temples. 'My parents were so proud of me and it was nice to be the one they bragged about for a change. Did you know my sister is an actual genius?'

He tipped his head from side to side. 'Sumi did mention it, yeah.'

'Of course she did,' I smiled. 'Jo is the miracle child and I'm just me. And my dad will never get over the fact I didn't want to sell toilets for a living.'

'That's got to be tough,' he said, biting into a chip. 'But I'm sure they're just as proud of you.'

'They wouldn't be if they knew I'd got the sack,' I replied. 'Isn't it ridiculous? There's no big story, no big scandal, I'm just a let-down. I was sad and lonely and I failed at my job, I got the sack and I don't want anyone to know because they'll think less of me. Honestly, I'd give anything to go back and change my mind, to not leave in the first place.'

John let it all sink in while I took a very cautious sip of wine. My natural response to dropping a truth bomb was to chug but I felt strangely relaxed. My nan was right, it was better out than in. Although, she was rarely referring to the truth when she said that.

'I suppose one good thing came out of your coming back when you did,' John said.

'What's that?'

'You got back together with your boyfriend,' he said, wiping his hands on a white cloth napkin. 'You've been very quiet about him tonight. What's going on there?'

It was a change of subject I wasn't expecting.

'Uh, everything is fine?' I meant it to be a statement but it definitely came out sounding more like a question.

John's features flashed into a quick 'yikes' expression before settling back into his sort-of smile.

'No, it is, really,' I said again, more certain this time. 'Things are still a bit complicated.'

Right by the door, I saw a couple in a pink booth, clearly on a date but clearly still quite new to one another. She kept fussing with her hair and he was finding every excuse he could to touch her. By my calculations, they were half a drink away from one of them having to buy a toothbrush on the way to work tomorrow morning.

'Amazing that you're both single now you're back,' he said. 'Maybe it's meant to be.'

'Maybe.' I searched my brain for something clever but came up with nothing. Patrick would have had the perfect literary quote ready to go. 'I still feel like I'm playing catch-up. Who knows where we might be now if I'd never left?'

The girl from the sofa practically skipped past our table on her way to the toilet, leaving the boy to stare after her and then, the second she was out of sight, chug his entire glass of water. Utterly hammered.

'You need two people to try to make a relationship work,' John said. 'I'm sure you weren't entirely to blame, these things don't usually work like that.'

'Perhaps,' I replied with a forced smile that I hoped made clear I didn't want to talk about it. 'I know, I know, all relationships are difficult.'

'In my experience, when a man wants to be with someone,' John said, breathing in deeply. 'He will do everything in his power to make it happen.'

I watched his face, a wistful smile slipping away into something more regretful and, suddenly, I wondered where his wife was tonight.

He set down his wine glass and gave me a look. 'I might have a whisky, do you want a whisky?'

Something in the air shifted, a tension that had dissipated suddenly rallied, separating us again.

'No, thank you,' I replied politely, treading carefully around his raw nerve. 'Whisky and I don't get along terribly well.'

'That's a shame,' he said as he stood. 'Me and a good bottle of Scotch are closer than those two lately.'

He looked over at the pink sofa where the girl had returned from the toilets and the boy was attempting to excavate her tonsils with his tongue.

'Young love,' I said, grossed-out and charmed in equal measures. 'You can't beat it.'

'Except with a stick,' John replied before folding his napkin and laying it neatly on the table. 'Excuse me.'

I watched the two of them going at it on the sofa until it felt indecent, which didn't take very long at all. All smiles and hands and red cheeks, they dumped notes and coins on the table before hurrying off into the night, holding the door open for someone as they left.

'You're a sight for sore eyes,' Patrick said, striding through the bar in his charcoal-grey trousers and white linen shirt. He leaned down and planted a firm kiss on my lips, his mouth warm and wet, alcohol on his breath. Without asking, he sat himself down in John's empty chair. 'Christ, I thought dinner would never end, thank you so much for waiting.'

'I totally forgot you were coming,' I admitted, searching the bar for John. Nowhere to be found.

'Charming,' Patrick said, smiling. He picked up John's wine glass and gave it a sniff. 'Pinot Grigio? Classic Sumi, never had a clue about wine. White and wet and in a glass as I remember. Where is she? In the ladies?'

'It's a Sauvignon . . . never mind. Sumi had to work, that's not hers,' I told him as I tried to fasten the top two buttons of my jeans without him noticing. 'How was your dinner?'

'Long,' he said as he picked up the wine glass and took a swig anyway, pulling a face as he put it down. 'Can't wait to get you home.'

'Rough day? Me too. Honestly, work today was—'

'Let's get out of here,' Patrick interrupted, skewering me with his light blue eyes. 'I've got a bottle of Valpolicella at home that will wash the taste of this away in no time.'

'OK, give me a minute.' I hurriedly fished around under the table for all my things, my shoes, my jacket, my backpack. I couldn't leave without saying goodbye to John but, at the same time, I really didn't want him to see Patrick. They just weren't fated to be best friends, why make a lovely evening awkward?

'If you're not a whisky girl, how about a cognac?'

John reappeared from the kitchen, dusting off a big, square bottle. 'I've had this for ages but it's still incredible stuff.' He looked up and saw Patrick in his seat. 'Oh. Hello.'

It might have been the least welcoming greeting I'd ever heard.

'Ahh,' Patrick stood up, hands on his hips, chest puffed out. 'The bartender.'

'The bar owner,' John corrected.

'Do you want a drink?' I asked Patrick hurriedly. 'John's got some amazing stuff.'

'We're about ready to close up,' he said before Patrick could reply. 'I was going to pour you one for the road then kick you out, I'm afraid.'

'Not to worry,' Patrick said, peering at the bottle in his hand. 'That's a pretty nice cognac though. Ever been to the Chateau de Royal Cognac?'

John shook his head as he tested the weight of the bottle in his hand.

'It's about an hour and a half out of Bordeaux, you should try to visit, incredible place.' Patrick stepped away from the table and picked up my bag, slinging it over his shoulder and narrowly missing clobbering me right in the chops. 'I'd better get this one home.'

He took my hand tightly in his and pulled me towards the door. I looked back at John with a smile I hoped conveyed how grateful I was for the burger and the wine and the conversation, how much I'd enjoyed hanging out with him, how much I wished I could have said a proper goodnight. It was, in all honesty, probably too much to fit into one smile.

John's eyes stayed locked on mine as I lingered in the doorway.

'Thanks for dinner,' I called as I clung to the door-frame. Better that than nothing. 'I'll see you soon.'

'You will,' he replied.

And it sounded like a promise.

CHAPTER TWENTY-THREE

The tennis club was not a natural venue for a wedding, second or otherwise.

I'd driven past it a thousand times but never bothered to take the right turn down the long driveway to see the place for myself. In my mind, tennis clubs were Wimbledon, Roland-Garros, champagne and strawberries and lots and lots of Robinsons squash. I'd expected civilized-looking types to be wandering around in tennis whites, shouting things like 'Jolly good forehand, wot wot', and I'd hoped for at least one Roger Federer lookalike to ease my distress at having to race home from work and take two different buses to meet Mum and Dad at their venue of choice for six thirty, on Thursday night.

I was disappointed on all counts.

'This is where Dad comes every Sunday?' I whispered in Mum's ear as we let ourselves through the fingerprint-smeared glass doors and inside the club. It looked as though someone had thrown it up as an afterthought in 1962 and hadn't bothered to update it since. Faded sky blue and primrose yellow panels that had been patched up with bits of painted plywood ran all the way around the bottom half of the outside, with big, mucky windows above.

'It's looking a bit worse for wear at the moment,' Mum agreed. 'But I'm sure they'll give the windows a rinse before the event. We haven't got a lot of time to find anywhere, you know. I'm grateful they can accommodate us at all.'

'No, you're right,' I replied, looking for the potential as we passed the changing rooms and entered a large, empty space.

'And this,' Dad said, holding his arms out wide. 'Is the event space.'

The tennis club was impossibly sad but Dad looked more relaxed than I'd seen him in a long time. It was weird to think this was my dad's happy place. When you think of someone in their element, you assume it's going to be a tropical beach or a five-star hotel or a no-holds-barred spending spree at Tiffany but here he was, surrounded by pine-clad walls and orange plastic chairs and the smell of stale smoke that was baked into every single surface despite a thirteen-year-old smoking ban, walking around like a pig in shit.

'Oh,' Mum said weakly, pulling her beige Marks & Sparks cardi tightly over her neon-pink boob tube as the regulars around the bar leered in her direction.

My phone began to vibrate in my hand. I looked down and saw Ted's name in all caps, screaming at me.

'I've got to take this,' I said, throwing Mum a supportive smile before run-walking back out to the foyer. 'Hello? Ted?'

'Snazz wants Beezer Go-Go as his guest on the first episode of the pod,' he announced, as though there was something I could do about this at almost seven p.m. on a Thursday evening.

'Right, OK,' I replied, wandering over to the notice-board. Lots of people trying to sell second-hand Ikea furniture at this tennis club.

'It's only a couple of weeks away, Ros. Can you get him?'

'Yes, absolutely I can.'

The Ros reflected back at me in the sliding glass door of the noticeboard did not look as certain as I sounded. Possibly because she had no idea who Beezer Go-Go was.

'He's going to want first-class flights and I'm sure there'll be a fee,' Ted said, audibly exhaling with stress. 'He's only getting two companion flights though.'

'Only two,' I clucked, pressing my fingers into the skin around my eyes and lifting it up and back. Did I always look this tired or had I aged considerably in the last forty-eight hours?

'And they're business, not first-class,' he warned. 'I can be flexible with the budget for this episode if he'll do it, what Snazz wants . . .'

'Snazz gets,' I finished for him, wondering where all this money was coming from. My salary was reasonable but it was not in any way, shape or form generous. It was days like this that I was furious I'd wasted all the time reading books and learning when I could have been playing computer games and practising talking shit into my phone camera for hours on end.

'I'm kind of in the middle of something,' I said, glancing over my shoulder to see my mum hanging by the doorway of the event space while a man in a rugby shirt climbed on top of an orange plastic chair to poke a fluorescent light with a snooker cue. 'Can we pick this up tomorrow?'

Ted tutted and muttered something under his breath that I couldn't quite make out but sounded a lot like my twenty-six-year-old boss was suggesting that I, his thirty-two-year-old employee, was an entitled little millennial.

'Fine, tomorrow,' he replied and immediately ended the call.

'And I don't know if you're thinking about a band or a DJ but we've got connections with both,' the man in the rugby shirt said as I walked back into the events space. 'My friend Keith does a brilliant disco, gets everyone boogying on the dance floor, does Keith. But if you're looking for live music, we had a Welsh turn on at the Valentine's dance, fantastic fella. His band performs modern covers in the style of Elvis, they're called The Wonder of Huw.'

'Ros,' Mum said, speaking in the voice of a strangled cat. 'Didn't you say you wanted to do the music?'

'Yes,' I said as smoothly as possible, agreeing enthusiastically with this imaginary conversation my mother and I had definitely, absolutely had. 'I am very particular about music, very much wanted to be in charge of that, so no need to bother Huw.'

The rugby shirt looked me up and down and shrugged. Clearly he considered this my loss. 'Shall we have a look in the kitchen?' he suggested.

'I promised I'd FaceTime Jo,' I said, looking past him into a stainless-steel miseryland. 'Show her the venue.'

'That's nice,' Mum said. She ran a fingertip along the windowsill and her shoulders sank. 'Don't let her go without us saying hello.'

'So she'll answer the phone to you, will she?' Dad chuntered as he followed on into the kitchen. 'Tell her we need to have a conversation about her last phone bill. There's a cap on her data usage for a reason, she's supposed to be in Cambridge to *work*.'

I returned to the lobby, smiling briefly at an older gentleman on his way into the changing rooms as I found my sister's contact info.

'What?'

Jo appeared on the screen in front of me, bored before we'd started.

'I'm at the tennis club where Mum and Dad want to have the wedding,' I said, flipping the camera to show her the lobby. 'It's a bit sad.'

'It's murder–suicide depressing,' she replied.

Jo's face truly was perfection, like a Disney princess come to life, little pointed chin, bright blue eyes and long, glossy brown hair she had pulled back in the perfect messy bun, one it would take me an hour to achieve.

'What do you want?' Jo asked, driving the heel of her hand into her eyes. Her dark circles only served to emphasize her fragile prettiness. Who looked better when they were tired? My genius sister.

'I thought you'd want to be involved,' I replied, flipping the camera back to selfie mode and rubbing at my own dark circles. 'Since you're not here.'

'Don't try to guilt-trip me because it won't work.' She shoved a pencil into her bun and pouted. 'I've only got two months until the semester starts, I haven't got time, Ros. I've said I'll show up but honestly, I don't know why you or Mum and Dad expect me to be happy about their celebrating the fact they're spent more than half their lives reinforcing one of the key institutions that props up the patriarchy.'

'Jo,' I said, too tired to get into it. Two months until the semester started and she didn't have time. Because it wasn't as though I had a job or anything.

'Marriage is death,' Jo declared, staring daggers right at me. 'It limits both parties, traps everyone financially and emotionally and forces people to become co-dependent. Did you know male suicide rates are soaring? It's not just women that suffer in this shitty society, men are just as at risk, they're not allowed to—'

'The man who runs the club was asking if we wanted a DJ or a live band,' I interrupted loudly, right as someone opened the door to the men's changing room and left it swinging back and forth to reveal the elderly gentleman stepping into a jockstrap. Why did this keep happening to me? 'Do you have a preference?'

'Remind me to bring my AirPods,' she groaned as I spun on my heel and turned to face the corner, praying that was not a glimpse into my future. Did all balls get that saggy? 'Do not, under any circumstances, allow them to get a band. My boyfriend is a musician and I would rather eat red meat than make him suffer through any local shit.'

Jo had AirPods? I didn't have AirPods.

'You don't eat meat?' I wondered out loud. 'And since when do you have a boyfriend? What happened to your girlfriend?'

'Meat is killing the planet and if you're not

247

plant-based, so are you,' she replied. 'Don't be so close-minded, you can have a girlfriend and a boyfriend at the same time, you know. He's obsessed with me, it's so cute, he's so cute, we'll probably move in together or whatever.'

I could not wait to see her try to explain that one to our parents.

'I've got to go, I'm cooking dinner for the homeless shelter by the halls,' Jo said, checking the time on an Apple Watch. Where was she getting all this stuff? Last Christmas, Mum and Dad had sent me an old-lady dressing gown from Marks & Spencer and a spiralizer. I lived in that bloody dressing gown. The spiralizer remained in its box.

'That's nice,' I replied, smiling at my little sister. 'How did you get into that?'

'Wilf's mum runs it?' she said, as though I might know who Wilf was. 'Wilf is my boyfriend? We're going to give a lecture on the importance of avoiding conflict diamonds while they eat. It's a cause Wilf feels, like, really strongly about.'

I chewed on the inside of my cheek for a moment.

'You're going to give a group of homeless people coming to a shelter to eat a meal a lecture on the ethics of the diamond industry?'

'They're homeless, not stupid,' she snapped. 'God, Ros, you're such a bigot.'

And then she hung up.

'Serves me right for calling, really,' I muttered, tucking the phone in the back pocket of my jeans.

The door to the men's changing room opened again and the gentleman walked out, thankfully dressed in crisp tennis whites.

'Good evening,' he said with a polite nod. I smiled back, unable to form words.

'Ros?' I heard Mum shout. 'Are you still on with Jo?'

'Um, she didn't answer,' I called back before joining them. 'I was just checking work emails, talking to myself.'

I was a terrible liar.

'Maybe we'll cut off her credit card,' Dad suggested. 'See if that gets a response.'

I said nothing. I did not have a credit card when I went to university, let alone one that my parents paid for.

'Shall we have a look outside?' rugby shirt proposed. 'You can have the rose garden as well as this room, in case you want a bit of outside space.'

'Rose garden!' I said to Mum, giving her an encouraging nudge. She forced a smile, attempting to reinflate herself for a moment as we ventured outside.

A moment was more than long enough. The rose garden was not a rose garden. The rose garden was a square of ancient Astro turf with a battered white picket fence around the outside and half a dozen plant pots filled with plastic flowers.

'Nice spot for the smokers,' rugby shirt said. He nudged one of the plant pots and I realized it was brimming with cigarette butts.

'We can make it nice,' I said as my mother's face fell so far, I'd have had to get down on my hands and knees to pick it up. 'Lucy'll help. You know she's amazing at this kind of thing.'

'If we burn it to the ground would there be time to rebuild?' she asked.

I was trying to work out just which shade of lipstick

to put on this particular pig when my phone buzzed again. Only when I saw the name on the screen, this time I was very keen to answer.

'Sorry!' I said, holding the ringing phone aloft again as evidence. 'Another important call. I'll be two seconds.'

'She's a producer,' Mum explained to our host with a warm edge of pride in her voice. 'She just got back from a very important job in Washington and they always need her help at her new job.'

'She's never off the bloody thing,' Dad clarified. Rugby shirt rolled his eyes and nodded in understanding as I skipped along to an empty bench next to the tennis courts.

'Hello?' I answered, breathless.

'What are you doing tonight?' Patrick asked. 'I want to see you.'

I shivered with delight.

'Sorry, I'm with my parents,' I told him, all regret. 'They're doing wedding stuff and I said I'd help.'

'That's a shame,' he said sadly, even though I could hear the smile in this voice. 'I finished my chapter early, I was hoping I might lure you out for a drink.'

'I wish I could but it would be at least . . .' I looked down at my watch. It was after seven now and we clearly wouldn't be done here any time soon. I'd have to go home, pick up some clean knickers, give myself a Vegas shower with a bunch of baby wipes and then scoot back across London. 'I think at least nine by the time I could get to you? Maybe even nine thirty?'

'Then I'll just suffer without you,' he lamented. 'I was just sat here, thinking about the first time we met.'

'Oh?' I replied, my body prickling to attention. I remembered the night with violent clarity.

'I remember walking into that party with my editor and all I wanted to do was turn around and walk out again,' Patrick said. His voice was rich and warm and heavy and I could taste him as he spoke.

'And I nearly didn't go in the first place,' I replied, my pulse quickening as my voice lowered. I heard liquid being poured into a glass. 'The Mapplethorpes' annual Christmas tree trimming. Mum bullied me into going.'

'I walked in and saw you and I couldn't believe my luck.' He took a sip of something and the sound of it sent tingles sparking all along my scalp. 'This gorgeous creature, all those wild brown curls and big eyes, just boring into me.'

Someone nearby was calling out scores for a tennis game but I was somewhere else entirely. A warm living room in East Mosely, the smell of homemade mince pies in the air mixed with a freshly cut Christmas tree and too many middle-aged women wearing the same Estée Lauder perfumes. I'd actually had my hair up that night but I wasn't about to spoil his fantasy with pedantic facts. It had certainly been down by the end of it.

'And you were wearing a white shirt and grey trousers,' I said quietly. 'And you were laughing about something then I caught your eye and you came over to say hello.'

'What did we even talk about?' Patrick asked. I imagined him lying on his bed, holding his whisky glass, loosening his top button. 'I can't remember.'

We talked about books we'd both read, the books he had written, we talked about the places he travelled to, the places I wanted to travel to, we talked about my job, we talked about the sad state of modern

Christmas number ones, we talked about homemade versus shop-bought Christmas cakes, we talked about the importance of Fleetwood Mac and my unpopular opinion that *Tango in the Night* was better than *Rumours* and we talked about how his editor was friends with the Mapplethorpes but didn't know my parents, how I was there out of daughterly duty, how he was there to meet some journalist who hadn't turned up and maybe that was all just meant to be.

'I have no idea,' I replied. 'Absolutely no idea.'

'I remember you said we should leave and get a drink somewhere else.'

'That was you!' I exclaimed, ducking to the left as a stray tennis ball swooshed past me and bounced off the plastic window.

'No, it was definitely you,' Patrick laughed. 'You asked me with your eyes, I translated it into words.'

My lips curved into a smile.

'And then we got in that taxi and . . .' His words trailed off into a deep, satisfied sigh. 'Where are you right now?'

I gulped and tucked my hair behind my ears.

'On a bench outside a tennis club in Worcester Park.'

'I wish you were here.' Patrick's breathing, the sound of a zip, a body moving on soft sheets. 'I wish you were doing what I'm doing right now.'

I stared at the grass in front of my feet, face hot, palms sweaty.

'What would you do?' he asked. His voice was slightly hoarse. 'If you were here right now?'

'Patrick, I'm at my dad's tennis club,' I whispered.

'Go into the ladies' room,' he instructed. 'Go into the ladies' room and do exactly what I tell you.'

I stood up without hesitation, only thinking about one thing.

'Watch out!'

Which meant I was not thinking about low-flying tennis balls.

'Oh, shit!' I wailed, dropping my phone and clutching my face. 'Shit bugger bollocks ow.'

'Goodness, I am sorry,' the elderly gentleman from the men's changing room tottered over. Clearly all his strength was in his backhand. 'Are you all right? Should I get the first aider?'

'Ros?'

Patrick's voice echoed out my phone speaker from the ground. 'Ros, are you there? What happened?'

I gave my assailant a pleasant smile and a thumbs up as my head throbbed. Trying not to pass out, I bent over and picked up my scratched but not shattered new phone.

'Ros?'

'I'm OK, I got hit in the head by a tennis ball,' I said, wandering back towards the rose garden, a little dazed and very sore. 'Give me a minute?'

'I think the moment's gone,' Patrick replied, clearing his throat. 'I might give today's pages another once-over if you really can't tear yourself away.'

'Sorry,' I told him, wincing as I poked my fingers into my new injury. Fantastic. What this week needed was a black eye from a septuagenarian tennis player.

'Can't be helped,' he said briskly. 'I'll see you tomorrow?'

'Tomorrow,' I agreed. His first scheduled visit *Chez Shed*. 'Maybe you should think about what you'd like me to do for you then.'

'I'll see you tomorrow,' he said with a soft promise.

'Rosalind, what the bloody hell happened to your face?' Mum asked, practically running across the club as I ended the call. 'You've been gone two minutes.'

'Stray ball.' I pulled my head out of her hands, turning away from her inspection. 'It's fine.'

'It's going to bruise,' she replied. 'We need to put some ice on that.'

'We usually have ice packs but I just defrosted the freezer,' rugby shirt said. 'Ice cream van should be around in a minute, we could stick a Mister Whippy on it?'

'Let's get you home,' Mum said, tenderly brushing my hair back from my forehead. 'I've got some arnica gel, that'll help.'

'Thanks for the tour,' Dad said to our host. 'Apologies, can't take this one anywhere.'

Rugby shirt looked me up and down and scoffed. 'I thought she was supposed to be some sort of genius?' he guffawed.

'That's the other one,' Dad explained, clapping me hard on the back before giving his friend a sharp salute. It hurt almost as much as my eye.

'Home, James,' Dad said, striding off towards the car. 'And don't spare the horses.'

CHAPTER TWENTY-FOUR

By the time Friday evening rolled around, I was prepared to call the working week, tennis-ball assaults aside, a success. I had Snazz's first podcast guests confirmed, the art department was working on the logo and the marketing team was shouting about our live recording at WESC (which I now knew stood for the World E-Sports Championships) reaching even the deepest, darkest little corners of the internet. Basement-dwellers would be risking the outside world from far and wide to get a glimpse at Snazzlechuff, live and in person. Even I had found myself wondering if he'd get a new mask made. There was a minor bump in the road when I tried to get Veronica to schedule in some rehearsal time but she insisted that he didn't need it, that too much prep would 'fucking ruin the magic'. When I raised it with Ted, he advised me that the magician works in mysterious ways and so, I had left it alone. It had been such a long time since I'd felt good about myself at work, knowing I was killing it was such a high.

At exactly five thirty, I switched my casual Friday Converse for a pair of black patent heels, checked my concealer, closed up my computer and bolted for the door. Patrick had rented some obscure French movie from his very cool video club and we had made plans to watch it *at mine*. After leaving the tennis club, I'd spent all evening pimping the place out to prepare for his arrival: new sheets, new wine glasses, knock-off Jo Malone candles I'd sent Mum all the way to Aldi to procure. As long as I kept the light low and the smell of the compostable toilet out of the bedroom, I truly believed I could pass off my current predicament as sexily bohemian. And if the candles weren't enough to distract him, I'd also spent my following week's food budget on a pair of stockings and suspenders that were definitely more six-star hotel suite than one-star shed. I needed about three hours to get into them but it would be worth it.

I was fifteen minutes into a mindless run around the M&S Foodhall when my phone rang with Patrick's name lighting up the screen.

'Hey, hi,' I beamed. 'I was just thinking about you.'

'Warm thoughts, I hope,' he replied. 'What time are you coming over tonight?'

I dropped a packet of prosciutto in my trolley and frowned.

'I thought you were coming to me?'

'Really? I thought you were coming here,' he said. 'I was going to make you dinner.'

'I was going to make *you* dinner,' I countered, hand hovering over a pre-packaged cheese selection. 'You said you'd come to me because it's Lucy's baby shower tomorrow and it's easier to get there from my place. Remember?'

He gave a long groan of recognition. 'Ohhh, the baby shower is tomorrow? I thought that was next week? My brain is like a sieve.'

'Lucy's baby shower is this weekend,' I confirmed. 'Next weekend is my mum and dad's vow renewal.'

'And what's the weekend after that?' he laughed. 'Your milkman's cousin's bar mitzvah?'

'The weekend after that is my birthday,' I said quietly, putting back the cheese.

'I know that, I'm just joking,' Patrick replied. 'You sound tired. Why don't you come here tonight and let me look after you?'

'Because you said you'd come to mine,' I said in as hushed a tone as I could manage. I would not be one of those women who had a full-volume slanging match on the phone in the supermarket. At least not in M&S, what would my mother think? 'Come on, Patrick, it's going to be nice, I was going to buy cheese?'

I would not give in. He was coming to my shed if I had to drug him and drag him and that was almost definitely illegal or, at the very least, frowned upon.

'Ros, don't take this the wrong way but this week has been a nightmare and I don't think I can deal with roommates tonight.'

I stopped in the middle of the aisle.

'I don't have any roommates,' I said, confused. 'What are you talking about?'

A pause.

'You don't?'

'I'm staying at my parents' house until I find a flat. I must have told you ten times.'

'That's what I meant,' he replied confidently. 'I meant your roommate-parents. I didn't want to offend you but the idea of dealing with anyone's mum and dad after the week I've had is just too much. Come to me, I'll open some wine, make some pasta, pull out the projector. I'll make you your own private cinema. It'll be wonderful.'

It did sound wonderful, or at least it would have sounded wonderful if we hadn't already made plans.

'I can't, all my stuff for tomorrow is at home,' I explained slowly, calmly. 'And it doesn't make any sense to go all the way back home and then come all the way back across London just to go all the way back again in the morning. The baby shower is ten minutes from my mum and dad's place.'

'Then we'll get it in the morning on the way,' Patrick replied. 'Look, you've clearly had a hell of day. Has that Snazz upset you or something? You never used to get this stressed out about little things.'

'I'm not stressing out about little things,' I said, grabbing the cheese. I didn't care if we were sharing it or I ate the entire thing myself, either way, it was coming home with me. 'I told Sumi *we* would be at the baby shower early to help her set up because you said you wanted to help.'

'You know what, I am really exhausted,' he said with a forced yawn. 'Why don't we watch the film tomorrow night instead?'

I felt my frustration rising. It was reasonable that he wanted to stay home after a long week but it was also reasonable for me to expect him to stick to our plans, especially when those plans made the most sense for the following day. My grip tightened around the handle of the basket.

'*After* the baby shower,' he added. 'Which is in my diary and I am very excited about.'

'Really?'

Patrick huffed down the line. 'Rosalind Reynolds, I can't believe you would doubt me.'

I rubbed my nose on the back of my hand to drive away any threatening tears. Frustration always made me tear up. Frustration, anger and any time there was an elderly dog in an advert.

'Now, you go home and relax, put your feet up, have a bubble bath or something and I'll see you tomorrow. Don't worry about coming over here, I'll be fine on my own. I'll meet you at the party whenever you want me there.'

I looked down at my high heels and thought about the twenty minutes I'd spent applying false eyelashes in the PodPad toilets and about the stockings and suspenders, wedged on top of the bathroom cabinet in the shed. What a waste.

'I'll miss you tonight though,' Patrick murmured, chasing away my annoyance.

'Good,' I told him, my annoyance building again as he laughed down the line. 'I'll see you tomorrow.'

My phone beeped to confirm he'd ended the call.

Tears welled up in my eyes as I stared into the cheese fridge. I had two choices. One, fill my basket with dairy delights, go home and try not to make eye contact with my redundant lingerie. Or, two, abandon my shopping and find an adventure.

'It's Friday, I'm wearing false eyelashes and cheese

backs me up,' I accidentally declared to an unsuspecting shelf stocker. 'Time for an adventure.'

'It gives me the runs,' clucked a little old lady at the side of me. 'You get off out while you're young.' She picked up a block of Wensleydale and looked me up and down. 'Well, fairly young.'

And there it was, decision made.

'Where are we going?' I asked Sumi, clambering out of the taxi and following her blindly down an alleyway. 'Why won't you tell me?'

'Because if I tell you, you won't want to do it and I'll let you talk me out of it and we'll end up at mine, completely rat-arsed, you whining about Patrick, me buying shoes I can't afford and both of us hungover for the baby shower tomorrow,' she replied. Sumi had thought this through.

'I will want to do it,' I promised even though I clearly had no way of knowing if that was in fact true. 'It doesn't matter what it is.'

She marched on, lips firmly clamped together.

'Is it a quiz night?'

No response. It was a fair guess though, Sumi loved quizzes. Mostly because she was much cleverer than anyone else in the world and quiz nights were the only place she could really let that light shine without feeling like an arse.

'Immersive theatre experience where we all have to pretend we're squirrels?'

I could have sworn I'd read about that happening somewhere round here on *Time Out*.

'Lesbian board game night?'

'What's a lesbian board game?' she asked.

'Monopoly but instead of buying property and going to prison you buy Birkenstocks and have to go to Ikea.'

'I have never in my life worn a Birkenstock,' she gasped, glancing down at her Guccis to make sure they hadn't heard. 'And I'd rather go to prison than Ikea.'

'Ikea has better food,' I argued.

'Just barely,' she sniffed. 'Those meatballs are gross, they're fake news.'

'Blasphemy,' I whispered under my breath.

'We are here,' Sumi announced, stopping in front of the nondescript door of an ordinary building. 'After you.'

'Is it an escape room?' I asked, my pulse suddenly racing. 'Because I should warn you, I'm not allowed in those.'

'No it isn't, and what do you mean you're not allowed?'

'We went to one as a team-building exercise in DC,' I explained as she gently pushed me through the door. 'And I got slightly over-competitive and made one of the other girls cry.'

She gave me a look.

'You couldn't make me cry if you tried,' she said, as much of a threat as a promise.

'Where are we?' I asked again, the distant sound of music thrumming through the floorboards.

'It's a dark disco,' she replied, handing two tickets to a man who appeared to be watching a beauty tutorial on his iPhone. He swapped her the tickets for two bottles of water and cocked his head towards a narrow death trap of a staircase behind him. 'We're going to dance.'

'Like, a goth disco?' I looked back at the staircase and wondered if it truly was steep enough to finish me off. Because if it was a choice between that and an entire evening of swishing around to The Cure, I couldn't honestly say which was the better option.

'No, you knob. A dark disco, a disco that takes place in the dark.' Sumi grinned as we heaved our way upstairs. 'It's the best thing ever, they play the most amazing music and you can dance however you want because it's pitch black, no one can see you. You're literally dancing as though nobody is watching.'

I clutched my water bottle to my chest.

'Is this a sex thing?'

'You're thinking of a dark *room*,' she replied. 'And no. At least, it wasn't last time I came. It's incredibly freeing. You can dance your arse off to Taylor Swift without worrying what anyone else thinks. Last time I was here they did a full hour of Spice Girls songs and, I swear, I thought someone had slipped some Molly into my drink I was so happy.'

'And you're sure they hadn't?' I asked before carefully inspecting the tamper-proof seal on my own water bottle.

'Unlikely, it's a sober party.'

It took a minute for the words to register.

'Excuse me?'

'It's a sober party,' Sumi repeated. 'No booze, no drugs.'

I almost fainted clean away.

'Is there at least fizzy pop and Haribo?'

'Ros,' Sumi wedged her water bottle under her armpit and took both of my hands in hers. 'There is only water. You will survive, you will dance and you will feel amazing. We need to seize these moments while we can. One day, we'll have different responsibilities, we won't be able to randomly nick off to a disco without a care in the world.'

'We won't?' I asked. What was she talking about?

'We will not,' she confirmed. 'Trust me, you're going to love this. And if you're very good, I'll buy you a Nando's on the way home.'

'Won't Nando's be closed on the way home?' I asked, allowing her to lead me towards a heavy black curtain.

'Dark Disco ends at nine,' she answered. 'You'll be home by ten, asleep by eleven and I swear it'll be the best night's sleep you've ever had in your life. You can thank me tomorrow when you're incredibly grateful not to have to deal with Lucy's baby-mama friends with a hangover.'

'I don't think I've been dancing sober since I was fourteen,' I said, weirdly nervous as I handed my backpack over to a much friendlier-looking woman, standing behind a folding table.

Sumi snorted with laughter. 'It's just dancing, Ros, not shagging, which you definitely want to be drunk for. At least the first time. Or for the first three years, depending.'

I followed her through the curtains into a small vestibule where the music suddenly became much louder. I had to find out what kind of curtains these were, I thought, fingering the heavy velvet with admiration. Maybe they'd help class up the shed a bit.

'My name is Jeremy, I work here at Dark Disco and, before I let you in, I'm going to run you through the rules,' said a mystery voice. I could still see Sumi's outline and a few stray chinks of light found her heavy silver necklace, covering her in stars. 'Once you get inside, it'll take a minute for your eyes to adjust to the low light conditions. Until they do, we suggest reserving your big dance moves. There is likely to be some accidental bumping into people but we do not condone unwelcome touching—'

'How will we know the difference?' asked a male voice.

'Oh, you'll know,' Sumi replied before Jeremy could.

'If you are touched in a way you do not find acceptable, in the first instance, please inform the person touching you that it is unwelcome as it could still be accidental. If it continues—'

'Kick him in the bollocks?' I suggested.

Sumi held up her hand for a high five which I just managed to hit.

'Violence of any kind will not be condoned,' Jeremy said firmly. 'If unwelcome touching continues, please come back here and inform either myself or Mary on the bag check-in. There is a night-vision camera installed in the disco for your safety although it will only be looked at if we have any complaints.'

'Yeah, this sounds like it's going to be a right barrel of laughs,' I whispered to Sumi. 'How did you even hear about it?'

'Wait until you get in there, it's amazing,' she replied while Jeremy placed neon wristbands on everyone's wrists. Mine was orange. Sumi's was pink. We immediately switched. 'John brought me and Ade a few months ago, I think one of his friends runs it? We had to drag John out at the end, you wouldn't think it but he's the full *Saturday Night Fever*. Surprisingly good dancer for a tall man.'

Jeremy clapped his hands loudly. 'Are we all ready to disco in the dark?'

Everyone cheered with varying degrees of enthusiasm and a second pair of black curtains opened, leading through to a pitch-black room where the party was already well under way. The bass thumped so loud, I could feel it vibrating from the floor, through the slender heels of my shoes and up my legs. My chest pounded with the music as my heartbeat was forced into a new rhythm.

'Sumi?' I yelled, totally thrown by just how dark it really was. 'Where are you?'

'Just dance!' she shouted back. 'Just let go!'

I watched her orange neon bracelet drift away from me, bobbing up and down as she air-punched her way across the dance floor.

I loved dancing as much as the next person, in that I danced when I was drunk or heard a Beyoncé song. When I was a teenager, we made up routines to every song on the charts and practised them until there wasn't a single drop of joy left in Britney Spears's entire back catalogue. Even two decades on, I couldn't hear 'Hit Me Baby, One More Time' without bursting into the exact choreography we'd recorded off *Top of the Pops*. I couldn't put an exact date on when we stopped going dancing every weekend – one minute we were hobbling home with our arms around each other, barefoot with our shoes in our hands, and the next we were putting each other in taxis and saying goodnight right after dinner. Maybe it was when we realized half the girls in the club were a clear decade younger than us, or maybe when working all week and going out all weekend became too much for our bodies to handle. And for some of my friends, a night at home was much more appealing when there was a significant other waiting for them there.

But this was a different kind of game. I didn't need any warm-up drinks to find the confidence to bust out my moves, there was no scanning the dance floor to find a safe space, away from the good dancers and the hot girls and the stag parties and the drunks. Everywhere was a safe space when no one could see you.

Slowly, I began to move from side to side, hips moving gently at first, my calf-length silky skirt swishing against my skin. Before I knew it, my arms had loosed themselves from my sides and began to swing back and forth above my head. I felt incredible. I was Britney, Beyoncé and Lizzo all rolled into one. Why hadn't anyone thought of this before?

With my eyes closed, I rolled and gyrated and, God help me, twerked on the spot, occasionally skipping across to another part of the room, just because I could. I hadn't felt this powerful on a dance floor since that time I got smashed on three-for-two Bacardi Breezers in the student union and decided to leap on stage and perform an interpretative dance rendition of the *Grease* megamix. I felt so free, I felt so young, I felt – someone crash into me.

'Fuck, I'm sorry,' a voice said, immediately backing away, their striped blue and green bracelet moving across the floor.

'That's OK,' I replied, as I waved the stranger on with a thumbs up even though he couldn't see my gesture. Maybe it was best to keep my eyes open, I decided. With slightly more awareness, I slipped back into my groove as my eyes adjusted to the darkness.

Now I could make out shadowy shapes of human beings as they rolled and thrust to the music, just the outlines of their bodies, like shadows moving to a Motown beat.

The more I surrendered to the music, the further away my problems felt. No need to worry about work, no need to wonder where I was going to live. Why concern myself with Mum and Dad's second wedding and Jo's antics and Nana's casual bigotry? Even my existential angst felt far away. So what if I couldn't bring myself to look at a newspaper? Sure, climate change was destroying the planet but we could figure it out! All that mattered was the music and the dancing and not getting twatted in the face again.

Only one niggling doubt remained.

Patrick.

I was annoyed he had backed out on our plans and I was annoyed that I'd let him get away with it so easily. Was it a mix-up or could he just not be bothered? Like Sumi had said when he sent that first text, he'd always had a tendency to be a little callous, a little carefree with other people's plans and feelings. But he wasn't malicious, he wouldn't let me down. Would he? No. So what if he was a bit flaky? These were simply growing pains, bumps in the road that would be smoothed out by time. For a moment I considered going back out to get my bag to text him. This was the kind of thing he'd get a kick out of. Not that he was a big dancer but he'd definitely enjoy a dark disco. Probably. Maybe in an ironic sense. I felt my arms sliding back down towards my waist in the time-honoured tradition of your mum dancing at her work's Christmas party.

'No,' I whispered to myself, forcing all thoughts of my sort-of-boyfriend out of my head and throwing my arms back up in the air, waving them around like I just didn't care, hoping that if I kept it up, it would become true again.

Before I knew it, my body was dripping with sweat, my black camisole sticking to me like a second skin as I sang out the words to every single song. We could have been in there for fifteen minutes or fifteen hours, I had no idea. Sumi was right, you didn't need a drink to do this and you definitely didn't need drugs. If I was any higher, I'd be a kite.

Someone's unknown body part bumped into my hip while I was gyrating wildly to some vintage Prince, knocking me out of my euphoria for just a moment.

'Sorry,' a male voice yelled over the music.

'No worries,' I called back, dancing towards the tall, slender shape. In the misty darkness, I could just about make out a smile as we tentatively orbited each other. A long dormant flutter came to life in my chest. How long had it been since I danced with a stranger in a club?

Slowly, we moved closer and closer until I had my back pressed up against his front and his hands rested on my hips. Every moment of contact connected sharply; there was no booze in me to make my decisions fuzzy but the darkness kept reality at a safe distance. It felt so good, leaning into his solid chest, to move with someone, to connect with another body. And it was just dancing, no big deal, nothing to feel guilty about.

The music switched to a classic Madonna song and suddenly my hips took on a life of their own. I felt myself twist and turn, grinding against my partner and finding him more than up to the challenge. Without really thinking, I turned around, looping my arms around his neck as my skirt rode up above my knees to make room for his thigh between my legs. We swayed back and forth, skin on skin, sweat mingling with sweat as the gospel chorus kicked in, the two of us moving together in time to the music. Life is a mystery, indeed.

It's only dancing, my mind whispered, my eyes closed and my body on fire as the sound of everyone singing drowned out the song and the pounding of my heart drowned out the voices of everyone singing around us. His hands moved down my back, slipping lower, his warm breath against my cheek . . .

And then without warning, the song ended and the music stopped. My dance partner and I froze, still pressed together, panting, sweating, on the precipice of something.

'That's a wrap on another Dark Disco, thanks for coming, everyone,' a voice boomed through the speakers. 'We'll be back next month, hope we won't be seeing you!'

And then the lights came on, unflattering fluorescent strip lights that were no one's friend. I looked up at the man's face and gasped.

'John?'

I dropped him faster than if he'd been on fire. Staggering backwards, I pulled my skirt back into place, searching for the right words, but I was still half lost in another world.

'Are you OK?' he asked, holding out a hand.

'There you are.' Sumi, glassy-eyed, sweaty and

utterly euphoric, bounced across the dance floor as everyone else began to filter out towards the doors. 'John! I wondered if you'd be here, we came last minute. How brilliant was that? I wish they would do it every week. Once a month is not enough.'

John and I were still staring at each other, him looking more than a little confused and me feeling utterly mortified. He pushed damp, messy hair away from his face, recovering just enough to give Sumi a smile.

'Yeah, great one,' he agreed, eyes drifting back in my direction. 'Glad you had a good time. I've got to go, see you tomorrow, yeah?'

'OK, weirdo.' Sumi pulled a face at me as John turned around and bolted for the door. Bouncing up and down on the spot, she grinned at me madly. 'Don't know what's wrong with him. Did you love it? Was it the best thing ever?'

'So good,' I replied, forcing weak enthusiasm into my voice.

'Ready for a Nando's?' she asked.

'Always,' I replied, forcing a smile and pushing away difficult thoughts I wasn't ready to deal with.

CHAPTER TWENTY-FIVE

'Do you think women glow when they're pregnant because of the baby or because they've had nine months off the sauce?' I asked Sumi, pressing a hand against my face, only shining thanks to my liberal application of highlighter. Lucy's baby shower was packed full of gorgeous, glossy pregnant women I had never met before and half-hoped never to meet again. They all squealed as they arrived, grabbing each other's hands with pincer-type movements and enthusiastically comparing bumps.

'I don't know but it's enough to put me on it,' she replied, eyeing the bar. Beyond the glasses of pre-prepared mocktails was a whole wall of hard liquor that we could not touch. For shame.

'You've done an amazing job on the party,' I told her, looking around at the picture-perfect shower. 'Lucy's never looked so happy.'

I'd turned up early as promised but there really was no need. Sumi had failed to mention the fact she'd hired an events company to take care of the entire thing, leaving me standing around like a complete tit, holding the world's saddest papier-mâché stork. Because Lucy and Dave didn't know the sex of the baby, she had gone to town with a gender-neutral bunny theme. Rabbits hopped all over the walls, girl bunnies in bows, boy bunnies in shorts and, Sumi quietly informed me, non-binary bunnies in shorts and bows, just to piss Dave off. A plush carpet of fake grass was spread beneath our feet and even the corridor down to the toilets had been turned into a rabbit warren with carrot-shaped soaps in the lavs. All the food was bunny-themed, carrot juice to drink, cotton-tail cupcakes, rabbit-food sandwiches and a huge carrot cake with a dummy on top. And in the middle of the room was the pièce de résistance, a giant eight-foot stuffed rabbit that I really hoped she had a home for after the party because there was no way it would fit through Lucy's front door. I also hoped Creepy Dave had been lifting weights in secret because I'd helped the delivery men bring it in and it was not light.

They'd even created a 'traditional' cigar lounge for Creepy Dave and his man friends and, even though there was nothing traditional about the baby's dad and awful friends even attending the shower, Sumi had provided exactly what he'd asked for. Through heavy wooden double doors was the smoking lounge of dreams, decanters full of Scotch, hand-rolled Cuban cigars and, at Creepy Dave's special request, a box full of Peperamis. It was a horrible, horrible dream come true.

'I should definitely get these people to do Mum and Dad's wedding,' I breathed, watching as another pregnant woman arrived, gleefully accepting her

272

bunny ears and tail from one of the waitresses. 'Do you think they could put an entire party together by next Saturday?'

'I think they could take over the world by next Saturday,' Sumi replied. 'Wedding planning not going well?'

'It's going OK, I think,' I said, utterly unsure. 'Although I did see a Post-it note on the fridge that said "Call Pam about cake" and then "Venue" with ten question marks, so that's reassuring.'

'As long as you've got cake,' she said. 'What else could you need?'

'Flowers, music, chairs, tables, decent food and a muzzle for Jo.'

She pulled me in for a hug then rested her head on my shoulder, bracing herself for another round of braying as the door flew open.

'Where did Lucy meet all these women?' I asked as our lucky thirteenth pregnant guest arrived. 'I didn't know there were this many pregnant women in all of England.'

'It happened when they moved,' she whispered, lowering her voice so that the mombies wouldn't hear. 'Suddenly there were all these shiny couples hanging around their house. Very straight, very white, literally no sense of humour.'

'So, Dave's friends?' I guessed.

'That's what I thought at first but there can't be this many people on earth who actually like him,' Sumi reasoned. 'Every time I went over there were more of them. I blame you for leaving. I think she was auditioning to replace you in case you never came back.'

'Looking for a shinier version with more functions?'

I asked, comparing myself to the sparkly herd of pregnant women, swarming around my friend.

Sumi shrugged. 'When you buy a new phone, you don't ask for a model that's worse than the one you have, do you?'

'When I buy a new phone, I accidentally send a text out to everyone I've ever met and end up getting spammed by personal accident lawyers morning, noon and night,' I replied. 'Is it me or do they all have the same handbag?'

'It's not you.' Sumi pressed her hand against her forehead and groaned. 'How have I got a headache when we didn't even drink last night?'

'It's only about to get worse,' I warned cheerfully, watching as the door opened. 'Patrick's here.'

'And he brought his friends,' she sighed happily. Behind Patrick was Adrian and behind Adrian was John. 'This should be fun.'

'Wow.'

Patrick, hair mussed, shirt, tie and trousers all tailored to perfection, swooped down on my best friend before greeting me, planting here-I-am kisses on both of her cheeks before she could protest. The charm offensive, I noted with relief, was on. His black tie was loosened slightly at the throat, the top button was undone and his sleeves were rolled halfway up his perfectly toned forearms. He looked as though he'd just stopped in on his way to compose an epic love poem or rescue a baby from a burning vehicle. He was perfect.

'This is incredible, Sumi. Did you do all this?'

'Yes,' she lied, giving me an almost imperceptible look of disapproval. 'Nice to see you, Patrick.'

'It's been a long time,' he said genially, bending down to give her a kiss on the cheek. 'Good to see you again.'

'Is it though?' she asked, smiling at the warning on my face. 'I'm joking, I'm glad you came. On time.'

He cleared his throat and stuck his hands in his pockets. He had never really known how to deal with Sumi, she was the only person impervious to his charms, his intelligence and his never-ending supply of witty comebacks. Sumi was Patrick's kryptonite.

'You look beautiful.' Patrick gave me a brief but tender kiss. 'I missed you last night, what did you get up to?'

'We went dancing,' Sumi answered for me. 'It was amazing, we had the most incredible time.'

'I can't believe you took my girlfriend out dancing and left me all alone at home to work,' he said, wrapping his arm round my waist. Girlfriend, I registered, stunned. He called me his girlfriend.

'You should have come with us,' Sumi said, bundling Adrian and then John into hugs, a much warmer welcome than she'd reserved for Patrick. I caught John's eye and then quickly looked away. 'Dark Disco is amazing, isn't it, John?'

'You were there too?' Patrick said, his tone light and breezy but the look he gave me was anything but. 'Now I really do feel left out.'

'If it makes you feel any better, I wasn't invited,' Adrian said as it became clear that John had no interest in joining in the conversation.

'Yeah but you were too busy with your *girlfriend*,' Sumi sang. 'Where is she anyway? This mythical

275

beast of a woman who's infected you with such an incredibly virulent strain of feelings?'

'Having a wee.' Adrian blushed. 'I think she's nervous about meeting you all.'

'Isn't this the part where you're supposed to say "Why would she be nervous?"' Patrick asked me.

'No,' Sumi, John and I all said all at once.

'I'll talk to her, if you like,' Patrick said, clapping Adrian on the back while Sumi made a very sour face, this time not even attempting to hide it. 'Tell her none of you bite.'

'At least he's trying,' Sumi said to me, loudly and very much in front of Patrick. 'Excuse me, I think the caterer is trying to get my attention. Go, have fun, drink a juice, do not kill yourself.'

'No one is trying to get your attention,' Adrian shouted as Sumi bustled off through the doors to the kitchen with her middle finger up in the air. 'So,' he said brightly. 'Where's the booze?'

'In the man cave,' I told him, pointing at the smoky fug clouding up the windows of the cigar lounge. 'Creepy Dave has whisky.'

His face fell to the floor. 'Are you serious?'

'Unless any of you brought a flask?'

John held out empty hands and Patrick groaned.

'Then it's carrot juice smoothies or baby bunny punch, pick your poison,' I told them. 'The carrot juice smoothie isn't bad but I'm pretty sure the punch is just loads of Um Bongo.'

'Fuck yeah,' Adrian cheered, disappearing to the drinks table.

'Are you going to tell me all about this incredible party I missed last night?' Patrick asked. I wasn't sure if he was speaking to me or John but, since John didn't look especially chatty, I took the baton.

'Sumi had a spare ticket so I went with her,' I explained, rushing over my words. 'And John was there. Only we didn't know until the end because it's in the dark. That's why it's a dark disco, you dance in the dark. Anyway, it ends at nine so I was home really early which was really great and we should go together next month, you'd love it.'

Patrick took a moment to let my word vomit settle.

'What kind of music is it?'

'They play everything,' I answered. 'Pop, disco, dance, everything.'

'Might not be my kind of thing,' he replied. 'But I'm glad the two of you,' his eyes flicked between us, 'had fun while I was slaving away over my edits.'

'We weren't there together, I mean, we were both there but we weren't there together,' I insisted before realizing I was probably insisting a little too much. 'But maybe we can all go together next time.'

'I'm going to get a drink,' John announced, walking away without asking if anyone else wanted anything.

'I'm sorry, I know he's part of the gang now and everything but I do not like him at all,' Patrick said quietly, curling an arm around my waist. 'Does he think all that brooding passes for a personality? He's hardly Heathcliff, is he?'

'Brooding was very sexy when I was a teenager but really, it is a textbook abusive relationship,' I babbled, happy to pull the conversation in another direction. 'Heathcliff is an absolute monster. We had a psychiatrist on The Book Report, reappraising *Wuthering Heights* as a romantic novel. It was fascinating.

Heartbreaking if you love the book, but totally fascinating.'

'Sounds interesting,' he replied. 'What's The Book Report?'

I blinked and smiled. 'The radio show I worked on in DC?'

'Of course, I'd forgotten the name,' Patrick said, pretending to choke back a sob. 'You'll have to send me the link to that one.'

Closing my eyes, I leaned into a kiss that quieted my concerns. All those nights I'd lain awake dreaming about him kissing me, why ruin it over a few forgetful moments?

'Thank you for coming today,' I said, wiping my lipstick from the corner of his mouth. 'It means a lot to me.'

'Just promise me you won't put me through this if we have kids,' he whispered as Lucy heaved herself out of her carrot-adorned throne and waddled towards us. 'And whatever you do, don't let them drag me into that cigar lounge.'

I mentally recorded his words, storing them in the safest corner of my brain so that they could be debated endlessly in the group text as soon as possible. I pressed my hand against my stomach to calm a strange feeling I wasn't entirely sure I liked.

'Lucy,' Patrick let go of my hands to take Lucy by hers, kissing both of her cheeks and matching her beatific smile with one of his own. 'I don't want to be rude but you've put on a few pounds since I last saw you.'

'Twenty-nine and a half,' she said with pride. 'I tried not to gain too much but, you know.'

'You look radiant,' he replied, instinctively choosing

all the right words. Lucy beamed over at me and I smiled back. 'When my sister had her first, she was tiny until her thirty-third week and then she blew up like a balloon. A gorgeous balloon but, you know.'

'What? Your sister had a baby?'

Patrick's sister was the most militant member of the anti-baby brigade I had ever encountered in my life. The first time I'd met her, she asked me if I wanted kids and when I said I didn't know, she screamed in my face that I should be sterilized before I 'panic-spawned' in my late thirties. Such a charmer.

'Two, actually,' he replied. 'Curtis is almost three and Manix just had his first birthday. I'd be amazed if there wasn't a third before long, she's dying for a girl. I've never known anyone take to motherhood like she has, she's a natural.'

Quite the turnaround for a woman who wore a T-shirt that said 'Feed Don't Breed' to her brother's birthday dinner four years ago.

'We haven't told anyone our names,' Lucy said, letting slip the light giggle she reserved for the opposite sex. 'They're top secret.'

'You haven't told anyone?' Patrick replied, his eyes big and blue. 'I don't believe you.'

'Dave made me promise I wouldn't,' she said, fanning herself with a cardboard lettuce leaf. 'And you know anything I tell one of them immediately works its way around the entire group.'

'You could tell me,' he offered. 'I swear I'll take it to my grave.'

'She's not going to tell you,' I said, somewhat stuck on the fact his sister had spawned. 'It was eight months before she told me she'd lost her virginity.'

'That's hardly a secret now, is it?' Patrick said, glancing down at her protruding belly. 'But I understand. Baby names are sacred. I was the only person who knew my nephew's names until they were born and I never told a soul.'

Maybe you should have, I thought to myself. Could have spared them eighteen years of schoolyard bullying.

'Ohh, Dave would kill me but I am dying to get it off my chest,' Lucy squeaked, looking around the room for potential witnesses. Apparently I didn't count. 'You're sure you won't tell anyone?'

Patrick crossed himself and leaned in as she wrapped her fingers around his ears.

It was unreal. Two weeks ago, she would have pushed him under a bus as soon as look at him and now she was about to confide her super special secret baby names to Patrick bloody Parker.

'I might go and get a drink,' I said, rolling my eyes as they gasped and giggled at each other.

'I'll take a whisky if you're going in there,' Patrick called as I walked away. 'Thanks, Ros.'

'"I'll take a whisky if you're going in there",' I parroted as I let myself into the cigar room, immediately choking on the thick, Cuban fug. It was every bit as awful as I'd imagined it might be. Leather recliners, tall bookcases, a poor woman in *Mad Men* cosplay, tasked with cutting and lighting the cigars, who looked about ready to throw herself through the window. I hoped she was being well paid.

'Ahoy there, Ros,' Creepy Dave crowed from his

oxblood throne. 'What are you doing in my lair? Husband-hunting?'

His assembled minions all guffawed while looking me up and down. Their wives must be so proud.

'I'm sorry, I appear to have walked into 1952 by mistake,' I replied, pouring a small glass of whisky and shooting it straight back. Bleurgh. It was incredible that you couldn't smell this hovel in the main room, Sumi must have rented every air purifier in London.

'We'll let you stay,' Creepy Dave's brother, Weird Dean, said. 'But only if you sing us a song.'

I took another swig of whisky before turning to face him.

'OK,' I replied. 'Roses are red, violets are blue, you're an arsehole, shut up.'

'Was that a haiku?' asked a voice in the corner. It was John, perched on a ledge by the bookcase. My lips parted to speak but my throat seized up at the memory of last night and everything slowed down for just a moment. His body against mine, his arms around me. And then I remembered he was married and I had a boyfriend and the world came hurtling towards me fast.

'Not quite,' I said, thinking for a moment and counting the syllables on my fingers. 'That would be, roses can be red, violets are often blue, shut up you arsehole.'

'I'm impressed,' he replied, showing off that down-turned smile of his while the rest of the menfolk went back to discussing I really didn't care what. 'Let me have a go. How's this? Last night was very weird, how can I apologize, I fucked up. Does that work?'

'Couple of syllables off but the sentiment is there,' I said, choking on a fresh plume of smoke as Creepy Dave puffed out. 'You don't have to apologize, I should apologize. I apologize. Apologies.'

The dimple in his left cheek made an appearance as he smiled.

'How come you're on the whisky?'

I looked at the glass and realized my hand was shaking.

'Desperate times?'

'Desperate measures,' John finished. 'Would you like to get some fresh air?'

With watering eyes, I looked back into the main room to see Lucy and Patrick still deep in conversation, Patrick talking and Lucy staring at him, positively rapt.

'OK,' I said, following him out the door and into the gardens. Patrick wouldn't like it, but I didn't like him cancelling on me the night before either.

It was another hot day. The notoriously reliable weathermen were still promising that the humidity would break soon and we would get an almighty downpour to test my father's shed roofing skills. I made a mental note to sleep in my cagoule for the next couple of nights.

'Did you have a good time last night?' I started as we stepped off the path and onto the lawn. Keep off the grass signs be damned. 'I mean before we saw you. And after we saw you, obviously, just generally, did you have a nice night—'

'Ros,' he said, cutting me off before I could talk myself off a cliff. 'You did know it was me, didn't you?'

'No!' I exclaimed, walking with all my weight on

the balls of my feet to avoid sinking through the soil in my spike heels. I was aerating it, they should be grateful. 'Of course I didn't, I would never.'

'What, because of Patrick?' John asked with a dark look.

'Yes but also because you're *married*,' I said, lowering my voice as I looked back into the Carriage House. 'I wouldn't do that to Patrick or your wife, it's not fair. If you're not happy then that's for you to work out bu—'

'What did you just say?' he interrupted again. 'My wife?'

'Will you stop doing that?' I sighed, moving further away from the party. 'Don't butt in while I'm talking, it pisses me off.'

He followed me across the lawn, his long legs catching up with me too quickly. 'I'll stop interrupting you when you start making sense. What are you talking about, my wife?'

'The giant blonde,' I replied, stretching my hand high up over my head. 'The really pretty woman from the bar, the one you're married to.'

'Oh, *that* wife.' He stuck his hands in his pockets and kicked a stone as he nodded. 'You mean the one I divorced two years ago?'

I looked back at him, mouth agape.

'You missed that part of the story, did you?' John asked, combing his hair out of his eyes. His forehead was already damp, it was so hot out. 'So you probably didn't get the bit where she was cheating on me then refused to give up her half of the business in the divorce because her dad gave us half the startup money. So now I have to work with my ex-wife, on the busi-nesses I built up from nothing.'

'I didn't know that,' I said, allowing my weight to fall back into my heels, anchoring myself into the ground. Everything suddenly felt unsteady. 'I'm sorry.'

He gave a dignified sniff and stared off into the distance while I took in this new information, adding it to my Facts About John pile. I already knew he worked hard and could be funny when he wanted to be. I knew he was a bit too tall but he was handsome and had quite nice hair. He was blunt and a know-it-all but he was kind and generous and caring when it mattered. And I knew that when we'd danced, I'd desperately, desperately wanted him to kiss me which made no sense, because . . . Patrick.

'I'm so sorry,' I said when we had both been quiet for altogether too long. 'Camille said she was "the wife" so, obviously, I thought . . . I didn't know about the rest of it.'

'Really must get Camille to add "ex" into her title,' he muttered. 'Force of habit, she's known her for years.'

'She didn't seem that keen,' I added and John showed a hint of a grin. 'It must be really hard for you, to have to work with your ex.'

'Well she gives about as many fucks about the business as she did about our relationship,' he replied, before shaking his head at himself. 'But I cope. I'll be able to buy her out someday. Not all of us get as lucky with our exes as you did.'

He began to walk on again and I prised my heels out of the recently watered grass, trying not to break my ankle in the process.

'Do you want to get back together with her?' I asked, trotting after him. I was starting to feel too warm once again in my Zara midi dress. Seriously, I should have burned it after the first time I wore it but I was still short on wardrobe options and would be until I got my first proper paycheck.

John looked at me over his shoulder and laughed out loud. 'Kate? Christ, no. We never should have got married in the first place. We weren't right for each other from the start but we were young, I was so sure she was the one. You know what they say, when you wear rose-tinted glasses, all the red flags are just flags.' He shielded his eyes from the sun. 'People don't change, you know, no matter how much time you give them. You just start to lower your expectations until, eventually, you're on the floor.'

John moved underneath a big oak tree. I stopped a little way away, just outside of the tree's shadow, and squinted up at him.

'That's not true,' I murmured.

'I'm not talking about your boyfriend,' he said stiffly.

'Yes, you are,' I replied. 'But it doesn't matter. I didn't expect Patrick to change, I don't want Patrick to change. I *want* things to be exactly how they were before.'

'But you can't turn the clock back, Ros.' He shook his head sadly and scratched his nose. For moment, I thought I saw the glimmer of tears in his eyes but in the next moment, they were gone. 'Trust me, I've tried.'

'You're not me, you don't know,' I said firmly. It was true, it was true, it was true. I had everything I wanted, everything I'd longed for. Patrick, my friends, my job.

'Ros, what's going on?' John stretched up to wrap his hands around an overhead bough. 'You're upset.'

285

'No, I'm not,' I answered as I snapped a leaf from one of the low-hanging branches, following its veins with my fingernail. 'Why would you say I'm upset?'

'OK, not upset,' he replied. 'You seem angry. I'm not like Patrick. I don't play games, I'm not clever with words and I don't say things I don't mean.'

'You've met him twice,' I reminded him, my temper beginning to flare. Perhaps he was right, perhaps I was angry. 'You don't even know him.'

John let go of the tree and took a step towards me. 'And does he know you?'

I crunched the leaf in my hand.

'What's that supposed to mean?'

'It means that when you're on your own you're funny and interesting and kind and I want to know everything about you. But when he's there, you're awkward and weird and always deferring to him,' he said, coming closer. 'If I had to choose, I think I preferred it when we first met and you were just rude.'

'I wasn't rude when we first met,' I replied, too heated to hear him. 'I was embarrassed. You were – doing what you were doing, after all.'

'I was referring to the part after that but good to know you haven't forgotten,' he muttered, eyes shifting awkwardly towards the sky. 'I don't like him, Ros. He's rude, he's pretentious and he doesn't care about anyone but himself.'

'Thank fuck no one's asking you to go out with him then!' I yelled, shocked at the fire in my voice. 'And he does care about other people, he cares about my friend and he cares about me.'

But as the words came out my mouth, my conviction

trailed off. Did Patrick care about me? As much as I cared about him?

'Right, if he's so brilliant then why are you standing out here, talking to me, instead of sitting in there and listening to him?'

I looked up at him, one, maybe two steps away from me, dark hair falling in front of his dark eyes that were more hazel than brown in the sun. I heard the sound of ragged breath and realized that it wasn't coming from me. Or at least, not only from me.

'Did you know it was me last night?' John asked quietly.

'No,' I answered honestly, my anger seeping away. 'Did you know? That it was me?'

He replied with a nod.

'I couldn't sleep last night for thinking about you,' he said, stepping closer.

I searched the grass for any response he might accept and that I could live with. From the moment I'd left Sumi to the moment I'd finally fallen asleep, I hadn't thought about anything else. And when I closed my eyes, it was John's face I saw in front of me, not Patrick's.

Neither of us said a word, neither of us moved an inch.

Even though we weren't quite touching, I could feel him through the heavy summer air. Last night we'd been pressed together, hip to hip, heart to heart, but he felt so much closer now. His hand reached for my face and I felt the very tips of his fingers graze my cheek.

'I'm sorry,' I said, breaking away and taking one small step backwards.

Then another, then another.

'I'm really sorry, John.'

He opened his mouth to say something but, before he could, I bent over to take off my shoes, turned back towards the Carriage House and ran.

CHAPTER TWENTY-SIX

'Where have you been hiding?' Patrick asked as I dashed back into the baby shower.

'I was outside,' I said, slipping my feet back into my shoes and looking around for Sumi or Adrian or Lucy, anyone I could talk to.

'Are you OK?' He pressed the back of his hand against my forehead. 'Do you feel all right? You're quite warm.'

'I need some water,' I replied, my cheeks still hot and flushed. I certainly couldn't talk to Patrick. 'Are you going to tell me Lucy's baby names or what?'

'Sorry, I made a promise,' he replied, holding his hand against his chest in mock shock. 'But if you want to try to wrestle it out of me, I won't stop you.'

'Maybe we should go,' I suggested. Lucy was back in her chair, surrounded by her acolytes, and Sumi was nowhere to be seen. Adrian, however, was by the bar, sipping a carrot juice smoothie and gazing into the eyes of a girl with long black coils all the way down her back. They were staring at each other so intently, it looked as though they were checking for cataracts. I was so happy for them both but something inside me swelled with sadness. I just wanted to leave.

'Already?' Patrick asked, almost disbelieving with relief. 'You mean I don't have to stay and schmooze?'

'It's OK,' I told him, one eye on the back door. 'You're not here to win over my friends.'

Still no sign of John.

'I'm not?' He was understandably confused. 'Then why am I here? I certainly didn't come to play What's in the Nappy.'

'You came to be here, with me,' I said, nodding and busying my hands by straightening his tie. 'You're here because I'm here. We're here together.'

'But we could be together at my place,' he whispered in my ear. 'Just the two of us, no one else. Wouldn't that be more fun?'

Yes, I told myself, that's what I wanted. What I'd always wanted. What I finally had. I turned my face up to meet him and pressed my lips to his and pushed away any and all thoughts of John McMahon.

'Let me find my jacket and we'll sneak out,' I said, running my hand down the front of his body, hooking my fingers in his waistband. If only I'd gone over to his flat the night before instead of meeting Sumi and going to that stupid disco. 'I'll meet you out front in a minute.'

Patrick did not need telling twice. Without a second thought of his new best friend Lucy, he strode out of the party and straight down the rabbit warren, while I searched for my denim jacket. I'd had it when I arrived and I'd put it down when . . .

'I helped them move the giant rabbit,' I whispered

to myself. There it was, a stonewash sleeve poking out from underneath the rabbit's left bum cheek. Creeping over, I bobbed down, trying to balance in my heels and long dress, and grabbed hold of the jacket. I tugged gently, but nothing happened.

'What are you doing?'

I looked up to see John looming over me.

'Clearly, I am trying to get my jacket out from underneath this rabbit,' I replied, yanking harder. 'What does it look like I'm doing?'

'Running away from a difficult conversation or molesting a giant stuffed animal.'

'I'm not running away,' I said, gripping the jacket with both hands. Why did a rabbit need to be so bloody heavy? 'I'm leaving to spend the rest of the day with my boyfriend.'

'In that case, why don't you let me help you,' John said, bending over to grab a handful of denim. He heaved my jacket out from under the wobbling rabbit and threw it into my arms. 'Here.'

The bunny teetered behind me as I stared at him, clutching my jacket to me like a safety blanket. I wanted to say something, do something, only I didn't know what. I wanted it to be all right and it wasn't.

'Ros! John!'

But we turned too late. The oversized cuddly toy fell face forward, right on top of the pair of us, knocking us both to the floor. I landed on top of John, pinned flat by an errant arm.

'Shit,' I said through clenched teeth, trying to roll out of a John, Ros and Rabbit sandwich without showing the entire room my knickers. 'Shit shit shit.'

'Ros?' John whispered urgently.

'What?' I replied, meeting his eyes as a rescue effort mounted beyond the rabbit. He was smiling. Without a word, he put his lips to mine and kissed me.

Short, sharp, electric.

I pulled back, stunned, just as the bunny was successfully raised by Adrian, Eva, Creepy Dave and Weird Dean.

'Are you hurt?' Eva asked, offering a hand to help me up and Ade pulled John to his feet. 'Do we need to call an ambulance?'

'I'm fine, thank you,' I insisted, still clutching my jacket in both hands. 'Also, you are very strong.'

'I teach CrossFit,' Eva nodded. 'Nice to meet you.'

'And you,' I murmured, catching John's eye and pressing my fingers to my lips. 'I'm just going to pop out and get some fresh air, excuse me.'

'I'll come with you,' he offered.

'No you won't,' I shouted, running out the rabbit warren and back into the real world, where Patrick was waiting.

CHAPTER TWENTY-SEVEN

'Anyone home?' I asked as I let myself into my parents' extremely hot kitchen the next evening and immediately downed a giant glass of water. It seemed as though the entire country had been stuck in a sauna and I wasn't coping. Maybe that was why my brain was messing with me. It was just too bloody hot for rational thought. I'd seen them talk about heat-induced psychosis on *BBC Breakfast* and if it was on the BBC, didn't it have to be true?

To atone for whatever it was that had happened under that rabbit, I had spent the rest of the weekend doing all of Patrick's favourite things: watching foreign films, preparing complicated food that ended up tasting like shite and melting as we walked around parts of a heatwave-stricken London that I, and every single other person I knew, was too afraid to travel through, even on the bus. It was prejudice against poverty that kept us away, Patrick explained, not the fact there was nothing to do and the one pub he wanted to go to had been closed because a secret cockfighting ring had been uncovered there a week before. We had to fight that prejudice by facing it, Patrick explained, he'd learned that in Yangon. He seemed slightly less chipper when we finally got back to the tube station and he realized someone had stolen his wallet out of his back pocket but still, it seemed like overall he'd had a nice time.

And I had barely thought about the kiss at all.

'I'm in here,' Mum called from the living room. 'Your dad's at the club and we're on sugared almond duty.'

Every Sunday for the last five years, Dad went to that bloody tennis club in his tennis gear, carrying a tennis racquet, and he came back three hours later, half cut, and passed out on the living room sofa until *Songs of Praise*. None of us had ever seen him play a single set of tennis. It really was a wonder their marriage had lasted so long.

I set my bag down on the back of my armchair and joined my mum on the floor, where she was surrounded by dozens of little voile bags and a plastic bag of sugared almonds so big it could have ended world hunger. My mother had her glasses on, her hair tied back and was wearing a string bikini. In fairness, she was looking amazing.

'Please tell me Dad put a hot tub in while I was at the baby shower?' I said, crossing my legs to sit down opposite her.

'Every year for the last five years I've told your dad we need to get air conditioning and every year he says the weather won't last,' she grumbled as she pulled a cardigan off the settee and slid her arms into the sleeves. 'This is the last year. I'm calling someone next week and getting it done. It's too bloody hot.'

'Don't put the cardi on for my benefit.' I peeled off my shoes and socks to reveal my slightly-worse-for-wear pedicure. 'I was going to ask if you'd got another bikini.'

'Two bikinis?' she clucked. 'Why would I need two bikinis? And we did talk about getting a hot tub at the bottom of the garden, your dad could have got a good deal on one, but you've got your shed instead.'

There was definitely a hint of accusation in her voice.

'How was the baby shower?'

I helped myself to a handful of sugared almonds and began filling bags.

'Good.' I replied, popping one of the sugared almonds in my mouth. 'Mum, how did you know you wanted to marry Dad?'

She grabbed another dozen bags, pulled them all open at the top and gave me a look. 'Is this because your dad told you I was pregnant when we got engaged?'

'No,' I replied in between sucks on the sweet. I'd forgotten how awful these things were. 'But also yes.'

'I didn't marry your dad because I was pregnant, I married your dad because I loved him,' Mum answered. 'Fancied him too, which I suppose is how I got in trouble.'

'"Got in trouble",' I repeated, chomping down on the almond. 'Thank god we don't say that any more.'

'You wait until you're pregnant and you'll find out

how much bloody trouble it is,' she said, slapping my hand away from the bag of sweets. 'Thirty-two years later and I'm still in trouble.'

'I just wanted to see if both flavours are equally disgusting,' I whined, feigning hurt and rubbing my hand. 'Why do we even have these?'

'It's good luck,' Mum answered. 'And I wanted them at the first one but your nan said we couldn't have them because they'd break her teeth.'

'And they won't break them this time?'

'They might,' she replied with a wicked smile.

'So you just knew?' I said, abandoning my task and lying back on the living room carpet. 'That you were going to marry him?'

Mum looked up at the living room ceiling and smiled a smile that was far too happy for someone who was contemplating some really quite dodgy Artexing.

'The first time your dad kissed me, I felt like I was floating,' she said. 'It felt like we were the only two people on earth who knew this incredible secret and I never wanted it to stop.'

'Gross,' I muttered.

'You asked.' Mum put down her stack of little voile bags and gave me a good, hard, maternal stare. 'What's going on? You've only been back two minutes, surely there isn't a proposal in the offing?'

I took a deep breath and looked at her, my mouth clamped shut.

'*Stiffen the sinews, summon up the blood,*' she trilled, one of her all-time favourite quotes. 'Out with it.'

'Do you remember Patrick? The one I was seeing before I left?'

She reached for her cup of tea as though it were something stronger. I wondered, for just a moment, if it was.

'You *do* remember him then.'

'I do,' she replied in a tone that suggested that, while she remembered, she did not necessarily approve.

'We've been seeing each other again.'

'Right.'

'My friends aren't especially impressed.'

'Should they be?' she asked, allowing me to sneak a second sugared almond. The blue ones were just as rank as the pink. 'As I recall, it didn't end terribly well.'

'It's complicated,' I told her. 'But we were both at fault.'

She sipped her tea in her cardigan and bikini while I carried on putting sugared almonds in bags, waiting for her next move.

'We met him once, didn't we?' she asked eventually. 'He was the writer, the clever one?'

'Yes,' I confirmed, pleased with the description. He'd like that, my former literature professor mother remembered him as clever. 'But you make it sound like a bad thing.'

'Not at all,' Mum replied. 'I'm clever, you're clever. But I wouldn't want it to be the first thing people thought of when my name came up.'

I'd never heard her complain when people went out of their way to tell her how clever Jo was, although, to be fair, the word used most often in that scenario was genius. Not that it bothered me *at all*.

'What's so bad about people thinking you're clever?'

'There are a million things a person can be and

clever is a decent piece of the puzzle,' she said kindly. 'But I would hope you would think of a lot of other words to describe me first. Kind, funny . . . snazzy dresser?'

With an eye roll and a snicker, I felt the sugared almond get sucked into the back of my throat and immediately spat it out into my hand. The sweets were out to get me. *Funny and kind.* Those were two of the words John had used to describe me. At least me when Patrick wasn't around. Clever Patrick.

'I don't know,' I said, arranging my sugared almonds into patterns on the floor. 'I always liked how clever he was.'

Mum added a blue almond to my pink trail. 'But?' she prompted, sensing the word before I could say it.

'Patrick is everything I ever wanted,' I began, not quite sure where I was going to end up. 'And now he wants me. Or at least I think he does. But something isn't quite right.'

Picking up a reel of white ribbon and a pair of scissors, Mum slowly rolled out the ribbon and began snipping it into six-inch lengths.

'Ros,' she said, rolling and snipping, rolling and snipping. 'Do you know why there are so many books about people falling in love and people getting their hearts broken?'

'Because we're all simple idiots?' I suggested.

'Not quite,' she replied as I swept my almonds into one tidy pile. 'It's because it fits quite nicely into the pages of a paperback. A real love story – a true, enduring love story with all its ups and down and compromises and ugly and petty and mundane moments – would be longer than a phone book and not nearly as interesting. Grand passion might make for a good read but it doesn't make for a happy life.'

'OK,' I said, filling an empty bag with almonds to avoid looking at the boob that was trying to escape from the left cup of her swimsuit.

'There's nothing glamorous about going to bed with a headache and waking up to find your husband has done the dishes but I'm telling you, dearest daughter, I'd take that over a thousand lovestruck Mr Darcys, any day of the week.'

I gasped. Speaking ill of Austen was tantamount to heresy in my mother's presence.

'Once the bloom is off the rose of romance, clever doesn't get you as far as you might like,' Mum said with her breast now flying free. 'Same goes for brooding and intense and mysterious. Basically anything you would have looked for in a man when you were studying for an English degree. Throw it all out the window.'

'Books do a real number on us, don't they?' I said with half a laugh.

'If it weren't books, it'd be films,' she nodded. 'At least you're literate, I don't take that for granted. What I will say is, all any mother wants is for her child to be happy and you don't look especially happy to me.'

I looked at her and frowned. 'Mum, your boob fell out.'

'Bloody hell,' she muttered, promptly putting it

away. 'That's all I need to hear. That you're going out with this clever chap because he makes you happy.'

'He's not just clever,' I replied, very interested in my toenails again all at once. 'He's lots of things.'

Mum raised her eyebrows in silent rebuttal.

'He's fascinating, I could listen to him talk for hours and never get bored,' I went on, absently stuffing nuts into the little gift bag. 'He's travelled all over the world, he loves to learn about new things, he's really driven. And he's funny, not ha-ha funny but still really funny. And not to go into detail but I still get butterflies every time I see him. That's important, isn't it? At least at the beginning.'

'Very important,' Mum agreed. 'And those are all wonderful qualities but they're not going to run out and buy you a box of tampons in the middle of the night when you've got the flu. What else do you like about him?'

'I can always buy them in bulk,' I replied. I'd expected listing Patrick's positive attributes to be an easier task but it wasn't coming as quickly as I'd expected. I couldn't in all honesty call him kind, even though he wasn't mean. He wasn't exactly generous in nature, even though he had his moments. And he could be as hot as the seventh circle of hell but he definitely wasn't warm.

'Does he make you happy?' she asked.

'Yes,' I replied immediately.

'Happy when you're with him, not happy that he's with you,' she corrected carefully.

'He does make me happy,' I said, looking for the truth. There was no point lying now. 'Only it feels so different to before. I get frustrated and anxious. I'm not always sure he's listening to me. To be honest, things aren't going exactly the way I thought they would.'

'Things rarely do,' she said, delivering sage wisdom with a light touch, in that way only mums seemed to know how. 'But you'll know what to do when you know what to do.'

'That does not feel helpful,' I smiled, my bag of almonds slipping out of my fingers and falling into my lap. I watched the candy-coloured nuts spill onto the hardwood floor before rolling away into adventure under the settee.

Mum shrugged and combed my hair back off my face, holding my eyes with a smile of her own. 'You'll work it out, Ros, no one else can do it for you. I know you'll sort it out, you always do.'

'Thanks, Mum,' I said, chewing on my bottom lip to stop my eyes from welling up. I hadn't realized just how much I'd missed her and not just while I was in America. Ever since Jo came along when I was four-teen, I couldn't remember us spending any real one-on-one time together. 'I should go and get some work done. Big week coming up.'

She gave a nod and set back to work on the sugared almonds. 'Make sure you're getting enough rest. You're working every hour god sends at the moment. I see that light on all night.'

'Yes, Mum,' I said, giving her a peck on the cheek. 'And for the record, the first thing I tell anyone about you is what a snazzy dresser you are.'

'Get on back to your shed,' she clucked, cracking the back of my legs as I scrambled to my feet, laughing. 'Let's wait and see the state of you when you're sixty.'

'If I make it to sixty . . .' I muttered, making a hasty exit via the kitchen and the biscuit barrel. There was too much to think about: Patrick, John, Lucy and the baby, and on top of that, work? Thank god everything made more sense with a Hobnob.

CHAPTER TWENTY-EIGHT

'Ros!'

The knock at the door of my studio was followed by a gurning Ted, weighed down by a cardboard box that was slightly too big for the doorframe. I swivelled around in my chair to watch him shuffle it this way and that, to no avail.

'All right there?' I called, remaining right where I was. It was Tuesday and I hadn't seen a single soul in my cave for more than a week. Whenever I emerged, Gollum-like, to grab something from the fridge, everyone on the main floor stopped what they were doing and watched me, as though I were a Victorian orphan rummaging through their personal snacks. So, no, I didn't exactly rush to help him out even though my self-imposed rudeness cut me to the bone.

'Won't . . . fucken . . . fit,' he grumbled before dropping the box on the floor and kicking it inside. 'There we go. Where there's a will and all that. How's your day going?'

'What's in the box, Ted?' I asked, unmoved by his

pleasantries. I'd only been working there for a couple of weeks but I already knew better than to trust a Ted bearing gifts.

'You're going to love it,' he replied. 'It's for Friday.'

The other half of my studio already looked like a warehouse, absolutely rammed with cardboard boxes. They were piled so precariously I had to text Lucy every time I went in there in case they collapsed on top of me and no one upstairs noticed. We had posters and flyers and badges and cardboard versions of all of Snazzlechuff's various masks for the WESC audience to wear, as well as USB sticks, water bottles, mini fans in case it was hot, scarves in case it was cold, and what looked like adorable branded flannels but I had been assured were little, tiny towels that the audience would whip around above their heads to show their appreciation. I had shown my appreciation for them by taking half a dozen home so I could double cleanse with wild abandon. Never had my face been so clean. Ted had spent more on branded merch for a podcast that still did not exist than he had on me. But still, I *was* getting free flannels so who was really winning?

My boss opened the box slowly, lifting one flap at a time and attempting to make a drumroll sound with his mouth but since he couldn't really roll his Rs, it sounded more like a wet fart, which somewhat sucked the tension out of the moment.

'Whaddya think?' he asked as he yanked a huge, furry tiger's head out of the box and held it aloft.

'Ted, did you sacrifice a tiger?' I whispered as he presented it to me, proudly. It was far too lifelike for its own good. 'I know the podcast is important to you but those things are endangered.'

'It's not real,' he scoffed, placing it very carefully on my desk where it stared at me, mouth slightly ajar, as though about to say something profound. Like, 'They're grrreat!'

'Why is it here?' I asked, turning it around to face the wall.

'Because Snazz's first mask was a tiger mask,' Ted explained, as though he were going through the fundamentals of astrophysics with a one-year-old. 'When he first started out, he wore a tiger mask so I had a new one commissioned in his honour. We're going to get someone to wear it around the convention to hand out flyers before we record, make sure we've got a packed house. I woke up in the middle of the night and it hit me, just like: tiger mask . . .'

'Brilliant,' I replied, wondering if Ted had a girl-friend. Or a boyfriend. It really didn't matter either way, but he did need to get out more. 'I think it's going to go well, there's already been loads of interest. A full house is pretty much guaranteed.'

And even though I couldn't quite believe it, it was true. I'd had more enquiries about this podcast than anything I had ever worked on before. Which was equal parts exciting and incredibly depressing.

'And Beezer Go-Go and PsychoBang know exactly where they need to be and when?' Ted asked, absently petting the tiger's head.

Beezer Go-Go and the questionably named PsychoBang, the co-hosts for our first episode, were both under twenty-one and already worth more than ten million apiece, according to the internet. And to think my mum wouldn't let me and Jo have a PlayStation because she said it would rot our brains.

'Everything is ready to go,' I confirmed. 'I've run through it all a dozen times, we're sorted.'

'And you're scheduled to record the rest of the series next week?'

'Yes,' I nodded. 'Happy summer holidays, Snazzlechuff.'

'I'll arrange something special,' Ted said, more to himself than me. 'We'll get a chef in to cook. Or I'll fly pizza over from Chicago. He loves Chicago pizza.'

'Is that even something you can do?' I asked. Ted gave me the same look you might give someone's toddler who had just found out you can actually take the things you see in shops home with you.

'I know gaming isn't exactly your vibe.' He added bunny ears to the term to try to make it more palatable. 'But if this goes well, maybe we'll, like, have a go at one of your book shows or something.'

'Really?' I felt my heart lift.

'Yeah, yeah, yeah,' Ted nodded. 'We listened to some of your old shows and they're, like, not shit.'

The highest of praise.

'You listened to The Book Report?' I asked, glowing from head to toe nevertheless.

'Not me,' he spluttered. 'One of the nerds that, like, *reads*. But you know. You're good.'

I was *good*. It was validation I needed to hear more than I cared to admit.

'Get this right and it's a big foot in the door for you, Ros.'

'And if I get it wrong, it's my foot and the rest of me out the door?' I joked.

'I love your sense of humour,' Ted laughed before looking at me with an entirely straight face. 'But yes, that is correct, I will have to let you go.' He carefully placed the tiger head back into the box, holding his breath until the tissue paper was replaced and the lid was safely secure. 'Protect this with your life.'

'To the grave,' I swore as he showed himself out.

Once I heard his footsteps tap all the way back upstairs, I poked into the box with my toe, opening the flap and lifting up the tissue paper. It was hideous.

'Get through this, make it a success, and the Washington situation won't matter,' I whispered to myself. 'No gaming, no teenagers, no Ted.'

The tiger stared back at me.

'Thanks for the vote of support, Tony,' I muttered, turning back to my computer.

This week was going to go on forever.

'OK, so where did you run off to on Saturday afternoon?' Sumi dumped her full-to-bursting bag down beside her later that evening. I'd tempted her away from work with the promise of treats at the latest addition to London's thrilling dessert scene, Yo, a café that specialized in and sold nothing but fro-yo. If there was one thing Sumi was powerless against, it was frozen yoghurt.

'Well, unfortunately you missed my performance,' I told her, craning my neck up for a kiss on the cheek. 'Since you hadn't arranged any entertainment, I thought it might be fun for me to pull that giant rabbit down on top of myself.'

'Oh, I know,' she replied. 'I saw the photos.'

I felt my nostrils flare. 'Who took photos?'

'Creepy Dave, Weird Dean, every single one of those pregnant women,' she counted off the culprits on her fingertips. 'And don't look like that because you would have done the same if it was them.'

'Not if it was one of the pregnant women,' I sniffed. 'At least not if she was really pregnant. Did John stick around long?'

'John?' Sumi looked up from her phone before slinging it into her bag. 'I thought he'd left with you two?'

I shook my head. I had decided it was best not to tell her about our conversation or about the kiss. There was nothing to tell so there was no point. It wasn't fair to put her in the middle of a thing that didn't even exist. But on the other hand, if I didn't tell her, I would explode then and there in the middle of the café and that would create such a mess for someone to clean up.

'I hope you can live with yourself, knowing you missed out on a thrilling fucking game of Stick the Pin on the Nappy,' she said, glancing over at the next table where a woman with a sleeping baby strapped to her chest was spooning frozen yoghurt into her mouth, over the top of the baby's head. 'It was a lot, I don't blame you for leaving, but you could have told me before you vanished. I'm still technically pissed off with you.'

'I could have and I'm sorry,' I agreed. 'I'm a shit.'

'Yes, you are, but luckily for you, I need to talk to you about something.' She piled her long black hair back over her shoulder, the annoyance fading from her face. 'Lucy enjoyed it though? I think she did.'

'She definitely did,' I said. I frowned as she pulled her phone out again, opened her emails and threw it back in her bag. She seemed too tense for someone

about to eat their body weight in frozen dairy delights.
'Sumi, what's wrong?'

'Evening, ladies,' the waiter came back around, pen and paper at the ready. 'What can I get you?'

Sumi looked up and stared at me, big brown eyes wide open and entirely serious.

'I want to have a baby.'

'I'll come back in a minute,' the waiter replied.

'Please come back with two large glasses of white wine,' I said.

'We don't serve wine,' he said quietly. 'Why don't I bring you some fro-yo samples while you work out what you'd like?' Before I could respond, he ran across the café floor and disappeared behind the wall of frozen yoghurt dispensers.

'What are you talking about?' I said, resting my forearms on the table and leaning towards her. 'You've never mentioned wanting kids before, what's going on? Talk to me.'

'Ros, I'm older than you,' she began.

'You're two years older than me,' I reminded her. 'You literally just turned thirty-five ten days ago.'

'And do you know what that is in lesbian years?' she asked. I shook my head. I did not. 'Well, it's thirty-five because lesbian years aren't a thing but, my point is, everyone's life is moving forward and I'm stuck. You went away and had this amazing career adventure in the US, Adrian is going to be married by Christmas at the rate he's moving and Lucy is *already* married, living in a gorgeous house, about to have an actual baby and the happiest person I have ever met. What am I doing with my life? Nothing.'

'Apart from your very important job? And your very

lovely architect girlfriend and being a badass?' I corrected. Shocked wasn't the word. Sumi, out of all of us, had always been the one who knew exactly what she wanted and went for it. She was living her best life before anyone even knew that's what they were supposed to be doing. I couldn't believe what I was hearing.

'I didn't want to put it up for debate until I was sure in my own mind,' she said slowly. 'It's not an overnight decision, it's something that's always been in the back of my mind. I'm not Lucy, I'm not going to meet a man and just "get" pregnant, am I? I always knew there would have to be planning involved and that's what I'm doing now. Planning.'

'And what does Jemima think?'

Sumi pursed her lips and looked upwards, blinking. 'Jemima isn't sure she wants a baby,' she replied. 'But I do. I know I do. There won't be a better time for me to do this and I've told Jemima if she doesn't want to do it with me, I'll understand but my mind is made up.'

The waiter reappeared and slipped half a dozen small paper cups of frozen yoghurt on the table. 'I'll just leave these here for now,' he whispered before melting away.

'You're really serious?' I said as Sumi dug into the salted caramel sample. Halfway to tears, breaking the news of the biggest decision she would likely ever make and she still wasn't about to miss out on her fro-yo. At least I knew it was really her and not some very sophisticated clone.

She looked up from her dessert to fix me with a very serious stare. 'When have I not been serious?' she asked.

'When you were going to adopt a dog from

Russia, when you decided we were all going to be vegan, when you said we should go to Japan for Christmas, when you went to look at that tiny house in Wimbledon and put an offer in and then cancelled it and then put it in again and—' I said, counting off examples on my hand.

'Fine, yes, got the point,' she said, cutting me off. 'But this is different. I can feel it in my bones. I want a baby and I don't want to wait until I'm any older to be a mum. I can afford to take care of a family on my own, I can afford to buy a house. Now is the time and I'm going to do it.'

I picked up a cup of yoghurt and dipped the tip of my spoon in thoughtfully. Lemon curd. It was OK.

'Go on then,' Sumi said. 'Tell me what you're thinking.'

'I'm thinking about how everything keeps changing,' I said with a sad smile. 'And how this is the biggest change yet.'

Sumi set down her spoon and sighed, pressing her palms against her face. 'Right, I'm sorry but I've got to say this. I love you, Ros, and I am so fucking happy you're back, but this obsession you've got with missing your old life, with how everything was better "before" has got to stop. Before didn't exist!'

I dropped my spoon on the floor and leaned over to pick it back up, hair covering my burning face.

'Lucy had already moved in with Dave before you left and I only stuck it out in that shithole because I knew you wanted me there,' she went on. 'We weren't ecstatically happy little elves, running around London shitting rainbows. We were broke kids, struggling to get by, struggling to be heard, and we made the best of it.'

'So you're saying you hated it?' I asked. I was stung. 'It was a nightmare, was it?'

'No, it wasn't a nightmare,' she said, holding her hands out and looking up to the ceiling as though it might help her out. 'It was brilliant and shit and fine and everything life is, depending on the day of the week. I loved my twenties but I'm also happy they're in the past. It's like you've convinced yourself it was utterly idyllic and I can't work out why. Where has this "Everything was great when I were a lass" attitude come from? I'm trying to tell you I'm ready to move on to the next chapter in my life and you're sat there wishing we were in our pyjamas in a house that didn't have a living room, eating the Chinese takeaway we could only afford once a month and wondering whether or not some dickhead is going to reply to your text? It's starting to get pathetic.'

I looked down at the other samples of yoghurt while I let her words simmer. Pathetic? I was pathetic?

'Will you talk to me please?' Sumi said, tapping two fingers on the table under my nose. 'Help me understand, Ros. I know moving back home isn't exactly a dream come true but you've got a good job, you've got that tit Parker back – which you'd think would have you cock-a-hoop – *and* you got to work in America for three years which is an opportunity most people would kill for—'

'And would they kill for the opportunity to be shit at the job and get fired?' I asked, raising my head sharply.

Sumi blinked at me, confused.

'I got the sack,' I said, dipping my spoon into the coconut. It was fine. 'I hated my life in DC. I was lonely and miserable and I got the sack. Does that help?'

I turned away and gazed out the window.

'What do you mean, you got the sack?' Sumi asked.

'They let me go,' I replied, remembering the conversation so clearly. Sitting there in my boss's office, the HR person explaining they were terminating my contract, my boss refusing to make eye contact, and me, just sitting there, overwhelmed with shame. 'I wasn't good enough and I got the sack. The end.'

'Why didn't you tell me?' she asked, softening her voice and reaching for my hand. 'Ros?'

'Because I was embarrassed,' I replied, closing my eyes and breathing in. As soon as I said it, I felt incredibly stupid.

'You were embarrassed to tell me you lost your job?' Sumi squeezed my hand and I opened one eye to see a small smile on her face. 'Seriously? Even though I know your deepest, darkest secrets?'

I sniffed and squeezed her hand back.

'Don't you dare,' I warned in a thick voice.

'Even though I know you had a wee in your cat's litter tray when you were twelve?' she said. 'Even though I know you found out the hard way that a blow job does not mean you blow on a penis?'

'Oh my god, shut up,' I groaned, pulling my hand away and covering my face.

'Even though I had to take you to A&E after you tried to use cotton wool as a makeshift tampon and were convinced you had toxic shock syndrome?'

'I was wondering if you'd like to order now?' asked the ashen-faced waiter. We looked up at his pale face and trembling lower lip and burst into hysterics.

'Two large originals,' Sumi said, gasping for breath. 'With chocolate chips for her, coconut shreds and strawberries for me.'

He nodded and left. No further questions.

'Tell me exactly what happened,' she ordered. 'I want to know all of it.'

'It was horrible, I felt so worthless,' I told her, so relieved I could have laughed. 'It was fun at first, being in DC, but then it got on top of me and I was just so lonely. There were days at the weekend when I didn't get off the settee because what was the point? And I didn't know how to get myself out of it.'

'Oh, Ros.' Sumi looked like she might cry. 'Why didn't you tell me?'

'I wanted to but I couldn't,' I whispered. 'I didn't know how to start the conversation without sounding pathetic. And ever since I got back, it feels like all these doors are closing to me. Lucy is further away, Adrian's got his girlfriend, even my parents don't want me around. And now you're going to take this incredible, incredible step, which I am so happy about and I'm sorry if it seemed as though I wasn't because I am, I really am.'

She nodded in silence, her face open and kind and there for me, and it was enough.

'It was easier before, everything was up for grabs. Something didn't work out, you just did something else. Now it feels as though I have one less choice, one less option every day,' I said, reaching for words I had struggled to find until now. 'I know it's not just me, I know lots of people are having a hard time right now, but I don't know how to fix it and I feel as though I used to, or we used to.'

314

'Don't get upset,' Sumi said, slowly, carefully. 'But have you thought about talking to someone about this? A counsellor maybe? Only, I've been seeing one to talk about all the baby stuff and it's life-changing. Not saying you need to or have to but just putting it on the table. It sounds like you've really been struggling.'

A rush of affection for my best friend ran through me. I'd dreaded this conversation, like I was trapped in a dark room all on my own, but now it was as though someone had pulled the curtains open from the outside. There was a light at last.

'Have you talked to Patrick about any of this?' she asked. 'What does he say?'

I clenched my jaw and made a fist, suddenly tense. 'I can't talk to Patrick about any of this,' I told her. 'I don't want him to know I got the sack, about any of it.'

Sumi raised an eyebrow but said nothing as the waiter reappeared with two immense-looking buckets of frozen yoghurt. He placed them on the table in front of us and backed away, eyes wide and transfixed, half bowing as he went. Either he was terrified of us or he was in love with us. Possibly both.

'I talked to John,' I said lightly.

'Oh,' Sumi dug into her dessert with a neutral expression on her pretty face. 'Did you now?'

'And I might have kissed him.'

She looked up so quickly, I was afraid her head would snap clean off. A spoon of yoghurt that had been headed for her mouth, sticking her in the neck.

'*What do you mean, you kissed him?*' she screamed.

'All right, calm down,' I whispered, smiling nervously at the mother and her stirring baby beside us.

'You literally just told me you're going to bring a life into the world and I didn't even raise my voice.'

'I'm having a baby, I'm not breeding chimeras,' she replied, her voice lowered by barely a fraction. 'What do you mean, you kissed John? When? Where? How? And again, what the fuck?'

'At the baby shower, under the stuffed rabbit, with my lips,' I groaned. Worst game of Cluedo ever. 'Technically he kissed me, I was the kissee, not the kisser. I don't even know how it happened.'

Sumi pffted loudly. 'It happened because he's obviously got a raging boner for you. How dare you sit there and tell me how terrible things are when you're casually getting it on with one of the most beautiful men my gay self has ever seen, Rosalind Reynolds, you are a disgrace.'

'Sumi!' I suddenly very much wished we had opted for an establishment that had wine. 'It's not like that.'

'Yeah, yeah, yeah, you're unhappy and confused and you don't know what you're doing and we'll get to that,' she said, waving away the last ten minutes of emotional revelations. 'You snogged John at the baby shower? Now with the details please.'

'That's it, that's the whole thing,' I insisted before biting my lip. 'Except we also had a bit of a dance at the dark disco. A sexy dance.'

Sumi gasped, loudly and dramatically, with her entire body.

'And just like with everything else, I have no idea what's going on.'

'Your honour, I refer you to my first point,' she replied. 'John's raging boner. Wait, you kissed under the rabbit? That is kinky.'

'It doesn't matter,' I said, my fingers finding my lips as my memory tiptoed back to the kiss. Short, sharp and electric. I could still feel it. 'It's not happening again. I just had to tell you before I exploded.'

'Whatever you say,' Sumi confirmed, resuming her serious expression. 'I am listening.'

'Did you know he was divorced?' I asked.

She nodded. 'Oh yeah. One of my mates at the firm did his divorce. That's how we met. Adrian thought he could train him up as a new wingman but me and Lucy couldn't put him through that off the back of a nasty break-up.'

'I heard it wasn't great?'

'The nastiest,' Sumi confirmed. 'You must have seen her at the bar, she's always there, haunting the place. Blonde? Pretty? Very tall. Two red horns poking out of her forehead and a forked tail sticking out her arse. Cheated on him with one of their friends and then refused to sell him the business. It's so messy.'

'Poor John,' I said slowly, my heart lurching at the thought of how hard that must have been for him.

'Not that it matters to you.' Sumi leaned back in her chair, a calm coming over her face.

'It doesn't?' I asked.

'No,' she replied. 'Because you've got Patrick.'

'Right, yes,' I agreed. 'Patrick.'

'I don't get it,' Sumi said, watching me shovel my fro-yo. It really was very good, even if it wasn't wine. 'All you've ever wanted was Patrick Parker. And now you've got him, you don't want him? Come on, Ros, you're not that kind of girl. What's going on?'

'I just want things to feel easy again,' I replied, sure of my answer for the first time in what felt like forever.

'I'm tired of being tired. And stressed and on edge. I want to wake up in the morning and have all the answers. That's all I want, for life to be easy.'

'Well, I can't help you there,' Sumi said sadly, sticking her spoon into my dessert. 'I'm a brown lesbian who's about to use a sperm donor to become a single mother. I don't know if I've ever known what easy feels like.'

'You know I love you,' I told her, pushing my yoghurt away. 'And I want you to know I'm here for you for all of it, start to finish. Except not the literal start or the literal finish because I don't want to look at your vagina. But everything else, I'm one hundred percent yours.'

'The further you stay from my vag, the happier I'll be,' she said with glistening eyes. 'Look at us making emotional breakthroughs over frozen yoghurt. Lucy would be so proud of us. And to think, I almost went vegan.'

I looked at her face, a face I knew as well as my own, and found myself smiling. It was so strange to see my Sumi without a smirk or a grin. Something had changed in her but it suited her.

'You've got to talk to Patrick,' she said.

'I know,' I said with a sigh. 'He's coming to the podcast recording on Friday and to Mum and Dad's ceremony. I need to figure this out.'

'Who knows?' she said, waving her spoon around in the air. 'Maybe I've been wrong about him all this time and he'll be wonderful. Maybe he'll be able to help you.'

I nodded but something inside me sank sadly. Even though I wanted to agree with her, I knew in my heart that I couldn't.

'You're going to have a baby, aren't you?' I said, finding a smile for my friend.

She nodded and rested her elbows on the table, cradling her chin in her hands.

'Ros?'

'Sumi.'

'Can I ask you something?'

I reached my spoon into her fro-yo and grabbed a scoop with a side of strawberries. 'Shoot.'

'How was the kiss with John?' she asked, batting her eyes at me.

'Oh, sod off,' I mumbled, looking away.

'Oh dear,' she grinned. 'You are in trouble.'

CHAPTER TWENTY-NINE

By Friday morning, I was a wreck.

The entire week had been eaten up by production prep and wedding planning, leaving me with only the odd minute here and there to worry about my own life. Thankfully, Patrick was caught up with a deadline and hadn't had time to see me before the podcast recording, which he'd sworn up and down on the graves of assorted family members that he was going to attend, and all my friends were preoccupied by their lives. Adrian with Eva, Sumi with work and Lucy with being 'too fat to live', to quote her directly. While I hadn't given an awful lot of thought as to when I would prefer to be pregnant, the height of summer seemed like the worst possible option. I was only carrying a food baby from all my stress eating and that was uncomfortable enough. I couldn't begin to imagine what an extra thirty pounds strapped to your ribs must feel like.

'Hey, Ted,' I tapped my boss on the shoulder, smiling brightly.

'Ros?' My boss yanked out his AirPods. 'What are you doing here? You should be at WESC, you should be backstage, you should be—'

'It's all sorted,' I said calmly, pointing to the great big box on the floor beside me. 'I was there this morning, the set-up, the soundcheck, it's all done. I just came back to get the tiger mask and see if there was anything else you needed.'

He pressed both hands against his face and breathed out a gargantuan sigh of relief. 'Thank fuck, Ros, thank fuck,' he laughed. 'Because for a minute there, I thought maybe you'd fucked up and I was going to have to fire you on the spot.'

'Wouldn't that be hilarious?' I replied, polite smile still pasted on my face. Clearly the fact my entire career depended on what happened that afternoon hadn't even occurred to me. 'No, everything is great. Snazz should be getting to the venue in about an hour so I'll head over now so I'm there to meet him. See you there?'

'See us all there, the entire company is coming,' he confirmed as a dozen pairs of eyes furtively peered up at me from behind their computer screens. It was like being watched by a whole family of meerkats. He lowered his voice and covered his hand with his mouth. 'Except Kelvin. We didn't invite Kelvin.'

I followed his eyes over to a young man across the room. He was wearing prosthetic elf ears and a deerstalker and was peering at his iPhone, laughing loudly to himself. I looked back at the appalled expression on Ted's face. I'd have invited Kelvin before any of the rest of them. At least Kelvin looked like he knew how to have a laugh.

'Right, see you in a bit,' I said, squatting down to pick up the heavy box, unassisted. But Ted had already replaced his noise-cancelling headphones and gone back to ignoring me, as had everyone else.

'As god intended,' I muttered, waddling out of the office and into the street.

Patrick's flat was only twenty minutes from the PodPad offices but twenty minutes was a long way to walk in twenty-nine degrees while carrying a giant cardboard box. Aside from a touch of tepid drizzle, the rain still hadn't come and the streets of London were full of people wearing next to nothing. I felt wildly overdressed in my jeans and T-shirt but it felt indecent to see the city down to strappy vests and little shorts when we were definitely more of a black-opaque-tights kind of a town.

I'd said I would pick Patrick up en route to the recording but I was nervous about seeing him. Not because I was worried I'd say something stupid or cock up in some way but because I had been sure that he was the answer to all my problems for so long and, suddenly, I wasn't quite so certain any more.

Pretending I wasn't sweating through my T-shirt, I stood in front of his door and juggled the box in my arms to reach for the doorbell.

Right before I pressed, I looked at the giant box and smiled. The tiger mask. It would be funny, wouldn't it? I thought it would be funny. Sumi would think it was funny. I was prepared to bet John would get a laugh out of it. But would Patrick? Without overthinking it, I whipped the mask out the box and, with one deep breath, I jammed it onto my head. Not ideal for my claustrophobia but it would be worth it, I thought, jabbing the doorbell, for the look on his face.

Sweat trickled down the back of my neck as I waited for Patrick to answer and, as the seconds passed, I began to question the sense of my plan. What if I ruined the mask and Ted got mad and fired me? What if my sweat ran into my eyes and mixed with my mascara and blinded me and I couldn't produce the podcast and I lost my job? Or even worse, what if Patrick didn't open the door at all because he clearly wasn't home? And then I tried to take the tiger mask off and realized it was stuck on my bloody stupid head?

'Oh shit,' I muttered, trying to work my fingers into the opening around the neck, tugging and pulling and twisting and wiggling. It was no good, the thing was stuck on, the fur matting against my skin, and the more I struggled, the tighter it seemed to squeeze.

'You're not going to pass out in a tiger mask,' I told myself sternly, desperately trying not to panic even as the mask got tighter and the world outside got darker and my breathing became more and more erratic. Abandoning the safety of Patrick's front step, I walked back out onto the street, searching for help, but of course there was no one around. I'd have taken any kind of human contact, even the youths my nana was so worried about, anyone who had the strength to yank this bloody thing off my head. And then, I saw them at the end of the road, two men walking towards me. Just as I was about to shout out for help, one of the two men came into focus. One of the two men was Patrick.

It really didn't matter who the second man was, I knew, with every fibre of my being, that Patrick would not feel like introducing me to a friend, colleague or family member while I was wearing a giant tiger's head. I had two options: I could run in the other direction even though I couldn't see very well, end up on the main road, get run over and find myself on the six o'clock news as 'Local Mad Woman Wearing Tiger Mask Causes Ten-Car Pile-Up'. Or, I could hide in his garden. I opted for the latter.

The garden was sparse in the middle, just a small patch of lawn, lined by tall privet hedges. Without any other options, I clambered up onto his wheelie bin, trying to hoist myself over the locked gate and into the neighbour's yard before I could be caught. It was only once I was halfway over the gate, the sharp wooden slats cutting into my soft middle, I realized I was stuck. Hanging in midair, my legs kicking the air in Patrick's garden, my tiger head and human arms flailing wildly in the neighbour's garden.

'What the hell . . .'

Shit. It was Patrick.

'It's a burglar, call the police.' I heard another man's voice behind me, tense but assertive. 'You're stuck now, son. Nowhere for you to go.'

I squirmed, sweaty and sore and utterly humiliated.

'Get down,' Patrick ordered. 'Get down and fuck off and I won't call the police.'

'I would if I could,' I yelled from the other side of the fence, kicking wildly.

'Probably on drugs,' the second voice stated. 'He's probably on the cocaine or the crack.'

If only, I thought to myself as I heard someone

approaching my rear end and watched a hand slide around the wooden door and unhook the latch from the other side. The gate opened, the hinges squealing as I slowly swung backwards until I was face to tiger face with Patrick.

'Blow me!' the other man gasped before raising his voice in my direction as the gate began to swing back and forth, the hinges squeaking loudly in protest at the extra weight. 'Don't you bloody well move, I've got a club in my bag and I'll knock you out as soon as look at you!'

'Ros?' Patrick said, staring up at me as the swinging gate slowed to a steady stop. 'Is that you?'

'No,' I replied in a voice thick with tears brought on by embarrassment and the fact I had several sharp wooden slats stabbing me in the guts.

'Then why have you got "RR" monogrammed on your backpack?'

'Because I'm Robert Redford,' I choked. Every part of me was in pain. 'I wear this mask when I'm in London so I can walk around without being bothered by my fans.'

'Ros. Get down.'

'I can't,' I whimpered as the gate swung to a stop and I finally caught sight of Patrick's face. He did not look nearly as amused as I'd hoped he might. 'I'm stuck.'

Without another word, I felt him grab my legs and tug as I tried to lift myself up and over the gate, only succeeding in tearing my T-shirt and scratching my stomach as I went.

'Take the bloody mask off,' he said through gritted teeth.

'I can't,' I said again as my feet touched the floor, quickly followed by my bottom as I crumpled to the ground. 'It's stuck.'

Patrick reached over and took hold of the tiger's head, yanking it roughly over my head and dropping it into my lap. I rubbed my ears and opened and closed my mouth, stretching my jaw. I was a sweaty mess, mascara and eyeliner everywhere, jeans and T-shirt torn and three deep scratches along my stomach. In my lap, I saw a big bloody smudge across the tiger's face. I looked up to see a silhouette of Patrick, features obscured by the bright sun shining behind him.

'Julian, this is my . . . friend, Ros,' he said, gesturing at me by way of explanation. I raised a hand at the older man who was now standing by the front door, and gave him a charming wave. 'Why don't you wait inside, I'll just be a moment.'

'Of course, of course,' Julian replied, never once taking his eyes off me as Patrick unlocked the front door. 'Is she . . . well?'

'I honestly don't know,' he answered. The older man paused on the doorstep for just a moment, taking in the whole scene, and then disappeared inside, shaking his head.

'What are you doing, you absolute lunatic?' Patrick asked, once the door was firmly closed.

'Surprise?' I offered, slowly raising my hands and attempting a smile.

He did not smile back.

'Did you hit your head or have you gone mad?'

I crossed my legs where I sat, wondering if perhaps I had. That would be a relief.

'That was my publisher,' he went on. 'He's here to talk about my book but now all he's going to be thinking about is the time he was attacked by a mad woman in a tiger mask. Is that the kind of thing you'd want people to think about when they thought of you?'

'I thought it would be funny,' I said quietly as he paced up and down the garden. 'I see now that it was not.'

'I don't know what has got into you,' Patrick yelled. He was very much not done. 'Ever since we got back together, you've been acting strangely. I know you were gone for two years but you weren't like this before. You didn't behave like this last time.'

'Three years,' I said, cradling the tiger's head in my lap.

Patrick's pale face was beetroot red with rage.

'What?'

'I was gone for three years,' I explained. 'Not two.'

'Three years, whatever,' he huffed. 'What the fuck were you thinking, hanging around outside my house in that ridiculous mask?'

'It's for the podcast,' I began to explain but it hardly seemed relevant now. 'You said you'd come to the recording this afternoon.'

'That's today?' he asked. I nodded but said nothing. 'Fuck. I forgot.'

'You forgot?' I repeated. Maybe I had hit my head.

'This book is killing me,' Patrick shrugged as though it was enough of a response. 'Julian came over to see if we could work through a tough chapter. Sorry. I'll come to the next one.'

'Are you kidding me?' I forced myself up to my feet

so we were at least somewhere near face to face. 'You're going to let me down again? You know this is important to me.'

'So your work is more important than mine, is that it?' he asked, his words hot. 'I've got to say, I don't remember you being this needy. You used to be a lot more easygoing and, I have to say, a lot more respectful of my writing.'

'I am respectful of your writing!' I exclaimed, wincing as I strained the six-inch scratch that now ran along my midriff. 'I'm incredibly respectful of your writing. But you said you would come to this, you asked me to pick you up and now you're just not coming? How would you feel if it was me constantly letting you down? This is really important to me.'

Patrick turned and slammed the neighbour's gate closed with an almighty bang.

'Everything is really important to you,' he snapped. 'It was important to you I be at Lucy's baby shower, it's important to you I be at your mum and dad's ridiculous second wedding and it was important to you that I be at Sumi's bloody birthday, even though my being there was so important to your friends that they'd already fucked off home when I got there.'

'You were three hours late!' I shouted back. Inside, I saw the net curtains flinch as Julian backed away from the windows. 'You were three hours late but you said you were working, so I understood. And please don't shit on my parents because that's incredibly rude. I haven't asked you to do anything out of the ordinary, I haven't asked you to do anything I wouldn't do for you.'

'And there's the difference, I wouldn't ask you to

328

do *any* of this,' he replied, head held high as we fought for the moral high ground. 'Did I make you come to my dad's birthday last Sunday? No.'

I shook my own head in disbelief. 'I would have loved to have gone with you to your dad's birthday! You told me you had to work Sunday night.'

'Can you lower your voice?' he hissed, looking over his shoulder at the completely empty street. 'You're being hysterical.'

'No, I'm not hysterical, don't be that man,' I replied, my senses white hot. I felt focused, I felt clear. 'This is what angry looks like, get used to it. I don't think it's going to be the last time you ever see it.'

He rolled his eyes and glanced back at the house to make sure his precious publisher wasn't listening. He absolutely was. 'All this because I'm not coming to your work thing? You should see yourself.'

I was, in fairness, very glad I could not see myself. I could feel myself and smell myself and that was bad enough.

'All this because you don't respect me enough to follow through on things you've committed to,' I corrected, all the receipts adding up to a total I could no longer ignore. 'This is not on me, well, the tiger mask is, but the rest of it is not. It's on you. You're not a nice man, Patrick Parker.'

'And what's that supposed to mean?' he cried, suddenly incredulous. 'You dump me to move to America, come swanning back into London with your desperate text messages and expect me to drop everything for you? Is that it?'

I felt the blood rushing around my body, skinned palms and bruised knees throbbing, the scratches on my stomach burning and my eyes ready to shoot laser beams. In that moment, I was invincible.

'Stop trying to rewrite the past,' I yelled, jabbing my finger in his direction. 'I did not dump you, you dumped me and you were glad to do it. I was in love with you, Patrick. Madly, hopelessly, head over heels in love with you and you lapped it up. As soon as I told you I'd been offered the job abroad, you didn't even blink before finishing with me.'

'That's not how I remember it,' he said with a shrug. I looked down and noticed two buttons of his fly were undone. The indignity. 'But I'm sure your version of events works better for you.'

I stood up as straight as my shredded knees would allow, mascara all over my face, jeans stuck to me with sweat and T-shirt stained with blood.

'I thought about you every day,' I said. 'And I see now it was *such* a waste of time.'

'Ros,' Patrick loaded my name with meaning, as though the simple act of saying it out loud was exhausting. 'I'm trying to prepare for an important meeting and I find you trying to break into my neighbour's garden, wearing a ridiculous animal head, shouting incoherently, but somehow I'm the bad guy? What are you going on about, what do you *want* from me?'

You are not going to cry, a voice whispered in my head. You're not going to cry in the street when you're already sweating, bleeding and carrying a tiger's head.

'I want you to want me,' I said. There was no point holding back now. 'That's all I ever wanted from you. I wanted you to want me the way I wanted you.'

And it was true. I wanted him to want me so badly, it burned me up inside. It was something so simple but it always felt like much too much to ask for. I stood there, raw and real and vulnerable, waiting for him to respond.

But he didn't say anything.

John was right. People didn't change, their expectations did. Patrick was the same charming, selfish, sexy, intellectual, inconsiderate person he had always been and I was still the adoring, lovesick doormat I had always been. My expectations of him were so low, a worm could have cleared them without catching his belly. Now I understood what I'd really wanted from him, I realized I was never going to get it. I couldn't change Patrick but I could change my expectations. My expectation of what I deserved.

'You've lost the plot,' Patrick grunted as I picked up the tiger mask, more backstreet moggy than regal feline at this point. 'Go to your work thing and call me later when you've calmed down.'

'No,' I said, balancing the mask in my arms. 'I'm not going to call you later.'

We stared at each other, each waiting for the other to speak, not knowing what we wanted them to say.

'Then just go.' Patrick's body stiffened as he became a stranger. I looked at his rumpled blond hair, his light blue eyes, the lines of his face that I'd memorized while he slept. He was someone else now. 'But don't start sending me "group texts" six months from now when you change your mind.'

'Bye, Patrick,' I said, pinching myself together at the seams. 'I hope your meeting goes well.'

'This is usually the bit where I say it's not you,'

Patrick yelled as I walked away, carrying my blood-stained tiger mask, quiet tears cutting a sharp path through my smeared makeup. 'But this is definitely you!'

'Oh, I know,' I called back without turning around. 'Isn't it brilliant?'

CHAPTER THIRTY

The World E-Sports Championships was the last place on earth I wanted to be. After a very uncomfortable taxi ride, I finally arrived at the convention centre, less than an hour before the podcast was supposed to start, still in my filthy jeans and torn T-shirt, carrying the poor, mauled tiger head. After finally convincing a wary security guard to let me and my access-all-areas pass inside, I began to wish he hadn't. It was like walking into a parallel universe – all around me were people speaking the same language as me but I only understood every third word.

The main foyer swarmed with kids in cosplay, screaming and shouting and, thankfully, paying me not a single sniff of attention. I couldn't even begin to imagine how many hours they had spent putting together their elaborate costumes, although if that's what they'd been doing while I was breaking my heart over Patrick Parker, they were one up on me. I made a mental note to buy a games console on the way home, it would be a better use of my time and energy.

'Ros, where have you been?' Ted barked as I climbed up the stairs to the backstage area. 'Jesus, Mary and Joseph, what the hell happened to you?'

'Pack of wild dogs,' I said flatly, handing over the tiger mask. 'I made it out alive but just barely. Is everyone here?'

In one corner of the room, I saw Snazz, wearing a shiny metal robot head, with his millionaire coworkers, Beezer Go-Go and PsychoBang, sitting beside him. All three of them were staring at me with wide and terrified eyes. Well, I assumed Snazz was staring at me, his mask was pointed in my direction at least.

'So, everyone mic'd up? Everyone know exactly what they're doing?' I clapped my hands and pointed at the three chairs and the giant screens on the stage to the left of us. 'Travis, they appear to have been struck mute. Have you tested their mics?'

Travis, the production assistant, coughed. 'Mics are fine,' he whispered.

'I know I look a bit mad,' I said, examining my bloodstained shirt as I spoke. 'Would you believe me if I said it was cosplay?'

'I'd believe you if you said you'd killed a man,' replied Ted. 'Are you OK, Ros? You do know you're shaking?'

'I don't *think* anyone died,' I said. 'I tripped and fell, that's all. I'm very clumsy, I fall over all the time. I'm amazed I haven't broken my neck at work yet.'

'You've never seemed especially clumsy to me,' Ted replied, glancing over at Travis and the rest of the PodPad team who were loitering in the wings. They all looked at each other, muttering to confirm my elegance and grace.

'Well,' I said in a high-pitched voice, a giant grin stretching across my face. 'Either you accept I tripped and fell, and we get on with the podcast, or I can tell you all the story about how I got stuck trying to climb over a gate while wearing the tiger mask then broke up with my boyfriend. Which would you prefer?'

'Must have been a steep fall.' Veronica emerged from the darkness of the arena and answered on everyone's behalf. 'I hope the stairs took a beating as well.'

'Stairs weren't as bothered as I would like,' I admitted, walking over to the sound desk and making sure everything had been set up as per my instructions. 'But I can't think about the stairs right now or I might lose my mind. Are you excited, Snazz? All ready to go?'

The robot mask moved a fraction but he didn't say anything.

'He's fine,' Veronica said, cuffing him around the back of the head in the way only a family member could. 'Bit of stage fright, that's all.'

'Stage fright?' I squatted down in front of the boy, gasped at the pain in my knees and immediately stood up again. 'You're online in front of fifty thousand people every single day.'

'That's not in real life though,' he replied. Inside the mask was a voice modulator and, when he spoke, he sounded like a robot. A sulky, teenage robot. 'That's just gaming.'

'That's still live,' I argued, pointing at Beezer Go-Go and PsychoBang, or Dustin and Greg, as they were known to their mothers. 'I was watching a stream of you calling both of these a pair of butt nuggets last night, that was live.'

'It's "fuck nuggets",' the ginger-moustachioed PsychoBang called out to correct me. 'He called us fuck nuggets and butt monkeys.'

'Thanks, Greg,' I replied before turning my attention back to my charge. 'You'll be absolutely fine. Everyone loves you and they're so excited to watch you play the game that you've chosen to play which I can't remember right now.'

'Street Fighter 2,' Greg piped up again.

'Street Fighter 2,' I confirmed. 'Thanks again, Greg.'

'I'm not doing it,' the robot said again. 'Don't want to.'

'Do you know what, I think there's a few too many people in here,' I said, turning around to look at the rest of the room. Greg and Dustin and Veronica and Tyler and Ted and everyone from PodPad apart from Kelvin looked back. 'Could me and Snazz get a minute on our own?'

'I'm not going anywhere,' Veronica said as everyone else began to pile out.

'Fine by me,' I replied. 'Pull up a pew.'

I grabbed a bottle of Snazzlechuff-Says-branded water and a Snazzlechuff-Says-branded flannel, sat down in the chair opposite my favourite gamer and began cleaning my war wounds.

'So, here's the thing,' I said, sucking in the air as I picked tiny splinters out of my palms. 'I understand that you're nervous—'

'Not nervous, just don't want to do it,' he interrupted. Veronica snapped her fingers and made a zipping motion in front of her mouth. The robot fell silent.

'Well, I would understand if you *were* nervous,' I

shrugged. 'Even though you're very obviously not nervous. But the thing is, if you don't do this, I'll lose my job. And between you and me, things aren't going that well for me at the moment. Ted really loved that tiger mask and I have fucked it right up. Almost certain that will be coming out of my salary.'

'I'll pay for it,' he beeped.

'While that is the nicest thing a human male has ever offered to do for me, I really would rather you did the podcast,' I said. Once my palms were clean, I turned my attention to the scratches on my belly. I looked like I'd lost a fight with all the cats from *Cats*, even Taylor Swift. 'It might not seem like it today but years from now, when you're not gaming any more, you'll be really glad you did this. You'll be able to play it for your kids. Won't that be cool?'

'In what, fifty years?' he scoffed.

I looked up at Veronica, somewhat alarmed.

'How young *is* he?' I asked.

'Snazz, you signed the contract, you're doing the podcast,' she said without taking her eyes off her phone as she tapped away. 'Ros is trying to be nice, I'm not. Get your arse in gear and get it done.'

'Does his mum not mind the swearing?' I asked casually, hoping she didn't decide to go full Naomi Campbell and beat me to death with her phone.

'His mum doesn't mind the money,' she replied, glaring at me with such force, any comeback I might have had dried up in my throat.

'What did you mean, when I'm not gaming any more?' Snazz asked, his voice so low the voice modulator could barely pick it up. I leaned forward and nudged his knee, putting on a smile.

'You might want to do something else when you're older,' I replied, eyes flitting over towards his agent, ready to duck any flying missiles. 'You might want to work with charities or travel the world or get a job at KFC like other teenagers. Who knows?'

'What if I wanted to do something else now?' he asked, even more quietly, his voice barely above a whisper.

'We should probably talk about that after the podcast,' I answered, just as quietly.

'What if I do it wrong?' Snazzlechuff asked, his robot voice growing a little bit stronger. 'I've never done a podcast before.'

'You can't get it wrong,' I promised. 'It's your podcast. It's literally impossible for you to make any kind of mistake.'

He looked down at his empty hands.

'And you'll help me?'

Holding my breath, I crouched down in front of him again, biting my lip against the sting of my injuries. 'Snazz, I'll do everything I can. I've had a very hard day and actually a really rough couple of months. I really don't want to lose this job. Will you do it for me?'

Slowly, he reached up and flipped a clasp behind his shiny, silver ear. The mask popped open and, all of a sudden, I was face to face with a teenage boy. He had blue eyes and blond hair and a scattering of acne on his left cheek. Above his top lip was the slightest hint of a wisp of a moustache and it took all my self-control not to lick my thumb and rub it right off his face.

'You can call me Max, if you want to,' he said with a shy smile.

'This is all very sweet but can we get this show on the road?' Veronica called as Max snapped the mask back shut. 'They won't let me smoke in here and I haven't had a cigarette in twenty-three minutes. If I don't get one soon, everyone's going to look as rough as you.'

I looked into the robot's face, hoping I was making eye contact with Max. I'd done the best I could but he was either going to do it or he wasn't, it was like trying to explain a logical decision to a cat.

'OK. So that's that. Now, I'm going to make sure everything is where it needs to be on stage,' I told Veronica while Max pulled a tiny gaming device out from behind his back and started zapping things, seemingly happy for the moment. 'It's all fine.'

Stepping through the curtains into the empty arena, I gazed out at the rows and rows of empty chairs. It was such a lot to put on a child, I couldn't imagine how he must be feeling.

'He'll be fine,' I muttered to the empty room, trying to convince myself. 'He'll be absolutely fine.'

On the third row from the front, I saw four white pieces of paper with my name on them. The seats I'd reserved from Adrian, Lucy, Sumi and Patrick.

'Lucy will appreciate the extra room,' I whispered, nodding mechanically. This wasn't the time for my breakdown. That would come after the podcast. And Mum and Dad's ceremony. And the reception. And lunch with the family on Sunday. But it would have to be before work the next day. So early hours of Monday morning. Perfect scheduling.

Before I had a chance to laugh in my own face, the security doors at the back of the room opened and people began to pour into the arena, racing to snag seats right at the front. Before they could see me, in all my torn-shirt glory, I slipped back through the red velvet curtains, grabbing a Snazzlechuff Says T-shirt as I went.

'Five minutes to showtime,' I told everyone as I skipped across the room. 'Looks like you've got some very excited fans out there. Everyone's going to love it.'

As I slipped into the backstage bathroom, I really hoped I was right.

'Team Snazzlechuff!' Ted bellowed, two minutes later as we huddled in the middle of the stage. 'My boyzzz! Is everyone good to go?'

Dustin, Greg, Travis and Veronica gave various grunts of affirmation then looked to Snazz for approval.

'Yeah,' he said with a mild shrug.

'This is going to be the pinnacle of my career,' Ted breathed, his face so white I was afraid he might faint. 'Ros, I want you to go out there and introduce everyone and then let's make some magic happen, my brosephs.'

'Don't you want to do the introduction?' I asked, waving up and down at the state of myself.

'Yes,' he admitted. 'But it's a better look for the company if a woman does it. We don't want people to think it's a sausage party over at our place.'

'Of course not,' I agreed, even though it absolutely was.

Standing up, I attempted to comb my fingers through my mess of curls before giving up and winding my hair up into a topknot. Ted handed me a microphone, branded of course, and curled his mouth into a disapproving frown.

'Have you not got a bit of lipstick?' he asked.

I answered with an ungodly glare.

'You look great,' he said, giving me the double-finger guns.

'OK, let's do this,' I declared, winking at my new friend, Max. 'See you on the stage then.'

Before I could think any more about it, I stepped through the curtains and onto the stage, soundtracked by an absolute thunderclap of applause. The last time I'd heard clapping on stage, it was because I'd abandoned my rendition of 'Don't Stop Believin'' halfway through the song during the Year Eight talent show. There was a reason I preferred to stay behind the scenes.

In the third row, I spotted Adrian, Sumi and Lucy, cheering so loud their voices soared above everyone else's in the crowd. But they weren't alone. John was sitting in Patrick's chair, whooping and cheering as loud as anyone. Pushing away a stab in my guts as I remembered the look on Patrick's face when I'd walked away, I smiled directly at my friends, stepped forward and turned on my mic.

'Hello, World E-Sports Championship!' I shouted. Everyone except for my friends immediately stopped clapping. I tapped the microphone, it was still on.

'Noob!' yelled someone at the back of the room, sending a ripple of hand-over-mouth dampened chuckles around the crowd.

'Fine, whatever,' I muttered. 'My name is Ros and I'm the producer of Snazzlechuff Says.'

I paused for applause but there was none.

'I'd like to thank you for coming,' I went on,

desperate to get off stage and into a drink. 'And without further ado, let's bring on our guests for this evening. First up, from Kansas City, Missouri, we have Overwatch legend, Beezer Go-Go!'

I stuffed the mic into my armpit and clapped as he sloped onto the stage, shoulders rolling in a denim jacket so big it looked as though he'd borrowed it from his dad, if his dad was a giant.

'Also joining us is one of this year's Fortnite World Cup runners-up. From Milton Keynes, England, it's PsychoBang!'

The teenage boy who had just inhaled three packets of Wotsits in a row rushed onto the stage, throwing his arms out wide, a PC-gaming Jesus Christ as the crowd howled his name. Definitely not someone who was going to struggle to form functioning relationships when he got older.

'And of course, last but not least, we have this year's Fortnite World Cup Champion, a Dreamcast Extreme Master, the most subscribed-to player on any streaming site in the world and host of PodPad's first gaming podcast, the one, the only Snazzlechuff!' I called out his name like a boxing announcer, riding the wave of screams echoing around the room. Rows and rows of teenage boys, teenage girls, grown men and even a few grown women leapt up, clapped their hands and stamped their feet as they waited for their hero to appear.

Only he didn't.

'Let's hear it for Snazzlechuff!' I shouted again, turning off my mic and sticking my head back through the curtains. Veronica, Ted and Travis were all standing around Max's chair, where he was still playing his game.

'Max,' I hissed. 'Get out here.'

'Don't wanna,' he replied without moving.

'That's not funny,' I said as the cheers began to fade away into discontented murmurs. 'You need to come out here right now.'

'No,' he said, looking up at me as defiantly as someone in a robot mask was able to. '*You* need me to come out there right now. I need to play Super Smash Bros.'

I looked at Ted but he was frozen to the spot. Travis ran over to the sound desk and began fiddling with unnecessary knobs.

'Veronica?' I said, helplessly.

'Kids today,' she shrugged. 'I'd give him a slap but it's illegal. Maybe somebody shouldn't have filled his head with ideas about giving up gaming.'

I gulped. How could it be anything other than my fault?

'I know!' Ted screeched. 'You put on the tiger mask and pretend to be him.'

'*I think they're going to know*,' I hissed, pointing at my tits. On the other side of the curtain, the crowd was beginning to get restless. 'Travis,' I ordered. 'Cue the video.'

He nodded and gave a salute, hitting a big red play button in front of him. In the arena, I heard the crowds hush as our Snazzlechuff Says introduction video began to roll.

'All right,' I said, dropping to my knees in front of the teenage maestro and feeling nothing. 'I am begging you. What do you need? Ted, did you get him that Chicago pizza?'

'Order the pizza, I repeat, order the pizza,' Ted barked into his iPhone. I could only assume he had the intern at Heathrow, ready to go.

'Don't want pizza,' Max mumbled inside his mask.

'Then what do you want?' I asked, utterly frantic. I had not come this far to fuck up now. 'Are you hungry? Thirsty? Do you want a new mask? The tiger mask? A real tiger? Ted, he wants a real tiger.'

'Cancel the pizza,' Ted screamed into his phone. 'I repeat, cancel the pizza and find us a tiger.'

But still, nothing.

Taking a deep breath in, I dug deep. There was only one thing for it.

'That's it, you're officially on my shitlist, Max,' I said, fixing him with the glare of a woman whose fucks had all but expired. 'Do you think I want to be doing this? No, I don't. I've spent ten years working as a radio producer, I have won awards for my culture programming, I have produced interviews with world leaders, I have shown Greta Thunberg the way to the toilet. *Michelle Obama once told me she liked my shoes.*'

I paused to let that sink in but the robot was unmoved.

'Yes, a real tiger,' Ted marched up and down the room, still bellowing into his phone. 'What other kind of tiger would I be talking about?'

'But forget everything else I've ever done,' I said, still focused on my target. 'Because this is what we're doing today and I have worked too hard for too long for you to cock it up now. I'm not going to get sacked because you can't even be bothered to go out onto that stage and talk about Street Cleaner Three with your two chuckle buddies.'

'Street Fighter Two,' he corrected sullenly.

'It could be Street Fighter Seventy-Eight for all I care!' I shouted. 'I am sick to the back teeth of putting all my energy into something when the other person could not give a flying fuck. Do you know how long women have been doing this? Forever, Max. For-Ever. So I will not eat your shit and call it ice cream, so either get out there and show me the same respect I've shown you or go home and stop wasting everybody's time.'

The robot head looked up at me, shining silver, all its bright lights flashing.

'You're amazing,' he gasped. 'Will you go out with me?'

I looked around the room to make sure everyone else had heard the same thing I had. From the looks on their horrified faces, they had.

'Absolutely not,' I replied.

'I'll be sixteen next December,' he said, a trace of teenage bravado forcing its way through the robotic effects on his voice modulator.

'Which means you're fourteen now,' I said, looking him dead in the robot eye. 'Max, you are a child, I am not going out with you.'

'Then I'm not going on stage,' he replied.

'Fifteen seconds left on the video!' Travis yelled.

'We could go to the cinema,' Max suggested. 'I can probably get into a fifteen but if you want to see an eighteen, my mum has to come with us.'

'Ten seconds!'

'Veronica?' I squealed, looking for help in all the wrong places.

'I usually put Maltesers in my popcorn,' Max added. 'But we don't have to if you don't want to.'

'Fine,' I said, panicking. 'We can go to the cinema. But we're not going to see an eighteen and it's not a date.'

'Seriously?' He leapt to his feet and tossed his

computer game to the floor. 'You'll go to the movies with me?'

'Hold the tiger,' Ted barked down the phone, staring at me. 'I repeat, hold the tiger.'

'Yes, seriously,' I confirmed, holding my head in my hands. 'Now will you please get on stage before the crowd tears this place apart?'

Silently, he grabbed hold of my hand and strolled out through the curtains right as the video finished playing.

'Let go of me,' I hissed, trying to shake him off as the crowd began to whoop and scream. 'I need to be backstage.'

'Aight WESC-ers!' Max said into his microphone. Everyone, except for Lucy who seemed to have doubled in size since Saturday, and Sumi who looked very confused, stood up and began chanting for Snazzlechuff. 'I have an announcement to make.'

The crowd lowered their volume to a reverent hush, almost silent save for the sound of four hundred and ninety-eight people clamouring for their mobile phones.

'It's kind of a big deal but I've been thinking about it for a long time, like, the last couple of weeks.'

The room gasped.

'As of today, I am retiring from competitive gaming.'

You could have heard a speck of dust fall off the head of a pin.

'Having discussed this with my girlfriend—' he raised my hand in the air.

'I'm not his girlfriend,' I said quickly.

'I have decided to spend more time travelling the

346

world and doing charities and going to the pictures with Ros. Thank you for all your support.'

And then the boos began in earnest.

'You're not Snazzlechuff!' shouted a girl with candyfloss-pink hair at the back of the room. 'You're an imposter!'

'From today, I am no longer a slave to the mask,' he shouted back, fiddling with the clasp on the side of his ear. The booing stopped, and all the air was sucked out of the room as he carefully unhooked the catch and let his mask swing open to reveal his face.

'My name is Max, this is my girlfriend, Ros—'

'Oh god, please make this end,' I groaned, covering my face with my arm as dozens of camera flashes popped below us.

'And I *am* Snazzlechuff!'

I stared at the crowd, trying to shake my hand free of Max's vice-like grip as five hundred people live-streamed my worst professional nightmare to millions of people all around the world.

'I am Snazzlechuff!' A voice bellowed in the crowd.

I peered through my arms to see Adrian standing on his chair, arms aloft.

'Yes! So am I! I am Snazzlechuff as well!' Sumi echoed, giving Lucy a kick as she climbed up onto her own seat.

'Don't make me stand up,' Lucy groaned as she reluctantly raised her hands halfway into the air, John beside her doing the same. 'Fine, I'm Snazzlechuff too.'

A girl I didn't know, three rows behind them, rose to her feet.

'I'm Snazzlechuff!'

'Me too! I'm Snazzlechuff!' shouted three different teenage boys, all standing at once, swiftly followed by an entire row by the back door. Slowly but surely, the entire room stood up, waving their arms in the air.

'I'm Snazzlechuff!' they chanted, individually at first but soon, all as one. 'I'm Snazzlechuff!'

Max grinned and wrapped his skinny arm around my waist as I tried to push him away.

'We're all Snazzlechuff!' he cheered. Dustin and Greg stood behind him, chanting along with everyone else.

'And I am so fired,' I groaned, watching Ted march off down the middle aisle and storm out the back door.

CHAPTER THIRTY-ONE

Saturday morning was announced by a single drop of water, landing directly on my face. Bloody condensation in the shed, I thought, rolling over and bumping into another body. Lying on her side, surrounded by a nest of pillows and cushions, was heavily pregnant Lucy, happily snoring away under my sheet. I sat up, the night before slowly seeping back into my memory, to see Sumi wedged onto the world's smallest sofa and, when I looked over the edge of my mattress, Adrian was curled up in a ball between the bedframe and the front door. Empty pizza boxes were stacked up at the side of the sink and my head throbbed with recollection. Patrick followed by podcast followed by Pinot Grigio.

After The Artist Formerly Known as Snazzlechuff's big announcement, absolute chaos had broken loose. And by chaos, I meant three teenagers turned their chairs over and had to be escorted out of the convention centre. After that, came the social media decimation, the Snazzlechuff Is Over Party, Hashtag

Cancel PodPad and, my personal favourite worldwide trending topic of all time, Who the Fuck Is Ros Reynolds? It was an excellent question and not one I was certain I could answer.

By the time I'd fought my way off the stage and down to find my friends, John had disappeared, late for work at the bar, and there was an email in my inbox from Ted confirming that since Snazzlechuff Says was not going ahead, my services would no longer be required at the office. Those weren't the exact words he'd used but I got the general gist. I'd been sacked. But this time, I wasn't overwhelmed by shame. It wasn't my fault. Or at least not entirely. And this time, I had my friends to support me, I would work it out somehow. We left the convention centre and went straight to the closest pub where I gave them a blow-by-blow recap of my Patrick predicament and proceeded to get very, very drunk.

Sacked, single and hungover. The perfect start to my parents' special day.

'Are you awake?' I asked Lucy as I saw one eyelid flicker.

'I'm thirty-seven weeks' pregnant, I don't sleep,' she muttered. 'I just close my eyes and hope that when I open them, the baby will have fallen out.'

'God, it hasn't, has it?' I rubbed my hand against my face. 'I felt something wet on my head?'

Lucy stared straight at me.

'Are you asking if I got up, straddled your face, waited for my waters to break and then got back into this position, all without you noticing?'

I looked up at the ceiling and back down at my friend.

'Yes.'

'You got me,' she grunted, closing her eyes again. 'Was it a boy or a girl?'

'You didn't have to stay over, you know,' I said, somehow managing to smile at the bodies crammed into my tiny space.

'Please,' Adrian grunted. 'As if we were going to leave you alone.'

'The first night is the most dangerous,' Lucy added. 'Sumi needed to be here to chop your hands off if you tried to change your mind and call him.'

I lay back on my bed and smiled happily. All my friends around me, all my friends (bar Lucy) hungover. Just like the good old days. Another drop of water landed on the top of my head. I looked up at the ceiling, which was moving too quickly, the room spinning around me.

'What's that sound?' I asked, leaning over Lucy to move the curtain.

'In England, we call that rain,' Adrian replied from the floor. 'Listen.'

'I thought that sound was in my head,' I groaned. It wasn't just raining, it was torrential. Water was splitting the sky in two, it was practically coming down sideways.

'At *last*,' Sumi said in a muffled voice, still face down on the settee. 'Maybe it won't be so bloody hot today.'

'But Mum and Dad's party.' I flexed my head left and right, wincing at the headache that was starting to scratch away at my temples. Outside the rain was coming down so hard, I could barely see the house. 'She's going to be so upset.'

'Rain on your wedding day is good luck,' Lucy replied. 'Don't worry.'

I flipped my legs out of bed, narrowly avoiding stepping on Adrian's face. 'What about rain on your fortieth-anniversary slash marriage-vow-renewal day?'

'I think it's fine and you should be quieter and we should all go back to sleep,' Sumi answered in a monotonous tone I recognized all too well. 'Ugh, what was that?'

'The roof is leaking,' I wailed as another giant droplet landed on my face. 'I knew it!'

But the roof wasn't just leaking, water was pouring in. At first, the drops turned into a trickle which turned into a steady stream, the gaps in the roof widening from minor cracks to gaping chasms until it was raining as hard inside as it was outside.

'This isn't good,' I said, eyes on the ceiling as I felt around on the floor for my trainers. 'We should get inside.'

'But we are inside,' Adrian protested, wiping a raindrop from his face.

'Inside the house,' I clarified, helping Lucy to her feet and shuffling a pair of flip-flops onto her feet. 'Come on! We need to go before—'

A huge chunk of my white plastic ceiling crashed to the floor, right beside Sumi's head.

'I'm up, I'm up!' she shrieked, rolling off the settee and onto the floor. Draping Lucy's arm over my shoulder, I propped up my pregnant friend, Adrian waiting with my cagoule held over his head as another piece of ceiling tile cracked loudly and fell onto the bed, the heavens opening onto my mattress.

'Grab the phones!' Adrian screamed as Sumi

unplugged her own from the wall charger. 'No man left behind!'

'I've got them, I've got them,' she yelled, holding four black phones aloft and hoisting her enormous tote bag onto her shoulder.

We rushed across the garden as quickly as we could given the size of Lucy, the protection of the cagoule doing absolutely nothing for anyone. I half expected to see an ark sailing down the neighbour's driveway at any minute.

'For what it's worth, I thought the shed was quite cute,' Lucy said, looking back sadly as the rest of the roof gave up the ghost, and water rushed out the front door.

'*Was* being the operative word in that sentence,' Sumi replied, hammering down on the locked back door as loudly as she could. 'Let us in!'

'I'm coming, I'm coming,' I heard Dad trill as he strolled through the kitchen with a steaming mug in his hand. 'What's the emergency?'

'The emergency is the death trap you built for me just collapsed,' I said, falling through the door, more puddle than person. I scraped my soaking hair back from my face to see Mum peering at us from the hallway, the cordless phone up to her ear.

'My beautiful shed,' Dad gasped, fingertips pressing lightly against the kitchen window. 'My poor, beautiful shed.'

'Your poor, wet-through daughter and her nearly concussed sodden friends,' I corrected. Sumi began filling the kettle while Adrian sat Lucy at the kitchen table. I pulled four mugs out of the cupboard and popped a teabag in each. A proper brew, the answer to all of life's crises. 'We could have died, Dad. The roof collapsed onto the bed.'

'It wouldn't have killed you,' he said sadly, watching as my waterlogged copy of *Starting Over* sailed downstream towards his alpine rockery. 'Wasn't heavy enough. Worst-case scenario would have been a broken leg.'

'Thank goodness for that,' I replied loudly, glaring at the back of his head as Mum walked into the kitchen, phone pressed to her chest, knuckles white around the handset. 'I'm sure Lucy and her unborn child are relieved.'

'Morning, Mrs Reynolds,' Adrian said, pulling out a chair. She sank into it wordlessly. 'We nearly died but everything's fine now. You look radiant this morning . . .'

'Nearly died,' Dad scoffed under his breath before narrowing his eyes at my friend. 'Adrian, did you fiddle with the roof?'

'That was the tennis club on the phone,' Mum said before Adrian could reply. Her face was ashen. 'They're completely flooded. They say there's no way they can have it up and running again by this afternoon.'

I bit my lip as the kettle whistled.

'That was fast,' Adrian commented as Sumi poured out the water.

'It's a fast-boil kettle,' Mum said, breaking into heaving sobs. 'Alan got it last month.'

'It's OK.' I rushed to my mum's side, hugging her into my damp pyjamas and looking to everyone else in the room for reassurance. 'It's going to be OK. We'll fix it somehow.'

'But the ceremony is supposed to start at one,' she

choked. 'Your Aunt Annette and Uncle David are already checked in at the Premier Travel Lodge. They'll be furious if they've had a wasted trip.'

'And our Kevin has set off to get Mum from the home,' Dad added darkly. 'I'll not convince him to do that again in a hurry.'

'It's *fine*,' I insisted. 'We'll find somewhere else, you will have your ceremony. I will fix this, I promise.'

Even if I didn't exactly have a fantastic track record of fixing things of late, I thought to myself.

'Sumi,' I said, firing out ideas before I could second-guess myself. 'What about the event planners you used for Lucy's party? Do you think they have any last-minute venues?'

'I'll give them a call but I wouldn't bet on it,' she said, immediately grabbing her phone. 'There's last minute and there's last minute.'

'I know someone who could help.' Adrian closed the fridge, a pint of milk in his hand. 'What about John?'

'What *about* John?' I replied, skimming through the (cursed) contact list in my phone. Dry cleaners, no. Hairdressers, no. Wong's Chinese, *maybe*.

'Adrian, you're so clever!' Lucy brightened immediately. 'We could use the upstairs room at Good Luck! It's so beautiful, with the big windows and the chandeliers, oh and there's the little stage at the front. It'd be perfect. Call him, Ros, I'm sure he'll let us use it.'

Tightening my grip on the back of my mum's chair, I smiled brightly at my friend. 'Why don't one of you call him?' I suggested. 'You all know him better than I do.'

'Technically, not true,' Sumi said with a wink as she fished four teabags out of four mugs.

'I wouldn't be comfortable asking him,' I said, enunciating each word with a knife-like degree of sharpness. 'And I would appreciate it if you would call him for me.'

'Fine, I'll call him,' Sumi said, cackling into her mug. 'It's a beautiful space, Mrs Reynolds, you'll love it.'

'You can't just reorganize something like this on the day, all the food was at the club and now it's all ruined,' Mum said with a sniff. 'Everything is ruined.'

'Mum, we've got all morning, we can do this,' I insisted. 'Adrian can call the florist, Sumi and Jo can sort out the food and me and Lucy can call the guests and let them know the change of plan. The bar isn't that far away, just in Borough Market. We can be there in half an hour. It's probably just as close as the tennis club.'

'I don't know,' she said tearfully. 'Maybe we should just cancel it.'

Everyone jumped as Dad slammed his coffee cup down on the kitchen counter.

'We'll do no such thing,' he declared. 'Sumi, call this John chap and tell him we need his help, money is no object. We're getting this done.'

We all stared at my father, shocked into silence by an unprecedented display of emotion.

'I promised you the most special day of your life, Gwen Reynolds,' Dad bellowed as he dropped to one knee before his wife, a triumphant finger in the air. 'We are renewing our vows today, come hell or high water!'

'Poor choice of words,' Sumi whispered to me, phone pressed against her ear. 'It's fucking biblical out there.'

As my mother collapsed into my father's arms and my friends cheered, I turned my attention out the window and watched the shed, as it collapsed in on itself. All the clothes that hadn't quite made it into my wash basket floated across the garden in a parade of slovenliness.

'Could you help me up, Ros?' Dad asked, stuck on the kitchen floor. I took hold of his hand and yanked him to his feet.

'We'll make it perfect, Dad,' I promised, determined to see this right.

'Not to throw a spanner in the works,' Lucy said quietly, staring down between her knees. 'But I think my waters just broke.'

'That seems to me like something you need a definite answer on,' Adrian asked from the seat beside her, leaping to his feet and climbing onto the chair as though expecting a second flood.

'I was trying to be delicate,' she replied, gripping the edge of the kitchen table and grimacing tightly. 'But either my waters have broken or I've just wet myself.'

'She hasn't had a drink,' Sumi commented, pushing her fingertips into her temples with her eyes closed. 'So, I'd say it's almost certainly the waters breaking thing.'

Mum wiped her face on the sleeve of her dressing gown and rushed over to Lucy's side. 'You're all useless,' she scolded lightly, throwing a tea towel onto the floor. 'Let's call Dave, he can come and pick you up.'

Lucy's delicate face seized up again.

'Perhaps just text him and tell him to meet me at

the hospital,' she suggested. 'I don't know that this is going to take very long.'

Everyone blanched at exactly the same time.

'But you're not due yet!' I protested, forcing myself not to think of what would become of the new pyjama bottoms I'd lent her. 'And people are usually in labour for hours, aren't they? Days, even?'

'Mum had me in two hours and my sister in three,' Lucy replied. 'And my sister had Lesley an hour after her waters broke. They both delivered early.'

I'd forgotten Lucy's sister had called her baby Lesley. Baby Lesley. Honestly.

'What do we do?' I asked, looking straight to Mum and Dad.

'I'll drive you to the hospital,' Adrian offered.

'No!' everyone shouted back at once.

'Fine,' he sniffed in response.

'I'll take her,' Dad offered, grabbing his car keys from the kitchen counter. 'Gwen, you've got your woman coming over to do your hair, I've only got to put my suit on. I'll take her.'

'I'll come with you,' I said, slamming my tea down on the table as Mum, unable to wait a second longer, reached for the mop.

'No, you've got more than enough to do,' Lucy insisted, rising carefully to her feet and we all rose with her. She smiled at Dad as he held out his arm. 'Shall we?'

'We shall,' he confirmed with a gallant nod before turning to my mum. 'I'll be back in plenty of time and don't worry about a thing. Rosalind has got this under control, haven't you, Ros? She can do this.'

I breathed in sharply, surprise spreading across my face in a smile.

'Yes, of course,' I promised, my chest swelling with pride. 'Like I said, we'll make it perfect.'

'Right,' he said, pulling an umbrella from the stand by the back door. 'Then everything's all right. We'll see you in a bit.'

We followed Lucy out the door and helped her into the car, choruses of good luck ringing all around her until they had backed out the drive and disappeared down the street.

'Now what?' Sumi turned to me with her hands on her hips.

'Now we plan a wedding,' I replied with a gulp. 'And we do it really, really quickly.'

'OK, then,' she clapped me on the shoulder and marched back into the kitchen with a determined stride. 'Let's do this!'

I stood in a puddle outside the front door and looked up at the grey, overcast sky.

'This has not been my week for good luck,' I whispered to the heavens. 'But if there was ever a time for that to change, it would be now.'

The sun peeked out at me from behind a storm cloud, just for a moment, before disappearing again.

'I'll take it,' I said before following my friend back into the house.

CHAPTER THIRTY-TWO

Reorganizing a wedding in a little over three hours was actually far less stressful than it could have been. Everyone involved in event planning, it seemed, was prepared for the absolute worst. The florists had barely batted an eyelid when I explained we would need to collect the flowers early and take them to the new venue ourselves. The bakers simply shrugged, put the wedding cake in a box and sent us on our way.

'Really decent of John to give your mum and dad the bar for nothing,' Adrian said as he span his car around the corner before firing it down the alleyway behind Good Luck Bar.

'Really decent,' I agreed from underneath a sea of flowers in the backseat. Pink roses, white geraniums and dozens of blushed-peach dahlias, striking me straight through the heart.

'Well, he's not really doing it for her mum and dad, is he?' Sumi said from the front passenger seat, carefully nursing the wedding cake on her knee.

'Shut up, Sumi.'

'He isn't?' Adrian asked.

'He's totally in love with Ros,' she nodded.

'*He is?*' Adrian gasped, grinning.

'Shut *up*, Sumi,' I said again.

She leaned across her seat to whisper in his ear.

'They kissed at the baby shower,' she told him.

'*Did they?*' Adrian wrenched up the handbrake and turned to me with his mouth wide open. 'No wonder you're not that heartbroken over Prick-trick Parker.'

'I am heartbroken,' I sniffed, realizing even as I said it that I wasn't in pieces. Too stressed, too hungover, too unemployed, I reasoned. No doubt the moment Mum and Dad left for their second honeymoon, I'd fall apart. Probably. 'I'm just too busy reorganizing a wedding and worrying about Lucy to show it.'

'Not too heartbroken to get off with John,' Sumi said in a stage whisper before raising her voice to me. 'Lucy's fine, Dave's at the hospital with her now. And I'm not joking, Rosalind, if you fuck up our free drink situation, I will never forgive you.'

'Oh, you shut up and get the cake out the car,' I ordered, slithering along the backseat, heart pounding as I tried to work out just exactly what I was going to say to John.

Since the rain had stopped, the sun had come out, brightening the sky to a bold blue but with none of the stickiness we'd been suffering all summer. It was a perfect day.

'Morning, Cammy,' Sumi sang as the bartender opened the back door to us.

'Morning,' she said, grabbing one of the buckets of flowers out of my arms and carrying it inside. 'The cleaner's already been in so it's spotless for you and I'll be working the bar.'

'Oh, we don't need you to do that,' I said from behind a jungle of dahlias. 'We've got a load of wine, we'll just leave it out the side for everyone to help themselves, we don't want to be any bother.'

'No way,' Camille said, shaking her head. 'John says you're VIP so you're VIP. Chef's making mini quiches as we speak.'

Adrian batted his eyelashes at me and made a not-at-all-attractive kissy face.

'You can't, it's too much,' I insisted, following her up the stairs into the private room. It was even more beautiful than I remembered. 'I've already sent my sister to Costco for a platter of sandwiches.'

Very much against her will, I added silently.

'Food's all arranged,' Camille argued, holding up her hands to let me know it wasn't her doing. 'Do you think your parents would prefer mini burgers, mini fish and chips or a mix of both?'

'Both,' Sumi and Adrian said together. I rolled my eyes and fumbled for my phone, shooting a message to Jo, telling her to stand down from sandwich duty.

'Both it is,' Camille confirmed. 'Right, I'll leave you to get the flowers where you want them. Sound system and speakers are all plugged in, you can connect your phone to the Bluetooth and we've got microphones over there if you need them. Didn't know if you wanted chairs or not but they're stacked in the corner. I'll get rid of 'em if you don't want 'em. If you need anything else, I'll be in the kitchen.'

'Is John here?' I asked, attempting nonchalance but

ending up somewhere in between 'shrill' and 'hysterical dolphin'.

Camille stopped halfway down the stairs and shook her head. 'Nope.'

'He's not?' I breathed out slowly. Was I relieved or disappointed? I couldn't tell. 'Good. I mean, oh. I mean—'

'Why don't you start getting ready?' Sumi suggested. 'Me and Ade will put the flowers out, we've got the cake, Jo's with your mum. All you need to do is put your frock on and have a quiet minute.'

'Thank you,' I said, feeling flustered all at once. 'You're amazing.'

'We are, it's true,' Adrian replied as he began unstacking chairs and placing them in rows, facing the front of the room. 'Now get out the way before I push you down the stairs.'

'Best friends ever,' I whispered, doing exactly as I was told.

At least I don't have to use the gents this time, I thought, letting myself into the ladies with a pair of heels in one hand and a garment bag in the other. I sat down on the pink leatherette bench in front of a large, well-lit mirror and took in the woman who looked back at me.

Once my hair was up in a twist that more or less looked as though I'd done it on purpose, I shuffled out of my mum's leggings and Dad's T-shirt (all my clean clothes having been lost to the great flood) and unzipped the front of the garment bag. I'd been worried about the bridesmaids' dresses, given Mum's recent sartorial adventures, but she had outdone herself. My dress was pale lavender, floor-length, sleeveless and truly beautiful. The material was soft, slipping between my fingers as I held it up against me before stepping into the gown and pulling it up around my waist. Checking my reflection, I picked up the two long sashes that fell from the waist and held them out like wings. What was I supposed to do with these? Letting them float back down to the floor, I turned my attention to my bra, unhooking it under my dress and slipping my arms out the straps.

'Ros?'

The door opened right as I whipped my bra out from inside my dress, the bodice and its wings flopping down around my waist.

'Don't come in!' I yelped, crossing my arms over my chest.

But it was too late. In the mirror, I saw John walk into the ladies as I lunged for the toilet stall, restraining my boobs with my hands.

'I didn't see anything,' he called. 'I swear.'

Pulling the dress back up over my chest, I leaned against the cool metal of the stall door.

'Camille said you weren't here,' I said as the top part of my dress drooped back down around my waist. Why wouldn't it stand up on its own? Was I really going to have to spend the entire day with my arms crossed to stop myself from flashing the entire family? What was my mother thinking?

'I wasn't, now I am. Can you come out please?'

Reluctantly, I unlocked the door and let it open, just a little. In the crack between the door and the wall, I saw his downturned smile, his brown eyes, his dark hair.

'Ros,' he said. 'Will you please come out the toilet?'

'I can't,' I explained. 'I can't keep my dress up.'

'I've heard a lot of excuses in my time,' John replied. 'But that's a good one.'

'I'm serious!' Emerging from the stall, I turned my back to show him the strange straps of my dress. 'The bodice won't stay up.'

'That's because you haven't fastened it.' John waved his hands in the air between us like he was casting a spell. 'Those straps are supposed to wrap up and around, aren't they?'

I grasped one end with my left hand, keeping my boobs firmly inside the front of my dress with the right. 'Are they?'

'I hate to be the one to tell you but you're a rubbish girl,' he said, taking the end of each sash in his hands. 'Turn around.'

Biting down on my lower lip, I turned my back to him and felt him reach around my waist for the long swathes of lilac fabric. He cinched them tightly around my middle before winding the fabric up around my chest then tying a neat bow behind my neck.

'How did you know how to do that?' I asked, marvelling at his handiwork in the mirror.

'I've put more women back into more complicated clothing than I care to remember,' he replied as I put my dress through the shimmy test. 'You pick up a wide array of skills when you work in bars for your entire adult life. Which reminds me, who do I need to speak to about outlawing jumpsuits?'

'Not me,' I replied. 'You only need wear one to a festival once and you'll never put yourself through it again as long as you live.'

'You look beautiful,' John said, straightening out the bow at the nape of my neck. I looked into the mirror and saw the pair of us staring back. Me in my lavender gown, John in a beautiful charcoal-grey jacket over his white shirt, grey tie and jeans, his hands resting on my shoulders.

And when he smiled, my stomach flipped.

'We've really got to stop meeting like this,' he said, his body warm against mine.

'Thank you for dressing me,' I replied. I wasn't ready to move just yet. 'And for everything else. You saved the day again.'

'Least I could do,' he said, removing his hands and digging them deep into his pockets, leaving my shoulders bare and cold. I felt myself sway backwards as he moved away and had to steady myself with one hand on the wall.

'And thank you for coming yesterday,' I said, folding my arms around myself as John slouched back against a rose-gold-painted radiator. 'You really didn't have to. I think it might have been better if no one had been there.'

'I figured I owed you one after the way I acted at the baby shower,' he replied with an apologetic smile. 'And besides, Sumi said you'd introduce me to Snazzlechuff. I'm guessing that's not on the cards now, is it? Unless I can crash your date.'

'Please do,' I groaned. 'He's already texting me. How do you let a fourteen-year-old down gently?'

John looked down at the floor, his black hair falling in front of his face. 'The same way you let everyone else down,' he said. 'Tell him you've already got a boyfriend.'

'But I haven't,' I said, noticing how hard I was breathing against the tight bodice of my dress. 'Me and Patrick, it's over.'

He looked up, his eyes wide and his face open. The downturned smile he always seemed to be fighting against slowly broadened.

'Really?'

'Really,' I confirmed. 'Turns out we both wanted different things.'

'And what is it that *you* wanted?' John asked, all hope and anticipation.

'I'm still working that out,' I replied, looking up to the pink-painted ceiling, arms securely wrapped around myself. 'I think it might take a while.'

'Oh,' he replied with an understanding but clearly disappointed nod, keeping his chin to his chest. 'I get it.'

I couldn't not smile. Once you knew how to read them his feelings were always right there on his face, he wouldn't know how to hide them if he tried. I had got too used to trying to read between the lines, translate signs and search for things that weren't really there. I'd forgotten what honest attraction looked like.

'I think it might be time for me to make some bold moves,' I said, reaching out and adjusting his tie. 'Make some big changes. I've been trying to bring back the past, and that hasn't worked out so well.'

John lifted his head in surprise. 'Speaking as someone who has been doing all kinds of bold, some might say crazy, things lately, I approve of your plan,' he said.

'What kind of bold, crazy things?' I asked, tilting my head back as he closed the space between us.

'Oh, you know.' He stopped right in front of me and I let go of his tie. 'Roller skating, going to baby showers, throwing last-minute weddings and birthday dinners, dancing with strange girls at dark discos. That sort of thing.'

'Sounds to me like you've lost it,' I whispered.

'I feel like I have,' John agreed in his deep, low voice. His eyes were big and round and dark. 'Because I can't stop thinking about you. Ever since we met, I just can't stop thinking about you. What you might be doing, where you might be doing it, wondering what I can do to spend more time with you.'

I didn't know how to answer. No one had ever said anything like that to me before.

'I'm sorry for the way I acted last weekend,' he said, his words heavy with honest regret. 'It was wrong and there's no excuse.'

I felt myself slip into that other state, my eyes half closed, my lips tingling and everything around us warm and fuzzy and insignificant as something pulled us closer and closer together.

'I was frustrated but I shouldn't have been so aggro.' He was so close that I could feel his breath on my skin. 'And I definitely shouldn't have kissed you like that.'

Our hands found each other, my left palm meeting his right, skin grazing against skin, with the lightest touch.

'You're right,' I said as I lifted my face to look at him. 'You should have waited.'

'Waited for what?'

'For this,' I told him, pushing up onto my tiptoes, lifting my lips to meet his.

'There you are!'

The door to the ladies slammed against the wall right before our lips could touch, my sister marching in with her bridesmaid's dress over her arm, completely oblivious to whatever she might be interrupting.

'How am I supposed to get this dress on?' she demanded. 'I'm literally a genius and I cannot work it out.'

John stepped backwards out of my arms, his eyebrows knitting together with regret at a moment lost. 'I'll be upstairs,' he said, lingering in the doorway for a moment. 'If you need me.'

I nodded and watched him leave, dizzy with denial.

'Who's that?' Jo asked, stripping off before the door was even halfway closed.

'That's John,' I replied. 'He's my friend.'

CHAPTER THIRTY-THREE

The wedding was perfect.

No one got lost on their way to the new venue, we managed to dress Jo on time and my nan hadn't offended a single soul in the entire seventeen minutes she'd been in the room.

'I can't believe you forced me into such a toxic heteronormative gender role,' Jo grumbled as we made our way down the makeshift aisle between two groups of chairs. We really should have been clearer about the dress code, I realized, as I spotted two of Dad's friends in actual tuxedos, Aaron from the garden centre in his shorts and flip-flops and Mum's friend from yoga, whose name I'd forgotten, in a fascinator so fascinating three rows of people behind her could see absolutely nothing.

'I know, I'm such a bitch,' I replied sweetly, nodding at Ruby and Bill from next-door-but-one. 'I'm forcing you to be an agent of the patriarchy, you're doing one nice thing to make Mum and Dad happy. It won't kill you.'

'It's a system of oppression,' she muttered while doling out doe-eyed smiles to Janet from the garden centre. 'You know, in ancient times, if the bride didn't go through with the wedding, one of the bridesmaids would be forced to marry the groom.'

'I don't think anyone here is going to make you marry your dad,' I assured her. 'Anyway, where's Wilf?'

'Eurgh, Wilf? Over,' Jo pouted. 'I'm in a throuple now. With a couple who are researching biomedical engineering at Magdalen.'

Winking at Dad in his new suit, we took our seats beside our nan in the front row.

'That's a terrible colour on both of you,' she grumbled. 'Washes you right out.'

'Nice to see you too, Nan,' I said, patting her hand, too happy to care. 'Jo was just telling me she's going out with a man and a woman at the same time. Why don't you two talk about that for a bit?'

Sumi and Jemima and Adrian and Eva sat behind us, all glowing with happiness. It felt good, I thought, to see so many cheerful faces in one room. And also my sister and my nan. I couldn't remember the last time we'd all been together, if ever.

A terrible instrumental version of Mum's favourite Elton John song began pouring through the speakers and everyone turned at once.

Gwen Reynolds was beautiful. Her dark hair was curled and pulled back, her clear skin shining and the gorgeous wedding gown we'd chosen together moved with her as she walked, floating lightly behind her. I felt myself tearing up as she came closer, trying to recall if I'd ever seen either of my parents look like this before. It was wonderful, I realized, that they could make each other this happy. I couldn't imagine how it must feel to have someone like that in your life, someone who actually wanted to be there, who could make you smile the way my parents were smiling at each other in that moment, even after forty years. And at the back of the room, standing off to the side, out of the way, I saw John, watching me watch my mum.

'Ladies and gentlemen, thank you for joining us today.'

Dad's best friend, Peter Mapplethorpe, stood in front of my parents, a solemn look on his face and a well-worn paperback open in his hands.

'He does know this is just a vow renewal, doesn't he?' I asked, trying to get a better look. 'Why has he got a bible?'

'It's *The Da Vinci Code*,' Jo replied, twisting her head to one side. 'What a knob.'

'We are gathered here today to celebrate the love between our friends, Gwen and Alan,' Peter Mapplethorpe said, imbuing his speech with great reverence as he clutched the sacred words of Dan Brown. 'But before I begin, if anyone here has any reason to object, speak now or forever hold your peace.'

An easy chuckle rippled through the crowd.

Then Nan stood up and everyone flinched.

'I've got something to say,' she announced. 'This is utter nonsense and I can't believe you've dragged me into this filthy city to witness it.'

I looked at Mum and Dad, panic in my heart, but they simply shrugged at each other and seemed to silently agree it could have been much worse.

'That it?' Jo asked, eyebrows drawn together, eternally unimpressed. 'Anything else?'

'I'll not hear from you, you harlot,' Nan sniffed. 'In my day, you'd have been strung up for your behaviour.'

I looked down at the order of service in my lap and noticed a late addition that hadn't been on Mum's original design. It was a line from an Emily Dickinson poem, one she quoted so often, I knew it by heart and had once put in a love letter to Patrick.

Forever – is composed of Nows –

I gave an involuntary sniff, my eyes welling up for just a moment. He used to use that letter as a bookmark, I remembered quietly, my heart softening against my will. Whatever book he was reading, my note was always tucked away inside although I'd never known if it was because it meant something to him or it was just convenient.

'I'll start again,' Mr Mapplethorpe said as I wiped away a confusing tear and tried to feel happy again. 'Do you, Alan, take Gwen to, um, still be your wife?'

'I do,' Dad confirmed, beaming at his wife.

'And do you, Gwen, take Alan to still be your husband?'

Another sob caught in the back of my throat as my parents beamed at one another. Before my mum could open her mouth to answer, three different mobile phones chirped into life, competing for attention with their different ringtones.

'Oh my god,' Jo groaned, rolling her eyes so hard I assumed she could see the inside of her skull.

'Sorry,' I called out, fiddling with my tiny handbag and searching for the offending phone as Sumi and Adrian did the same. 'I thought I'd turned it off.'

'It's Lucy!' Sumi squealed, waving her screen in my face. 'She's had the baby!'

'It's a girl!' Adrian added. 'Or at least it says it is. Looks like a hairless cat.'

A picture of a very sweaty but very happy-looking Lucy shone out from Sumi's phone, a tiny scrunched-up version of a human wrapped in a white swaddling cloth tucked into her arms.

'Should I start this again or shall we not bother?' Peter Mapplethorpe asked, rather upset at being interrupted for the second time. We all put away our phones and turned to the front of the room, guilty smiles on our happy faces.

'Yes, please do,' Mum said, taking Dad's hand in hers. 'We're not going anywhere.'

'No rush,' Dad agreed with a nod, beaming at his wife. 'It's only been forty years. I've got my fingers crossed for another forty.'

After the vows were said, music struck up as everyone began to cheer and I turned in my seat to look at my friends, and to avoid the intensely passionate kiss my parents were sharing in full view of everyone.

'I can't believe you pulled it off,' Sumi said, resting her chin on my shoulder as my uncle Kevin led Nan off into a corner to pass judgement on everyone quietly and by herself. 'Well bloody done, you.'

'Well bloody done us,' I corrected, leaning my head against hers. 'There's no way I would have managed all this by myself.'

'Have you spoken to John?'

'Yes, Sumi,' I replied.

'And what did you say?'

'Shut up, Sumi.'

'Someone should say something,' said Adrian,

craning his neck to get a better look around the room as people rose out of their seats and then sat back down. 'No one seems to know exactly what they should be doing.'

'I'll do it,' Jo said, standing immediately. 'I'll make a speech.'

'You stay where you are,' I ordered, pushing her back down into her seat. The last thing people wanted to hear was how what we perceived as love was nothing but a chemical reaction and the statistical probability of divorce after the age of sixty. 'I'll do it.'

Edging my way down the row of chairs, I hopped up onto the stage where Mum and Dad were still lost in a world of their own.

'I'm going to say something,' I said, picking up the microphone and switching it on. 'Let people know what's going on now, if that's all right?'

'Oh, love,' Mum pressed her hands to her heart. 'That would be wonderful.'

Dad took the microphone out of my hand and banged it against the palm of his hand, silencing the room with a screech of feedback and warming up a few migraines.

'Everybody,' he said, speaking far too loudly into the mic. 'Our eldest daughter, Rosalind, would like to make a speech so, yes, let's let her do that.'

'Not a speech,' I said quickly. 'I was just going to tell them what the plan was for the afternoon.'

'Well, you're doing a speech now,' Mum said as she stepped down off the stage and took my seat in the front row. 'Let's hear it.'

Dad handed me the microphone as everyone began to applaud and, for the second time in two days, I found myself on stage in front of a group of people with no idea what I was going to say.

'Erm. I recently read a book called *Starting Over*,' I began, trying to keep my eyes on the back of the room, away from my friends, my sister and John. 'It was very interesting, all about how we shouldn't stay so attached to our past that we can't move on with our future. You know, I think we all do that a bit these days, don't we? It used to just be our grandparents but now it's everyone, talking about how brilliant things used to be back in the day when people weren't so angry all the time and we didn't fall out with the neighbours over who they voted for and before Facebook ruined everybody's life.'

'Where's she going with this?' I heard Adrian not-quite whisper to Sumi who didn't seem to have an answer and looked as though she was holding her breath.

'The thing the book tried to say is that nostalgia can be toxic,' I went on, sure I had a point. 'It can poison us if we let it, it stops us from finding joy in our present. We're so in love with our idea of our past, we can't trust that there are good things waiting for us in the future. And we have to move on. We have to make bold steps and believe in ourselves and in each other. And that's why I think it's so amazing that my mum and dad didn't just want to celebrate all the time they've spent together, they wanted to look to the future as well. Today is just as much about celebrating what's to come as it is toasting to the forty years they've been married.'

'Thank fuck for that,' Sumi said on an exhale.

'I'd like to make a toast to all the wonderful things we've already experienced together,' I said, reaching out as Adrian stretched up to hand me a glass of champagne. 'And to all the amazing things that are still to come.'

Everyone raised their glasses and made happy noises, toasting Mum and Dad with smiles on their faces. I couldn't help smiling too.

'Oh and also, we're doing appetizers now and then food so please get out the way while we rearrange the tables and don't fill up on snacks,' I added before turning off the mic and climbing down from the stage.

'Smashed it,' Sumi declared, clinking her glass against mine. 'Ten out of ten.'

'I think I'm getting better at public speaking,' I said, my smile growing as I made eye contact with John and he winked.

CHAPTER THIRTY-FOUR

Everyone was laughing and talking and eating and hugging, the way it should be at a wedding. John was serving up drinks behind the bar, Sumi and Jemima were on the dance floor and Adrian and Eva were sitting beside my sleeping nan, completely oblivious to everything around them and gazing into each other's eyes, while Nan snored away, head right back, propped up against the wall.

Before anyone could miss me, I slipped downstairs and out the back door of the bar, skirting around the alleyway to watch a busy Saturday afternoon in Borough Market. The sun had gone back in, leaving us with a pale grey sky and, thankfully, tolerable temperatures.

'Now or never,' I said to myself, taking out my phone and hitting the call button. '*Stiffen the sinews and summon the blood.*'

She answered immediately.

'Yes?'

'Veronica?' I asked with shaking hands.

'Ros.'

'How are you?'

'What do you want?' a cigarette-fried voice barked down the line.

Hardly able to believe what I was about to say, I launched into my pitch. 'I've been thinking about what you said,' I told her. 'And you're right.'

'I'm always right,' Veronica agreed. 'What specifically was I right about this time?'

'About having a podcast of your own,' I replied, pulling the phone away from my ear at the sound of commotion down the line. 'Veronica?'

'Get off the phone, you little arse,' the agent shrieked, the sound of a teenage boy wheedling in the background. 'Yes it's Ros and no, she doesn't want to talk to you. Let go of my fucking arm.'

I winced as Veronica and Max bickered back and forth, ducking underneath an archway as I felt the first drop of rain fall from the sky.

'Max wants to know if you're free to go to the cinema tomorrow and do you want to go ice skating first?' Veronica asked, a wheeze in her voice. Clearly she had only won the fight on a conditional basis.

'Tomorrow isn't great,' I said slowly. 'And I'm not much of a skater.'

'She can't do tomorrow,' I heard her yell away from the phone. 'Great, now he's crying. What were you saying? A podcast?'

I nodded furiously. 'Yes, you should have a podcast. Wait, what do you mean he's crying? Is he all right?'

'He's right as a fucking bobbin,' Veronica replied. 'Came home from that shitshow yesterday, bounced up and down on his trampoline for three hours then

379

booked the entire family a holiday to Florida. We're going to Harry Potter world on Tuesday. He wanted to invite you to that too but I said he might be coming on a bit strong.'

'I like Harry Potter,' I began before immediately correcting myself. 'But no, you're right, bit much. Anyway, sorry, podcast. You should have a podcast. You have a fascinating story and helpful advice and I've never met anyone like you. You should have a podcast.'

She considered my suggestion for a moment.

'At PodPad?'

'Hmm, no,' I said. 'I don't work at PodPad any more. After yesterday, we decided to part ways.'

I held the phone away from my ear as she cackled loudly down the other end.

'Good, everyone there was a complete twat,' she replied, clearing her throat and hacking up what sounded like at least half of one lung. 'But if you're not there, how are you going to get me a podcast?'

'I'm going to launch my own network,' I announced. 'For women and non-binary creators, only interesting stories and a strictly zero-arsehole policy. I'm calling it BroadCast and I want you to be my business partner.'

Veronica coughed again before taking a long, thoughtful drag.

'You mean you want me to invest in it?'

'Yes.' Honesty was, after all, the best policy. 'I mean, I'm going to do it either way but I'd love to have your expertise on board. And your cash.'

'Convenient that I've got loads of my own cash and a fourteen-year-old investor who's completely in love with you,' Veronica said, her creaky voice warming up with what sounded like a smile.

'Would it be ethical?' I asked, holding out my hand and feeling another raindrop fall. 'I mean, to have Max invest in it?'

'Probably not but since I'm in charge of his finances, I'm not terribly worried,' she replied. 'The only problem we have is if you shit the bed and lose all his money. Here's how I see it, you're an intelligent woman, Ros. An intelligent woman who is passionate about what she does. For fuck's sake, you very nearly got a half-decent podcast out of a grumpy teenage game player who likes to wear animal masks. How impressive is that?'

'Quite impressive?'

'And if that's not enough, I'm an even more intelligent woman with a lot of business savvy behind me,' she continued, selling herself on the idea as she went. 'I know how to make things work. And you're right, there are a lot of stories out there and someone should be telling them. Stories by women, stories for women, fuck it, even stories by men who aren't shit-scared of women. Not that I've ever met many of those. Someone should be doing it.'

'And that someone is me and you,' I told her, a thrill running through me, all thoughts of PodPad and Washington and the past fading away. Failures were only failures if you didn't learn from them and I had learned *so* much. See? I had learned *something* useful from *Starting Over*. 'You don't have to decide right now,' I said. 'But—'

'Fuck it, let's do it.'

A loud cheer was followed by a heavy cough and the flick of a cigarette lighter.

'Seriously?' I hopped up and down on the spot, registering a few strange looks from people passing by. Nothing like an adult bridesmaid doing a jig in the middle of Borough Market outside in the rain to attract attention.

'Get your arse to the Snazzlechuff compound at nine a.m. Monday and we'll start our plan of attack before I have to drag my arse around Hogwarts for a week,' she confirmed. 'Now, are you sure you're out for Florida?'

'I'm sure,' I replied, looking sadly up at the grey sky.

'All right then,' she replied. 'Fuck off and enjoy your Saturday, I'll see you Monday morning.'

And the call ended with a beep.

I dashed back towards Good Luck Bar right as the rain began to fall again in earnest.

'Be still my beating heart, Rosalind Reynolds, you look spectacular.'

Right as Patrick appeared.

'What are you doing here?' I asked, swiping a damp strand of hair off my face and taking him in: the hopeful smile, his beautiful grey suit, his light pink shirt and big black umbrella.

'I got the email with the change of venue,' he explained. There was something oddly hesitant about his demeanour, something I wasn't used to.

'That's not what I meant and you know it. What are you doing here?'

Underneath his umbrella, Patrick's face fell. 'I came to see you,' he said quietly. 'I was really hoping you might be pleased to see me.'

My eyes widened and my mouth dropped open. 'Are you being serious? After everything we said yesterday?'

'It was just a fight,' he said, coming closer. I backed away, towards the door of the bar, listening to the happy sounds mixing with music just a few steps away. 'Couples fight, don't they? I know we never did before but they do, you know. And I'm sorry, I'm truly very sorry.'

And I thought I was lost for words before.

'We never fought before because I didn't let us,' I told him as the rain fell with more enthusiasm. 'I always agreed with you so you wouldn't be upset, that's why we never argued.'

'It doesn't have to be like that this time,' Patrick said, his light blue eyes clouded over like the sky. 'It can be the way we said it would be, total honesty. After you left, I tried to sit down and write and I couldn't. You know how easy it is for me to turn everything off and focus on the work? But I couldn't do it, there was something blocking me. I thought I was angry with you but eventually I realized, I was angry with myself.'

It was a lot to take in all at once. I'd fantasized about being with Patrick for so long but it turned out hearing him apologize was more erotic than anything else I could have even dreamed of.

'I haven't been fair. I wasn't fair last time either and I'm sorry. And I won't lie, I liked seeing you all fired up like that,' he said with a hint of a wolfish smile. 'Let's give it a real try this time, all in, double or nothing.'

He reached an arm out from underneath his umbrella

to hand over a small package, carefully wrapped in brown paper and tied with string. He held the umbrella over my head as I took it in my hands, and the rain fell on him instead of me, his light grey suit shifting shades, drop by drop by drop.

'This is for you.'

'Patrick,' I gasped as my cold fingers worked their way through the packaging. It was one of his copies of *Jane Eyre*. His only first edition. I looked up and saw his blond hair plastered to his forehead, half a smile on his face.

'I can't take this.'

'Yes, you can,' he insisted. 'They're like us, don't you see? I had to get a good kick in the ego before I could understand what was at stake. Now we can be together properly.'

I frowned at the book and then at Patrick. 'You're comparing us to a couple who could only get together after the hero was ruined by his first wife, who he locked in the attic, and ended up blind after she set the house on fire, and the heroine ran out on their wedding, turned down another proposal and became rich enough in her own right to feel socially equal to the man she loves?'

Patrick nodded eagerly. 'See? Just like us.'

If I hadn't been certain before, I was certain then.

'I'm sorry,' I said. 'But I can't take it because I don't want to give it another try. There's no point, it won't work, and I know you're going to laugh but seriously, it's really not you, it's me.'

Patrick's strong arm faltered slightly, straining equally under the weight of holding the umbrella outstretched and the blow to his pride. 'Why are you being like this?' he asked, bluster creeping back into his voice and sweeping away the raw edges I had just heard. 'Isn't this what you wanted me to say? I'm sorry, I'll try harder, you were right?'

'It's exactly what I wanted to hear.' I stopped and sighed. 'But it turns out I was wrong about a lot of things. Most things, in fact. You're asking me to go backwards and I realize now, I can't, no one can. You can only go forwards, you have to keep going forwards or you'll die. I don't want that.'

'That's sharks, Ros, not people,' Patrick replied, his arm slowly retracting, the umbrella covering his head again and not mine. 'You're thinking of sharks.'

He smiled down at me with an expression I knew all too well. Condescending but humouring. Pleading eyes, lips curving upwards just a touch, brow lightly furrowed as though he wasn't quite sure what he'd done wrong in the first place. But there was impatience as well, he wanted me to hurry up and accept his apology, and then life to go on according to his plan.

'It's sharks *and* people,' I told him, the heat gone out of my end of the argument. I didn't want to fight when there was nothing to fight for. 'Don't you think it's weird that I never told you I loved you because I was worried it would scare you off? That's mad. If you're afraid someone will walk away from you if you tell them you love them, why on earth would you want to be with them in the first place?'

'It's a word that gets thrown around a lot,' he muttered as he suddenly became very interested in his own feet. 'I don't like to rush it.'

'It's OK, I know you don't love me,' I said, pressing the book back into his hands. 'You never did. You loved how much I loved you and that's very much not the same thing.'

It was strange, to be standing there, looking at Patrick Parker, all sad-eyed in the rain. Too many of my fantasies had started this way. But this was definitely an ending, not a beginning.

'I wish you would give us a chance,' he said, even though he was already tucking the book away inside his jacket. 'I know you, Ros, you'll regret this.'

'That's the thing, isn't it? You don't know me at all.' I moved in towards him and rested my hands against his lapels, looking up into his light blue eyes. 'I was never really me when I was with you. That was a sort of edited version of me and I don't think I'd be happy if I had to be her all the time.'

'Do you remember the first time we met? Do you remember how it was in the beginning?' he murmured as he tilted his chin down towards me, playing his last hand. 'Give me another chance. Whatever it is you want, you can have it.'

I shook my head. He wasn't listening. As usual.

'I think I already have everything I need.'

With a tiny tug on his lapels, I kissed him on the cheek and took a step backwards into the pouring rain, leaving Patrick Parker in the past.

CHAPTER THIRTY-FIVE

I went back into the wedding, swiping at myself with half a dozen napkins and skipping around the edges of the party to avoid my friends. I needed a moment, just a moment, to myself.

The chain that had been wrapped around the door to the roof terrace was gone, I realized, as I made my way to the other end of the room. With a quick glance over my shoulder, I pushed on the bar that opened the door and felt it give, slipping outside by myself. The rain couldn't make its mind up, slowing down to a light drizzle with a bright blue sky above. I searched for a rainbow but couldn't find one.

The view from the terrace was a beauty. All of London, new and old, sparkling fresh, straight out of the shower and shining just for me. Along the riverbank, different-coloured umbrellas danced around each other, streaming past the *Golden Hinde*, the Globe, all the way down to the Tate Modern. Across the Thames, St Paul's was almost glowing in the sun, thankful for its long-awaited bath. On my right, I saw the Tower of London battling for attention with The Shard. Centuries-old stone, competing with a decade's worth of glass and steel, past versus progress, separated by a river and somehow managing to co-exist.

'Oh, it's you.'

I heard the door open behind me and turned to see John stepping out onto the terrace. I smiled and turned back to my city.

'I was on my way to give someone a bollocking but, since it's you, I'll let you off. I haven't got the permits to open this up yet, I don't want anyone falling to their death,' he said, leaning against the low railing beside me. 'Ros, you're wet through. Here.'

He shrugged off his warm jacket and wrapped it around my shoulders like a blanket.

'I don't want to ruin it,' I protested, even as I pulled it around myself. I hadn't realized how cold I was until someone offered me a chance to get warm.

John waved away my concern and moved to stand beside me, resting his forearms on the railing to gaze out over London.

'I just met your mum,' he said. 'She's really lovely.'

'Yeah,' I nodded, smiling warmly. 'She is. I'm lucky.'

'She reminded me a lot of my mum . . .' he added before letting the thought trail away. 'What are you doing out here? I thought I saw you leaving.'

'I went out to make a call, got wet, came back,' I explained. 'I came out here to think.'

'About?'

I inhaled, wondering how much to share. It had been easy to talk to him before, when he was the married, slightly annoying bartender. But now he was someone completely different and I wasn't sure how but the rules had changed.

'I was thinking how annoyed the Tower of London must be,' I said, pointing down at the old fortress. 'You know, you're just there, minding your own business for a thousand years, doing everything that's asked of you, and then someone comes and builds a giant bloody skyscraper right across the road. I'd be furious.'

'I hate The Shard,' John said, turning his nose up at the glass colossus to our right. 'It's just *there*, isn't it? Everything around here has a reason to exist, the market, the theatre, the bridges, the tower. And then that's just there to be there. They could so they did. I hate it.'

'Bold take,' I said, smiling. I nestled into his jacket and breathed in. It smelled like him.

'So, what was the phone call you had to think about?' he asked. 'Because I should have mentioned we have a strict no-stripper policy at this bar.'

'It was about a job,' I laughed. 'I'm starting my own podcast network.'

'Ros, that's terrific,' John exclaimed, grabbing hold of my hand and squeezing. 'What a brilliant idea. That's perfect, now you can do whatever you want.'

'And then Patrick showed up and we had a chat,' I added. John loosened his grip on my hand but he didn't let go. 'He wanted to give things another try.'

His fingers tightened around mine again.

'Did he now?'

'And I told him I didn't want to.'

John considered this news, nodding as he stared straight ahead. A light breeze blew his hair in front of his face, dark wavy locks dancing over his forehead.

'None of my business but I think that might be for the best,' he said finally.

'I agree,' I replied. This time I was the one who gave his hand a squeeze. 'I need to work out who I am and what I want without the thought of him looming over me. I need to stop thinking about what might have been and get on with what is.'

'Seems to me that you've got a lot of things to be excited about,' John said, raking his hair away from his face.

'The present doesn't look too shabby,' I agreed. 'Trying not to get hung up on the future.'

'Well,' he said as he turned his body away from London and towards me. 'If we're focusing on the present . . .'

'The thing is,' I started before pausing for a moment to take him in. His black hair curled in the damp air that followed the storm, brushing the collar of his shirt at the nape of his neck. His big, dark eyes, his broad face with its strong nose and wide mouth were all focused on me so intently but there was nothing in his expression but hope.

'The thing is, I don't know if this is the right time to be rushing into . . . something,' I said as I let go of his hand. 'I'm sorry.'

'I don't want to be your rebound,' he said solidly, eyebrows creasing in towards each other. 'And I absolutely want you to take all the time you need. But there is one problem.'

'What's that?'

John leaned in towards me and my body moved to him, our fingers winding around each other, furling and unfurling, one hand learning the other, the light pressure of his thumb stroking circles around my palm.

'I think I might be in love with you.'

'Really?' I asked, snapping out of the moment.

'Oh my god, the look on your face,' he laughed, shaking his head in wonder. 'Is that so hard to believe?'

'It's just I've got so much going on, you know, just so much stuff.' Words bubbled out of me as though someone had shaken up my bottle of pop. Keep talking, change the subject, he doesn't mean it, he can't mean it, don't let him say it again. 'With my job and the podcasts and Lucy's baby and Sumi's going to have a baby, did you know that? And I need to find somewhere to live now my shed is gone and . . .'

I tailed away, running out of words.

'I only understood half of that but, sure,' John said, staying right where he was as I backed away. 'I'm not going to push you, Ros. Only, life is short and when you meet someone who makes you feel excited to be alive, who you can talk to about anything, who makes you laugh, who makes you want to get up in the morning just because there's a chance you might get to see them that day? I reckon you should tell them how you feel.'

Before I could reply, I noticed something above his head.

'Look,' I said, pointing to the sky. 'A rainbow.'

As he turned to see what I saw, a bright, bold rainbow that started somewhere near Big Ben and stretched all the way over to Whitechapel, I suddenly realized.

The way he felt about me was just how I felt about him.

'John?'

He turned back to face me.

'Ros?'

'I've had a chance to think about it.'

'Oh good,' he said gravely. 'You gave it a whole minute, thank you.'

'I think I am not ready to be in something new. But . . .' I rested my hands on his chest as his eyes widened with surprise and a slow smile spread across his face. 'But I also would really like to kiss you right now if that's OK.'

'You've got good instincts,' he whispered, stroking my damp hair out of my eyes. 'You just need to trust yourself more. I say, go for it.'

I reached up to wrap my hands around his face and pulled it down to meet mine, pressing my lips to his and holding him as close as I possibly could. The sodden fabric of my dress soaked through his shirt and I could feel the warmth of his skin against mine. It was wonderful. As my mouth opened to his, he curled his arms around my shoulders, sliding his hands down my back and circling my waist before lifting me up off the floor.

And just for a moment, I felt like I was floating.

TWO MONTHS LATER . . .

I chose the desk closest to the window.

Veronica couldn't argue, she was having her own four walls built into the back of the office, complete with a state-of-the-art air-filtration system so she could smoke away to her heart's content. I did remind her it wasn't technically legal to smoke in a workplace but she simply reminded me there wasn't technically a workplace at all without her investment and so we came to a silent agreement.

The glazier was finishing up on our glass door, polishing up the sign as I popped my last pencil in its pencil pot.

'What is it you do here, anyhow?' he asked, giving the BroadCast logo a last rub with the sleeve of his boiler suit.

'We're a podcast network,' I said proudly. 'We make podcasts.'

'Any of them about serial killers?' he asked hopefully.

'Not yet,' I said, shaking my head apologetically. 'But give it time.'

'Hasn't been a good serial killer in ages,' the man lamented. 'You should do one about Shipman. I'd have known right away if he'd been my GP. Shifty fucker, that one, you could see it in his eyes.'

'Are you all done with the door?' I asked, very keen to be talking about literally anything else.

'Yeah, I'll wash my hands and be out your way,' he nodded, taking his mucky boiler suit and filthy mitts into the bathroom I had just stocked with brand-new white hand towels.

Looking around the office, I felt a surge of pride. Once Veronica and I were in agreement, things had moved quickly. Luckily, she knew a teenager who knew a man who got all the online end of things organized – our website, our domain names, our social media handles – and I got in touch with a few friends who I thought might be interested in working with us. It turned out, I was right. They all jumped at the chance to have their voices heard and now, just a few weeks later, we were a real company, moving into real offices with desks and chairs, white walls, lots of windows and a positively gorgeous all-glass recording studio. We already had show sponsors, I'd hired someone to sell advertising, we had a marketing person starting on Monday. I couldn't quite believe it.

'Where do you want this?'

A giant succulent pushed through the door with a six-foot-four man attached.

'Just down by the wall?' I said, grinning as John lowered my plant carefully to the ground. 'Thank you.'

'It's looking good!'

John had been our unofficial moving co-ordinator, fixer and all-round hype man from day one. He brought us food when we worked late, he drove me home when I missed my last train and, as Veronica said to his face the first time they met, he had 'shagged a smile' onto me that I simply could not wipe off. I'd always assumed sex with Patrick was the best sex could ever possibly be but, apparently, that was only because I didn't know better. Sex with someone you fancied like mad was great but sex between two people who fancy each other like mad *and* really cared about one another? Another stratosphere.

John crossed the office floor in three strides and put his arm around my shoulders as I leaned into him. He sniffed the air and pulled a face.

'Is Veronica here?' he asked.

'Left four hours ago,' I groaned. I knew that filter would not work.

Outside, I heard a ruckus on the street and turned to see Sumi, Adrian and Eva banging on the glass, faces pressed against my freshly washed window. Next to them, and very much not participating in the banging, Lucy waved as she rocked her pram back and forth.

'Argh, look at it!' Sumi crowed as they barged through the door, leaving fresh palm prints as they went. They spread out across the office, Eva hopping up on a desk, Sumi rattling the water dispenser, Adrian going straight for the big, pink retro fridge. 'Ros, it's brilliant.'

'I still think it's just an elaborate front for a knocking shop,' Adrian said, his face bursting with delight as Eva laughed out loud.

'Why aren't any of you at work?' I asked, planting

my hands on my hips theatrically as John greeted them all with hugs and kisses. 'Does no one have a job any more?'

'I had a doctor's appointment,' Sumi said, frowning as she prodded a tender spot on her stomach. Getting pregnant wasn't proving to be as easy as she'd hoped but she wasn't giving up. Adrian had offered to 'lie back and think of England' if she wanted to 'get it done the good old-fashioned way' but Jemima had voiced a stern objection about the idea of raising anything with Adrian's DNA and Sumi had politely declined, explaining it was still early days and, quite frankly, she'd rather eat her own face than have sex with him.

'I trained classes this morning,' Eva explained, her CrossFit-honed muscles rippling in a strappy vest, even though it was no longer strappy-vest weather. Eva loved a bit of nice athleisure wear.

'And I'm rich,' Adrian shrugged as he admired his girlfriend's rippling muscles. 'So, yeah.'

'How do you put up with him?' I asked Eva but she just smiled and laughed and they gazed at each other with the same gooey intensity I'd seen on both their faces every day since they'd met. Her birthday was in a week and it couldn't come fast enough. The sooner Adrian put the beautiful diamond ring I'd helped him choose on her finger, the better.

'We wanted to bring you this.' Lucy stooped to produce a small gift bag from the tray underneath the pram. Underneath a very comfortable-looking selection of blankets, Baby Penny slept on, already well accustomed to ignoring our nonsense.

Lucy handed me the bag as my other friends cheered,

John peering inside as I tore out the tissue paper in the top. It was a giant mug with something printed on the side.

'"You don't have to be mad to work here but it helps",' I read, holding it out in front of me. 'Thank you, it's exactly what I was missing.'

'It was that one or My Boss Is a Bitch, Get Me Coffee,' Sumi explained.

'But I'm the boss?' I said.

'Exactly,' Adrian replied.

'Are you done?' Lucy asked. 'We were going to take you out for supper.'

The toilet flushed and the glazier re-emerged with sparkling clean hands. My poor towels. 'I'll be off then,' he said, picking up his bag. 'See you next week.'

'Thanks, Dave,' I called. He touched the brim of his baseball cap on his way out the door, completely ignoring the others.

'You're hiding other men in the loos now, are you?' John asked, squeezing the back of my neck.

'Yes.' I tilted my head back into his hand and melted. 'That was my lover, Dave. He might not look like much but it's the experience you can't beat.'

'Oh, don't let me forget,' Sumi said as John clipped me gently on the back of the head and the others began piling back outside. 'One of the girls at work is moving and she needs someone to sublet her flat for a couple of months. It's tiny but it's nice, not far from here actually. Remind me to give you her number.'

'Anything that isn't my mother's yoga studio,' I replied gratefully, grabbing my keys from my desk. Since shedmageddon, I'd been living in my parents' house proper. All well and good while they were on their month-long second honeymoon but now they were home and three was most definitely a crowd. It was one thing to know your parents were going through a mid-life sexual renaissance, it was quite another to be in the next room while it was occurring.

I quickly paused behind my desk to scribble down an idea in my notebook before it vanished. A podcast of ASMR bedtime stories for adults, especially adults who had to sleep with earphones in every night. Well, not every night, I thought, looking up at John, who was holding the door open for everyone. Officially speaking, we were still taking it slow, but the tooth-brush in his bathroom and the drawer of my things beside his bed certainly had a sense of speed about them.

I was cautious, I was taking things day by day, but I was also fairly sure I was in love.

'Ready?' he asked as our friends assembled on the pavement outside, laughing and whooping and then scolding each other on behalf of the baby.

I looked at him, I looked at Sumi, Adrian and Lucy and at the October sun, starting to set against the London sky. And then I turned to gaze lovingly at my office, my desk, my chair, my mug. It was all starting to come together.

Picking up my bag, I slid the strap across my body and straightened my hair before taking John's hand in mine.

'Yes,' I said with a smile. 'I'm ready.'

ACKNOWLEDGEMENTS

They say it takes a village to raise a child and I say it takes a medium-sized city to make a book, perhaps something like Birmingham or Seville.

Firstly, thank you to my agent, Rowan Lawton, the greatest cheerleader in the land. I could not and would not want to do this without you.

I owe so many thanks to my HarperCollins family, it's hard to know where to start. To Lynne Drew, without whom there would be no book (and not just this one, literally there would be no Lindsey Kelk books, full stop), thank you for all your wisdom, guidance and support. Martha Ashby, your keen Yorkshire eye is always appreciated. Felicity Denham, you're the best at what you do and I could not appreciate you more. I might be sat in a room, pouring my guts into a laptop but it takes killer editorial, sales, rights, marketing, publicity, production, art, design, logistics and legal teams to make sure this book finds its way into your hands. I'm lucky to be held together by some of the very finest out there, in the UK and all over the world.

The last year has been a lot. Who thought it would be a good idea to move house, plan a wedding and write a book all at the same time? This idiot. And this idiot would be completely on her arse without the love and support of Kevin Dickson, Della Bolat, Terri White, Emma Gunavardhana, Danielle Radford. Also, he won't ever see this but I couldn't get through a day without my big brother, so thanks Bobby. I owe a lot of thank yous to a lot of people that will never be properly expressed (I mean, I still haven't sent all the thank you cards out from the wedding) but I hope everyone in my life knows how much I appreciate and love them.

Special thanks to Caroline Hirons and the fantastic, not-at-all-Snazz-like, Max Hirons, for their insight into the minds and wardrobes of teenage boys.

To Jeff, thank you for all that you do, all that you are, and for taking care of me and our cat children. I love you very much. I can't believe we got married. Lol.

Being an author is a very weird and often lonely job. I mean, it's hard to go out for a drink after a hard day when your only office-mate is a cat, so thank you to Mhairi McFarlane, Kevin Dickson (again), Paige Toon, Giovanna Fletcher, Louise Pentland, Marian Keyes, Sarra Manning, Rosie Walsh, Rowan Coleman, Julie Cohen, Lia Louis, Isabelle Broom, Andrea Bartz for understanding and supporting and being absolutely brilliant. Sometimes it was just a tweet or a DM, sometimes it was an entire bottle of wine or a weeping three a.m. phone call (sorry about that) but I really want you to know it was appreciated.

There will never be a time I'm not completely stunned by the fact I get to do this for my job. The fact you chose to read this book means I am forever in your debt and you have my endless gratitude.

If you've enjoyed *In Case You Missed It*, read on for a taste of *One in a Million*, also by Lindsey Kelk.

The room at the end of the hallway on the first floor had been empty for as long as we had been at The Ginnel. It was a tiny, awkward sort of space with a glass front and only one small, square window to the outside, slightly above head height. It was too little to be a meeting room and too dark to be an office and, so far, no one who had been to look around had been interested in setting up shop.

Until today.

The first thing I noticed as I approached the working home of my newest client was the panels of white paper that had been sticky-taped to the glass wall, effectively closing out the rest of his co-workers and pretty much defeating the object of being in a co-working space in the first place. The second was the sign on the door. It was a nameplate that appeared to have been pilfered from a 1970s polytechnic. Everyone else had identical signs in the same, slightly retro serif font but Dr S. E. Page MPhil PhD had got ahead of the game and glued a narrow blackboard with block white lettering onto the door himself.

Charlie and Martin had been positively joyous when our subject selected himself but what could they know from one look? There was no reason to think just because he wasn't some kind of Adonis he wouldn't be interesting. For all they knew he could be an amazing photographer or he might have a dancing dog or any number of incredible, Instagram-worthy skills. He already had more letters after his name than anyone I'd ever met and my sister knew some truly insufferable academic types who seemed to have been put on this earth solely to rack up qualifications.

'There could be any number of reasons he's covered up the windows,' I told myself, tracing the edges of the white paper through the glass. 'This space would make a decent dark room. Or he could be super light-sensitive.'

Inside the office, I heard papers rustling. I knocked, stepped back and waited.

The rustling stopped but he made no attempt to answer the door.

'Or he's an actual serial killer,' I suggested to myself. 'Making himself a nice skin suit for the autumn.'

I knocked again. Louder.

Still nothing.

'Once more for luck,' I said under my breath, rapping as hard as I could for as long as I could.

My hand was still mid-air when the door opened. The tall, skinny man had tied back his long hair in a man bun. His beard was still enormous, and not in a cool, hipster way and though it was huge, it completely failed to disguise the annoyance on his face.

'Dr Page?' I enquired with a forced, friendly smile.

'Is something wrong?' he asked, looking me up and down.

'No,' I replied. 'At least, it wasn't the last time I checked.'

'Right, you can go away then?'

He phrased it as a question but it definitely felt more like an instruction.

'I'm sorry, I'm Annie,' I said quickly before he could close the door again. 'We're office neighbours. I work upstairs? I came to say hello, welcome you to the building.'

He pushed his smudged spectacles up his nose with a long, slender finger.

'Right,' he said. 'Hello.'

And then he slammed the door so hard, I felt it rattle my fillings.

'Bugger,' I whispered, the door a fraction of an inch from my nose.

There was the slightest of chances this was going to be more difficult than I had hoped.

'That was quick?' Miranda looked surprised to see me back in the office so soon. 'How'd it go?'

'He only answered the door after I cut up my knuckles knocking for half an hour, asked if anything was wrong and then told me to piss off,' I replied. 'So not great.'

'So, he isn't a natural conversationalist,' Mir shrugged. 'How did he look?'

'Think Tom Hanks in act two of *Castaway*, only without the social graces necessary to make friends with a volleyball,' I said, punching the call button for the lift. 'He's the least likeable human I've ever met – and I've met Jeremy Kyle, Katie Hopkins and the man who plays the Fox in the Foxy Bingo adverts.'

Miranda grimaced.

'We'll work it out,' she promised. 'Or we'll call it off. It doesn't matter, it's only a stupid bet.'

'Oh, absolutely not,' I replied. 'There's no way we're not winning this. I'm not giving them the satisfaction.'

'You know you could just shag Charlie and get this out of your system,' she said, holding her hands up in front of her to create a human shield. 'Not saying you have to; just putting it out there as an idea.'

'I don't know what you're talking about,' I said primly, tossing my long ponytail over my shoulder. 'Don't worry, Mir; one way or another, we're going to win this.'

I walked over to the huge whiteboard in the corner of the room and uncapped a bright blue marker. On one side of the board, I wrote the word 'followers' and added a big fat zero underneath. On the other, I put down the number thirty. Thirty days to make this man the internet's latest leading attraction. Taking a step back, I folded my arms and stared at the board as though it might have the answers I needed.

'This is going to be a piece of piss for you,' Miranda said. 'A month is practically forever. You've got this.'

'Yeah,' I replied. Now I had the numbers literally staring me in the face, I was suddenly not quite as sure as she was. Zero to twenty thousand with nothing to go on. Inside thirty days. 'I've got this.'

Hopefully, the more times I said it, the more likely I was to believe it.

DISCOVER LINDSEY'S

I heart SERIES

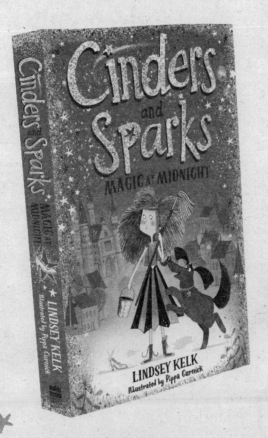

There are lots of ways to keep up-to-date with Lindsey's news and views:

lindseykelk.com

 facebook.com/LindseyKelk

@LindseyKelk

 @LindseyKelk

Or sign up to Lindsey's newsletter here
smarturl.it/LindseyNewsletter